She kissed him again ...
you?"

"It's complicated."

She pulled her head back and stared into his light brown eyes. After a year and twenty-one days, after letting her think he was dead, he needed a much better explanation. "Tell me about it."

She wasn't letting him run away after giving her a whisper of sweet talk and "it's complicated." She needed a hell of a lot more than that. She slid down his body and planted her boots on the ground. "Sit down, Wade."

"I already told you. I can't—"

"We can do this the easy way or the hard way."

He frowned. "What?"

The hard way, it was. She stalked around him until she had the uphill position. From there, it was easy to shove his shoulder and hook his legs out from under him. As soon as his butt hit the dirt, she was on him. After taking away his rifle, she flipped him onto his belly and cuffed his hands behind his back.

"Wade Calloway, you're under arrest."

COLORADO WILDFIRE

BY
CASSIE MILES

First Published in Great Britain 2016
By Mills & Boon, an imprint of HarperCollins*Publishers*
1 London Bridge Street, London, SE1 9GF

© 2016 Kay Bergstrom

ISBN: 978-0-263-91896-0

46-0216

Our policy is to use papers that are natural, renewable and recyclable products and made from wood grown in sustainable forests. The logging and manufacturing processes conform to the legal environmental regulations of the country of origin.

Printed and bound in Spain
by CPI, Barcelona

Cassie Miles, a *USA TODAY* bestselling author, lives in Colorado. After raising two daughters and cooking tons of macaroni and cheese for her family, Cassie is trying to be more adventurous in her culinary efforts. She's discovered that almost anything tastes better with wine. When she's not plotting Mills & Boon Intrigue books, Cassie likes to hang out at the Denver Botanical Gardens near her high-rise home.

To the most excellent uncles, Charlie and C.J. Climp.

And, as always, to Rick.

Chapter One

Sheriff Samantha Calloway hadn't cried this much since her husband went missing and was presumed dead. She swabbed the moisture from her cheeks with the back of her hand. These tears didn't come from sorrow. Smoke had got into her eyes.

She parked her white SUV with the sheriff's logo at a deserted intersection, climbed out and rested her elbows on the front fender to steady her binoculars. Beyond a wide field that was green with the new growth of early spring, she could see the approaching wildfire.

Though the crimson flames were far away, barely visible behind a distant ridge, smoke consumed the landscape. A stinging haze draped the spires of pine and spruce at the edge of Swain County in the high Rocky Mountains.

When she licked her lips, she tasted ash on her tongue. Her pale blue eyes continued to ooze with tears.

Caleb Schmidt, a deputy who had been with the sheriff's department for thirty years, one year longer than Sam had been alive, had followed her to this location. He got out of his vehicle and strutted toward her. A short, wiry man, Caleb thrust out his chest and swung his arms when he walked. Maybe he thought the posture made him look bigger. He pulled the dark blue bandana down from his mouth and squinted at her through his thick glasses.

"It's time," he said in a voice of doom, "time to start emergency evacuation procedures."

"Not yet."

"Doggone it, Sheriff, we gotta hustle and—"

"I've been in contact with the proper officials," she interrupted. "Fire Marshal Hobbs will tell me in plenty of time if we need to evacuate."

Caleb scoffed. Before he could say anything more, she stretched out her long arm and tugged on his bandana. "Where's your smoke mask?"

"Where's yours?" he retorted.

This morning when she'd started out, she had two boxes full of disposable ventilator masks that she'd gone to the trouble of ordering even though they weren't in her meager budget. Before noon, she'd given them all away without saving one for herself. Her late husband, Wade, would have pointed to her behavior as an example of her too-too-responsible attitude. And, she admitted to herself, Wade would have been right. Sam knew she couldn't take care of others if she didn't take care of herself first, but the other way around felt more natural.

"The wind's picking up," Caleb muttered. "The fire's on the move. I hear it's already burned two thousand acres. I'm advising you to reconsider."

"If I had reason to believe it might reach town, I wouldn't hesitate to get everybody out." Her five-year-old daughter was smack-dab in the middle of Woodridge at the sheriff's office in the two-story, red stone Swain County Courthouse, where the dispatch/911 operators were keeping an eye on her. Sam's regular babysitter had an asthmatic toddler and had driven down to Denver to get away from this awful smoke.

"We gotta be smart, gotta move fast." Caleb would not give up; he was a feisty little pug with a bone. "It ain't going to be easy to get some of these old coots to leave their houses."

He was right about that. A mandated evacuation of Woodridge would be a nightmare. Her county was the smallest in the state in terms of acreage and population. They didn't have a ski resort or a condo development or fertile land for farming. The entire sheriff's department consisted of twelve people, including Sam.

She swabbed the moisture from under her eyes and stared at her deputy. "I'm not going to change my mind. No mandatory evacuation unless the fire marshal says there's an imminent threat. Is that clear?"

Grudgingly, he said, "I guess you're the boss."

You got that right. None of her six deputies had been thrilled when she took over her husband's job as sheriff. That was over a year ago, and she'd been duly elected last February for one big fat obvious reason: she was the best qualified. As a teenager, she'd done volunteer search and rescue. She'd been top of her class at the police academy. Not to mention her three years' experience as a cop in Grand Junction before she married Wade. Still, her deputies second-guessed her at every turn.

"Deputy Schmidt, I want you to stay right here and keep an eye on things. That's an order."

"Yes, ma'am," he said, properly chastised.

The two-lane asphalt road pointed south was one of the few direct routes toward the flames. "Except for firefighting personnel, no vehicles are allowed to pass."

"And what are you going to do?"

She spotted the black Range Rover she'd been waiting for. "I need to go with Ty Baxter to check on a property."

"It's that FBI safe house. Am I right?"

"You know I can't tell you." Not that the location was a well-kept secret. "And you're not supposed to say anything about the safe house, either."

He mimed zipping his lips, fastening a lock and throwing away the key. Then he pulled up his bandana to cover his mouth and marched toward his vehicle.

FBI special agent Ty Baxter jumped from his Rover and came toward her with long strides. In his Stetson, denim jeans, snakeskin boots and white shirt with a yoke and pearly snaps, he could have looked as phony as a drugstore cowboy. But Ty pulled it off. After all, he was the real deal, the son of a local rancher.

He'd been her husband's best friend. They'd gone to school together, played football together and dated the same girls. Ty had won the heart of the prom queen. The whole county had been heartbroken when he and Loretta moved to Denver to pursue his career.

He gave her a big hug. "Looking good, Sam."

"Liar."

She knew better. Her blue eyes were bloodshot. Instead of makeup, she had jagged smears of ash across her face. Under her beige cowboy hat, her long brown hair was pulled back in a tight braid that hung halfway down to her waist. Her boxy khaki uniform wasn't designed to flatter. Not to mention the heavy-duty bulletproof vest under her shirt and the utility belt that circled her waist. On top of all that, she was fairly sure that she had pit stains.

"How's Jenny?" he asked.

"Getting taller every day."

"Like you."

Sam was six feet tall in her boots. "I kind of hoped she wouldn't inherit the giraffe gene."

Ty grinned and his dark brown eyes twinkled. "Both her parents are giraffes."

Wade had been six feet five inches tall. Whenever Sam was with Ty, her thoughts drifted toward her husband. The two men had been close. They even looked kind of alike. Both were tall and lean. Both had brown eyes and dark hair. Ty had been with Wade when he died.

She shook off the memories and returned Ty's easygoing smile. "You got here from Denver really fast."

"I was already on my way when I called about the safe house. Sam, there's something important I need to tell you."

She nodded. "We can talk on the way. We'll take my SUV. I need to be able to hear my dispatcher."

After reminding Deputy Schmidt to keep this route blocked, she got behind the steering wheel. When Ty joined her, he was carrying a gym bag from his Rover. Before he buckled up, he reached inside and took out his smooth, black, lethal-looking Beretta 9 mm semiautomatic pistol.

"Whoa," she said. "Are you planning to shoot the fire?"

"I like to be prepared." He clipped the holster to his belt. "Don't you?"

Prepared for what? Sam was wary. First, Ty had mentioned "something important" he wanted to talk about. Now he was packing a gun. She had a bad feeling about what fresh disaster might be lurking around the next corner. Hoping to avoid bigger problems, she asked about his family. "Are your twins still playing T-ball?"

"They're getting pretty good," he said, "and Loretta signed on to be coach of their team."

"Good for her." Sheriff Sam was happy to support women who broke the stereotypes.

"Surprised the hell out of me. I never thought my Loretta was athletic, but she's getting into sports."

"Imagine that."

Apparently, Ty had forgotten that Loretta was a rodeo barrel racer and a black-diamond skier. Because his little Loretta was capable of looking like a princess, he forgot her kick-ass side. Wade had never made that mistake with Samantha.

The first three miles of paved road swept across an open field. Under the smoky haze, the tall prairie grasses mingled with bright splashes of scarlet and blue wildflowers. Then the road turned to graded gravel, still two lanes but bumpy. The scenery closed in around them as they entered a narrow canyon.

While she guided the SUV through a series of turns that followed the winding path of Horny Toad Creek, they chatted about family and how much Ty and Loretta missed living in the mountains. His dad wanted him to move back to Swain County and help out at the ranch.

"That would mean giving up your career," Sam said. "There's not much need for an FBI special agent around here."

He exhaled a sigh. "You and Wade had the right idea. Decide where you want to live, and then find a way to make a living."

When she and her husband started out, she hadn't been so sure they'd made a good decision. They were newlyweds with six acres and a good well outside Wood-ridge. She'd just quit her cop job and was trying to make ends meet on one salary. Within two months, she was pregnant. While expecting and unemployed, she was able to oversee every step of the construction.

The house they built was perfectly tailored for them. She'd even made the kitchen counters a few inches taller so she didn't have to stoop when she was chopping to-matillos for green salsa. She and Wade had made love in every room and on the deck and in the garage…

"The turn is coming up," Ty said as he squinted to-ward the left side of the road.

"I know where it is." She checked on the safe house whenever she was in the area. It hadn't been occupied in months.

He took a water bottle from his gym bag, unscrewed the lid and poured a splash over a red bandana. Like Caleb, he tied the bandana across the lower half of his face.

She couldn't stop herself from being Miss Know-It-All. "The fire marshal says the weave of a cotton bandana isn't fine enough to prevent ash particles from getting through."

"Don't care," he said. "The wetness makes breath-ing easier. Here's the turnoff."

After a quick left, she drove on a one-lane road that ascended a rugged slope. The safe house clung to the side of a granite cliff and faced away from the road. If she hadn't known where she was going, Sam would never have found this place amid the rocks and trees.

When she exited her vehicle, the smoke swirled around her ankles in a thick miasma. From the wraparound porch of the house, she and Ty had a clear view of the wildfire.

The blaze danced across the upper edge of a hogback ridge. With the sun going down, the billowing clouds of smoke turned an angry red. It looked like the gates of hell. A chopper flew over the leaping flames and dropped a load of retardant on the forest.

She watched as Ty wandered around to the side of the house toward the long attached garage. "Looking for something?"

"I'm being thorough."

She noticed his hand resting on his belt near his holster, ready to make a quick draw. What was making him so suspicious? "Is there something I should know about?"

He joined her on the porch. "Long as I'm here, I might as well look around inside."

His fingers hovered over a keypad outside the front door. He glanced over his shoulder at her. "Do you happen to…?"

"Remember the code to deactivate the alarm?" She grinned and rattled off six digits. The Swain County sheriff always had the code. When the alarm went off, it rang through to her office, and she had to come up here to turn it off.

Before she could follow Ty inside, her cell phone rang. It was the fire marshal—a call she needed to take. As she answered, she signaled to Ty to go ahead without her.

"Marshal Hobbs," she said, "what can you tell me?"

"The fire is mostly contained." His voice was raspy. Sore throats must be an occupational hazard. "You won't need to evacuate the town, especially not if it rains tonight like it's supposed to."

"That's the good news," she said. "What's the bad?"

"Well, Sheriff, I've got a favor to ask. The chopper

pilot spotted three hikers on the road by Horny Toad Creek. I can't spare the men to pick them up. Could you take care of it?"

"No problem," she assured him. "I happen to be in that area right now. How do you know they're hikers?"

"The pilot said they were wearing backpacks. You know the look."

"I sure do. Keep me posted on the fire."

When Ty came out of the safe house, she waved him over to her SUV and told him about the hikers who needed a pickup. "I can't imagine any sensible reason they'd hike near a wildfire. These guys must be thrill-seekers or morons."

"Or reporters," Ty said.

"Same thing."

She'd had her fill of reporters after Wade's death. They wouldn't leave her alone, constantly pestered her for interviews or photos of her and Jenny. All she ever wanted was to grieve in private. But Wade's accident was news.

One year and twenty-one days ago, he'd gone bow hunting with Ty and two other feds, including Ty's boss, Everett Hurtado. A kayaker on the river had lost control in the rapids, and Wade had jumped into the frigid waters to rescue him. The kayaker had survived. Wade had been swept away by the white water. His body had never been found.

As Sam started the engine in her SUV, dark thoughts gnawed at the edge of her mind. She had plenty of things to worry about: the fire, the hikers, the lack of ventilation masks and Ty's "important" news. But she could never escape the pain and the sorrow that had taken up permanent residence inside her. She'd never forget the loss of her husband. He was her soul mate, her dearest lover and best friend.

As she drove along the road that followed the twists and turns of the creek, she turned her head toward Ty. *Might as well get this over with.* "What's this important thing you want to tell me?"

"You know, Sam, I can hardly look at you without thinking of Wade."

"Back at you, Ty. You were one of his best friends. You grew up together." She guided the SUV into a more open area that deviated from the path of the creek. "Is this important message about Wade?"

"How do you feel about him? Are you, maybe, looking at other men?"

"Hell no." There was no other man, and there never would be. She only had room in her heart for Jenny and for Wade.

The road straightened out. The right side was a field behind a barbed-wire fence. To the left, a gently rising hillside climbed into a thick, old growth forest. If the fire got this far, these hills would go up like dry tinder.

Ty cleared his throat. "I was just thinking..."

"If you're going to say that it's time to move on, that I should get out there in the world and start dating, forget it. Don't you dare tell me how to grieve."

He pointed across the windshield to the left side of the road. "Over there."

In the shadow of a tall cottonwood, she spotted a dark green sedan that apparently had gone across the shoulder and run into the shrubs, rocks and trees at the side of the road. She parked behind it. "Maybe our three hikers came from that car."

"Makes sense," Ty said. "Maybe they had an accident and are trying to walk back to civilization. But why didn't we see them on the road? Why would they go toward the fire?"

She left the SUV and went to investigate. The green sedan blended into the trees and shrubs, which was why the helicopter pilot hadn't noticed it. She saw the outline of a man's head and shoulders behind the steering wheel.

He wasn't moving.

Chapter Two

A rising sense of dread crept up her spine and raised the fine hairs on the nape of her neck. Unlike the distant threat of the raging wildfire, this trouble was only a few steps away. Sam adjusted the holster on her belt for easier access to the Glock 23 she'd used to win marksmanship contests at the academy. Never once had she fired her pistol on the job: her stun gun was usually enough. But her cop instincts told her that this situation might require more firepower.

"Sir," she called out as she moved closer to the vehicle, "I'm with the sheriff's department. Show me your hands. Sir?"

Ty came up beside her. He held his Beretta at the ready. "I suggest we proceed with caution."

"Ya think?"

He immediately backed off. "I'm following your lead, Sam."

Even if Swain County wasn't a hotbed of criminal activity, she knew the standard procedures and would adhere to them as much as possible. She pulled her pistol from the holster and went to the driver's side. The window was down. Fully expecting to find the driver sleeping or drunk, she angled around until she could see inside.

"Sir, are you...?" The words froze in her mouth.

He'd been shot in the chest. The front of his plaid flannel shirt was drenched in blood from his neck to his gut. *Oh God, what do I do next? What's the procedure?* She should check for a pulse, assess his condition. But she didn't need to touch his pale jowls to know the flesh would be cold. His sightless eyes stared directly at her.

"He's dead," Ty said.

"Yes." She could barely speak. Her throat was dry.

"We need to be careful. The killer might still be nearby."

Gathering her courage, she backed away from the sedan and scanned the area, peering through the smoke at the rocks, shrubs and trees. No one else was in sight, but these hills were full of hiding places. A murderer wouldn't put up a billboard to announce his presence.

But would he run away? Was he waiting for them? Harsh little flashes of tension and fear made it impossible for her to concentrate. *Oh, Wade, I miss you.* He would have known what to do. He was a born leader; giving orders came easily to him. Somehow, she had to pull herself together.

She cleared her throat. "We have to find the hikers."

"Do you think they did this?"

"I don't know."

But she didn't think those three men with backpacks were in this area by coincidence. Either they were friends of the deceased who were on the run or they were killers.

Ty gently touched her shoulder. "Are you all right?"

"This is my first murder case."

"I'm here to help."

She'd seen dead bodies before, usually people who passed away from old age or due to an accident. And she'd arrested plenty of bad guys who had hurt someone else. The local violence had always stopped far short of murder.

"I can do this," she said.

"Hell yes."

She slapped her Glock back into the holster. "I want this investigation to be done right." She took out a pair of baby blue latex gloves and slipped them on.

"Do you always have gloves in your pocket?"

"Not my pocket. My utility belt." She passed a pair to him. "I keep them in here."

"Isn't that the place where you should be packing a second magazine for your Glock?"

"Here's the thing, Ty. I've never fired all thirteen rounds from this gun. I'll carry one mag of extra bullets, but the second one is overkill. But I've found the gloves come in handy. I am a mom, after all."

"Uh-huh."

"Last time I used my latex gloves was at Jenny's kindergarten class when we were making a collage of forest animals."

He nodded slowly. "What's our next move?"

That was a good question. Swain County didn't have the facilities to deal with a murder. They had a small clinic and a dentist who doubled as county coroner but no hospital for an autopsy. For forensics, she used a fingerprint kit that she usually carried in her SUV. She had no access to DNA data analysis or a mass spectrometer or any other fancy tools.

In usual circumstances, she'd step aside and happily

turn this investigation over to the Colorado Bureau of Investigation or maybe the Grand Junction police. But today was different. Today, there was a wildfire that just might reach this car and obliterate the scene of the crime.

She took her cell phone from her pocket. "First, I'm going to take photos of the crime scene and dust for prints. Then you and me are going to load this body into the back of my SUV and cart him to the nearest hospital."

"Why move him?"

Pointing toward the flames, she said, "So the body won't be incinerated along with the rest of the evidence."

With her phone camera, she took a picture of the windshield and the front end of the car, which was crumpled against the trunk of the cottonwood. The damage wasn't severe, causing her to think the car hadn't been going very fast at the time of impact. Pleased with herself for drawing that conclusion, she made a complete circle around the sedan, taking pictures of the whole car. No skid marks in the gravel behind the car. The driver hadn't applied the brakes.

A theory began to form in her mind. The man behind the steering wheel was already dead when the car hit the tree. Her conclusion fit the evidence. Wade would have been proud of her. He'd always said that she was a natural-born cop, not surprising since her father was a captain in the Portland PD.

She returned to the front window and made observations, sticking her head inside. The dead man was covered in blood, but the rest of the front seat was fairly clean. She looked over her shoulder at Ty. "I don't think this sedan is our primary crime scene."

"What do you mean?"

"I think he was killed somewhere else and then put in the front seat, which is why there's no spatter. And he didn't crash this car. It was pushed off the road into the tree."

"How do you know that?"

After outlining her prior conclusions, she stepped away from the window so he could see the final bit of evidence for himself. "No keys in the ignition."

He peered inside, taking care not to get blood on his white shirt with the pearly snaps, and then he cursed. "I recognize this guy."

Had she heard him right? "You know him?"

"He's a cop." Ty pulled his head out of the car and stood up straight. "A state patrolman. I think his name is Morrissey. Wade introduced us."

Her husband had been well acquainted with all the law-enforcement guys who worked in and around Swain County. Like her own deputies, they hadn't been as friendly with Sam. "We'd better do everything right. The staties can be as annoying as you FBI guys. Lieutenant Natchez is a real pill."

"Agreed. I've met Natchez." Ty whipped out his cell phone. "Do you want me to contact him?"

"I guess that's the right thing to do."

If the situation had been reversed, and someone had found Deputy Caleb Schmidt's body, she'd want to be among the first who were informed. She wasn't looking forward to seeing Natchez. Somehow, he'd get everything turned around and make this murder her fault.

While Ty placed the call, she continued photographing

the inside of the vehicle, starting with the front driver's side and working her way around. No blood at all in the backseat. When she opened the passenger-side door, she saw a handgun. An attractive piece, it was a Colt revolver with an inlaid copper-colored design on the grip.

The weapon belonged to her husband.

WADE CALLOWAY EXERTED every bit of his willpower to keep himself from charging down the hill, grabbing his wife and planting a big, hard kiss on her soft, pink lips. The urge almost overwhelmed him. He couldn't stand to watch her anymore. Ducking down behind a tall boulder at the edge of the forest, he squeezed his eyelids shut, fighting his desperate need to be with Samantha, his angel.

Now wasn't the time or the place.

If he showed his face, she'd be in danger.

What the hell was she doing on this road? Why did she have to be the one who discovered the body? His fingers curled into a fist, and he hammered the ground beneath his boots. Life was not fair!

For more than a year, he'd fantasized about what it would be like when he came home to his sweet wife. She'd come running toward him with her long brown hair streaming behind her in a silky banner. Her clothing—always flimsy in his imagination—would outline her slender legs and supple torso. Her laughter would ring out, and their perfect daughter would join in with hugs and kisses. Jenny and Sam would treat him to a hero's welcome.

He peeked around the edge of the boulder. Samantha stalked around the vehicle. He couldn't actually see her scowl from this distance, but he could tell that she was frustrated and annoyed. More than annoyed—anger radiated from her in waves that were even hotter than the wildfire.

He had a real bad feeling that this hostile version of Samantha was the woman who would greet him when he stepped out of hiding. He could hope for her forgiveness but didn't expect it.

His life—which used to be so very fine—had become one snafu after another. The murder of Drew Morrissey was the latest blunder. Somebody should have been watching the bum, keeping him from getting shot. Not that Wade intended to waste any tears on Morrissey. The man was a traitor to his uniform. Protecting him would have been a smart strategy. Morrissey was cowardly and weak. He might have turned on his partners in crime. Most likely, that ratlike tendency to squeal was probably why the scumbag was dead.

Wade had found the body behind the steering wheel of his car about a half hour ago and had staked out the area, hoping that the killer or killers might come back. And if they did, what would he do? He wanted to take these guys into custody, to lock them up and throw away the keys. It wasn't that easy. He'd spent the past year in protective custody, waiting to testify and make things right.

Three days ago the legal case had collapsed for the umpteenth time, and Wade decided he wasn't willing to wait, especially not after he'd caught a glimpse of a man in the federal courthouse whom he vaguely remembered. The name hadn't come to him. But he'd seen this guy before. And that was enough of a threat to get him moving. If the bad guys had seen him and knew he was alive and waiting to testify, Samantha and Jenny would be in danger.

He'd escaped from his handlers in Texas and made his way back here. Last night, he'd slept in the FBI safe house, thankful they hadn't changed the security code from the time he was sheriff. From the house, he'd picked up some important supplies: two semiautomatic pistols and a hunting rifle. In the attached garage, he'd found a lightweight Honda motorcycle with heavy-tread tires that made it suitable for off-road or on-road driving.

He had intended to find Samantha and Jenny this morning, to take them away with him. A lot of people, including his supposed friend Ty, would tell him that he shouldn't return to Colorado. The whole reason they faked his death was so nobody would come after Samantha or Jenny to hurt him. But Wade couldn't stay away.

He'd find a way to keep his family safe. It might not be comfortable or pretty, but at least they'd be together. That was what he should have done in the first place. The time apart had been gut-wrenching.

He peeked out from behind the rock again. Damn, she was pretty. He wanted to caress every inch of Samantha's beautiful body, to smell the clean fragrance of her shampoo, to taste her mouth and stare into her cool blue eyes. Not even the boxy sheriff uniform could disguise her long legs and well-toned arms.

Not to brag, but he'd done some bodybuilding of his own. One of the ways he'd distracted himself for all these months was by working out. He'd tightened his six-pack, and the biceps and triceps in his arms were sharply defined. Would Samantha notice? He couldn't wait until she ran her long, slender fingers down his chest and commented on his new physical conditioning.

From the road, he heard her bark an order at Ty. "Just do what I say. Do it now."

Wade chuckled under his breath. "That's my sweet, delicate angel."

He craned his neck so he could see the road more clearly. She had the door of the sedan open and was messing around with the dead body. What the hell was she doing?

Chapter Three

She might not be an expert on how to process a crime scene, but Sam was in charge here. Ty needed to remember that little fact. Swain County was her jurisdiction. And she wanted to move the body of Colorado state patrolman Drew Morrissey into the rear of her SUV before this scene was engulfed in flames and all the evidence destroyed.

"Come on, Ty, let's do it."

He groaned. "Didn't your friend the fire marshal tell you that the burn wouldn't get this far?"

"Marshal Hobbs said the town would be safe. This location is miles and miles away from there." She slapped her hands together to start the action. "You take his head, and I'll take his legs."

Ty slipped into his black FBI windbreaker to protect his white shirt, but he still complained. "Why do I get the messy end of the body?"

"Don't be such a wuss. You're stronger than me and the top half of the body is heavier."

Also, she intended to use the few minutes when she was alone by Morrissey's car to shove Wade's copper-handled revolver under the seat. Removing evidence would be wrong. She was certain about that. Hiding the evidence might be kind of, maybe, a little bit acceptable. *It's not. I know better.*

But she needed a couple more minutes to figure out what to do about a gun that should have been locked in a case at her house. *It could be the murder weapon.* Maybe she'd tell Ty about it before Morrissey's supervisor got here. She definitely didn't want Lieutenant Natchez to use her husband's fancy revolver to tie her to a murder scene.

When Ty pulled Morrissey away from the seat, the man's head flopped forward against the steering wheel. Seeing him was different than touching. The stench of death cut through the smoke as she helped Ty manipulate the dead weight. Morrissey's arms dangled. His legs were as floppy as a rag doll. There wasn't anything she could do about the revolver until Ty had the body halfway out of the seat.

In a quick move, she ducked inside the car, shoved the weapon under the passenger's seat, emerged and slammed the driver's-side door. She faced Ty. "Okay, let's roll."

He held Morrissey under the armpits with his legs sprawled. "What the hell was that dance about?"

Instead of replying, she grabbed the dead man under the knees. "I won't be carrying my share of the weight like this. Let me get him around the middle."

Morrissey's blood smeared her khaki uniform. She should have put on her windbreaker; Ty was smart to do that. They stumbled a few steps toward her vehicle.

A burst of gunfire echoed against the canyon walls. She looked over her shoulder toward the road in front of them. Through the smoke, she saw the shapes of two men diving across from the right side to the left where the green sedan had run into the cottonwood trunk.

Ty's reaction was immediate. He dropped Morrissey, ducked behind her car and yanked his Beretta from the holster. "Take cover, Sam."

Her brain wasn't so agile. It took a few beats to register the obvious. Somebody was shooting at them. She needed to return fire, needed to find cover, needed to move. *Move!* But she stood there like a statue, holding the lower half of Morrissey's legs. She looked down. His sneakers were untied.

Ty's voice wakened her. "Sam, move! Damn it, move!"

She dropped Morrissey and bolted like a jackrabbit, dashing to her SUV, where she whipped open the driver's-side door to use as a shield. A bullet pinged against the door. If she'd been standing in the open, she would have been hit in the center of her bulletproof vest. Thank God she was wearing it today.

In the academy and during other training exercises, she'd been in dozens of simulations. But this was her first real-life firefight. As she drew her Glock, her focus tightened. Time seemed to slow. She remembered what was supposed to be done. *I can do this.* Her confidence returned and with it came courage.

When she spotted a backpack in the middle of the road where the two men had been, she yelled to Ty, "The hikers, these guys have got to be the hikers. The marshal said there were three."

From the opposite side of her SUV, he shouted, "I saw only two."

The hikers continued to lay down a steady barrage of gunfire. That was a lot of ammo. She regretted using her storage for a second ammo magazine as a carryall for latex gloves. Ty was aiming at a big, chunky boulder that was about ten yards down the road. She guessed the hikers would try to move toward the wrecked sedan, where they'd have a better angle.

Bracing her gun hand against the window frame of her vehicle, she popped a bullet into the space between the rock and the sedan. The action of her Glock felt good in her hands. She was a fairly good shot, the best in the Swain County Sheriff's Department...which wasn't saying much, given that Caleb was second best.

"Cover me," Ty yelled.

Peering through the space between her car door and the windshield, she fired in the direction he'd been shooting. Every bullet counted. She squeezed the trigger seven times, rapid-fire. Her ears rang with the percussive noise.

In a low crouch, Ty darted to the right side of the road, concealed himself in a ditch and took aim. He fired several times in quick succession.

A man staggered out from behind the boulder into the road. With one hand, he clutched his gut. Blood spilled through his fingers. With the other, he tried to steady his weapon. Ty fired again. The man crumpled to the dirt.

One down, two to go. She saw the second man run from the cover of the boulder toward the cottonwood tree where he could hide in the shrubs behind the car. He was closer to her than to Ty. Keeping her head down, she maneuvered toward the sedan.

The heavy smoke hanging over the trees made her think of a battlefield. Adrenaline pumped through her veins. She was on high alert, shivering and sweating at the same time. She dodged around the body of Morrissey on the ground. Her gloved hand touched the trunk of the sedan. She saw the hiker beside the tall cottonwood.

Ty ran toward the sedan, blasting as he came. She raised her weapon, took aim. She had the best angle—a head shot that was perfectly aligned. Before she could squeeze the trigger, the hiker was hit. He threw both arms in the air as he fell. *Two down, one to go.*

She could have sworn that shot came from behind her, uphill to her left. But when she looked, she didn't see anything but a couple of ragged-edged boulders and a dark wall of pine trees. Squinting, she tried to catch the glint of sunlight off a rifle barrel. If there was a mysterious marksman, he'd have to be using a high-powered rifle. A handgun wouldn't be accurate from those trees.

"Are you okay?" Ty called out.

"I'm fine. You?"

"There's another hiker, right?"

When the wind rippled the tall buffalo grass, she glimpsed him in her peripheral vision. He was half up the hill toward the trees. His pistol aimed directly at her.

She wheeled to face him. Somebody else fired first, and his bullet hit the hiker in the upper right chest. The hiker let out a fierce scream. He turned on wobbly legs and stared uphill to the point where she'd been looking. Then he went to his knees and curled up on the ground, moaning.

She rushed toward him, kicked his gun out of his reach and unhooked her handcuffs from her belt. With his shoulder wound, it seemed cruel to force the hiker onto his belly, but she wanted to be sure he was subdued and no longer a threat.

Breathing heavily, she got a lungful of smoke and coughed before she called out, "Ty, have you got the other two?"

"The one in the road is dead. The other is unconscious. I secured his wrists with a zip tie."

Her attack tally turned to a roster for emergency care: two wounded and two dead, including Morrissey. It was time to call for an ambulance. Proper procedure would have been to dial up the EMTs when they first discovered Morrissey's body. But she'd figured that the local emergency personnel would already have their hands full, being on call for the firefighters and treating patients with smoke-related illnesses.

As she reached for her cell phone, she looked uphill and saw a tall man in a cowboy hat with his arms raised over his head. This man had fired accurately through the smoke from a significant distance; obviously he was an excellent marksman. He was dangerous. She should have been scared but, for some reason, she wasn't.

She gave herself a mental slap. *Shape up, girl.* Just because he had his hands up, he was far from harmless. She could see the rifle strapped across his back and the two holsters on his belt. She lifted her gun and pointed it at him.

"Don't shoot," he yelled.

The sound of his voice sliced through her defenses and turned her insides to jelly. "Wade?"

It couldn't be. He was dead.

But that was her husband walking down the hill. She'd recognize his bowlegged gait anywhere.

He'd come back to her. Either that or she was dead, too. She must have been killed in this shoot-out, and her darling husband had come to greet her and escort her through the Pearly Gates. Their poor little Jenny was an orphan. She shook herself. No way. They couldn't both be dead.

Ty stepped up beside her. "This is what I've been trying to tell you."

"He's still alive."

"I'm afraid so."

She slammed her Glock into the holster, dug in with her toes and started running up the hill. There was not one single instant of hesitation on her part. Maybe she didn't know why he was back or where he'd been. But she didn't care. He was back. Wade was alive!

For a year and twenty-one days, her heart had been frozen solid. With one sight of him, the glacier shattered, and a warm, gentle feeling spread through her. As she ran, she heard the sound of her own laughter. Not a fake ha-ha but a real, bubbling, delighted sound. As she got closer to him, the smoke seemed to disappear. The whole world was bathed in golden sunlight.

With a giant leap, she flung herself into his arms. The equipment on her utility belt and her armored vest got in the way, but she did her best to have full body contact. Clinging to him with all her strength, she wrapped both legs around him. He felt different, more muscular. He felt right.

Her lips joined with his. There was nothing shy about their kiss. No clumsy fumbling around. No misdirected pawing. When it came to sex, they had always been good together. His tongue plunged into her mouth, and she welcomed the taste of him.

Neither of them was fresh and clean, and she should have been grossed out. Instead, it was the opposite. She nuzzled the bare skin of his throat inside his collar and inhaled his musky, manly aroma. Wade had never worn cologne, and that was fine with her. She liked the way he smelled.

His lips tickled her ear as he whispered, "I missed you, Samantha, missed you so damn much."

"Me, too." She kissed him again. "Where were you?"

"It's complicated."

She pulled her head back and stared into his light brown eyes. After a year and twenty-one days, after letting her think he was dead, he needed a much better explanation. "Tell me about it."

"There isn't time. I shouldn't have come down here, but I couldn't be this close and not touch you. You're an angel, so damn beautiful. But I've got to take off, can't stay here."

She wasn't letting him run away after giving her a whisper of sweet talk and "it's complicated." She needed a hell of a lot more than that. She slid down his body and planted her boots on the ground. "Sit down, Wade."

"I already told you. I can't—"

"We can do this the easy way or the hard way."

He frowned. "What?"

The hard way, it was. She stalked around him until she had the uphill position. From there, it was easy to shove his shoulder and hook his legs out from under him. As soon as his butt hit the dirt, she was on him. After taking away his rifle, she flipped him onto his belly and cuffed his hands behind his back.

"Wade Calloway, you're under arrest."

Chapter Four

Wade should have known better than to think he could pop back into her life and erase the past with a hug and kiss. He needed to do more, a lot more. But what a kiss! Her lips were delicate soft pillows but her need was hard. Her tongue had tangled with his for an aggressive battle that drew him closer, deeper.

Remembering, he licked his lips. A single kiss from Samantha was better than a week in bed with most women.

He rolled to his back and sat up with his legs stretched out in front of him. After Samantha pulled both guns from his holsters, she stood a few feet away and gave him *The Look*.

An involuntary grin tugged at the corners of his mouth.

"What's so funny?" she demanded with her arms folded across her chest.

Maybe he was still giddy from that amazing kiss, but *The Look* amused him. She meant for her scowl to be menacing, to strike terror into his heart. Instead, he saw a strong, sensible woman who was plenty ticked off but fair enough to hear him out.

"A question," he said. "What are you charging me with?"

"Let's start with attempted murder, two of them." Her

eyebrows pulled down, and her full lips thinned into a straight, angry line. "That was you, shooting from the trees."

"Let's call it self-defense," he said. "More accurately, defense of you and Ty."

Right on cue, his old pal tromped up the hill. "We could have handled it."

"You're welcome," Wade said.

"Incorrigible," Samantha growled. "The least you could do is pretend to be sorry. You have so much to apologize for, Wade. Not just to me but to all your friends, all the good people who showed up at your memorial service. Your sister couldn't stop sobbing, and she claimed to be glad your parents were dead so they wouldn't have to go through this tragedy. And then there's Jenny."

He watched *The Look* fade from her face, replaced by an empty gaze and vacant sadness that could never be fully expressed. When she spun on her boot heel and walked away from him, it was a knife in his heart.

She muttered, "I can't stand to look at you."

"Samantha, wait." He heard the desperation in his voice. "I can explain everything."

As she continued to put physical distance between them, she straightened her shoulders. "Ty, I'm going to contact Dispatch and tell them we need an ambulance, maybe two. Keep an eye on our suspect."

Wade's head dropped forward on his chest. Earning Samantha's forgiveness was going to be harder than hell. It was one thing to say that he'd faked his death so she and Jenny would be safe, and another to prove it.

"You're in big trouble." Ty hunkered down beside him on the hill. "Consider yourself lucky that all she did was throw you on the ground and slap on the cuffs."

The handcuffs were mostly a joke between them. Long ago during a particularly wild session in their bedroom, he'd shown her how to pick these locks. With his hands still behind his back, he dug into his pocket for the Swiss Army knife he always carried. His gaze locked with Ty's. He wanted to trust this guy he'd known since high school, wanted to believe that Ty was on his side 100 percent. Ty was one of a handful of lawmen who knew Wade had faked his death. He'd been nothing but supportive. But Wade had been betrayed by others. He had to be careful.

While he opened the knife and went to work on the cuffs, he said, "Kind of a coincidence, don't you think?"

"What are you talking about?"

"You and Samantha just happened to be on this particular stretch of road. You just happened to find Morrissey's body."

"Accusing me? Really?" Ty sat back on his heels. "You're a real piece of work, Wade. Do you really think I'd put Sam in danger?"

He wasn't sure what he thought or whom he believed in. "How did you get to be here? In this particular spot?"

"I sure as hell wouldn't call down an ambush on myself."

"Tell me," Wade said.

"Sam received a call from the fire marshal, who told her that the chopper pilot spotted three hikers near Horny Toad Creek. The marshal couldn't spare the manpower to pick them up, so Sam volunteered, since we were in the area."

Ty's story sounded plausible and bore no resemblance to the conspiracy theories that were running rampant in

Wade's head. It wasn't likely that the pilot, the marshal and Ty were in cahoots. Still, he said, "And why were you and Sam in this area in the first place?"

"I asked Sam to come with me while I checked out the safe house. And, yes, I had an ulterior motive. As soon as I heard about your escape, I figured you'd hightail it back here. And I wanted to warn Sam, maybe even take her and Jenny into protective custody."

"The hell you will." The pocketknife he was using to pick the cuffs slid across the metal and nipped into his thumb. "I know what protective custody is like. I'm not putting my wife and child through that."

"How are we going to keep them safe? When word gets out that you're alive, the cartel will use them. They'll threaten harm to your family unless you turn yourself over to them."

Wade wasn't sure how many people knew that he was still alive and waiting to testify against a former DEA agent and a member of the Esteban cartel who were in prison awaiting trial. He was the witness who could make sure those men were convicted of murder, conspiracy, drug trafficking and gun smuggling. His testimony would seal the deal…if he lived long enough to get into the courtroom.

"I've got a bad feeling," Wade said. "I think too many people already know."

"Is that why you broke out?"

"You make it sound like a great escape."

"Wasn't it?"

"Nothing so dramatic," he said. "After this last trip to the federal courthouse in Austin where—as you know— the trial was delayed for the seventh time, I went back to the safe-house motel with my handlers. Later that night, I climbed out the bedroom window."

"You just quietly sneaked out, huh? I heard you knocked both guards unconscious. One of them has a bad concussion."

"Not true. I wouldn't hurt anybody."

Ty cast a cynical gaze at the carnage spread across this smoky mountain meadow. "Yeah, you're a peaceful pussycat."

"I'm telling you that if my handlers were injured, I didn't do it. Whoever hit them could have been after me."

"None of the people who know you're alive have reason to want you dead."

Wade thought differently. Three days ago in Austin when he was leaving the courthouse, he caught a glimpse of a face he'd seen before. He didn't know the man's name but seeing him set off alarm bells. He needed to get back here, back to Samantha and Jenny as quickly as possible.

He regarded Ty with a steady gaze. His friend's easy-going manner was well suited to his ranching background, but Wade wasn't fooled for a minute. This laid-back cowpoke could move as fast as a rattlesnake's strike. Ty was sharp and smart. He was a good man; he'd earned an FBI Shield of Valor for his work on a kidnapping case.

The question was: To trust him or not to trust him? Even if Ty was brave and loyal, he was also a federal agent who wouldn't want to risk his job. "I'm going to ask you for a favor, Ty."

"Shoot."

"Don't tell anyone you saw me today."

Vertical worry lines creased between his brows. "That's asking a lot, brother. Those guys you shot are going to mention the mystery rifleman. And the forensic investigators are going to find bullets from the rifle."

Wade nodded toward the gun on the ground. "There it is. You can say that you were using it."

"You got it from the safe house, didn't you?"

"The rifle and two handguns," Wade said dismissively. There were more important issues at stake. Yes, he'd breached the sanctity of a federal safe house. So what? The place was never used. "I'm asking you for twenty-four hours. By nightfall tomorrow, I'll know what I need to do."

"I knew you spent the night in the safe house. As soon as I walked through the door, I could see that the dust on the floor had been disturbed."

"Yeah, yeah, yeah, and I ran water in the sink. And I ate a can of beans, left a dirty cup and messed up the sheets in the bedroom. Sue me." He heard a tiny click as the lock on his cuffs sprang open. "I need you to focus. Will you give me twenty-four hours?"

"If you can convince Sam, I'll do it."

Wade wished he was more sure of himself as he watched Samantha hike up the hill and stand beside Ty. Turning her profile to Wade, she spoke to his friend.

"My dispatcher contacted police and ambulance services in Glenwood Springs. They said they'd be here in half an hour, but I'm guessing it'll take longer. We need to do as much first aid as we can."

"I'll work on the guy by the sedan. And I'll get a tarp from your SUV to throw over Morrissey's body. His lieutenant is on his way. He'll want to see that we're showing respect."

"Even if Morrissey doesn't deserve it," Wade put in.

"Truer words never spoken." Ty backed down the hill. "I'm going to leave you two alone now."

Her thumbs hooked in her belt, she tilted her head down and stared at the buffalo grass beneath her boots. She'd left her hat in the SUV, and he noticed that her braided chestnut-brown hair wasn't as shiny as it used to be. Still beautiful but a little bit thin, her hair looked as if she hadn't been able to spend much time taking care of it. Managing the responsibilities of the sheriff's office was a lot of work.

A new wave of guilt splashed over him. Though he'd made sure that all her bills would be paid, he'd left her with a lot of loose ends. "Samantha?"

Her lower lip stuck out in a pout. "What?"

Her features weren't as tense as they'd been before. The deep sorrow had faded. The anger was gone, too. With a shock, he realized that he couldn't read her mood. They used to be in perfect harmony, perfect understanding. He'd lost that connection.

"Samantha, look at me."

She slanted a gaze in his direction. "I don't know what to do."

He swung his arms apart and made a grand gesture to show the cuffs dangling from his left wrist with the right side completely free.

"Ta-da!" He jumped to his feet. Like a magician, he took a bow. "The Great Wade has escaped the surly bonds."

Her blue eyes twinkled as though she was about to laugh. Instead, her chest heaved and a harsh sob exploded through her lips. In reaction, she slapped her hands over her mouth.

He caught her before she could run away from him. Gently, he peeled her hands away from her face and brushed a kiss across her knuckles. Her mouth trembled as she held back tears.

"It's okay," he murmured. "Everything is going to be all right."

Sobs overwhelmed her. He gathered her close and cuddled her against his chest, holding her shoulders while she poured out a torrent of tears. He patted her shoulders and stroked her hair, her silky-soft hair that smelled of flowery shampoo in spite of the fire and the smoke.

More than anything, he wanted to tell her that he loved her. This was the wrong time, too soon. And he was scared. Wade Calloway wasn't afraid of much. He was tough enough to take on a dozen rotten cops and a drug cartel, but he knew that Samantha could destroy him. If she denied his love or had given up on loving him, he might as well be dead.

"I have to go," he whispered to her. Ty had mentioned an officer with the state patrol was on his way, and then there would be the ambulances.

"I know." Her deep shuddering sobs had subsided to sniffles. Using his shirt, she wiped her face. "I heard some of the stuff you were telling Ty. You want to keep up the pretense that you're dead."

"And if the wrong people know I'm still alive and kicking, you and Jenny could be threatened." Her nose was red, and her cheeks were puffy from crying, but he thought she looked adorable. "You can't tell anybody you saw me. Within twenty-four hours, I'll have this straightened out."

With her right hand, she reached behind her back.

Keeping her voice low so Ty wouldn't overhear, she showed Wade his fancy Colt .45 with copper-inlaid handle. "I found this in the car with Morrissey, and I'm guessing it was put there to throw suspicion on you."

"Good guess." He took the gun from her and stuck it into his belt at the small of his back. "You kept this gun locked up at the house, didn't you?"

She nodded. "They must have broken in to get it."

A thief had violated the home he and Samantha had built together, their sanctuary, the house where their daughter slept. "Did you notice the break-in?"

She shook her head. "Half the time I leave the doors unlocked."

"That stops now," he said. "You can't trust anyone. Understand? Not anyone."

"What about Ty?"

Much as he hated to cast suspicion on his friend, Wade would rather err by being too cautious. "Trust him but keep your guard up."

"Of course I would. Ty told me a whopper of a lie about my husband being killed in the Roaring Fork River. Oh, wait, you told me that very same lie." Her bloodshot eyes narrowed. "Can I trust you, Wade?"

"I'll make this up to you. I promise."

"Not what I want to hear." She gripped the front of his plaid flannel shirt with both hands and pulled him close. "You need to listen to me, listen hard. You've spent a year trying to handle this by yourself. Don't make that mistake again."

"What do you mean?"

"You need me." She released his shirt and stepped back. "You need my help."

She was right. During the past year, Samantha had

proved she was capable of taking care of herself, their child and the entire population of Swain County.

He couldn't ask for a better partner.

Chapter Five

Sam's first-aid kit was suitable for scraped knees and poison-ivy rashes. Not life-threatening injuries. She knelt beside the unconscious man with the shoulder wound, which she had managed to bandage while still keeping his hands cuffed behind his back.

Wade had slipped out of his cuffs easily, which was as she'd expected. Arresting him was more of a symbolic gesture, a way of showing him that she refused to be ignored and would never be kept out of the loop again.

She still couldn't believe it. Her husband was back. He was alive. She wiped the smile from her face and tamped down her sense memory of how his arms felt when he embraced her and how his lips tasted when they kissed. *Not now!* She had to wait, couldn't allow her emotions to run rampant. And the anticipation was making her as edgy as a prairie dog surrounded by lawn mowers.

Her focus needed to stay on the practical aspects of how to handle his return from the dead. He'd promised to talk to her later tonight. The waiting was hard, but she believed him when he said it was necessary. And he'd spoken of possible danger to Jenny.

A worse brand of anxiety sped through Sam's veins when she thought of her daughter. Jenny was her precious girl with jagged bangs across her forehead that she'd cut all by herself and a strong singing voice that the church choir director said was remarkable. If anything happened to her precious five-year-old daughter...

Sam's attention returned to the injured man. He wasn't bleeding badly, but his chest heaved as though he was struggling for breath. A punctured lung? Internal bleeding? Where the hell were the ambulances?

If he died, it was her fault. Never mind that she hadn't fired the bullet that caused his wound. It didn't matter that the injured man was trying to shoot her and Ty before he was brought down by the expert marksmanship of her husband. Sam was the sheriff; therefore, she was responsible.

A fat lot of good all her training did. Yes, she was certified in CPR. Yes, she'd taken dozens of first-aid classes from the Red Cross. She'd heard of sucking chest wounds and septic shock and all sorts of emergency treatments for all sorts of injuries. However, until this moment, she'd never had to test those procedures.

She needed help. Why were the ambulances taking so long? She had to get out of here, had to get back to Jenny.

She stood and called to Ty. "I've got an idea. We could forget about the ambulances, load these guys into my SUV and drive them to the hospital. It'd be faster."

He was in the road, standing over the first man he'd shot, the dead man. In his gloved hand, he held a wallet. Though she was at least thirty feet away from him, she heard him muttering under his breath. Angrily, he wheeled around and shook the wallet at her. "Do you know who this guy is?"

How could she possibly know? "I'm sorry. Why should I recognize him?"

"Do you ever look at the BOLOs we send you?"

A bunch of law-enforcement offices, ranging from the FBI to the local Fish and Game warden, sent out computer notices or faxes of APBs and BOLOs to "be on the lookout" for certain license plates or vehicles or individuals. She always took a look at them and often hung them on the bulletin board. Ultimately, they became scrap paper that she handed to Jenny, who drew pictures with crayon or marker on the back. Passing a BOLO to her kid wasn't something she'd mention to Ty. She'd once caught Jenny drawing lipstick and purple eye shadow on a felon's mug shot.

Her ears pricked up as she heard the sound of a motorcycle engine cranking to life. Ty had heard it, too. He glared up the hill toward the place where Wade had disappeared into the trees.

"Oh, that's just great," Ty growled.

"A motorcycle," she said. "Why is that a problem?"

"I'm guessing that your husband swiped a very nice little Honda from the safe house. A good bike, it's got heavy tread for off-road and goes a decent speed on the highway."

"He wouldn't have taken it if he didn't need it."

"But it belongs to the FBI."

"Don't even think about whining. I had to dig deep into my sheriff's department budget to buy disposable smoke masks, and the FBI can afford to leave an entire house standing empty."

"Point taken." His tone became more conciliatory. "I just hope he doesn't wreck it, that's all."

She walked down the hill toward him. "Let's get back to what you were talking about. Tell me who our dead man is."

"Tony Reyes," he said. "He works for the Esteban cartel, and he's on the short list of Most Wanted for both the US and Mexico."

She'd heard horror stories about the drug cartels: beheadings, torture, brutal murders of women and children, and human trafficking that amounted to a slave trade. Never in her wildest imagination had Sam thought she'd be in contact with this type of criminal. Swain County was a lazy little territory with one semicharming town and a couple of local ranches. Nothing ever happened here, and that was the way she liked it.

"Why does this Reyes person rate so high on the Most Wanted list? What has he done?"

"He's an enforcer. He kills people, especially cops."

Like Morrissey. The murdered state trooper lay at the side of the road covered with a tarp. If the smoke hadn't already been blocking the sun, she would have sworn that the day turned darker.

She hated the way these pieces were falling into place. Had Reyes been the one who took Wade's gun from her house? Did he know where she lived? "Are these the people Wade is testifying against? How did he get mixed up with a drug cartel?"

"It's worse than that, Sam."

"Worse?" Her frustration erupted in a burst of absurdities. "What could be worse? Vampires? Zombies? Oh, wait, maybe Wade actually is dead and he's the zombie."

"What?" Ty looked concerned.

His frown made her laugh. Her grandma always said that nothing was so terrible that you couldn't laugh about it. *Oh, Granny, you're so wrong.* For the past several months, Sam had few reasons to giggle. Even now, after learning Wade was alive, her chuckle sounded a little hysterical.

As she paced up and down on the road, she indulged in wild speculation. "Let me see, what could be worse? Did Wade do something to upset the Nazis or the terrorists or, maybe just maybe, he's being pursued by undead Nazi zombies."

"Are you done?"

She paused by her SUV, leaned forward from the waist and rubbed at the two bullet holes in the driver's-side door. "This has been a lot for me to absorb. First, I've got a dead husband who isn't dead. Then I find out that my daughter might be in danger. And now you're talking about drug cartels."

"It's more than drugs. There's also evidence of human trafficking. A cache of high-tech weaponry was discovered, thanks to information from Wade."

The scope of these crimes sobered her. They were dealing with very evil, very scary people. "Is this as bad as it gets? Is there more?"

"Rogue cops," he said. "Wade witnessed criminal acts and transactions between the cartel and law enforcement. We're not sure how far the corruption spreads."

"Is that why you and Wade hated Morrissey?"

He nodded. "My boss is running the task force. They were keeping an eye on Morrissey, hoping he'd lead us to others. And there are a lot of others. Cops, patrolmen, inspectors, DEA agents, maybe even FBI agents, who are taking kickbacks from the cartel."

Literally, there was nobody she could trust, nowhere she could turn for help and no way to escape. The idyllic time in her life was over. When she and Wade were first married, they'd been so happy while building their house, having a healthy baby and making their dreams come true. Now the future looked a hundred times more complicated.

Ty had his cell phone in hand. "I need to tell my boss about this."

"Wait." She stopped his hand before he could lift the phone to his ear. "You aren't going to tell your boss about Wade, are you?"

"Come on, Sam, you can trust him. Everett Hurtado is a decent guy. Kind of a bureaucrat, he probably won't even come out here into the field."

"You promised Wade." She'd overheard that much. "You gave him twenty-four hours."

"Like I told you, Hurtado is running the task force. He already knows Wade is alive and escaped from custody. He's the one who suggested I come up here and poke around at the safe house."

Also to make contact with her. If his boss had been looking for Wade, it stood to reason that Wade would be drawn to his family and would show up in Swain County. Ty's SSA might not be as upstanding as he thought. "Your supervisor doesn't know where Wade is. You can't tell him. Not until tomorrow."

"Okay, fine."

This was important. She stuck out her hand and pinned him with a gaze. "Deal?"

When he shook her hand, he gave an extra little squeeze. "If I didn't know better, I'd think that you and Wade were out to ruin my career."

"Maybe I am," she teased. "Then you and Loretta would have to move back here and go to work on your daddy's ranch."

"The twins would love that."

He turned away to place his phone call, and she saw the red and blue flashing lights from a Colorado State Patrol vehicle—a Crown Vic, silver with a blue-and-black dash and a logo. Most of the staties were nice guys who were willing to do the paperwork on traffic citations, but she was seeing law enforcement through a different lens. Both Ty and Wade had agreed that Morrissey was corrupt. Why not his boss?

She'd never particularly liked Lieutenant Trevor Natchez. When it came to appearances, he was one of the most by-the-book officers she'd ever met. His white-blond hair had a short military cut. His shirts were always crisp. The dark stripe down his beige trousers was never rumpled. According to rumor, he washed his vehicle at least once a day. His vocabulary, however, was gross. It always surprised her that someone with such a high regard for cleanliness could talk so much filth.

Natchez swore constantly. Whenever she was around him, Sam used a mental (bleep) so she wouldn't be distracted and wouldn't show him that his bad language bothered her. He enjoyed irritating her and never failed to come up with borderline sexist comments when they met. Given those ugly characteristics, she halfway expected Trevor Natchez to be up to his elbows in dirty dealings.

After he parked his vehicle behind hers, he climbed out from behind the steering wheel, straightened the flat brim on his uniform hat and strode toward her.

"If it ain't Little Miss Sheriff," he said with a sneer. "What happened to my man Morrissey?"

She glanced around him to look at his car. The inescapable dusting of ash from the fire must be driving him nuts. "You left your flashers on," she said. "Were you hoping to keep the crowd at bay?"

"When I want advice from you, honey, I'll ask for it."

She directed him to the tarp, squatted beside it and held back the corner to reveal Morrissey's face. The folds of his chin were slack. His skin had taken on a grayish hue. Sam couldn't stand the dead man's stare and had pulled his eyelids down.

For a brief moment, Natchez seemed shaken. He clenched his jaw, and his thick blond eyebrows lowered so much that she couldn't see the blue of his eyes. He flipped the tarp to cover the dead man's face and tilted his head upward. While he scanned the skies as if looking for heaven behind the clouds and smoke, a litany of profanity spewed from his mouth.

"Where did you find him?"

"In this car." She pointed. "Shot in the chest, he was behind the wheel, but there wasn't any spatter. He must have been killed somewhere else."

"Did you come up with those conclusions all by your cute little self?" He glanced at Ty. "Or did this FBI stud help you?"

Ty ended his phone call and greeted Natchez with a pat on the back and a handshake. The two of them were as friendly as could be. They stood over the body of their fallen comrade and said a few things about what a truly great guy Morrissey had been, quick with a joke, sharp as a tack, a credit to the uniform, blah, blah, blah…

Earlier, Ty hadn't been so complimentary. He'd as much as told her that Morrissey was under suspicion for working with the cartel. She supposed Ty's conversation with Natchez fell into the "never speak ill of the dead" category.

Natchez scanned the area. His gaze paused on each of the dead or injured men. "What happened here? Did our sexy lady sheriff pitch a fit?"

Her hand rested on the butt of her gun. It would have given her great pleasure to shoot this man between the legs and ruin his perfectly neat uniform. "We were ambushed."

"No way."

"My dispatcher has already put in a call to the ambulances," she said. "They should be here any minute."

"Who told you to move the body?"

"Nobody had to tell me anything," she snapped. "These murders were committed in my county, and I have jurisdiction over the investigation."

"The heck you do. Morrissey was my man. I should be the one who looks into his murder."

She got in his face. This was one of those times when Sam was glad for her giraffe-like height. Natchez was an inch or two shorter than she was, and she made it seem like even more by stretching her neck and straightening her shoulders. "Here's the deal, Lieutenant Natchez. The investigation is mine. But I'm aware that I don't have the facilities to do thorough forensics."

"Damn right you don't."

"Neither do you. The state patrol doesn't have a coroner. You can't do an autopsy."

He opened his mouth, no doubt to swear, but nothing came out. Maybe Swain County was too small and too limited in resources to handle this case, but Natchez wasn't equipped for doing a murder investigation, either.

"I suggest," she said, "that we request assistance from the FBI on these cases."

"Good plan," Ty said as he held up his cell phone. "I just talked to my supervisor, and he mentioned the same thing."

Natchez gave a nod. "I'm okay with that. If you need my help, I'll do whatever I can."

Ty asked him, "Is losing a man going to cause you any problem in scheduling?"

"To tell the truth, Morrissey was cutting back on his hours. He used more sick time than a teenage girl getting out of gym class with the cramps."

She turned away. Where, oh where, were the ambulances? There was no hope of providing sensitivity or enlightenment to Natchez. She tried to ignore him, but he was like a rash that wouldn't stop itching.

Natchez swaggered around the scene with Ty. They paused beside the dead man on the road, whom Natchez recognized immediately from a BOLO. Well, of course he would. The guy probably had every notice on file going back ten years, probably practiced with them every night like flash cards.

"I heard a rumor, Ty. Maybe you can verify. I heard that Wade Calloway is still alive."

Too much! Hearing her husband's name on the tongue of this bigmouthed jerk sent Sam right over the edge. In a couple of quick strides, she was beside Natchez. With her right hand, she yanked his wrist behind his back, putting a nasty crease in his shirtsleeve. Her left hand held her stun gun at his throat.

"Never speak of my husband again, unless you intend to humbly and without profanity praise him for being an American hero. And show some respect for me, the grieving widow."

"Yes, ma'am."

Finally, she'd got through to him. All it took was an outrageous act of violence on her part.

Chapter Six

When Sam drove past the supermarket on the east edge of Woodridge, she noticed more activity than usual in the parking lot, and she wondered why. Typically, if a blizzard was predicted, everybody rushed to stock up on food and necessities. The fire might be having the same effect, even though gathering more supplies wasn't a good idea if your house might be burned to rubble.

On the wide main street that went through the center of town, every slanted parking space was taken outside the diner, the coffee shop and the two taverns. This was something she understood. People liked to huddle together and reassure each other when trouble was near.

She wished that she could do the same.

But she couldn't talk about Wade's return from the dead or the possible danger from a criminal cartel. Not even Ty knew the whole story; she hadn't shown him Wade's gun that had been planted in Morrissey's car. Besides, Ty wasn't here. He'd gone with the ambulances. One would deliver the wounded to the hospital in Glenwood Springs. The other would transport Morrissey and Reyes to wherever their bodies would be autopsied.

Sam was alone with her problems.

Somehow, she had to cope.

After a stop at the one traffic light in town, her SUV cruised past the Swain County Courthouse, where the 911 dispatchers were babysitting her daughter. Sam's bloodshot eyes bored a hole in the two-story building, wishing she could see through the chiseled red stones to where her daughter was drawing or skipping rope in the wide corridors or sitting at a desk and rearranging the clutter.

Before she picked Jenny up, Sam needed to be certain that her house was safe from intruders. Somebody had sneaked inside to steal Wade's revolver. They might come back, might want to grab her to get to Wade. Worse, they might come after Jenny.

The threat to her daughter enraged her, made her as fierce as a mama grizzly. But it also terrified her. Was she tough enough to keep her child safe? Sam couldn't take that chance; she needed to get Jenny far from harm's way.

Luckily, the solution was obvious: her dad was a captain in the Portland, Oregon, police department. Sam had already called him and arranged for Jenny to visit Grandma and Grandpa. The approaching fire provided a good excuse for sending her daughter to safety, while she herself stayed here and helped Wade investigate.

About six miles outside town, she made a left onto a curvy asphalt road that she paid extra to have cleared by the snowplow in the winter. Now, in springtime, the drive was green and pleasant with the new growth of shrubs and leaves sprouting on the trees. Runoff from the snowmelt made a sparkling rivulet in the ditch beside the road.

After her SUV passed the neatly lettered sign that marked Kendall's Cabin, her nearest neighbors, she drove around a stand of aspen to the two-story log home that she and Wade had built. The peaked roof above the second floor covered a balcony that stretched across the front of the house and provided shelter for the wraparound porch. A huge cedar deck jutted from the south end of the house outside the kitchen. At this time of year, she and Jenny usually ate dinner at the picnic table on the deck, where they could watch the hummingbirds zoom around the hanging feeders filled with red-tinted sugar water.

She could hardly wait until Wade joined them again. He loved cooking on the grill with the flames leaping high—maybe he loved the flames a bit too much. His burgers were usually burned. Her nose twitched as she remembered the charred aroma of her husband's cooking.

They were about to become a family again. Or were they? He had betrayed her in the worst imaginable way. How would she ever forgive him?

In her parked car, she sat and gathered her thoughts. Before her husband supposedly died, she'd never thoroughly appreciated him. Wade had always been affectionate, giving her pats on the butt and subtle hugs and surprise kisses on the nape of her neck. She'd yearned for those gentle touches almost as much as she missed having him in her bed.

Her life had been shattered by his fake death. She'd gone through the steps of grief from denial to anger to bargaining to depression to acceptance. Now she was back to anger. She flung open the car door. She needed to take action and not stew in her own fury. Her number one chore was to make sure the house was safe for Jenny.

Just in case there was somebody lurking, she drew her weapon as she climbed the three stairs to the wrap-around porch. Had she remembered to lock the door this morning? No, she hadn't. The handle turned easily. She silently chastised herself for being too complacent as she stepped over the threshold.

Nothing appeared to be disturbed in the living room. Some of Jenny's stuffed animals were arranged on the plaid sofa as though they were watching television. A long bar with tall stools separated the kitchen from the living room. The dining room was to the left of the kitchen and the deck was to the right through the sliding glass doors.

She prowled across the hardwood floors. On the kitchen bar, there was a note, written in crayon. It said, "Great minds think alike. The house is all clear. Lock the front door. Come to the bedroom." Instead of his signature on the bottom, Wade had drawn a cross-eyed green frog.

Sam holstered her gun, charged across the room to the entry, where she'd already flipped the lock. She climbed the stairs two at a time and pushed open the door to her bedroom.

The extra-long four-poster bed with the denim-blue comforter dominated the room. She didn't see him, but her husband's black cowboy hat was hanging on the post nearest the door. She unbuckled her heavy utility belt and draped it over a chair. Then she took off her hat and perched it on the post opposite his.

"I remembered," she said. "Never put your hat on the bed."

He came out of the adjoining bathroom with a pair

of pliers in his hand. "Hat on the bed is bad luck. Don't know why, don't know how, but that's the fact."

Before he could set down the pliers, she pulled him into her arms and planted a firm kiss on his mouth. The taste of his lips and the feel of his hard, sinewy arms wakened all her senses and made her feel truly alive. It was as though her nerve endings had been paralyzed and were now—suddenly and provocatively—reconnected. Electricity sizzled through her. She could almost hear the pop and crackle as the tension that had held her captive for one year and twenty-one days released.

He swung her in his arms, lifting her feet off the ground while their lips were still joined. The dark anger lifted. Pure joy bubbled up, and she couldn't hold it inside. She broke the kiss, threw back her head and laughed. When he waltzed her backward and shoved, she easily toppled onto the bed.

"Wait." She lay on her back, holding him off with both arms. "What did you mean when you said something about great minds thinking alike?"

"When I left you by Horny Toad Creek, my first thought was about Jenny. I needed to make the house safe for her." He pushed one of her arms out of the way. "I knew you'd do the same thing."

He was correct. Not a surprising conclusion given that they both loved their daughter more than anything in the whole world. She fended him off with one arm. "How'd you get here so fast?"

"I rode cross-country on that Honda I swiped from the FBI safe house. My route was likely faster than going the long way around on the regular roads. That's why I beat you home."

"Plus, I had to wait for Lieutenant Natchez and the ambulances."

"I thought you'd have to go all the way to Glenwood with the wounded," he said. "The crimes were committed in your jurisdiction. That means you're in charge, right?"

Of course he'd see it that way. He'd been sheriff for nearly ten years and handled things mostly by himself. That wasn't her way. She took her responsibilities seriously and did as much as she could. But if somebody else could do it better... "I don't have the resources to investigate a murder. No forensic laboratory. No CSI team. And the county coroner is a dentist. I handed jurisdiction to Ty and the FBI."

His mouth tensed. "You did what you thought was best."

He would have looked angry, but a couple of dimples appeared amid the stubble on his cheek and softened the chiseled lines of his face. His light brown eyes, a color that reminded her of champagne, sparkled. His flash of anger was gone. She knew exactly what was on his mind.

She sat up on the bed and pushed him away. "There are a few things we need to discuss before this goes any further."

"I don't mind talking, but make it fast." He held her chin and darted close for a quick little kiss. "Please make it fast."

When he stepped away from her, she felt his absence. Her fingers itched to trace the ridges of his abs and tweak the hair on his chest and tangle in his rumpled brown hair. She needed to make love with him, to reassure her body that he was really here with her again. But she wouldn't rush things. This time, they played by her rules.

"I haven't forgiven you, Wade. You know I'm not the sort of woman who holds a grudge, but you destroyed me with your betrayal. It's going to take more than your handsome smile to patch this relationship back together."

He sauntered across the bedroom to the dresser, folded his arms and sat on the edge with his long legs stretched out in front of him. For a long moment, she just stared at that fine-looking cowboy, *her* cowboy. His shoulders were bigger than before and the sinews in his forearms were more sharply defined. He had big hands, big wrists.

He cocked an eyebrow. "Well?"

Discombobulated, she stuttered, "Well, w-w-w-what?"

"What's it going to take to make you happy?"

With a mental effort, she swept her thoughts into a pile and started with the most important. "It's about Jenny."

"I can't wait to see my girl."

"That's not going to happen." She braced herself for an explosion before she continued, "The only way I'll feel comfortable about her safety is if she's out of the area. I already called my dad. He and my mom are flying out here in his Cessna to pick her up."

Wade's disappointment was palpable. The pain of being separated from Jenny for more than a year had to be devastating. She wished it could be another way.

"What about tonight?" His voice was husky. "Just an hour."

"It'd do more harm than good."

"Does she remember me? What does she say?"

"She draws pictures of you, of all three of us. She makes portraits of a happy family that doesn't exist.

Not only does she talk *about* you, but she talks *to* you, like you're an imaginary friend."

He winced.

Though she wouldn't wish this kind of guilt and sadness on anyone, she needed him to be sensitive to his daughter's needs before he thought of himself. Jenny loved him, and that love hadn't changed when he was supposed to be dead.

Sam rose from the bed and paced across the room, showing him her back. Breathing hard to let off steam, she rubbed at her midriff. Her lungs were constricted by the bulletproof vest she wore under her uniform shirt. "You put us through hell, both me and Jenny."

"I'm sorry."

His voice was as faint as a sigh. She heard his sadness. But it wasn't enough, damn it, not enough. She whirled to face him. "I've overheard Jenny having a chitchat with her imaginary daddy about how Mommy isn't fair. And, guess what, she's right. Mommy's not fair. Mommy makes demands and enforces the rules. Mommy is always going to do what's best for her little girl."

He didn't contradict her. "What's best?"

"I don't want her to see you tonight and then be forced to leave you tomorrow morning. She doesn't deserve that sort of heartbreak."

She watched his Adam's apple bob up and down as he swallowed hard. "I hate what you're saying, but I understand."

"And you agree, right? Promise me you won't try to see Jenny tonight." When he didn't reply immediately, she added, "Not only is it bad for her, but the other problem is obvious. Jenny's just a kid. She won't be able to keep your secrets."

"You didn't tell your dad about me?"

"Hell no." Sam's overprotective father, Jake Lindstrom, would never approve of an undercover investigation with her mysterious husband who had faked his own death. "I told him that the fire was a strain on our resources in Swain County, which meant more sheriff work for me. And Jenny's regular babysitter had gone to Denver. Plus, all this smoke can't be good for a kid."

"And he likes any excuse to fly across the country in his pretty little five-seat aircraft."

Her dad had been a pilot in the navy and never lost his love of flying. His greatest extravagance was a Cessna 185 Skywagon, named *Lucky Lindstrom*, which was one of her dad's nicknames after he survived a supposedly lethal gunshot wound. He planned to use the Cessna for circling the globe after he retired from the Portland PD. Until recently, her mom had been rigidly unenthusiastic about his plans and refused to set foot in the plane.

"Mom has finally accepted *Lucky Lindstrom*, maybe because Dad allowed her to reupholster the seats and get her own pink headgear for talking to the tower. She's coming with him."

"When do they get here?"

"They'll fly into the Glenwood Springs airport tomorrow morning." Her dad would have made the trip without stopping overnight, but her mom liked to take it easy. "They'll call when they get in."

He crossed the room and took her hands. "You're right about the way we should handle this with Jenny. I can't promise I won't be watching my little girl tonight, but she'll never know I'm near."

"How's that going to work?"

"I'll find a way. You won't see me, but I'll keep an eye on you both, keep you safe while you sleep."

She liked the idea of being cared for, having her protector back on the job. "Like a guardian angel."

"Samantha baby, I'm no angel."

"Don't I know it."

He was the only person who called her by her full name. And he was definitely the only one who dared refer to the nearly six-foot-tall sheriff who wore a Glock on one hip and a stun gun on the other as "baby." The intimacy of those two words melted something inside her. Her defenses were gradually unraveling.

"Samantha." His tongue rolled over each syllable. "Let's go to bed."

She snatched her hands from his grasp. "I have other demands."

"Bring them on."

"First, let me do this." Her fingers flew down the front of her uniform shirt, unfastening the buttons. There was nothing erotic about this striptease. Her moves were purely practical; she needed to get the bulletproof vest off.

"Can I help?"

Unlike her, he was sexy. His voice, his eyes, his lips, even his dimples—the whole package was a major turn-on, except for one very important aspect...the smell.

"You don't get to touch me," she announced as she ripped apart the Velcro straps, "and I won't touch you." She tore off the vest and stood before him, wearing her bra and her boxy uniform trousers. "I usually like the way you smell, but we need to take a shower. Right now. Both of us."

In a flash, he was peeling off his clothes. "I had

planned to clean up before you got home, but I got distracted. That's why I had the pliers in the bathroom."

"To fix the leak," she said as she sat on the edge of the bed and shucked off her boots. The faucet in her bathroom sink had been dripping for over a month—just one of those chores she intended to handle but never found the time.

"I already had the toolbox out," he said, "and I figured it would only take a sec."

Oddly, his willingness to take care of a mundane household task was almost as exciting as his bare chest. This was how they had been for years as wife and husband, partners in life who managed the daily chores. And then, at night, they turned off the lights and got down to business. She didn't know why that familiarity was so very sexy, but it was. Her ability to resist him was completely undone. She stepped out of her trousers and into his arms.

He pulled her into the bathroom and turned on the shower. Steam rose in a moist cloud and wrapped around them. All day long, the smoke from the fire had assaulted her senses. This steam was soothing, healing.

Wade tugged off the last bits of their underwear. Again, this wasn't a smooth romantic moment. She didn't hear the strain of violins or feel the brush of an angel's wings. His actions were practical. *Getting down to business.*

Then he looked her up and down...slowly. At each place his gaze touched, her skin prickled, from her throat to the tips of her breasts to her stomach to the apex of her thighs. A shudder rocked her body. The determined control she'd used to manage her sensations and emotions shattered. His glance had set her free.

His cheeks dimpled when he smiled. "Can I make a demand?"

"You can try."

"Tomorrow morning, I want you to get on the Cessna with your parents and Jenny. Go with them. I want you to be safe in Portland until this is over."

Not a chance.

Chapter Seven

Sam didn't give him an answer. Not yet. Right now, while she and Wade were naked and facing each other, she didn't want to argue. It was time to savor the moment.

She closed her eyes, hoping to shut out all the responsible things she should be doing—finding the rest of the ventilator masks, investigating the murder of Morrissey, checking in with her deputies to see what troubles the fire had brought and rushing back to town to pick up Jenny from the courthouse.

Not now. She claimed this reunion with Wade for her own. *This is my time.*

Finally, she could be a woman again. When she'd first heard that her husband was dead, part of her had died, as well. She'd stopped noticing other men, didn't even try to flirt. She'd lost the desire to kiss, embrace or even touch. Now that Wade was back, she meant to make the most of their time together. They would be getting down to business…a lot.

Her eyes popped open. Undressed and unembarrassed, she stepped into the frosted-glass shower stall and turned around to face him again. As the steaming water cascaded down her spine, her appreciative gaze devoured the tall, handsome man who stood just outside the shower door. She couldn't decide whether she wanted to pull him closer and feel his body against hers or just stand here and stare, dumbstruck with admiration. He'd been working out. She could tell.

"While you were dead," she blurted, "I didn't date other men."

"It would have been okay if you did." He braced one hand against the edge of the shower door. "Don't get me wrong. I wouldn't be happy if you found a new boyfriend, but I'd understand."

"Would you?"

"I'd try, but then I'd probably kick his ass."

He stepped into the stall and closed the door. Though they'd designed the shower to accommodate their size and height, there was no way to avoid each other.

It's time. She was ready to make love. Or was she?

With her backside pressed against the green tiled wall beside the faucets, she felt strangely reluctant to touch him and seal the deal. Though she wanted him with every fiber of her being, this might be too much, too soon. Was it because she hadn't forgiven him? Or because he seemed to think she'd be willing to hop onto her father's aircraft and leave him to investigate alone?

She really wished he hadn't suggested that she run and hide. She wasn't a child. He seemed to be putting her in the same category as Jenny. Oh my God, Jenny! Sam thrust out an arm and reached for the shower door.

He caught her wrist. "What are you doing?"

"I need my cell phone from my trousers. What if Jenny calls and I don't answer? She'll be freaked out."

"I'll get it," he said firmly. "You stay here."

Her first instinct was to get the phone herself, the

way she'd been doing everything by herself. While he was gone, she'd been mother and father to their daughter. How could she trust anybody else to get it right? But she had to trust him. If she was going to bring Wade back into her life, she had to accept him as a full partner. "Okay, you go."

As soon as he left the shower, she felt his absence. During their separation, a chill had crept into her bones and taken up residence. What if he died again? Loneliness was never more than a heartbeat away. She was crazy to invite him back into her life while they were surrounded by danger. If something happened to him, if he left her...

The door to the shower opened, and he held up the cell phone. "There were no calls or texts. I'll put it by the sink."

She nodded.

He stepped back inside, close to her. With his thumb, he tilted her chin up and studied her face. "Were you crying?"

She honestly didn't know. "I don't think so. It's just spray from the shower."

"I hurt you, Samantha. And I'm sorry, so damn sorry."

"I know."

With one hand he stroked, slowly and rhythmically, up and down her arms. With the other, he picked up the tail end of her long braid. "Did you want to wash your hair?"

"Not enough time." Using a barrette she kept in the shower for precisely this purpose, she hurriedly fastened the braid in a knot on top of her head. "I'm not late to pick up Jenny, but I ought to leave soon."

"You're worried about her," he said.

"You bet I'm worried." She grabbed the soap and started lathering up. "Ty said that one of the men we shot was part of the Esteban cartel. Those guys are mad-dog killers."

"Jenny will be fine. Nobody knows I'm alive."

"The people you escaped from," she pointed out. "They know. And that jerk Natchez said he'd heard a rumor about you."

"What did you tell him?"

"First, I got the drop on him with my stun gun." She grinned at the memory. "I told him to show some respect for a grieving widow."

His laughter echoed inside the shower stall, and she felt herself beginning to relax. This man wasn't a stranger or someone she'd just met. He was her husband. They had a long history together.

He took the soap from her hand and turned her around. "Have you missed having me wash your back?"

"Maybe."

"Relax, Samantha."

She rested her arms against the tile wall while he massaged her shoulders and spine. His touch sent quivers of wild, exotic excitement across the moist surface of her skin. "Do you remember what you told me the first time we showered together?"

He spoke in a lecturer's voice. "In the western United States, water is a precious commodity. Even if the frequent droughts haven't affected the water flow or pressure, it's up to each of us to conserve water. I convinced you that getting naked was the environmentally aware thing to do."

"How could I refuse? I'm a total eco-slut."

He turned her around so the shower spray sluiced down her back to rinse off the soap. "I'd like to start on the front side. Those breasts look like they need a lot of attention. Do we have time?"

"We do if I don't leave tomorrow."

His gaze searched her face. "What?"

"I'm not leaving with my dad tomorrow." No matter how much she wanted him, she had to take a stand. "You need me. When you came up with the idea of faking your death and going into hiding, you cut me out of the investigation."

"I was protecting you and Jenny. Being stashed away in safe houses with bodyguards watching your every move isn't fun. I didn't want that for you and Jenny. I wanted you to have a normal life."

"By turning me into a widow?"

"The witness-protection thing was only supposed to last for a couple of months, but—"

"I don't want to hear it," she said. "The plan—whatever it was—didn't work."

His intention had been to do the best for his family. She believed that. But he and Ty and the FBI had gone about it all wrong; their scheme had turned into a mess.

"You're right," he admitted. "It's ended up with all of us being in danger while the bad guys are still at large."

The strangeness of standing here naked and discussing their situation had not escaped her. She was conscious of the tight nubs at the tips of her breasts and the hot water sliding over her hips. But she couldn't stop talking. The need for argument overwhelmed her. Instead of making love, she was stating her case. "Why did you choose this moment to make a run for it?"

"At first, I just wanted to grab you and Jenny and

disappear. After I found Morrissey dead and the other three men started attacking, I knew I couldn't let this go. I need to end the threat."

"Yes," she said with relief, "and I need to help you. Please, Wade. We can solve this together."

There wasn't enough physical space in the shower for him to escape her, but it was obvious that he wanted to put some distance between them. He turned his head to the side, avoiding eye contact. As if that weren't enough, he turned away.

And she didn't stop him.

She could hardly believe that she was here, naked and as horny as she'd ever been in her whole life, with the man she acknowledged as her soul mate, and she wasn't touching him, kissing him, not even grabbing his muscular ass.

Her breasts weighed heavy with desire. From low in her belly came a steady pulsating throb. *Do it, just do it now.* But she clenched her fingers into fists and drew back. *Not yet.* She hadn't forgiven him. And she was anxious about Jenny. And she needed him to accept her as a partner.

"All right." His voice was low and ragged. "We're a team."

Her impulse was to wrap her arms around him and press her body against him, but she held back. Instead, she glided her hand between his shoulder blades. "It's going to all work out."

He pushed open the door of the shower and stepped out. "After you finish up in there, you should pick up Jenny."

When he closed the door, she was alone in the hot-water spray with the steam whooshing around her. She'd clung to her reservations by refusing to forgive. She'd accepted her responsibilities, starting with getting her daughter from the courthouse. She'd stated her demands and won the argument.

And she was miserable.

WADE HAD HOPED to share dinner tonight with his daughter and wife. He'd hoped for laughter and for hugs. In the best of worlds, he would have had a T-bone on the grill, a cold beer in his fist and an old Johnny Cash song on the outdoor speakers. Instead, he was hiding, lying flat on his belly in a storage space amid the rafters in the garage. He'd widened a space between the boards so that he had a clear view of the deck on the south end of the house. The smoke didn't seem to be causing him a problem with visibility.

At half past five, the shadows grew long, but there was still plenty of daylight. Ten minutes ago, Samantha had parked her SUV near the front door, which was just beyond his range of vision. He'd asked her to bring Jenny out on the porch, and he waited anxiously to see his little girl.

He'd heard her voice. When they pulled up in front, she was belting out a song, "Let It Go." He had to wonder if her mom had coached her to warble that tune; it had meaning for him. He was the one who'd taken her to the movie, and they used to drive along in the car together, singing at the top of their lungs. His voice sounded like an elk's bugle during mating season, but his daughter was musically talented. He wanted to get her a piano... if Samantha ever let him back into the house.

Their argument in the shower had taken him by surprise, not that he expected her to forgive him right away.

He'd put her through hell, and he regretted every tear she'd shed and every sigh of longing that had passed through her soft, full lips. Though he was willing to spend the rest of his life making it up to her, he didn't know how many more incidents like the shower he could take without going crazy. You couldn't put a woodpecker in a redwood forest and tell him not to poke, couldn't expect a fox in the henhouse to go vegan. His wife was a sexy, desirable woman, and he was a man.

They'd been only seconds away from full-on sex. He'd been aroused. And she was, too. He knew her well enough to see the signs. She wanted him with all the frustrated, pent-up desire of being apart for over a year.

Then she'd stopped short.

From inside the house, a screeching alarm sounded. Had somebody broken in? Wade couldn't see the north side of the property. Instantly alert, he braced himself, wrapped his hand around the long barrel of his hunting rifle and prepared to drop from the rafters. Taking action would be a relief after all this waiting. Then his cell phone buzzed.

This was a burner phone, and only Samantha had the number. During his cross-country run after he escaped from the Texas safe house, he'd picked up half a dozen throwaway phones. She was calling him on the one he'd given her.

Her voice was loud in his ear. "How do I kill this stupid alarm? I tried the off button, but it doesn't work."

"It's not exactly state-of-the-art." He'd purchased the burglar alarm several years ago and stashed it away in the garage. Before she went to pick up Jenny, he'd finished hooking it up and shown her how it worked. "Did you unplug it?"

"Duh! Of course I did." In the background, he heard Jenny asking her mom about who was on the phone. Samantha replied to their daughter, "It's the guy who fixed this thing."

Jenny yelled at the phone, "Don't quit your day job."

He chuckled, "Did you teach her that?"

"Would you please focus? What do I do about this screaming thing?"

"It's got batteries," he said. "Open the panel on the bottom and pop them out."

The alarm went silent.

"Thank you," she said. "I knew there was a reason I never wanted this alarm hooked up."

"Uh-huh." From what he'd seen, she'd rather leave the front door wide open and roll out a welcome mat for intruders. "It's motion-sensitive. Promise you'll turn it on tonight before you go to bed."

"I'll think about it."

While he watched, the sliding glass door opened, and Jenny came onto the deck. She carried a sketch pad and a flat pencil box he'd given her. Humming to herself, she set down her drawing tools and climbed on top of the picnic table to check the red liquid in one of the hummingbird feeders.

His daughter was so remarkable, so beautiful that she took his breath away. Her thick brown hair, which was the same rich color as her mother's, hung straight past her chin. The front was cut with weirdly slanted bangs. When she looked up at the feeder, he could almost see the blue of her eyes. He wanted to be closer to her, close enough to count the freckles he knew were splattered across her nose.

He whispered into the phone, "She's taller."

"Growing like a weed."

When Jenny stood on tiptoe in her pink high-top sneakers, her T-shirt with a multicolored, shiny heart came untucked from her red skirt. A sparkly bracelet flashed on her wrist. Though she liked being a princess, his little girl could outrun and outswim a lot of boys her age.

When she started singing to herself, he was overwhelmed by a fierce longing. He clenched his jaw so he wouldn't open his mouth and call out her name. Earlier today, he'd watched Samantha from afar. Seeing his daughter was different, more primal and visceral. The way he'd handled being apart from his wife was to think about her all the time, to write her letters that were never sent and record messages that were never spoken. With Jenny, he shut down the "daddy" part of his brain... and his heart. He couldn't stand thinking of her and not being with her. He loved this child more than life itself.

"Samantha," he growled into the phone, "we need to get this solved right away. I can't wait much longer. I need my family."

"Soon," she promised.

As she disconnected the call, she came onto the deck. With her fists braced on her hips, her gaze scanned the surrounding forest and focused on the garage. When she smiled, he knew it was meant especially for him.

Chapter Eight

Throughout dinner, Sam knew that Wade was watching. His voice on the phone had sounded so desperate that she almost called him back and invited him to join them. Not a good idea.

If Jenny saw her daddy, she'd never allow herself to be bundled off to Portland, even with the very special bribe of being able to ride in Grandpa's little plane and a promise that she didn't have to go to school. Jenny needed to go with her grandparents, to get away from here, to be safe.

And so, Sam didn't signal her husband. He could *not* join them. Later, there would be time for them to be a family again. For now, he could only watch. Having him as an audience made her feel self-conscious, as if the deck on the south end of the house was a theater stage and she was standing in the spotlight.

While serving their spaghetti dinner, she found herself striking poses that showed off her long legs in skinny jeans. On top, she wore a floaty tunic in a lavender print. This might be the most flattering outfit she owned. Her legs were most definitely her best feature, and the long tail on the tunic covered up her too-skinny bottom.

After slurping a long spaghetti noodle, Jenny stared across the picnic table. "How come you're all dressed up?"

"I'm not." She glanced toward the garage. Though she couldn't see Wade, she figured he was there. The storage area under the slanted garage roof made a good hiding place.

"Are too," Jenny said. "You never wear that shirt unless you're going someplace special."

"I've been slogging through smoke and yuck all day," Sam said. "After I took a shower, I felt like putting on something nice."

"Do you have a date?"

"What?" Sam had zero social life. "Why would you ask that?"

Jenny shrugged. "There's something weird about you."

At age five, Jenny was just beginning to be embarrassed by her mother. Though she enjoyed the perks that came from having her mom be sheriff, she had told Sam many times that she hated the uniform. If Jenny had her way, all the sheriff's badges would be bedazzled with pink rhinestones. But that wasn't going to happen anytime soon. Sam was still the mom, still the boss, and she didn't need to explain herself to her daughter.

She cleared the dinner plates. "As soon as we're done here, we'll get you packed."

"We have to fill up the hummingbird feeders. I betcha the fire makes them hungry."

"I bet you're right."

The devastation of the forest would affect the local fauna, from the tiny birds to the black bears and mountain lions. No matter how civilized the mountains were, this was still a habitat. Nature came first.

After filling the feeders, she checked her email and talked to the dispatchers at the courthouse. Then she personally contacted each of her six deputies and informed them that they'd be on call until the fire was completely contained. The real reason she needed her team to step up was so she'd have the time to investigate with Wade. But she couldn't come right out and say that Wade was back; telling the truth was not an option. Nor did she dare to attempt a cover story. Sam was a terrible liar and wouldn't be able to hide her excitement about Wade's return from the dead. Deputy Schmidt sounded suspicious and didn't like that the FBI had taken over the investigation of the murders. She'd cut him off midsentence and ended the call.

When this was over, there would be fences to mend. It occurred to her that when this was over, Wade would be back, and he might want to be sheriff again. And she might want to step aside and let him take over. That would be a huge change. Though she welcomed the extra time to be with Jenny and to work on the house, she'd miss wearing the badge and having folks depend on her.

As soon as she went through her evening rituals with her daughter and got Jenny tucked into bed upstairs, Sam heard a car pulling up in front of the house. It was just after nine o'clock, which was a little late but not outrageous.

In usual circumstances, she wouldn't think twice about charging onto the porch, but a touch of paranoia slowed her step. Why hadn't this visitor called first to let her know they were coming? Since she'd followed Wade's suggestion about pulling all the curtains after dark, she had to peek around the edge of the window. A dark blue truck parked next to her SUV. In the glow from the porch light, she saw Justin Hobbs, the fire marshal, climb down from the driver's side.

Her fears dissolved in a puff of smoke, which was kind of appropriate for a fire marshal. Though she didn't know Justin well, he had a reputation for being a reliable, stand-up kind of guy. When he wasn't in the midst of an active fire, he tended to be unassuming and to fade into the woodwork, even though he was a big man with a barrel chest and a full black beard.

Before he knocked on her door, she opened it and held her finger across her lips to indicate quiet. "Do you mind if we talk outside? I just put my daughter to bed."

Chagrined, he mimicked her finger-across-the-lips gesture. "Sorry, Sam, I should've called first."

"You've got enough on your plate." She led him around to the deck, which was on the opposite side of the house from Jenny's bedroom. Reaching inside the sliding glass door, she turned on the porch light so that Wade could see and hear what was happening, and she wouldn't have to explain later.

She turned to Justin. "Tell me about the fire."

"It's still burning but seventy percent contained."

From the edge of her deck, she looked toward the southeast, where the night sky was tinged with an ugly red haze. The flames weren't visible from here, but their destructive light colored the smoke and blurred the stars. "I thought we were expecting rain tonight."

"I'm still hoping," he said. "I wanted to let you know that a couple of properties are in the path of the blaze."

His calm demeanor told her that there weren't people living in the cabins. Still, the idea of a house going up in flames disturbed her. "Where?"

"They're near the place called Hanging Rock."

"Eyesores." She knew the exact location. "One of them is missing half the roof. Windows are broken. The wood siding has aged to a dead gray. If those houses burn, I say good riddance. They're probably haunted, anyway."

"Do you believe in that stuff?"

She gestured for him to have a seat. "Can I get you something to drink?"

"I'm fine." He held up a half-full water bottle as he sank into a chair. His bulk filled the rough wood frame, but she wouldn't describe him as being overweight. He was big. "And you didn't answer my question. How about it, Sam? Do you see ghosts?"

When she heard about Wade's death, she'd tried to contact him on the other side, even consulted with an Arapaho shaman. There hadn't been a tiny glimmer of awareness. But, of course, he hadn't really been dead.

"I'm not sure about ghosts," she said, "but the local high school kids like to sneak around those deserted houses looking for some old-time prospector. Hanging Rock is a prime location for parties."

"I guessed as much. I sent a couple of my firefighters down to check the houses out, and they reported finding a lot of junk and discarded beer cans."

"Are the houses still standing?"

"Yeah, and they might survive the fire, depending on which way the wind blows."

She sat in the chair across from him, close enough that she could smell his heavy cologne. Like her, Justin had changed from the clothing he'd worn all day while working near the fire. He probably used the cologne to mask the stench of smoke.

"Anyway," he said, "it might be a good idea to track

down the property owners and notify them of the situation."

"No problem. I'll pass that task to the clerk at the courthouse."

They sat in silence for a long moment. She wondered why he drove here to deliver the message personally when he could have called. The poor man looked as if he was struggling to keep his eyes open.

He snapped his thick fingers. "I almost forgot. I brought you a box of disposable ventilator masks. They're in the back of my truck. Twenty-four of them."

"Thanks so much." She reached over and gave his knee a friendly pat. "I started off the day with a box of my own but gave them all away."

"How's your little girl?" He leaned forward. "Does the smoke bother her?"

This was a good opportunity for Sam to try out her first lie about Jenny. "Actually, the smoke is kind of a problem for her, and her regular babysitter had to take her little boy into Denver. The poor kid has asthma."

So far, so good. The first lie was out there: Jenny was having trouble with the smoke. That wasn't such a stretch.

"Sorry to hear that," he said.

The second lie, which was more complicated, stuck in her throat. She didn't want to tell anybody that Jenny was going to Portland; bad guys could buy plane tickets to Oregon. She needed a different destination. "I'm going to send my daughter to stay with a friend of mine in Denver for a few days."

"Woodridge is perfectly safe. I can guarantee that."

"Getting my daughter out of town is partly for me," she said. "Worrying about the fire while taking care of the other things a sheriff needs to do is making me real tired."

She clamped her lips shut to keep from doing any more talking. Most lies fell apart because the liar kept embellishing until nothing made sense. "Yep, I'm exhausted."

"You do a fine job as sheriff. Everybody says so."

"Well, thanks."

"Do you mind if I ask you something personal?"

He stretched out his long arm and did exactly what she had done, placing his huge hand on her knee. She didn't get a sexual vibe, but his touch was more intimacy than she wanted. How could she refuse to answer his question? It seemed rude. Maybe if she ignored it, the question would go away. "I want to thank you for the way you kept me informed today."

"That's my job."

Right off the top of her head, she couldn't recall if Justin was married or not. She thought not. And he wasn't wearing a wedding band. She scooted forward as though getting out of her chair. "I'll go with you to your truck so I can pick up those masks."

"Sam, you've been a widow for over a year. As far as I can tell, you're not seeing anyone. Is that right?"

Before this nice man could go any further, embarrassing them both, she took his hand in both of hers. "It's by choice, Justin. I'm not dating anybody because I'm not ready to move on. I'm too much in love with my husband."

"Wade was a good man."

"Sometimes, I feel like he's still close to me, still watching over me."

Justin rose from the chair. A very big man, he matched

Wade in height and was far more massive. "I appreciate your honesty."

"Let's go get those masks."

She glanced toward the garage, where she suspected
Wade was hiding. Even if he wasn't physically close, she
hadn't lied to Justin Hobbs about her feelings. Wade was
her soul mate, the only man she would ever love. That
was truth.

WADE SWUNG DOWN from the rafters and crept from the
garage toward the front of the house, where he watched
Hobbs and Samantha saying their goodbyes near his
truck. Hobbs towered over his tall, slender wife and was
as wide as two of Samantha put together. Though Wade
was in excellent physical shape, he was glad he wouldn't
have to wrestle with Hobbs to win Samantha's love.

She loved him. Good to know. She wouldn't let him
near his daughter and threatened to throw him out of
the shower, but she still loved him. And he felt the same.

They needed to dig into this investigation and get
things figured out soon, real soon. Having Hobbs drop
by turned out to be useful. He'd said something that provided Wade with a starting point.

Samantha waved farewell to the fire marshal who had
the hots for her…no pun intended. As she strolled back
to the front door, she was humming, not paying attention at all to her surroundings. If somebody came after
her, she wasn't ready.

"Samantha," he hissed from the shadows at the side
of the house by the wood box. "Over here."

"What are you doing?" she whispered back. "Jenny
is upstairs, and if she sees you…"

"She won't. I've been watching."

"From the garage, right?"

It was the most obvious place. He wasn't about to give her a prize for guessing correctly. And he didn't plan to push his advantage and insist on coming into the house, where he could sleep comfortably. For tonight, he'd patrol outdoors and make sure his family was safe. Starting tomorrow, he and Samantha would start investigating.

"I set up that alarm for a reason," he said.

"To make me crazy?"

"Protection." He kept his voice low. "These are dangerous men, Samantha. If they knew I was alive, they'd use you to get me to do whatever the hell they wanted. They know I'd lie for you and Jenny. I'd commit treason. I'd kill for you."

"You're scaring me, Wade."

"That's the idea."

He'd meant to lecture her on taking safety precautions and staying alert. But when she was this close, his physical need overruled his brain. He clasped her upper arms and pulled her deeper into the shadows, into the darkness.

His kiss was gentle for about three seconds. Then she moaned. His mouth pressed harder against hers. His tongue pushed past her teeth and tangled with hers.

He started dragging her closer but stopped himself. If her lean body pressed against his, he didn't trust himself to be prudent. He'd tear off their clothes and make love to her right here in the open with no thought of the possible consequences. He was so damn weary of being cautious. He wanted his woman.

First, he wanted her safe.

He ended the kiss and spoke in a rush. "Go inside and set the alarm. I'll be out here watching tonight."

"Okay."

"What time do you take Jenny to the airport tomorrow?"

"Early," she said. "I talked to my dad, and he said they'd be here around seven thirty or eight."

Good. She'd been smart to make arrangements with her father, who was a cop and a man who loved gadgets. The security at his house in Portland was top-notch. Leaving early in the morning made it unlikely that the bad guys would take notice, and he'd overheard the story she'd told Hobbs. "Are you telling people that Jenny is in Denver?"

"In Denver with a friend of mine. That should be vague enough to keep anyone from looking for her."

"You lied to Hobbs. Do you have any reason to suspect him?"

"Justin?" Her voice must have been louder than expected because she clapped a hand over her mouth. "I barely know him. We're just friends."

"It sounds like he wants to be more than friendly."

She leaned so close that her breath tickled his ear. "He's not the only one."

Being around her was torture, pure and simple. He ached with need for her. He couldn't stand breathing in the scent of her lavender soap, hearing the teasing lilt of her voice and feeling her skin, her silky skin. Her full, soft lips taunted him. If he kissed her again, he would surely lose all control.

"Get a good night's sleep, Samantha." He took a backward step away from her. "Don't look for me tomorrow. I'll find you, and we'll get started."

Hobbs had given him the location where they would start. The place where Wade had witnessed a crime was near Hanging Rock.

Chapter Nine

Sunrise painted the clouds and smoky haze with eerie shades of blue and gray, slashed with streaks of yellow and red where the sun tried to break through. As Wade rode away from the airport in Glenwood Springs on the safe house's motorcycle, he thought of the old saying: *red sky at morning, sailors take warning.* Though he was nowhere near the sea, he needed to be careful. *Take warning.* No one could be trusted. There was more than his own safety at stake; Samantha would be with him as soon as she dropped off Jenny and headed back in this direction.

For the nine hundredth time, he considered the risks involved in working with her. She was a decent markswoman, an experienced cop and smart at figuring out puzzles. Those attributes counted as pluses. She had one big minus: Samantha was gullible. With a big smile on her face, she wanted to believe that everybody was good at heart and that nobody lied or cheated.

Before he got to the airfield, he turned the bike onto a side road and drove about a hundred feet to a thick stand of aspen trees on a hillside. He saw no other vehicles and doubted that anyone was following him. Why would they? Nobody but Ty knew about the bike, and

Wade's helmet disguised his identity. Still, just in case he felt threatened, he'd left himself a back-door escape; he could take off through the forest on this sweet little Honda.

After he dismounted and stretched his legs, he looked down at the crossroads. Samantha would take this route back to Woodridge, and he figured he could catch her along here. If her father landed when expected, Wade had less than a half hour to wait.

He took out one of his burner phones and put in a call to Ty. His old pal's voice sounded puzzled when he answered.

"What's the matter?" Wade asked. "Didn't recognize the number?"

"Burner phone," Ty guessed. "Where are you?"

As if Wade would answer that question. "What happened at the hospital?"

"Two dead, two survivors. Both of the men who made it are low-level thugs associated with the Esteban cartel. Both have criminal records. Both are from Denver. And, wonder of wonders, neither of them mentioned seeing you. They barely noticed me."

They were both watching Samantha. He didn't blame them. "Are you still at the hospital?"

"That's not how the FBI works, my friend, and you know it. Give us a murder and we swing into action like a well-oiled investigative machine."

They were a machine, all right. But the feds weren't always a model of efficiency. Wade had experienced a year's worth of glitches while they tried to mount their case. Most of the agents, like Ty, were effective lawmen, but others were half-assed losers, like the two guys who were supposed to be watching him at the safe house and let him slip out a window. Well-oiled? No way.

Ty continued, "We've got CSIs going over the car, which is not—as we suspected from the lack of blood spatter—the primary crime scene."

"He was shot somewhere else."

"Correct," Ty said. "Autopsies are scheduled for this afternoon in Denver. And I left an agent at the hospital to keep an eye on our prisoners. It'll be another day or two before they're ready to be transported."

It was too much to hope that the thugs would provide useful leads or make a deal with the feds to inform on their colleagues. These guys were low-level. If they ratted out their bosses, the cartels would take extreme revenge. Still, Wade asked, "Did you get anything from questioning them?"

"The two survivors claim to be working for the one who died. They know nothing."

"Probably not far from the truth," Wade muttered. "Where are you?"

"My dad's ranch." Ty's voice brightened. He loved coming home. "This is our command central. My SSA is coming up this afternoon to coordinate the investigation."

If Supervisory Special Agent Everett Hurtado was getting involved, it meant something bigger than Morrissey's murder was going down. "What's SSA Hurtado looking into?"

"For one thing—" Ty lowered his voice "—he wants to find you. I don't know how long I can keep you out of this. If Hurtado asks me directly, I can't lie to his face."

Though Wade didn't want to broadcast his location, Hurtado was one of the few who already knew that he'd faked his death. The SSA still belonged in the "do not trust" category, but keeping Wade's whereabouts a secret from Hurtado wasn't worth Ty losing his job. "You can tell him, as long as he understands that I'm not going to turn myself in or go back into custody."

"Why not? We can all work this together."

During his time in protective custody with nothing to do but think, Wade had run through many scenarios. No matter how he looked at the smuggling operation, one conclusion remained the same: someone in law enforcement was the ringleader, and it wasn't the DEA agent who was already in prison. This ringleader, the big kahuna, kept the other dirty cops in line and saved the Esteban cartel from getting arrested.

Was Hurtado the ringleader? Wade didn't know, couldn't be sure. "You said that nabbing me was one thing Hurtado wanted. What are the others?"

"Only one other," Ty said. "Something big is going down real soon. It has to do with weapons being sold to the cartel. Big guns were stolen from a US Army arsenal outside Colorado Springs, stuff like rocket launchers and bazookas."

He couldn't drag Samantha into the middle of this war. But he couldn't leave her alone to fend for herself. "We've got to put an end to this. How did Hurtado hear about the weapons deal?"

"I don't know."

"When does it happen?"

"Again, we're not sure. The fire might have thrown off the timing. These cartel boys are secretive. They don't like making a move when there are choppers flying overhead and firefighters swarming across the landscape."

Wade had to think Hurtado was getting his information from a snitch. Morrissey might fit that bill. If he was passing secrets to the FBI and some of the bad guys found out, it was a sure motive for murder. "What can you tell me about Morrissey? Did you get any leads from his death?"

"We've got no suspects. Following procedure, I talked to Sam last night and filled her in on the details."

In her role as sheriff, she needed to stay apprised of the situation. The crimes had been committed in her county. While Wade was gone, Ty had kept him posted on how Samantha was doing as sheriff. *Stellar* was the word he used most often. Not only did she keep a lid on the few crimes that happened in Swain County, but she'd instituted new programs for helping the homeless and dealing with domestic violence. She was also involved in educating the kids about the dangers of drugs, which was a topic that had got complicated after recreational marijuana was legalized in Colorado.

According to everything he'd heard, she was a damn good sheriff. The last thing he wanted to do was usurp her authority.

He made one last stab. "Anything else you can tell me?"

"Not a thing, nada."

Wade wasn't sure if Ty was holding back or just didn't know any of the details. SSA Hurtado was running the show for the FBI, and he wouldn't want Ty stealing the spotlight. Hurtado didn't have much use for Wade, either.

Sooner or later, they'd have to confront each other. Wade wasn't looking forward to seeing Hurtado at the ranch. He said goodbye and ended the call.

Seated on the Honda, he waited for Samantha to

come chugging along the road in her SUV. Without the smoke, this would have been a spectacular spring day with the breeze ruffling through the green aspen leaves that would turn to golden coins in autumn. A shaft of pure sunlight cut through the clouds and the haze to splash against a jagged pillar of granite that stood like a sentinel at the edge of the forest.

His memory cast back to another spring day when he'd walked among these white aspen trunks and listened to the wind rattling in the leaves. Wade had lived almost his whole life in Swain County. He knew the terrain, the landmarks and the houses. The inhabitants changed from year to year, but there were those who still remembered when Wade and his younger sister and the Baxter kids dashed around like a pint-size gang. A far cry from a drug cartel, their most reckless prank was turning loose three chickens inside the house of their rival.

Deputy Caleb Schmidt was the one who caught them. He still hadn't stopped teasing Wade about the stunt. For Wade's thirtieth birthday, Caleb presented him with a chicken-shaped cake. Foolish pranks and small disagreements were the norm for Swain County. Not arms deals and smuggling.

He spotted Samantha's SUV. Only a few other cars and trucks had used this back-road route, and no one appeared to be following her. He waited an extra minute, watching, and then he zipped down the hill on the Honda and turned onto the road behind her.

Though his motorcycle wasn't built for high speeds, he had no problem catching up with her thirty-five-mile-per-hour pace. Samantha was an excellent driver, better than him, and she maintained a steady, unflappable speed while he rode up beside her window and flipped up the face mask on his helmet.

She grinned and shouted something he couldn't hear over the noise of the engine. He gestured for her to follow him. In about seven miles they'd be in Swain County. Four miles after that was a turnoff. If nothing had changed in the year he'd been away, the turnoff would lead to a small farmhouse and horse barn that was occupied only in summer. When he was sheriff, the family who owned the place asked him to check in occasionally to make sure they hadn't been vandalized. He'd never found a disturbance at this remote property.

He parked his bike on the far side of the barn where it wouldn't be visible from the road. Samantha parked in the same area. She left her car and rushed toward him, talking as she approached.

"I had a dream about you," she said. "You were holding my hand and dragging me toward Hoppy Burger in Grand Junction, the place that has a rabbit with huge ears on the logo. But you weren't wearing a shirt. And I kept telling you—no shoes, no shirt, no service." She came to a halt in front of him but didn't stop talking. "By the way, you look really hot in that leather jacket."

"You're pretty hot yourself. I like you out of uniform."

"I can tell you've been working out. It shows in the abs."

"There wasn't much else to do."

"Okay, back to my dream. At Hoppy Burger, I told you that you couldn't go in. And you pointed to me. I looked down. And I wasn't wearing a shirt." She tossed her head, and her long braid whipped back and forth.

"Here's what I think it means. You're breaking the law, and now I'm about to join in your life of crime. Think so?"

Retelling dreams wasn't something he did, but he liked to hear Samantha talking and to see a sparkle in her big blue eyes. He slipped an arm around her slender waist. Without the bulletproof vest, her body was soft, feminine and pliant. She molded herself to him.

"It means," he said, "that you want to get naked with me."

"No deeper meaning? No complex interpretation? You think I just had a sex dream."

"Baby, that's the best kind."

As she snuggled closer and nuzzled the crook of his throat, his pulse thumped faster and louder. Wade was a grown man who ought to have self-control. But as soon as she touched him, his reaction was about sex and nothing else. The blood drained from his brain and rushed to his groin. He was hard. His hand slid down her back, pausing at the flare of her hips and then gliding down to cup her bottom. He adjusted her position until she was rubbing up to him in exactly the right way.

She whispered, "I'm ready to make love."

The thrill that ripped through his veins nearly knocked him off his feet. Those were the words he wanted to hear from her, but he hadn't expected her to say them so quickly. He thought there would have been more discussion, probably another apology on his part. He'd been prepared for a long talk about Jenny and her parents and the Cessna. Only after that would they move on to sex.

Her direct approach was different.

He didn't complain.

"This way." He took her hand and led her through a

side door into the horse barn—a long building with a center aisle and stalls on either side. He turned on the lights, which were just a couple of bare bulbs. The barn felt musty from being closed up, but the smell wasn't bad if you didn't mind hay, leather and horses.

He climbed a wood ladder to the loft, and she followed. When he opened the hinged window that overlooked their vehicles, a cool breeze swept inside. This area above the stalls was tidy but not spotlessly clean.

Her boot heels clunked as she paced on the bare, unvarnished wood floor. "Does anybody live here?"

"In the barn?"

"On the property, smart guy."

"The owners don't usually return until June." He crossed the loft and took her hand. This would be their first time together in over a year; he should have taken her somewhere classy. "This old horse barn isn't good enough for you."

"What did you have in mind?"

"Like on our honeymoon. We stayed at that five-star hotel in Hawaii."

"My best memories of that week aren't about the champagne and orchids and fancy sheets." She tossed him an over-the-shoulder glance and ran the tip of her tongue over her top lip. "I remember getting dirty with you in the jungles and sandy on the beach."

"Are you telling me I didn't have to pay for all that luxury? Would you have been just as happy wearing flip-flops and sleeping under the stars?"

"Don't get me wrong. I love the deluxe treatment." Her voice lowered to a sexy growl. "But I don't mind making love in a barn with the right man."

This warm, sexy version of Samantha spurred him

into action. He didn't want to wait too long and give her a chance to remember how angry she was with him. In a storage cabinet, he found a variety of camping equipment stacked on wide shelves. He rummaged through the gear and dragged out two sleeping bags, which he unzipped and spread on the floor. He peeled off his leather jacket, folded it and placed it at one end for a pillow.

The bed was made. He sat back on his heels and flashed a smile. "Join me."

"How did you find this place?"

"The same way I find everything. I was out wandering and stumbled upon this house and barn." He smoothed the sleeping bag. "I've slept here before."

"When?"

He sensed a shift in her mood. The urgent sexy Samantha had taken a step back. "I've known about this loft since I was a teenager. If I hadn't been able to use the safe house, I would have come here."

"Since you were a teenager, huh? Have you ever brought other women to this loft?"

This was not a discussion he wanted to have. Not when they were so close to reconciliation. Staying on his knees, he took her hand and held it to his lips. "There are no other women."

"Good answer."

"I know."

She rewarded him with a grin. "I have a feeling that no matter where we went, you'd be able to find shelter, food and a quiet place to make love. You know every inch of Swain County."

"Am I that predictable?"

"Not in any way." Finally, she lowered herself into

the nest of sleeping bags. "A man who fakes his death, spends more than a year in protective custody and then escapes from the FBI is not a stodgy old stick-in-the-mud."

The first thing they took off was their holsters. He placed both of their handguns within easy reach, which might be a mistake given the way her temperament was fluctuating between seductive and scary. They both pulled off their boots. She shucked off her denim jacket, and her fingers went to the top button on her blue-striped shirt.

"Wait," he said. "Before we take off our clothes, there's something I want to do. May I unfasten your braid?"

In answer, she turned so she was facing away from him. He held the length of her shining brown hair in his hand. At first glance, the color seemed to be a simple brown. Further study revealed shades of deep mahogany and shimmering strands of gold. He unfastened the band at the end of the braid and started spreading the long strands across her back.

"This is turning out okay," she said.

"It's all good." Her hair, like liquid silk, slipped through his fingers.

"We're a team, investigating together. When do we start?"

"Soon." He pushed aside the curtain of hair and leaned close to nibble her earlobe.

"When?" she demanded.

His focus wasn't on crime solving. All he wanted was to savor the taste of her body, inhale her clean scent and caress the perfect softness of her skin. "Later today, we need to meet up with Ty at his ranch."

"Uh-huh."

"But we start at Hanging Rock."

Chapter Ten

Hanging Rock. The two words rattled ominously in her head. Last night, the fire marshal had mentioned properties at Hanging Rock that were in danger of burning, and Sam was certain that Wade had been listening. What could possibly be of interest at Hanging Rock?

"Those houses," she said. "Nobody lives there."

"Where?"

"Hanging Rock."

"I can't do this." His stroking of her hair abruptly ceased. "I can't split my attention. Either we talk about the investigation or we make love."

"I want both." She twisted her head and looked over her shoulder so she could see him. "First, love. Then investigate."

"I can do that."

His focus switched from her hair to the task of separating her from her clothing. He pulled her across his lap, kissed her mouth and opened her blouse. Of course, he didn't do all those things at the same time, but the way he shifted her from one position to the next was smooth. She was still reveling in one set of sensations when another started up. He went from her lips to her chin to her breasts to her throat, her shoulder, her elbow.

He was everywhere at once. It was as though he had magic fingers.

While her breasts were tingling from his kisses, he spread her knees and unzipped her jeans. Magic fingers were inside her pants. Her breath caught in her throat and her skin prickled and her muscles flexed and relaxed in a throbbing crescendo as he teased her to a shuddering release she hadn't felt in over a year.

She exhaled a contented moan. "I'm so glad I chose sex first."

"We're not done."

"Good." To be completely honest, she couldn't stop thinking about sex when she was with him. This morning when she'd awakened with a gasp, she'd been completely aroused. Her dreams were—as he suggested—more about sex than anything else, and she was ready to re-engage that part of their relationship exactly as it was before.

Forgiving him would be harder. She was leery. Though she didn't think he'd deliberately misled her, she could see him pushing her out of the investigation in a misguided attempt to protect her—similar to the way he'd faked his death to keep her and Jenny safe. What kind of lunatic reasoning was that?

She held his face in her hands and stared deeply into his copper-brown eyes. There was more to their relationship than just sex. They'd built a home and a life together. They had a child. But the sexual component was overwhelming. It always had been. From the very first time she'd laid eyes on this tall, lanky cowboy with the dimples and the lazy smile, she'd wanted him. And vice versa. On their first date, they'd spent the night together, and she wasn't that kind of girl.

She whispered, "I never could say no to you."

"Yesterday in the shower," he said. "Was that the first time?"

Her head bobbed. "That should give you an idea of how angry I was."

She doubted she could resist him again. Her first orgasm was only a taste of what she knew would happen later. With Wade in control, she was in for a spectacular ride.

Again, he started with her hair. His hand tangled in her long mane, which he twisted into a knot at her nape. She couldn't move without causing her hair to pull. Slowly, slowly, he brought his mouth closer to hers. His kiss started as a light peck. His tongue flicked against her lips, teasing her. When she tried to move, he tightened his grasp on her hair, making sure she stayed exactly where he wanted her. His gentle nibbling became more demanding. The pressure increased. He tugged at her hair, pulling her chin up. His kiss was hard and savage. He took her breath away.

Breaking free of his grasp, she flung herself into his muscular arms. She wanted to be part of him, wanted him inside her. Under his skillful direction, they shed their jeans. In seconds, he had them positioned on the sleeping bags. He poised above her, ready to enter.

Though almost unconscious, she managed to speak. "Wait."

His body tensed. "Why, Samantha?"

"We need a condom. I'm not on the pill anymore."

Having sex with anyone else had been unthinkable for her. She'd quit worrying about birth control.

He grabbed his jeans, took out his wallet and produced a plastic-wrapped packet. "I came prepared."

But he hadn't mentioned the condom until she brought it up. Wasn't he worried about an unwanted pregnancy? Maybe it wouldn't be unwanted. While he was supposedly dead, she'd thought about having more children. She wanted Jenny to have a younger brother or sister… someday.

For right now, all her needs and desires were wrapped up in the man who parted her thighs and entered her slowly. When they joined, her inner walls clenched around him. In moments, they began the familiar yet wonderful rhythm of their mating.

His deep, rich voice murmured in her ear, "I love you, Samantha."

She couldn't stop herself from saying, "I love you back."

Giving her trust to him was a very different matter.

SAM WOULDN'T HAVE minded making love again and again, but Wade had only the one condom, which he'd purchased in a men's bathroom, just in case. The idea of having unprotected sex and possibly making another baby was in her mind, but there were too many other things to discuss, and she was anxious to start their investigation.

Basking in the afterglow, she was too comfy and content to leave their sleeping-bag nest, but she'd put on her blouse to ward off the chill in the horse barn. Wade had slipped into his jeans. She noticed that he was going commando.

"Before we get started at Hanging Rock," she said, "I have some questions."

"Me first," he said. "How was Jenny this morning? Was she okay about going with her grandparents?"

"Okay but not thrilled. Sometimes she's a little fussbudget, worrying about everything, from which stuffed animal to pack, to which pills she needs in case she gets airsick."

"Does she get airsick?"

"Not a bit." Sam didn't know where Jenny had heard about airplanes making your tummy jump; must have heard it from one of the kids at school. "And she worries about leaving me alone."

"Ouch." He winced. "Kids shouldn't have to feel that way."

"It's natural. She thinks you're gone and I'm the only family she's got left. If she loses me…"

"I understand."

She knew how deeply he connected with those feelings. Wade had lost his father to cancer when he was twelve. He and his sister were raised by a hardworking single mother—an unsung heroine in Sam's opinion. That gracious lady lived long enough to hold her granddaughter in her arms. Her death in a car accident nearly broke Wade's heart.

His eyebrows crinkled in a frown. "I never should have put you and Jenny through this."

Though she agreed, there was no reason to rub salt in his wounds. "My first question—what exactly did you witness?"

Stretched out on the sleeping bag with his fingers laced behind his head, he gave her an optimum view of his bare chest. "I've told this story a couple hundred times to the cops and lawyers. It probably sounds like a police report."

"Then it ought to be clear."

"I responded to a late-night call from the dispatcher at nine forty-four and took care of the problem. I was—"

"Hold up. What problem?"

"Mrs. Burroughs."

Thelma Burroughs was a sweet old woman who'd lost her husband two years ago. Ever since, she'd been hearing burglars, vandals and escaped convicts prowling around her property. Her calls to 911 came three or four times a month.

"Funniest thing," she said. "After you disappeared, I assigned Deputy Schmidt to Burroughs duty so I wouldn't have to leave Jenny at night. That dear little lady hasn't had anywhere near as many emergencies."

"I never minded visiting her. She gave me cookies." He cleared his throat. "I saw her and was headed home when I noticed lights in an area that should have been deserted."

"Hanging Rock?"

"You catch on fast."

One of the duties of sheriff was to do an occasional drive-by at Hanging Rock to chase away teenagers who might be using the dangerously run-down cabins for parties or for crash pads. Several times, she'd found kids sleeping under a rotted roof that might collapse at any moment.

He continued, "Though that area is uninhabited, there are several dirt roads that get close. As I approached, I saw vehicles parked along the shoulder. The scene was quiet."

"So you knew it wasn't a high school beer party."

"I killed my headlights, hid my vehicle and approached on foot. One of the vehicles parked at the side of the road was a state-patrol Crown Vic. Later I ran the plates to find out who it was. Care to guess?"

"Morrissey," she said. "Did you get other plates?"

"I did." His tone was formal. She could tell that he'd practiced this speech for courtroom presentation. "One was the DEA agent who is now in jail. Others were traced to cartel connections."

"No other cops?"

"I couldn't see all the cars," he reminded her. "There were others parked along another road. I didn't take the time to get the plates. I suspected serious business when I spotted the armed guards outside one of the cabins."

Her heart beat a little faster. Though these events had taken place over a year ago, she was scared about what he was going to find. "Armed guards?"

"Armed with semiautomatic assault weapons, similar to AK-47s."

"How can you be so calm?" She reached over and shoved his shoulder. "You should have gotten out of there."

"I'll remember that advice for the next time," he said. "I eased up close to a rear window so I could hear what was being said inside. The glass had been broken out. I was able to see over the sill. There were seven, possibly eight, men in a room where most of the drywall had been torn off the walls, leaving bare unpainted boards and wall joists. There was trash on the floor. The only light came from a battery-powered lantern on the table and from Maglites carried by some of the men. Two wooden chairs. A man sat in one and a woman in another. They both had their hands tied behind their backs. A big guy in a black leather jacket with fringe stood over them, yelling in Spanish. I could only pick up the gist of what he was saying. These two had betrayed him and cost him a lot of money. He turned toward my window. I'll never forget that face."

"Did you know him?"

"I recognized him from a BOLO Ty sent me. He was part of the Esteban cartel."

Though the APBs and BOLOs she used as scrap paper were aged and dated, the danger never grew old. She had to wonder if she would have been as alert as her husband. "I only remember one from the cartel. They called him El Jefe, which is Spanish for *boss*, even though he wasn't at the very top of the leadership."

"That was the guy. El Jefe."

His ugly face had printed itself in her memory. She read danger in his cold dark eyes and sneering mouth. "You should have run."

"You might be right." As though pulling himself together, he sat up, shoved his arms into his beige cotton shirt and rolled up the sleeves. "El Jefe took out a handgun—a Glock like the one you carry—but didn't pull the trigger. He passed the gun to a DEA agent who had been working undercover in this area."

"You knew him?" she said.

"We'd met. I remembered him because he had the same initials as me—W.C., which stands for William Crowe. Not a real friendly guy. Most of the undercover agents aren't."

Sam steeled herself. She doubted she'd like the next part of what he told her, but she wanted him to think she was cool, unaffected and ready to do an ace job of investigating. Maintaining that facade, she asked another question. "Did you recognize any of the other men in the room?"

"Some faces seemed familiar. Most likely, they were cartel men I'd seen on other BOLOs. And two cops from Glenwood that you probably knew from when you worked there. One of them retired and left the area. No one has been able to reach him. The other died under suspicious circumstances."

She counted the tally. "Four men from law enforcement—two cops, Morrissey and William Crowe."

"One cop is on the run. The other and Morrissey are dead. And the DEA agent is in prison."

She swallowed hard before asking, "Why?"

"Crowe talked back to El Jefe in Spanish, said something about how this wasn't sanctioned by his boss. He handed his cell phone to Morrissey and told him, in English, to make a call. Crowe said they didn't have to do the dirty work unless their boss said so. Before Morrissey could make the call, El Jefe pointed a gun at the DEA agent. In English, he said that there were fifty thousand reasons why they should follow his orders."

He paused to take a breath and let his story sink in. She wanted to hear that the good guys in white hats rode over the hill and rescued those people, but she knew this story didn't have a happy ending.

"The woman was unconscious and slumped over," Wade said. "The man had been severely beaten and he was also pretty much out of it. Crowe aimed the Glock and pulled the trigger. He ended their suffering."

She drew the obvious conclusion. "He was arrested because of your eyewitness account."

"That's right."

His shoulders slumped, and his copper-colored gaze turned inward as though trying to see his way clear.

"You had to turn him in," she said.

"Yeah, he's guilty as hell. Yes, he murdered those people in cold blood. Dana Gregg and Lyle McFee…"

He shook his head. "They're the victims here. It's important to remember them."

"But you're still thinking about Crowe."

"I regret sending him to prison. He didn't have a choice. He was looking down the barrel of El Jefe's gun. If Crowe hadn't killed them, he would have been a dead hero. That's too much to ask."

Though he'd told this story dozens of times, the emotion seemed to touch him. In his voice, she heard an echo of the terrible helplessness he must have felt while watching a murder take place. And his remorse about pointing an accusing finger at an undercover agent in a no-win situation.

"There's nothing you could have done differently. You couldn't change what happened," she said. "Not by yourself."

"I know."

"It's not like you could call for backup. A cartel murder is way out of Deputy Schmidt's comfort zone."

"The larger problem was that I didn't know how many others from law enforcement were involved," he said. "I made the decision not to tell anyone until I talked to Ty."

His words stabbed a knife blade into her gut. *He couldn't tell anyone. Not until he talked to Ty.* What about his wife? What about her?

"Why couldn't you trust me?"

Chapter Eleven

This confrontation was painfully inevitable. Wade should have told her, should have trusted her. She was right. He was wrong.

A year ago when he'd witnessed the murders, Wade had wished that he could have come up with a reasonable excuse for why he came home very late that night, crawled into bed for a few hours and left before she was awake in the morning. But there had been nothing he could say without unraveling the whole story. To his credit, he hadn't lied to her. But he'd dodged her questions and had done everything he could to keep from having a serious conversation.

"You had every right to know," he said.

Avoiding his gaze, she sat up in the nest of sleeping bags and started getting dressed. "At first, I thought you were having an affair."

"What?" Blindsided, he stared at her. "Why?"

"Think about it, Wade. You were out late, and you were secretive about where you'd been. When I wanted to talk, you claimed to be too tired and fell into the bed. Or you came up with some other distraction. You were acting real sneaky, mister."

"Maybe."

"I should have pounced on you."

"Why didn't you?"

"Your kisses told me a different story. You didn't have the lips of a cheater. The way you held me wasn't a lie. On the night before you supposedly died, we made love and it was…" She sighed softly. Her gaze lost its sharp focus. "It was something special and hard to describe."

He remembered. "I didn't want to leave you. It was tearing me apart inside. Believe me, Samantha, if I could have told you, I would have."

"Transcendent," she said. "That night, we were more than lovers. Transcendent, we were soul mates, destined to be together—even when we were apart—for all eternity."

He was so lucky to be with this woman. More than her physical beauty, she glowed from the inside. The fact that she could still care about him, after all he'd put her through, was nothing short of a miracle.

Had he done the right thing by leaving her and going into witness protection? Faking his death? He wanted to believe that everything would turn out for the best, but he couldn't be certain.

"I couldn't tell you," he said. "Some of the blame goes to Ty. He pointed out to me that you aren't an actress or even a very good liar. If you'd known that I faked my death, you would have behaved differently."

"Understatement."

"You might even have felt like you needed to tell others, like my sister or Mrs. Burroughs or your parents."

"I might have."

She wriggled to get her jeans up to her waist and

fastened the button. Getting dressed signaled an end to their intimacy. Though he could have spent the next few hours—or maybe days or maybe forever—making love to her, they were now bound to investigate. When she pulled her long, silky, beautiful hair up into a high ponytail and twisted it into a bun, he got the message: time to switch gears.

He made one more attempt to gain her forgiveness. "I thought I was protecting you and Jenny."

"I'm aware of that theory. What you don't know won't hurt you. That works okay for a little girl like our daughter." She jammed her feet into her boots. "But I'm a grown woman. I can handle the truth."

Another apology would be too much. He could have offered a promise that he'd never lie or skirt the truth again. But he wasn't sure. Another situation might arise when the best solution involved deception.

He reached for his boots. "Anyway, that's my story. That's how it went down."

"You're not done yet. What happened after the murders?"

He wasn't proud of what he did at Hanging Rock. It would have been a hell of a lot more satisfying to brag about how he rescued the victims and rounded up the bad guys. But that wasn't what happened. Instead of being a hero, he ran away and hid.

"It was one of those times," he said, "when I was glad for my misspent youth of playing hooky and hiding in the forest. I slid back into the trees and turned invisible while the men left the old house and went to their vehicles."

"What did they do with the bodies?"

"I'm getting there," he said. "Nobody was rushing. A bunch of guys were standing in a group smoking. El

Jefe was already in his car, which happened to be one I had the license plates for. At one point, the four lawmen clustered together. I couldn't hear everything they were saying. Basically, Crowe was telling the others to keep their mouths shut."

"Trying to get away with murder," she said.

But he couldn't condemn the DEA agent for his actions. If Wade had been in a similar situation, he wasn't sure he'd have been willing to sacrifice himself for two other people who were going to get shot anyway. "Or he could have been thinking of how to get in touch with his handler. Of the four lawmen, Crowe was the only one who was supposed to be undercover."

"You're still trying to believe in him."

"I can't help feeling responsible. It's my testimony—only my testimony—that's keeping him in prison."

"Oh, please." She rolled her eyes. "I'm sure there's other evidence. When you gave them the Hanging Rock location, I assume the FBI forensics team worked their magic."

"The murder weapon was gone," he said.

"No surprise there."

"They found blood on the floor, enough to get a DNA match to the victims. The bodies had disappeared."

"And you didn't see them being moved?"

"Like I said, I couldn't keep track of everybody. It was night. Including the guards posted outside the cabin, there were twelve or so guys moving around. Cars and trucks were parked in different places. The other side of the cabin was out of my sight line. They could have thrown the bodies in the back of a truck on that side."

"Or they could still be at Hanging Rock," she said.

"The FBI made a thorough search."

"But it never hurts to take another look."

He nodded. She had read his mind.

AFTER THEY CLEANED up the sleeping bags, closed the window and left the horse barn, he sauntered toward the edge of the corral, leaned his elbows on the top of the fence and gazed toward the enclosed circle. There weren't any horses right now, but the owners would soon return for the summer, and they'd bring their three mares and two stallions.

Samantha joined him and gave his elbow a nudge. "I've been thinking. Jenny is big enough to start learning how to ride."

"I want to teach her." He'd been four when he first got on a horse at Ty's father's ranch, but there was no way he'd allow his precious daughter to go galloping off without a helmet, safety gear and proper training. "Do you really think she's ready?"

"She wants to start."

He should have known, should have been there for his daughter. His gut twisted. He felt empty inside, but not from lack of food. He craved another sort of nourishment—the fulfillment that came from being a father.

He'd missed too much of her life. A year didn't sound like long until you broke it down into weeks, hours and minutes. Every minute he was away from Jenny felt like forever. "If I had known I'd be gone as long as this, I never would have agreed to the plan. I was only supposed to be dead for two months."

"How was that going to work?"

"They arrested William Crowe and the cartel guy

I'll always think of as El Jefe. The case against these two was based on my testimony."

"It's hard to get a conviction when you don't have a body," she said. "You must have given a real convincing statement to get a judge to hold these guys."

He pointed to his jaw. "Who wouldn't believe this face?"

"Those dimples look like trouble to me."

"I wish the judge had said that, wish he'd thrown the case out of his court and set everybody free. But it wasn't really about the trial. The feds wanted to use the threat of prison to get El Jefe and Crowe to talk."

"But they didn't take the deal."

"Nope."

"They couldn't hold the prisoners indefinitely. Was there another scheduled trial?"

"They went through a bunch of legal actions. I was actually delivered to the courthouse in Austin three times."

"How long?" she asked. "How long were they going to drag this thing out?"

"Until they got what they wanted."

"Surely they have enough evidence on the cartel to start making arrests."

Proving a case against the cartel wasn't the main issue. They'd broken a ton of laws and had done so without fear of reprisal. Anybody who crossed them ended up dead. "The Esteban cartel is bulletproof. Lawbreakers tend to disappear. If they're arrested, they have access to excellent lawyers. It's amazing that they've managed to hold on to El Jefe so long. If he gets released…"

Wade's muscles tensed. If the cartel decided he was

a threat to them, the danger would be extreme. He was glad that Jenny was far away and well protected.

Similar thoughts must have been occurring to Samantha. "Are we ever going to be safe?"

"I sure as hell hope so."

"But you can't promise," she said. "And it sounds like witness protection is the only way we can escape the cartel. We'll have to start over and change our names. We'll lose our house and friends."

"That's what I was trying to avoid by faking my death."

The life they'd built in Swain County when he was sheriff had been just about perfect, and he didn't want to give it up. He'd expected to have another kid or maybe two with Samantha and to grow old together.

"You sacrificed over a year of your life, over a year of our life together. Let's make damn sure it wasn't in vain." Turning away from the corral, she dusted off her hands on her jeans, straightened the front of her denim jacket and fixed him with a steady, blue-eyed gaze. "We have to close down this smuggling operation. You and me."

Never mind that the FBI, the Colorado Bureau of Investigation and the state patrol had failed to produce viable results. Samantha was on the job. He had no logical reason to believe in her. But he did. "Any questions?"

"Fill in some blanks. What kind of smuggling are we talking about?"

"You name it. Illegal weapons, drugs, even human trafficking."

She couldn't hide the shudder that rattled her shoulders. Human trafficking was the most heinous of crimes— ripping apart families, turning young women into hookers or drug mules, forcing young men into work that could only be described as slavery. He had thought of those victims while in witness protection. His sacrifice was nothing compared to those families'.

She asked, "How does the operation work?"

"Our backyard in Swain County and a couple of other remote mountain areas are a distribution hub. Using the back roads, the cartel is able to meet with their suppliers. According to Ty, an arms deal is going down real soon. The weapons were stolen from a US Army arsenal."

"We know about the cartel," she said. "But who are the suppliers?"

"A network of dirty cops and agents from DEA and ATF who are taking payoffs and staties like Morrissey."

"Why wasn't he arrested?"

"He was questioned. Ty and his boss were trying to turn him into a snitch to get to the ringleader." He stared directly into her eyes. "That's who we're after. We need to find the ringleader."

"Is his identity a secret?"

He nodded. "The feds have been digging for almost two years, and they still don't have a name."

The ringleader arranged the deals and the distribution. He procured items to be smuggled, set up the transfer of goods and sold to the end market. His involvement touched every part of the transaction. No doubt he was paid every step of the way. And yet he remained anonymous.

"How does he pay the others?"

"It's a cash business."

"Have you looked into bank balances?"

"The FBI used their forensic accountants to check

out major suspects. They found nothing. I'd assume it's a cash business."

"Let's get started at Hanging Rock." She strode toward her SUV. "I'll drive."

He caught her wrist and turned her toward him. Her fingers climbed up his chest and laced behind his neck. For a long moment, he stood and stared at her, memorizing the pillowy fullness of her lips, the cerulean blue of her irises and the arch of her eyebrows. When they kissed, he lingered tenderly, tasting the sweet flavor of his beautiful wife. She felt so good in his arms. She felt right.

Then he took a step back. "Be careful, Samantha."

Chapter Twelve

On the drive toward Hanging Rock, Sam peered through the windshield at thickening smoke and a cloud of dust kicked up by the heavy-duty tires on Wade's motorcycle. He'd insisted on riding alone while she stayed in the SUV—a precaution that made sense if he needed to disappear quickly. He was supposed to be dead, after all. And she agreed that they needed to choose the right moment for him to emerge from the shadows. Following that logic, he'd chosen a route that went the long way around to avoid well-traveled roads where he might be seen.

She'd be glad when this charade was over. They needed to find evidence that would nail these smugglers and make Wade's testimony irrelevant. More than that, they needed to figure out who was running the show—the ringleader.

While driving, she handled sheriff-type business. Her first call was to Deputy Schmidt, who was never going to forgive her for getting into a shoot-out yesterday and not calling him in to help. He promised to keep people away from the fire zone and take care of the 911 calls, most of which were related to traffic and vehicles.

Next, she spoke to the fire marshal. Hobbs assured

her that the blaze was 90 percent contained but there were still hot spots that might flare up. He expected to have firefighters on active duty in Swain County for several more days.

Sam took a couple of deep breaths to calm herself before contacting Pansy Gardener, the main 911 operator/dispatcher. Pansy was as perceptive as a fortune-teller. Keeping a secret from her wouldn't be easy. That sweet, rosy-cheeked little woman with the fluffy bangs and the silver bun on top of her head would guess from the tone of Sam's voice that something had changed.

During the past year, Pansy had become expert in reading Sam's moods and had often sent her home with instructions to take a long bath and unclench her muscles. Sage advice, and Sam was grateful for it. If she hadn't listened to Pansy, she might have tensed into a frozen statue and then—*blam!*—shattered into a million pieces.

Last night when Sam picked up Jenny, Pansy had been suspicious, and that was before she'd really connected with Wade. All she'd done at that time was kiss him and cuff him. Now that she'd made love with her "formerly dead but not a zombie" husband, the change in her was obvious. She could feel the glow that radiated from the inside out. Her whole being was energized and bubbling with vitality. She had her passion back.

Before hitting the dispatch button on her console, Sam rubbed the corners of her mouth to erase the smile that Wade's fine loving had put there.

"Hey, Pansy, it's me."

"You sound funny. Do you have a cold?"

"It's the smoke," Sam said with a fake cough. "I'll be available today, but I might be out of touch. Most of my time will be spent with the FBI, looking into the murder of Drew Morrissey."

"I can hardly believe it," she said. "We got ourselves a real mystery in Swain County. Is that what I'm hearing in your voice? Are you excited about the investigating?"

"A man is dead. That's no reason for excitement." She wouldn't be shedding any tears for the likes of Morrissey, but surely there was someone who would grieve. "I spoke to the fire marshal and he tells me the blaze is pretty much contained."

"When did you talk to him?"

"Last night. Then again this morning."

"Well, well, well…" Pansy gave a sardonic chuckle. "I have something important to say. Let's make this a private conversation."

Immediately, Sam switched the channels on the police console. She didn't want this conversation broadcast to every other unit. "What did you want to tell me, Pansy?"

"It's the other way around," she said. "You and Justin Hobbs, eh?"

"What? Why would you think—"

"You saw him last night, and then you saw him first thing this morning. Winner, winner, chicken dinner. Congratulations, Sheriff Sam. It's about time you got some loving."

"What?"

"Don't bother denying it. I can hear that growl in your voice. You had sex."

There were a dozen ways this story could twist around and become an embarrassment. She needed to end the potential gossip right now. "There is nothing between me and Justin Hobbs."

"Whatever you say. Wink, wink."

"I swear, Pansy. He's a nice man, hardworking and a good fire marshal—"

"And big," she said. "Don't forget big. You know I love you, Sam, but you're taller than ninety percent of the men in this county. Justin is a real good fit for you. He's got to lose the beard, though."

Sam groaned. If only she could tell Pansy about Wade… "Promise you won't gossip. Tell no one."

"You got it."

"If anyone asks, I got Jenny out of town. She was having a little trouble with the smoke, and I can't skip work to take care of her, not with this murder investigation."

"It'll be good when you're married again," Pansy said. "Then you can stay home whenever you want. Not to mention the other benefits."

Wink, wink. "I'll check in later."

Wade led her farther on a dirt road that ascended through the pine forests in a loose zigzag. The usually bright scenery took on a dark, sinister quality. When she peered over the edge of the drop-off, she didn't see trees and shrubs and springtime flowers. Instead, it was a witch's cauldron of smoke. The fire marshal—who would hopefully never hear Pansy's wild accusations— had said that the blaze was under control. But that didn't mean the fire was out.

On the slope opposite her road, the devastation was severe. Charred boulders poked out from scorched earth. The towering, majestic trees had been turned to scraggly, burned matchsticks. Occasional bursts of orange skittered and died. This wasn't an active blaze, but it was still dangerous.

After a sharp right turn, Wade drove half a mile down a one-lane road, slowed his bike and stopped without dismounting. She pulled up behind him and parked. Before she left her vehicle, she put on a white ventilator mask and grabbed another for Wade.

As she approached the bike, he took off his helmet and flashed a huge grin. His dimples winked. His teeth appeared extra-white against the dirt and ash smeared across his face. Riding a motorcycle through a fire zone probably wasn't the smartest way to get from here to there.

"For the rest of the way, you're riding with me." He handed her the helmet. "Put it on."

Apparently, she was going to find out exactly how dumb it was to ride through flames. She thrust the mask at him. "This is for you."

He snapped the elastic strap that held the white mask over the nose and mouth. "Do I look like a doctor?"

"It's not a costume," she said. "It's practical."

"Wish I had an extra pair of goggles for you."

"I'll manage."

She blinked, and her memory flashed back to a time several years ago when they'd been on a motorcycle together. For a couple of days, they'd been free and wild, zooming down the highway on a big, powerful Harley-Davidson. She'd leaned her cheek against his back and wrapped her arms around him while the powerful engine vibrated between her legs. Oh yeah, she remembered very well. But that kind of memory wasn't going to help their investigation. She needed to focus.

Today was different. They were experienced, responsible, and she certainly wouldn't confuse this feisty little Honda with a Harley hog. The rugged off-road tires were impressive, but there was barely enough room for her to sit behind him. "Why can't I take the SUV? This road looks wide enough."

"The bike has better maneuverability. The SUV is safer here, farther from the fire. It gives us a second way to escape."

Escape from what? Her thoughts jumped to worst-case scenarios. A spark from the fire could turn the houses they were searching to flaming infernos. Cartel thugs armed with AK-47s might stage an assault. Leaving her trusty SUV right here was a good plan. If anything bad happened to the bike...

She plunked on the helmet, flung her leg over the seat and clamped her arms around his middle. Bouncing along on the dirt road felt like riding a bucking bronco, but she didn't care. In spite of the potential danger, being with her husband and taking charge of her life filled her with a sense of well-being.

At any moment, disaster could come crashing down on them. The consequences might be terrible. They could be injured, even killed. For now, they were partners. For now, she was happy.

Through the tree trunks and the dulling haze of smoke, she spotted the two ramshackle cabins. Both one-story structures were made of wood that had weathered to a tired gray. Both were anchored by stone fireplaces. They weren't exactly alike but similar, like first cousins. Not side by side. Nor did they face each other. They were angled, as though one cousin had insulted the other and was leaving in a huff.

Her other visits to Hanging Rock had taken place after dark, and her only reason for being there was to chase away the teenagers who might have the roof collapse on them and get hurt. She'd never taken the time to look around.

When she got off the bike and removed the helmet, she strode between the two cabins, staring at one and then the other. The house on her left was smaller and more square. The one on her right was in better shape. It had a front window that actually hadn't been broken, probably because the filth was holding it together.

A few tattered ribbons of yellow crime-scene tape decorated the less decrepit cabin. She pointed toward it. "Is that where the murders happened?"

"See for yourself." He stepped onto the porch, which was missing a few boards, and jiggled the door handle. Not locked, the door popped right open.

Inside the front room, the old floorboards were discolored in two large, irregular patches. Dried blood from the two victims. Like Wade, she wanted to know and remember their names. "The man and woman— what were their names again?"

"Dana Gregg and Lyle McFee."

"What did they do to upset El Jefe?"

"These two weren't upstanding citizens. They had long rap sheets and bad reputations. When they siphoned off a hundred thou on a drug deal, El Jefe got mad."

She gave a sniff and was glad for the mask protecting her nose. The place smelled like a foul combo of ashes from the fireplace, dried vomit, mold, feces, urine and something else she couldn't identify. "Why did the cartel use this place?"

"First rule of real estate." He snugged an arm around her waist and pulled her close as he whispered, "Location, location, location."

He pulled aside their ventilator masks for a quick but tasty kiss. Tempting, but she pushed him away. "Not here."

"Why not?"

"I can't stop thinking about all the teen sweethearts who used this place for their love nest." A particularly gross thought struck her. "You never came here, did you? When you were in high school?"

He shrugged. "Once or twice for keg parties."

"But not with a girlfriend, right?"

"Give me some credit. I may not be high class, but this?" He gestured to the rusted-out lawn chairs, graffiti on the walls and piles of rubbish. "This is just about as low as you can go."

"Whatever was I thinking? You're such a perfect gentleman."

"When you think about it," he said, "it's lucky that the cartel never bumped into the high school crowd. Ty told me that Hanging Rock was used to make exchanges. And they stored contraband here."

"Aha!" Finally, she had a starting place. "We need to make a thorough search. If they left stuff behind, there has to be a hiding place."

In a sudden move, he pinned her to the wall. Craning his neck, he looked through the open space that was once a window. He whispered, "Did you hear that?"

Keeping silent, she shook her head.

"I think somebody's out there." He pulled his Beretta from the holster and ducked so he wouldn't be seen.

There seemed to be no other choice than to draw her gun. During the year she'd been sheriff, she'd unfastened the snap on her holster only once. Since Wade's return, it was twice in as many days. She didn't like being in this position. She'd always thought that if force was necessary, a stun gun could be used. But her little zapper wasn't good for long-range shooting, and this situation required a lethal response.

The danger Wade kept talking about came closer. Following his lead, she moved carefully from one window to the next. The boards creaked under her feet. There didn't seem to be much of a wind, but the tree branches outside shifted and the shadows moved as though they'd taken on a life of their own.

Hoping to get a view from the back side of the cabin, she crept down a short hallway toward the kitchen. Disgusting! Nobody had used this room for cooking in a very long time—at least she hoped they hadn't. Part of the ceiling had collapsed. The wallpaper that hadn't been scrawled on with graffiti peeled away in strips. The sink was filth encrusted. Same with the countertops, the tiles had been pulled off to expose the bare, rotting wood. An eight-by-ten rag rug was spread carelessly over the torn green linoleum.

"Samantha," Wade called.

She dashed back into the front room in time to see him put his gun away. "What?"

Through the open front door, he showed her a family of white-tailed deer. "There are our intruders."

Relieved, she clasped her free hand over her heart. "I'm glad to see them. But I'm not."

Protecting wildlife was a passion of hers, and she knew that Wade felt the same way. She heard the emotion in his voice when he said, "When I see deer and a fire in the forest, all I can think is *Bambi*."

And he was a hunter. "Fires are an inconvenience for you and me, but for the deer and the chipmunks and raccoons and bears and moose and even the snakes, their whole world is destroyed. Their food supply is gone. The water is polluted. They have no shelter."

"Did Hobbs mention if this one was started by natural causes?"

"He hasn't said anything yet." She couldn't allow herself to get sidetracked, thinking about fire safety. Her focus needed to stay firm. "Back to business."

"Yeah, ma'am."

"When the FBI searched in this cabin for the bodies, did they find a root cellar?"

"I don't know."

Her grandma in rural Oregon had a root cellar with shelves full of canned fruit, homemade applesauce and Mason jars with pickled beets. She used to take Sam down there and show off all those racks of supplies, telling her that a well-stocked household would never go hungry.

"These cabins are in a remote area," she said. "And sometimes you can't get to a store. If there were ever people living here, they'd need a good-size pantry and root cellar."

"That's not how most of these cabins are constructed." He took her hand and led her onto the porch. After they went down two steps to solid ground, he bent over and pointed at the rocks and concrete of the foundation. "No room for a cellar."

"It doesn't even look like there's a crawl space to get under the house."

"My guess is that they slapped down rocks and cement, leveled it off and started building. It would have been easier to add a second floor than to mess with a cellar."

She remembered the struggles when they were building their own house. "I suppose you're right."

He glanced over his shoulder. "The fire is getting closer."

"That gives us a reason to get out of here fast."

"I hope the sounds I heard were only those deer." He looked toward the other cabin. "I should check around."

"Let's take a quick look in the kitchen first."

She went onto the porch, through the door and down the hallway. There was something about that rag rug on the floor that didn't seem right. Hands on hips, she stared down at it.

He pinched his nose behind the ventilator mask. "It reeks."

"The rug bothers me," she said.

"Because it doesn't go with the rest of the decor?"

"It's almost a match in terms of ugly and dirty, but not quite as tattered. Did you notice any other rugs?"

"I don't think so. Your point?"

"This rug is newer, and I'll bet somebody brought it here to use as a cover-up." She cleared the surface of the rug, moving aside the clutter, empty boxes and a wood chair with a candle melted onto the seat. With Wade's help, she peeled back the rug to reveal a floor of torn and battered linoleum.

Bending down, she checked it out. "I was really hoping we'd find something here, like a secret escape hatch."

"Our search is a long shot," he said. "I sure as hell don't think the FBI is infallible, but they're good at gathering evidence."

"Forensics is half skill, half luck and half instinct."

He squatted down beside her. "Is that something you learned at police academy?"

"The three halves are from my dad the cop." When she was a child, she used to play crime scene with her dollhouse. "Let's try one more thing. Grab the edge of that linoleum and pull it back."

"It's going to wreck the floor," he warned.

"This place is already a wreck."

Working together, they separated the ugly green flooring from the plywood below. The glue and the tacks that held the linoleum in place were long gone, so it wasn't a difficult task.

Under a large section that was flush with the wall, Sam found what she'd been looking for.

A trapdoor.

Chapter Thirteen

"Beginner's luck," Wade said as he stared down at the stained, battered plywood lid of a trapdoor.

"What does that mean?"

"On your first investigation, you've outsmarted the FBI."

He couldn't see Samantha's smile behind her ventilator mask, but she was practically wriggling out of her skin with excitement. "You don't think the FBI found the cellar?"

"I doubt they even looked. It doesn't make sense to have a cellar in this kind of cabin. You saw the rock foundation. Like you said, there's not even a crawl space."

But here he was, looking down at a trapdoor that had to lead somewhere. The thick grime crusted around the edges of the plywood door told him that it hadn't been opened recently. He thought of that night so long ago when he witnessed the murders that changed his life. Had the trapdoor been used? Was this a place where the smugglers hid their wares between transfers?

Samantha took her Maglite from a pocket in her denim jacket and waved it over the trapdoor like a magic wand. "Open sesame."

"Are you expecting me to lift it?"

"Might as well use those great big muscles of yours."

The crude trapdoor didn't have hinges, just a carved-out handhold at one end. He yanked off the lid to a small opening in the floor. When she aimed her light into the darkness, he saw a wooden ladder that looked as if it had been hammered together by a four-year-old.

"The good news," he said, "is that if the ladder breaks, there won't be far to fall. That space can't be more than six feet high."

She slanted the flashlight beam to see farther inside. "Before you go down there, you should take off your sexy leather jacket. It'll get filthy."

"What about you?"

She flipped her denim collar. "Washable."

Before descent into a smugglers' pit, only a wife would worry about getting his clothes dirty. Only Samantha would call his jacket sexy. And he agreed both ways. He liked having her fuss over him, and the fact that she considered him sexy was a definite plus.

He tossed his jacket over the back of a chair, dropped to the floor and stuck his leg down to find the first step of the ladder. With a bounce, he tested the crude rung before putting his whole weight on it. Halfway between the floor and the cellar, he paused on the ladder and sucked down a deep breath. He hated enclosed spaces. Not that he was claustrophobic. Because he was six feet five inches tall, he needed more room to spread out. At least, that was what he told himself as he forced his legs to keep going down the ladder. He stepped onto a dirt floor. A thick darkness surrounded him.

Samantha handed the Maglite down. Before flashing it in all directions, he tried to take another couple of breaths. His lungs felt pinched. The ventilator mask was smothering him. He tore it off.

She was already down the ladder. Standing in front of him, she took his chin in her hand and forced him to look directly at her. "I forgot about that thing you have with small places."

"I'm fine."

She pulled off her mask to give him a little kiss. "Let's get this done."

Taking the Maglite from him, she swept the beam across the dirt floor. Like the upstairs, there was clutter. Nothing appeared to be contraband. The space contained only discarded junk.

Neither he nor Samantha could stand upright without bumping their heads against the floor joists. The walls were dirt and cinder block. Tumbled-down shelves lined every wall of the cellar that seemed to be roughly the same size as the kitchen above it. The beam from her flashlight lingered on the pipes and plumbing fixtures that congregated in the area below the sink.

Closer to them, two black garbage bags were piled against a wall.

Samantha's fingers clamped onto his arm. Under her breath she mumbled, "Oh God oh God oh God oh God…"

Her panic made him stronger. He took the wavering Maglite from her. "This is a good thing," he said.

"Not for them."

The bags covered only part of the bodies. Legs in jeans stuck out the end. The desiccated, blackened feet were shoeless.

"Dana Gregg and Lyle McFee." Their names were a

mantra. The victims should never be forgotten. "I meant it's good that we've found the evidence."

"Does that mean the feds don't need you to testify? An eyewitness account is always helpful, but the bodies will provide the type of physical evidence that wins convictions. There will be ballistics, maybe even fingerprints." From another jacket pocket, she pulled out a pair of baby blue latex gloves. "Don't forget these."

She was right about the physical evidence being important, and it was possible that his testimony wouldn't be needed. But Samantha was forgetting the ringleader. Until the smuggling operation was dismantled, there would be danger for them and for others in Swain County.

He took the gloves and gave her a hug. "You don't have to get any closer to those bags if you don't want to."

"For a minute there, I thought I was going to throw up." She stepped away from him and waved her palm in front of her face like a fan. "I'm still flushed, but I'm mostly fine. And I want to see."

Stooped over, they moved across the uneven dirt floor, kicking clutter out of the way as they went. The distance was only a few steps, and he scanned with the light to show himself that the walls weren't really closing in. He hated being underground, hated the darkness. But he couldn't leave until he'd done what was necessary.

He wished Samantha wasn't here. The beam from the Maglite glistened on a long strand of hair that fell across her delicate cheekbone before she tucked it behind her ear. She was so lovely—gentle but strong, sexy and sweet. He wanted to protect her from the ugliness of life.

When they were standing directly over the garbage

bags, he said, "I understand that you want to be part of the investigation."

"I'm good at this, Wade. I found the cellar."

He didn't think the sight of two corpses that had been stashed in a hole for over a year was a requirement for being a good investigator. "You don't have to look. Once I tear open that bag, you can't unsee what's inside."

"If that's true, there isn't any reason for you to look, either."

With a jolt, he realized that she was correct. There was nothing about the victims that would make a difference if he saw it. Since he'd never known Dana or Lyle in real life, he couldn't identify them. And he didn't remember what they were wearing when he'd witnessed their murders. He had a vague impression of a man with a mustache and a woman with bleached-blond hair. "It's okay. I can handle this."

"But it doesn't really matter, does it?" She took a backward step and pulled him with her. "Let's get out of this dark, awful pit. I need to cool down. It's really hot in here, isn't it?"

He took his burner phone from his pocket. "I'll call Ty. His boss was supposed to be at his ranch today. We can have him meet us here and let the FBI take care of this evidence."

Like Samantha, he had become aware of the heat. A light sweat broke across his back. The stench of smoke had become nearly overwhelming.

From overhead, he heard the unmistakable sound of a footfall on the cabin floor. Not a deer. Someone had found them.

Wade looked toward the open trapdoor and saw an

orange flickering light. Fire! Before he could react, the door slammed shut.

A nightmare coming true, he couldn't believe it. They were trapped below a burning cabin with no way to escape. He should have insisted that one of them stay at the top and keep watch, should have done more to secure the area, and he should never have brought her along. No time now for recriminations and apology. He had to make this right.

A crash sounded above them. The person with the nearly silent footfalls no longer felt the need for stealth. Not a good sign.

"I can hear it," she said. "I can hear the fire crackling."

He passed her the cell phone. "Call Ty. Tell him where we are. And then you might want to call your buddy the fire marshal."

"I know what Justin Hobbs would tell me." She sounded angry, which was better than scared. He didn't want her falling apart. "He'd say that this cabin was burning too fast. It wouldn't go up like tinder. The flames need time to spread. Somebody set this blaze. Somebody did this to us."

He had come to the same conclusion. The slamming trapdoor was his first clue. "Make the calls. I'll get the trapdoor open."

There hadn't been a latch on the plywood board that served as a lid. If the wind had blown it shut, he should be able to push it back without any trouble. He climbed onto the ladder and gave a shove. The board shifted but clunked back into place. Something was on top of it, something heavy.

She was standing behind him, holding up the phone. "There's no signal."

They couldn't count on help from anywhere else. He looked up at the trapdoor. Maybe if they both pushed, they could move the board. "Switch places with me. If we work together, I think we can lift the board."

"And then what?" She pointed to the front edge of the trapdoor where the harsh light of the blaze was visible. "We'll be in the middle of a fire."

If they got the door open, would they be adding oxygen to the fire, causing it to burn harder? Were his enemies waiting outside the trapdoor to ambush him? The most obvious exit wasn't the best escape. But he had to do something.

Following his instructions, she stood on the second rung of the ladder, bracing her back against his chest. Planting his feet on the earth floor, he reached up. With his height, he ought to be able to lift the trapdoor a foot or so. When he placed the flat of his hand against the door, he discovered that the plywood surface was hot. Already on fire?

"Ready?" He prepared for a major effort. All those hours of working out might pay off. "Push now."

With their combined strength, they managed to lift the plywood a few inches. The flames licked through the opening and seared the hairs on his arms.

"Put it down," he said.

They dropped it with a thud.

She turned on the ladder and aimed the Maglite in his face. "I couldn't see much, but I'd guess the beat-up fridge in the kitchen is now on top of the trapdoor."

"That must have been the crash we heard."

"Are you okay?" she asked.

"Are you?"

She rubbed her hand up and down her sleeve. "My trusty jacket took care of me."

He tightened his arms around her. Even now, even when they were close to death, he found pleasure in her embrace. "I left my sexy leather jacket up there. By now it's toast."

"If we get out of here alive, I'll buy you another."

"And I'll wear it when I take you on our second honeymoon in Hawaii."

They had so much to live for, this couldn't be the end.

Stepping back from the crude ladder, he circled the cellar with the beam from the Maglite, searching for inspiration. He'd done a lot of the construction work on their house. This little cabin was built on a stone foundation, nothing fancy, nothing too solid. In the root cellar, the walls were cinder block and loosely cemented stone. How hard could it be to break through?

He selected a portion of wall that was away from the trapdoor and away from the sink where extra care might have been taken to keep the pipes from freezing. If his directions were accurate, they'd come out on the west side of the cabin.

Moving the first cinder block was the hardest. The wall was a flat surface with nowhere to get a grip. Avoiding the main foundation support, he reached up to the highest cinder block. He wedged his fingertips into a space between the wood floor and the block and pulled hard. He would have given a lot for some sturdy workman's gloves instead of the flimsy latex.

"What can I do?" she asked.

"Look for a shovel."

"But you need the flashlight here."

"Use the phone."

The damn thing was useless for making calls; it might as well be demoted to flashlight status. He tugged again and the cinder block moved. This plan was going to work. With a new confidence, he yanked the brick halfway out of the wall.

Wearing her ventilator mask, she returned to his side. "No shovel, but I found a tire iron."

"I'll take it."

Smoke from the fire seeped through the floorboards. He pulled up his mask but still coughed. The tire iron was the perfect tool for tearing out the cinder blocks. In minutes, he'd made a hole in the wall that they could crawl through.

He inhaled a gasp of smoke. His eyes were watering. Sweat poured down his back. The last obstacle was the cemented stone wall. It hadn't been properly maintained. Jagged cracks cut through the concrete. If he'd been in a better position, he could have knocked it down with his bare hands.

Reaching up and picking at the stones with the tire iron was slow progress. There had to be a better way. "The ladder."

"What about it?"

He was too wiped out to explain. "Bring the Maglite and come with me."

Staggering across the uneven dirt floor, he struggled to keep his focus clear. His plan was to take the crude stepladder, lift it over his head and use it as a battering ram to break through the wall. Below the trapdoor, he snatched the ladder and headed back toward his hole in the wall.

The trapdoor overhead glowed red. With the added weight of the fridge, he guessed that the plywood would collapse in seconds. The fire would be in the root cellar with them.

Wade had to move fast.

Samantha did a good job of providing support, helping when she could and staying out of the way otherwise. She seemed to instinctively know where he needed the beam of the flashlight.

He placed the ends of the ladder into the space he'd made in the cinder blocks. It was about shoulder height. Using both arms, he rammed the ladder against the stone-and-concrete wall. He muttered under his breath, "Come on, move, damn it."

Samantha held the light steady. "You're getting it. Try again."

He thrust the long wooden frame harder, again and again like a piston engine. And he felt the wall give. In only a few more strokes, he would break through.

In a burst of red embers, the trapdoor caved in. Half of the refrigerator crashed into the cellar. The fire followed. Flames leaped toward them, clawing the air and consuming the last bit of oxygen.

One more time, he slammed the ladder against the stones. This time, he felt the wall break apart. He adjusted the ladder so Samantha could climb up and push her way through the hole.

"Go," he said. "I'll follow."

She did as he said. In seconds, she was up and out. Now it was his turn. The heat from the fire seared his backside as he removed a few more stones so he could make it through the narrow space that had been an easy fit for Samantha.

He heard shots fired. Two of them.

Chapter Fourteen

Sam took aim at the neatly uniformed Lieutenant Natchez, who stood in front of her with his hands raised above his head. When she'd first spotted him lurking around in the forest, she'd shouted the standard "Police! Freeze!"

He didn't respond, and she wasn't in a patient mood. Whipping out her Glock, she'd fired two warning shots.

"My next bullet," she growled, "will be accurate."

"Knock it off, Sam. You know who I am. You can't shoot me."

Oh, but I can. Anger surged inside her, causing her pulse to race. She would have taken great pleasure in shooting off both toes on his shiny boots. What kind of jerk wore high motorcycle boots when he was driving a car?

Gritting her teeth, she tamped down her emotions and controlled herself. After the hell she'd just been through, dealing with Natchez was no big deal. In the root cellar while she was facing a terrible and almost certain death, she hadn't dissolved into tears or started wailing.

A desperate need to survive had held her together. She was different now. Controlled. Focused. Nothing was more important than closing this investigation—nothing. She hadn't got her husband back from the dead only to lose him again.

She sighted down the barrel of her Glock. "Did you set the cabin on fire?"

"Hell no."

She glanced over her shoulder at the cabin. The most intense part of the blaze was in the kitchen, which was further evidence—as if she needed more—that she and Wade had been targeted. This fire was arson.

"What are you doing here, Natchez?"

"My job," he snapped at her. "I'm doing my job, trying to find out who killed my man Morrissey."

An evasive answer if she'd ever heard one. "You've got one more chance to give me an honest answer. Why are you here? Were you following me?"

He looked down at the dirt beneath his boots and scowled. "I spotted your vehicle on the back roads and decided I should see what you were up to. Then I lost track of where you were and drove around. When I saw this fire, I figured you had something to do with it."

Looking past her shoulder, he gaped. His eyeballs popped wide open. His military-cut blond hair stood on end. He let loose with a string of curses that was amazing in its scope and variety.

She'd already guessed what he saw: Wade.

Her supposedly dead husband strode up beside her, pulling off his ventilator mask as he approached. She'd done the same. Though the air outside the cabin was hazy, it was nothing compared to the suffocating blanket of smoke in the root cellar.

"I knew it." Natchez crowed. "I knew it even before Morrissey told me. You're still alive."

Without hesitation, Wade yanked his gun from the holster and pointed it at the state patrolman. "The next time I hear you curse, I'm going to punch your teeth out. There's a lady present and she doesn't need to hear any of your bad language."

"Sure thing, Wade. You got it." His hands dropped to his sides.

"Not so fast," Wade said. "Keep your paws up."

She couldn't believe that Wade would suspect Natchez of being the clever ringleader who had outsmarted the local police and the FBI. This jerk had less intelligence than a tree frog. Oddly, his stupidity was what made her think that Natchez wasn't one of the dirty cops.

Natchez leaned toward them. "This is some kind of big-deal undercover operation. Am I right? Yeah, I am. Tell me what's going on. I want to know."

"I thought you had your hands full," she said. "You were busy doing your job, investigating Morrissey's death."

Petulant as a kid with a busted toy, he said, "Turns out I don't have jurisdiction. The feds are doing the autopsy."

"Their results?" Wade asked.

"Cause of death was two gunshot wounds to the chest. Ballistics on the bullets indicate a Colt .45 revolver."

Remembering Wade's fancy Colt with the inlaid grip that she'd removed from the car, she shuddered. All they had were ballistics. Morrissey wasn't killed in the car, so there wasn't a primary crime scene to search for clues. Not much to go on, and it all pointed to Wade. On top of everything else, he was being framed for murder.

"Your gun," she whispered in his ear.

"I know," he muttered.

"You just can't catch a break."

His beige cotton shirt was torn to shreds when he'd

crawled through the stone and cinder blocks. The exposed flesh on his chest and torso was dirty and marked with bloody scrapes. He looked as if he'd come off a battlefield. Ash and smoke made dark smears across his forehead and under his cheekbones.

She wasn't accustomed to seeing her handsome cowboy as a fierce, macho warrior, and she liked this dangerous new image. The leather jacket wasn't the only sexy thing about him.

Wade snarled at Natchez, "Have you reported this fire?"

"Not yet."

"Do it," he ordered. "Contact the fire marshal on the console in your car. And wait here for him."

According to Justin Hobbs, the fire was almost out, 90 percent contained. He wouldn't be happy to learn about renewed flames at these cabins.

"I can't waste my time waiting around," Natchez said. His lips pinched with the effort of holding back his expletives. "I got things to do."

"The FBI forensic team will be here soon," Wade said. "There's evidence for a federal case in the root cellar under the kitchen. It shouldn't be moved."

Natchez puffed out his chest. "Are you asking me to guard the evidence?"

"Yes."

Wade holstered his gun and strode toward the faithful little motorbike that stood close to the cabin that wasn't aflame. At least their transportation was still intact. She trotted along behind him.

"Hey, wait," Natchez called out. "Aren't you going to tell me how you faked your death?"

Slowly, Wade turned. He gave Natchez a cold, hostile look. "I don't have anything more to say."

She got onto the bike behind him and held on tight as they chugged down the hill to where her car was parked. The jostling of the motorcycle should have kept her adrenaline pumping, but when she leaned her cheek against his back, she felt herself beginning to relax. She was tired. Not even noon, and she was already tired. How was she going to make it through the rest of the day?

"I've got an idea," she said. "Hide the motorcycle and ride in the car with me. We could go back to the house and get cleaned up."

"We can't quit now. We're making progress."

She wasn't seeing the same picture that he was. "How do you figure?"

"We found the bodies. That was your smart thinking."

Yes, indeed, she'd used some sharp observation and clever logic. Because of him, they had been in the right place at the right time. They worked well together. Though she'd like to spend more time developing intimacy, she had two bodies to deal with. And she needed to catch the person who set the cabin on fire and tried to trap them inside.

He guided the motorcycle to a stop behind her SUV.

"I'm keeping the bike," he said. "I might need it."

She dismounted and took off the helmet. Her ventilator mask hung by the elastic strap around her neck, but she didn't put it on. With a sigh, she adjusted her focus and turned the dial back to investigating.

"Natchez," she said. "He turned up at the very moment when we got attacked. Seems like too much of a coincidence."

He shut off the engine on the motorcycle, got off and paced along the road, stretching his shoulders and back. "I wouldn't be surprised if Natchez was part of the smuggling operation. Those state-patrol guys have a lot of autonomy. He could cruise anywhere in Colorado in his Crown Vic, and nobody would question his right to be there."

"Which would make it easy for him to facilitate the smuggling."

"Making sure the goods got from point A to point B."

She nodded. It was easy to imagine Natchez meeting schedules and bossing other people around. He was a middle-management type, a lieutenant who would never become captain. "He's the sort of guy who follows orders."

"But not the boss," Wade said, "not the ringleader."

"Why was he following me? Someone must have given that order. But why?"

"Because of me." He stopped pacing and leaned against her SUV. "He said that Morrissey told him I was still alive. If a snitch like Morrissey knows, the word is out. Natchez was watching you in the hope that you'd lead him to me."

So far, she was following everything he said. "Did Natchez start the fire and trap us in the cellar?"

"That's a negative." His smile activated dimples on both sides of his mouth. "His uniform was spotless. No way had he been playing with fire and pushing refrigerators across the grungy linoleum."

"But maybe he saw who did it."

"I hadn't thought of that." He pushed away from her SUV. "We might need to lean harder on Natchez and get him to talk."

"What are we doing now?"

"We need to go to the Baxter ranch to see Ty and his boss, Everett Hurtado. I'll meet you there."

As he stepped around her, their hands touched. Their fingers linked. In this small way, they joined together.

Investigating together was something new. Their connection as a married couple had grown from an intense love and trust. They'd shared the experience of birthing a baby, of raising her and of watching her grow. Before Wade faked his death, Sam had believed there was nothing stronger than their relationship. Not anymore. They were working together, thinking with one mind.

Their relationship wasn't perfect, not by a long shot. There were cracks in their perfect bond. She didn't trust him implicitly. She had doubts.

She lifted their linked fingers and kissed the scarred skin on his knuckles. He was trying so hard to make everything right, but when she looked into his light brown eyes, she didn't lose herself in his gaze.

"Back there, in the root cellar," she said, "I had a really bad feeling. I was scared that we might not make it out alive. I thought about Jenny. It would be so hard for her."

He dropped a light kiss on her forehead. "It was hard for you. When I was supposedly dead, it had to be hard."

"I thought about that. In the cellar when the fire was coming closer, I tried to imagine if it would be worse to lose you again or to die together."

"I vote no on both options," he said.

So did she, but the dark thoughts about possible future disasters were still there. Before he disappeared and supposedly died, she was a happily-ever-after type of woman who preferred to live on the sunny side of the mountain. Tragedy had forced her to look at the shadows. After all those nights when she was sleeping alone, aching for the company of a good strong man, she was left with a bone-deep chill. It was going to take a while to warm up.

She stepped away from him. "See you at the Baxters' place."

"Do you have any extra windbreakers in the back?" He plucked at the tattered sleeve of his shirt. "I look like a scarecrow."

"You might be in luck." She went around the SUV and unlocked the rear. "As you well know, the annual budget for the sheriff's department is pitiful. But I had several of the extra-extra-large windbreakers left over from when you were the big boss man, literally."

He dug into a duffel bag and pulled out a navy blue windbreaker with *Sheriff* stenciled across the back. Though the jacket was wrinkled, it was an improvement over the ragged shirt.

From inside her jacket, Sam heard the "Let It Go" ringtone for Jenny. A twinge of worry went through her as she walked around to the front of the SUV to answer.

The voice on the other end was her mother. "Sam, we have a problem."

Chapter Fifteen

The arrangements she'd made with her parents to take Jenny out of town was the one thing Sam thought she'd done right. She'd got her daughter away from possible danger. And now her mom was calling about a problem.

Clenching her jaw tightly, Sam asked, "What's wrong, Mom? Was there something I forgot to pack?"

"It's the Cessna, the *Lucky Lindstrom*. We ran into some mechanical problems outside Salt Lake City and—"

"Are you all right? Is Jenny all right?" Panic shot through Sam. A plane crash?

"There was never any danger," her mom said. "We're all fine. Well, your dad is grumpy but that's just him."

Sam's panic lessened. "Let me start over. Is something wrong?"

"Well, we had to land at this strange little airfield in the middle of nowhere. Not really nowhere. It's Utah and the landscape is pretty doggone gorgeous. You've got your snowcapped mountain peaks and your interesting rock formations. Lots of cows—you call them cattle, right?"

While her mother talked, Sam's tension ratcheted up a few notches. Cora Lindstrom was known for her ability to chat endlessly. Sam might be standing here for hours if she didn't move things along. "Long story short, Mom."

"We're renting a car and driving back to Colorado."

Hysteria screamed inside her head. Sam couldn't think, couldn't reason. They couldn't come back. That wasn't according to plan. "Let me talk to Jenny."

It took only a second before Sam heard, "Hi, Mommy." The sound of her daughter's voice had a calming effect. "Grandpa is unhappy about his little airplane, and Grandma says he ought to get rid of it."

"It looks like you won't get all the way to the beach in Oregon."

"It's okay," she said. "Grandma brought Poppy the puppy on the airplane. When Poppy comes to Colorado, we have to watch her or she'll get lost in the woods."

Sam felt her breathing return to normal. "I love you, kiddo."

"Love you back."

"Put Grandma on the phone."

Explaining the situation to her mother was going to be difficult. She couldn't tell her that Wade was alive because Cora would then want to tell Jenny. But if Sam didn't tell her mom what happened to Wade, the threat from the drug cartel and dirty cops didn't make any sense.

She had to convince her parents to go somewhere else, to take Jenny and stay away from Swain County. The threat was real. Less than an hour ago, she and Wade had been close to death. She had to keep Jenny safe.

Sam's mind was blank.

After stumbling through a bit more conversation with

her mom, Sam made an excuse to get off the phone. Later, she might come up with a believable explanation that wasn't all smoke and mirrors. She refused to take the same lying path that Wade had followed. But how could she tell the truth?

She disconnected the call, stomped around her vehicle and glared at her husband, who was sitting on the back catching his breath. This was his fault. One lie led to another and another.

"Problem?" he asked.

"That was my mom."

"Is Jenny okay?"

"She's fine." She waved goodbye to him. The last thing she wanted was input from him. "Later."

While she drove on back roads toward the Baxter ranch, Sam tried to figure out what to do about Jenny. As long as her parents kept their distance, her daughter was safe. If they got too close to Swain County, the ringleader might decide that the way to get to Wade would be through Jenny.

Wade's survival seemed to be breaking news. Natchez said that Morrissey had told him. Who told Morrissey? Was the person who told him the same person who killed him?

Whoever murdered Morrissey had used Wade's gun to do the job. Life would have been easier if Sam had found fingerprints when she dusted the Colt. That weapon was spotless. She'd even checked the bullets and found nothing. It was no surprise that the gun was clean. Wade had been fairly sure that the ringleader was in law enforcement, and cops knew better than to leave prints.

On the final approach to the Baxter ranch, she took off her denim jacket. She'd left early in the morning when it was chilly, layering up with a white tank top and a blue-striped cotton shirt. She unbuttoned the front of the shirt and untucked the tail to let it hang down to cover her holster. Not that anybody would be surprised to see Sheriff Sam with a weapon strapped to her hip.

Maybe because of her five-pointed, tin-star badge, people expected her to be strong, cool and self-controlled. Most of the time, she expected that from herself. Not right now.

She stood on a precipice of tears, paralyzed and staring down into the abyss, unable to decide what she should do. She wanted to point her SUV west and keep driving until she found Jenny and could carry her away to safety. But she also needed to be here with Wade and complete the investigation so he could rejoin their family.

If only he'd talked to her before he came up with the ridiculous plan to fake his death, things would be different. She would never have allowed this charade to play out for more than a year. She would have got results… or died trying.

A sane voice in her head reminded her that she knew very little about this sort of investigation. She didn't live in a world where each decision might make the difference between life and death. If she'd been involved from the start, she might have already been a casualty.

Making a right, she drove her SUV through the gate and down the long asphalt driveway that arrowed toward the front door of the two-story main house. The Baxter ranch had been in business since a few years after World War II and was the largest cattle-raising operation in the county. The herd ranged from five to ten thousand, depending on finance and marketing. Sam had heard they'd cut back on the number of cattle while they were in a transition period. Ty's older brother, Logan, was taking over the major operations from their dad. He and his wife lived in the main house with Mama and Papa. Mama Baxter, Maggie, was one of the kindest women Sam had ever known. Also, one of the most hardworking; she never took a break.

Sam found a place to park her SUV near one of the outbuildings. As she headed toward the main house, she saw Wade standing on the wraparound front porch talking to Maggie Baxter. Actually, he wasn't doing much talking. Mama was giving a serious lecture. With both fists planted on her round hips, she glared at Wade through her wire-rimmed glasses.

As Sam came closer, she caught a taste of what Mama was saying to Wade, starting with how faking his death was the dumbest thing she'd ever heard and ending with how he'd broken the hearts of his friends and his dear, wonderful family. *Thank you, Maggie.*

Though she hated to interrupt the tirade, Sam made some noise with her boot heels when she climbed the steps onto the porch. Mama came toward her with arms outstretched. She was a sturdy woman but only about five feet tall. When Sam embraced her, she had to bend over.

Mama was crying. "Isn't it wonderful? Wade didn't die after all."

She looked over Mama's head to where her husband stood with his shoulders slumped and a look of shame and misery on his face. Sam really hoped he was aware of the sincere grief he'd caused this good, kind woman.

Mama lifted her tearstained face, looked up at Sam and said, "I could just kill that inconsiderate butthead.

Who does he think he is? Pulling a stunt like that? I should turn him over my knee like I did when he was a kid."

She'd spoken loudly enough to be sure Wade heard. In case he hadn't been paying attention, she repeated, "Inconsiderate butthead."

He took a step toward them. "I'm sorry, Maggie."

"I know you are." She patted his cheek. Her mouth drew into a bow as though she wanted to give him a kiss. But she didn't, and she didn't accept his apology, either.

He edged past them on his way to the front door. "I need to clean up before Ty's boss gets here."

"Upstairs bathroom."

"Can I borrow some clothes?"

"Ty keeps some things in the middle bedroom—the one with the bucking-bronco wallpaper. They ought to fit. Help yourself."

"Thanks." His gaze flicked back and forth between them. "Once again, I'm sorry."

He disappeared into the house.

With her thumb, Sam wiped the tears from Mama's cheeks. "You never really spanked those boys, did you?"

"Corporal punishment wasn't much of an option. In fifth grade they were as tall as I am. The threat was enough." She took Sam's arm and bustled toward the door. "Come on inside and have some lemonade. How are you feeling about all this?"

"Pretty much the same as you," she said. "Mad as hell about being lied to. But incredibly happy that he's alive."

In the huge kitchen where meals were prepared for the ranch hands and family, Mama had a young woman from town helping out. Sam knew her, and they exchanged greetings while she went to the refrigerator for a bottled water. Mama poured them each an ice-cold glass of lemonade, which she placed on the kitchen table along with a plateful of snickerdoodle cookies.

As soon as she sat at the table, Sam finished off half the water with one long glug.

"I guess you're thirsty," Mama said.

"Being nearly burned alive has that effect."

Mama and her kitchen helper both plunked down at the table. "Tell us all about it."

Sam knew it went against protocol to talk to civilians about an ongoing investigation, and she would steer clear of actual information or evidence, like finding the dead bodies or possible suspects. But she really wanted someone else's opinion on what was happening between her and Wade.

Taking a bite of snickerdoodle, she started talking about being "trapped" inside one of the cabins near Hanging Rock. There was no need to embellish the horror she'd experienced in the root cellar. The truth was bad enough.

"Were you scared?" Mama asked. "Never mind— that was a dumb question. Of course you were scared. Why did you do it?"

"What do you mean?" Sam asked.

"Why did you go looking for evidence with Wade?"

"The last time he got involved in this investigation, he deceived me and disappeared for over a year. If I had been involved, that never would have happened. From now on I want to work with him."

Mama Baxter gently placed her hand atop Sam's. Behind her glasses, her blue eyes were leaking again. "You could have both been killed. Your little girl would have had to grow up without a mother or father."

"And that's why I can't be too angry with Wade. He didn't tell me the truth because he was trying to protect us."

And now she was trying to protect Jenny. It occurred to her that Maggie's feelings and opinions were a mirror image of her own. She might be the best person to talk to about how to handle her parents about bringing Jenny back to Colorado.

Ty and Logan rolled through the back door into the kitchen, laughing and poking at each other like a couple of schoolboys. The two brothers were tall and lean, but the resemblance ended there. Logan's hair was an uncombed mass of blond curls. He had a big sloppy grin and his nose had been broken more than once. When he greeted Sam, he lifted her out of her chair in a hug and swatted her behind. Ty would never do such a thing. His brown hair was neat to match his handsome features and his attitude. The FBI was a good calling for him. Both men kissed their mother and grabbed cookies.

Ty checked a message on his cell phone. "My boss will be here real soon. I told him to land in front so he won't spook the horses in the corral."

"The horses will be fine," his mother said.

"Yeah," Logan chimed in. "Your boss isn't the only person who comes here in a chopper."

"Sorry for trying to be considerate."

Sam hadn't seen Ty since yesterday, and she had questions about the guys who attacked them. Ty had gone to the hospital with them and might have information. Plus, he'd know about the FBI forensics on the car where they found Morrissey's body.

She cleared her throat. "Before your boss gets here, you and I should talk."

"Why is that?"

Did she really have to tell him? "I need to be aware of the evidence you've obtained on the murder and the men who ambushed us."

"But I already talked to Wade."

"But I'm the sheriff," she said.

"I talked to your husband."

The three women fired hostile glares so powerful that he took a backward step. Ty got it. He backed down as fast as he could.

"I didn't mean that the way it sounded, Sam. I swear I didn't. Ask me anything. I can't hand over my official FBI report, but I can show it to you on my computer."

Though it hadn't been her intention to put him on the spot, Sam took advantage of the situation. "There's something else I've wanted to ask ever since Wade came back."

"Go ahead. Shoot."

"What really happened on the day you and your boss and my husband got together and faked his death?"

Chapter Sixteen

The moment Wade strode into the kitchen, Sam felt a change in the energy. There was something strong and vital about him, something the two Baxter men lacked. And her husband was number one when it came to handsome. In her opinion, he was almost too gorgeous with the dimples and the deep-set eyes and the chiseled cheekbones. His brown hair was wet and spiky from the shower. The smears of cellar dirt, ash and blood had been erased, and there was an aura of freshness about him as he finished buttoning a clean flannel shirt.

Though she was fairly sure that her heart was jumping out of her chest, Sam squashed the mad attraction that she felt for the man she'd married. She needed to make adjustments in their relationship. She had to learn to trust him again.

"I should be the one to tell this story," he said.

"What story?" Sam had already forgotten what she'd asked.

"About that day," he said. "The day when I didn't die in the river."

She gave a nod and leaned back in her chair at the kitchen table. Every eye in the room focused on him. Even the woman who was helping Mama with the cooking had stopped chopping and stirring to stare. Wade had that effect on people. He was compelling, a natural-born leader. But trustworthy?

"I remember every damn detail," he said. "The way the sun flashed on the river rapids, a granite ledge where some fool painted his initials in green, the frigid cold of the water, everything. I remember the hum the tires made on the highway and the crunch when we drove on gravel. I heard the echo of a bird song."

Logan asked, "Why do you remember so much?"

"It was the worst day of my life. My feet were heavy as bricks. I could barely lift them because I was sure, one hundred percent sure, that I was walking in the wrong direction."

She couldn't avoid being sympathetic toward him, but she had a very different perspective. Sure, he felt guilty for deceiving her. But she had to live with that deception, to plan his funeral, to file insurance claims, to give away his clothes. Either way, it was painful.

"I'll start at the beginning," Wade said. "At nine o'clock in the morning, Ty picked me up at the house. I kissed Samantha and Jenny goodbye."

She remembered, too. At dawn's first light, they'd made love before Jenny was up and demanding breakfast. Their morning sex was the fourth time in less than twenty-four hours. Not unheard of for them, but a little overly energetic for a married couple with a four-year-old.

At any time in those twenty-four, very intimate hours, he could have told her what was going on. He could have changed the plan. But he didn't.

"I packed all the stuff I'd need to go hunting. I had a new, handcrafted reflex bow I wanted to test," he said.

"Our cover story was that Ty and me were taking his boss and another fed out in the woods for the day. In the days before, we had plotted our route. It wasn't easy to find a spot near the white-water rapids that was feasible for bow hunting."

"I used a couple of GPS computer programs," Ty put in. "We had to make it believable that Wade could have been swept away in the current and his body never found."

It was obvious to her that Ty wasn't as emotionally invested in their story. His voice was calm, almost callous. If the shoe had been on the other foot, Ty's foot, would he have been so laid-back?

"The kayakers," Wade said, "were two federal agents from the navy. We borrowed them from their headquarters in San Diego. They were in great shape and expert in kayaking. When we got to the site on the river, they acted out what might happen if one of them lost control and I jumped in to save him."

"Would you?" she asked. "If the kayaker had really been in trouble, would you have tried to rescue him?"

"I don't know. It took a long time to figure out how it would have been possible for me to be in a position to help."

"That didn't stop you from wanting a demonstration," Ty said. "I couldn't believe you. Being thorough is one thing. You were obsessive about how the rescue attempt would have worked. You even got your ass in that freezing water."

"So did the guys from San Diego," Wade said.

"They were wearing wet suits." Ty jabbed an accusing finger in Wade's direction. "You had me worried, buddy. You weren't acting entirely rational."

"Hey, you and your boss were the ones who thought I should die. It wasn't my first choice."

"You're not blaming this on me," Ty said. "You could have backed out at any time, but you didn't. And you went a little crazy. Remember what you did to your bow. That was a beautiful piece of equipment, and you smashed it all to hell."

When they'd brought Wade's personal effects to her, the pieces of his hunting bow had broken her heart. "It was black walnut and maple. You loved that thing."

Wade shrugged. "Ty's right. I snapped."

"We were talking about how injured the kayaker ought to be," Ty said. "And trying to get a clear picture of how Wade could get in the water. Would he lose his backpack? How far along the river would he go before he got sucked under?"

The picture he was painting had become a little too vivid. Sam summarized what happened next. "You boys acted it out, and Wade went into custody as a protected witness."

"I got into the back of a van. The federal marshals were driving. They told me to lie on the bench until we were a good distance out of Colorado."

"They must have done that because they were taking you on the highway," she said. There were many traffic cameras along the main highway routes. The lenses shouldn't be able to see into the rear of a van, but it was better not to take chances.

"All the way to Texas. I must have gotten out of the van and gone inside, but I don't remember. Several days blurred together. All I could think about was you and Jenny. I missed you so much it hurt."

Sam believed him. His eyes were sad. The lines

in his face seemed to be more deeply etched. But she hadn't forgotten what happened to her when he went missing.

"Should I tell you more about what happened at the river?" Ty asked.

Sam had been kept away from the search and the investigation. "I want to know."

"My boss and I talked to the sheriff's office in Pitkin County, the Colorado Bureau of Investigation and the state patrol. Here's a twist for you. I think Morrissey took our statements. Search-and-rescue teams were deployed to locate Wade's remains."

Ty's mother interrupted. "I always thought it was strange that they couldn't find Wade. Every couple of years, the river claims a victim. But the bodies usually turn up."

"It helped," Ty said, "that we were in law enforcement. The local cops accepted our statements without question. There was nothing suspicious about it. Everybody saw this as a tragedy."

"Including me," Sam said in a small voice.

The river accident made for high drama as the kayakers, the cops and the searchers frantically attempted the rescue of a man they all liked and respected. The moment when she'd been told was far different.

Since Ty was busy at the scene, the task of notification should have gone to Deputy Caleb Schmidt or one of the others. But Maggie knew better, and she took charge. As soon as Ty called his mother, she grabbed Tyler's wife, Loretta, and the twins, who were staying at the ranch. They all went to Sam's house.

When Sam opened the door and saw the tear tracks on Maggie's cheeks and matching sorrow from Loretta, she knew something terrible had happened. Maggie didn't say a word until she'd shooed Sam into the kitchen to make a fresh pot of coffee and sent Jenny back to the ranch with Loretta and the twins. Then she sat down with Sam.

Quietly, she had received the news that her husband was dead.

Thinking of that moment turned Sam's blood to ice water. She'd felt empty. The air had left her lungs. The strength had vanished from her muscles. She hadn't been able to stand or move.

She remembered reaching for her coffee mug. Her arm seemed disconnected from the rest of her body, as though it was someone else's arm. Her hand fell limply to her lap. Her head weighed a thousand pounds, and her neck wasn't strong enough to hold it up. She drooped forward in her chair. Before she passed out, Maggie grabbed her shoulders and gave them a shake.

Maggie's lips moved. She must have said something, but Sam couldn't comprehend the words. Every woman who married a lawman—even a sheriff in a rural Colorado county—had to prepare herself for the possibility that her husband might not survive his shift.

Her mom, Cora, knew the drill and had advised her daughter to make sure their wills were properly updated, life-insurance policies were paid up and monetary accounts were in either his or her name.

When she looked around the kitchen table at the Baxter ranch, she realized everyone was watching her. They were concerned, and she appreciated their kindness. But there were some things she couldn't explain.

"I grew up knowing what to do," she said. "My mom taught me. When a cop, like my dad, dies, you've got to take care of business. Wade and I had discussed everything. We both wanted to be cremated and to have the ashes spread from the highest point on our property. There was only one problem with that." She looked over at him. "No ashes."

He winced. "It feels like I should say I'm sorry."

"Not necessary." She rose from the chair and stepped into his embrace. "Having you back is a dream come true. I must have imagined it a million times. In the first months after your fake death, I kept thinking I saw you on the street or driving past in a car. You didn't do any of those things, did you?"

"I wanted to," he admitted. "My handlers wouldn't let me. They take the witness-protection thing real seriously."

"It damn well better be serious." None of this was a joke. Her life had been shredded for the sake of this investigation. "I used to go down to the Roaring Fork, where the kayak accident supposedly took place, and stand and stare at the water. I never got you a gravestone."

"That's a mighty good thing." Maggie rose from her chair. Though she was by far the oldest person in the room, her ears must have been the sharpest. She cocked her head and pointed skyward. "I hear your boss's chopper, Ty."

Arm in arm with her husband, Sam walked toward the front porch with the others. The midsize helicopter angled around and made a landing near the fence at the edge of the road. The whirring blades churned up the dust and blew the hair back from her face.

It was an impressive entrance…and an expensive one. She hated to think of how her meager sheriff's budget compared with the vast resources of the FBI. Swain County could barely afford to buy disposable ventilation masks to use in a wildfire. Keeping her husband away from her for more than a year with a couple of marshals guarding him must have cost a pretty penny. If they didn't shut down the smuggling operations and put the ringleader out of business, that money would have been wasted.

Everett Hurtado disembarked from the FBI chopper and strode toward the ranch house. In his black suit and blue shirt with a silver-striped tie flapping in the wind from the rotors, he projected an authority figure. She didn't like him.

The first time she'd met the slender man with cold obsidian eyes and black hair was a few hours after Maggie came to her house to tell her about the accident. Hurtado had accompanied Ty. His intention was to pay his respects, but she'd sensed something phony about him. Big surprise! The whole accident and death were phony. But she hadn't got the same feeling from Ty. He radiated guilt and also sympathy, knowing how hard the faked death would be on her.

Watching Hurtado approach with two other agents trailing in his wake, she made a decision. She didn't want to be part of whatever planning session they were going to have. In a closed room with all those guys, she'd have to shout to make her voice heard, and she wasn't in the mood for that kind of struggle. She knew what she needed. Her agenda was clear: investigate with Wade and keep her daughter safe.

The decision about how to handle her mom was still dangling over her head. Sam knew the best person to give her advice on that topic was Maggie Baxter.

She gave Wade's arm a squeeze and looked up at him. "Don't go anywhere, and I mean don't leave this house, without telling me."

"Aren't you going to wait around and say hello?"

"I'd rather get cleaned up."

She didn't offer further explanation.

Wade had told her that the ringleader—the man who coordinated with the cartel and facilitated the exchange of merchandise—was someone in law enforcement. In her mind, Everett Hurtado's name belonged on that list.

For that matter, it could also be Ty.

Wade leaned down to whisper, "That call from your mom. What was it about?"

"We can talk about it later."

They used to discuss everything. His opinion was important to her. Now she was reluctant. Her love for him was undeniable, but she didn't want to confide in him. She still didn't trust him.

Chapter Seventeen

Ty escorted Wade and his boss and two other agents who were eerily similar in appearance into the front office used by his father. From what Wade had gathered, most of the real work of the ranch was being done by Logan and the ranch manager while Papa eased into retirement. The desk in Papa Baxter's office was tidy and pristine. His computer had a light coat of dust and looked as if it was seldom used, which was probably accurate. The old man liked the things that computers could do, but he had a hard time typing. Like a lot of cowboys, his hands were calloused and beat up.

The five of them could have fit comfortably in a conversational area that had a sofa and padded leather chairs, but Hurtado opted for the throne-like seat behind the big desk. The other three men worked for him. Wade didn't; he had the luxury of not following orders.

Instead of hunching around the desk, he took one of the leather chairs and stretched his long legs out in front of him.

He wished that Samantha was here with him, but he completely understood why she'd gone off in another direction. He hated briefings almost as much as she did.

If there hadn't been so much information the FBI had that he wanted, he would have left.

"Gentlemen," said Hurtado, "we'll start with the good news. Wade?"

He sounded as if he was taking roll call. "What?"

"I have a hospital report. You'll be happy to hear that neither of the survivors from yesterday's shoot-out mentioned seeing you. Their stories are consistent— full of lies but consistent. Both are expected to make a full recovery."

He hadn't killed anybody. Actually, he considered that to be very good news. Wade had never been the sort of lawman who wanted a high body count. The fewer people injured the better. "Have they been identified?"

Hurtado gestured to his matching set of agents. One of them rifled through a briefcase that contained several file folders. His twin agent whipped out a small computer, fired it up and started scrolling. The competing technologies were interesting, and Wade found himself silently rooting for the guy with the briefcase. Even more interesting was Hurtado, sitting behind the big desk with an attitude of smug superiority. There was so much about this guy that Wade disliked. How did he let Hurtado talk him into witness protection?

The briefcase won the race. He rattled off names of the survivors and the third man who had died. The names meant nothing to Wade.

When he looked at the photographs the briefcase guy handed to him, he felt a jolt of recognition. "I've seen him before. Right before the most recent start to the trial, he was at the federal courthouse in Austin. Do you have an address for him?"

Ty picked up the photo and gave it a hard look. "I'm

pretty sure I don't know him. Are you thinking he might be a local?"

"I've seen him around and about." His brain couldn't fill in that last blank. "In Austin, I knew he looked familiar."

"That's what got you spooked," Hurtado said. "You thought this guy recognized you. And you assumed that he would report back to his superiors that Wade Calloway wasn't dead."

"And my family would be in danger."

"If you had told us—"

"But I didn't," Wade interrupted. "Could we move this along? I have a couple of questions."

"Next point of discussion," Hurtado said. "That would be the murder of state patrolman Drew Morrissey. I should tell you right now that Morrissey was my snitch."

Wade had suspected as much. When he'd witnessed the murders, he'd identified some of the cops in the room. The next logical move for SSA Hurtado would be to find a contact, like Morrissey, and offer him a deal in exchange for informing on the others.

While Hurtado bragged about his communications with his snitch, Wade wondered how he could have talked to a supposed insider for over a year and yet failed to learn the name of the ringleader. Either Morrissey was so low on the totem pole that he couldn't see the top or he was playing Hurtado.

The briefcase guy spread photographs across the desktop while Hurtado explained, "These are the pictures taken by Wade's wife before she attempted to move the body."

Wade straightened in his chair. "Samantha Calloway is Swain County sheriff. She's been duly elected to that position, and that's how you should refer to her."

"I recommend not making her angry," Ty said.

One of the twin agents snickered. "Are you scared of her?"

"Damn right," Ty said, "and you should be, too."

"It was quick thinking on Sheriff Calloway's part that got us these photos," Hurtado said. "She didn't have a crime-scene processing kit and made do with her camera phone and emailed the photos to Ty's phone, and then he sent them on to me. As you can see from the pictures, it's obvious from the lack of blood spatter that Morrissey was *not* killed in this vehicle."

This was old news for Wade. "Do you have any clue about the primary murder scene? Has anybody checked out his home? Or the last place he was seen alive?"

"Good questions," Hurtado said. "We've been to his apartment. The bed doesn't appear to have been slept in. A canvass of the neighbors indicated that no one saw him last night."

Maybe he'd been killed the night before. "What was TOD from the autopsy?"

"Time of death was between ten in the morning and noon. His last meal was bacon and eggs."

"That doesn't help much," Ty said. "He could have had breakfast anywhere."

Hurtado stood behind the desk, supposedly to shuffle the array of photos. Wade thought the real reason he was standing was to be able to look each of them in the eye and assert his authority.

"I deeply regret Morrissey's death," Hurtado said with gravity. "I blame myself."

"You think somebody found out he was a snitch?" Wade asked.

"Why else would he be killed?"

Off the top of his head, Wade could think of a dozen reasons, starting with Morrissey was an irritating jerk. He was lazy, always trying to figure out a way to get out of paperwork. But he was quick to grab credit when he worked with the deputies in Swain County. "He was a pig."

"Excuse me." Hurtado lifted an eyebrow. Like his hair, his brows were very black.

"He came to a barbecue at my house," Wade said. "I hadn't really planned to invite him, but there he was. He ate enough for three people and slopped sauce all over himself."

Thinking back, Wade recalled that night, a casual get-together of men and women mostly from the community and from local law enforcement. Natchez had been there; he had to drive Morrissey home after he'd had too much to drink. Wade remembered talking to both of them about custom-made weaponry. He'd just got his black-walnut-and-maple bow and led a group into his study, where he unlocked the weapons case. His Colt .45 with the fancy copper inlay on the grip had been in there. Morrissey had commented on it.

Had he been the one who'd stolen the gun from the house? But why? It didn't make sense for him to steal the weapon that was used to kill him.

As if reading his mind, Hurtado said, "The autopsy gave us some interesting data to work with. Ballistics indicate that the murder weapon was a Colt .45 revolver. There aren't many of those antiques still around."

Ty shot him a glance. "Didn't you have one of those?"

"Still do. A collector's piece with copper inlay on the grip, it's locked in my gun cabinet at home."

He lied without hesitation. The gun had been wiped clean of prints and was, therefore, useless as viable evidence. If they figured out who had gone to the trouble of stealing the gun and planting it, they'd probably be looking at the murderer. Who would go to so much trouble to implicate Wade in the crime? It had to be somebody who knew he wasn't dead. Otherwise, why frame him?

His gaze lingered on Hurtado. At best, he was annoying. At worst...a murderer?

Wade left the comfortable chair and stalked toward the desk. His suspicions were out of hand. Or were they? Hurtado wouldn't be the first FBI agent to go rogue. "I have a question."

Hurtado shuffled impatiently through the photos. "I'd rather stick to my agenda. There's an order to be followed. I want to make sure we don't miss anything."

A spurt of righteous anger prompted Wade to say, "Yeah, you wouldn't want to overlook something important, like the bodies of Dana Gregg and Lyle McFee."

"Who?"

"The victims. The two people whose murders I witnessed. At least show them the respect of recalling their names. Dana Gregg. Lyle McFee."

"Don't lecture me on victimology."

Wade didn't think he was using the term correctly. And he didn't care for labels anyway. "This isn't about your policy for vics or perps or anybody else. It's about human decency. These two people made mistakes in their lives. They weren't saints, but that doesn't mean they deserved to be murdered. It's our job to find justice for them."

Usually, he wasn't one for big declarations, but sometimes it was important to speak out. Hurtado used the FBI to build up his own power and status. He liked swooping around in helicopters, wearing sharp suits and giving the guys who worked under him a hard time. He'd forgotten that the job was about protecting those who couldn't help themselves.

He focused his black-eyed gaze on Wade. He was angry. His features were set in granite, and his lips barely moved when he said, "Are you done with your tantrum?"

"Not really," Wade said in an aggressively cheery tone. "Have your forensic guys drawn any conclusions from the evidence we uncovered at Hanging Rock?"

"Nothing yet," he snapped.

Wade couldn't resist another dig. "I wonder why they didn't find the root cellar the first time they went looking."

"At least they didn't burn the building down."

"Neither did we," Wade said. "It was arson."

Hurtado's stony mask twitched into a frown, and Wade took that as a sign. The SSA was weakening. He knew he was in the wrong. "Fire Marshal Hobbs says it was arson. A fire with accelerant started in the kitchen. By the way, he's not happy with you."

"He'll have to stand in line before he takes his shot."

"You've made a lot of people angry, Wade."

"I know." But there was only one person whose opinion mattered: Samantha. If she could find it in her heart to forgive him and trust him again, he'd be able to live with the rest of the world hating his guts.

"I have a bit more to say about Morrissey." Hurtado had returned to his all-important agenda. "The nature of the relationship between an agent and a snitch is a complicated one. At times, I praised him and offered him bribes. The reverse was also true. And I had to keep in mind that a snitch is, by his very nature, a liar who is without loyalty and…"

He droned on with his lecture. The matching set of agents he'd brought with him listened intently. Wade was glad to see that Ty wasn't similarly impressed. He'd left his chair beside the desk and stood at the window, gazing out at the front porch.

As Wade took a position beside him, he wondered if his pal Ty was thinking about what he'd given up on the ranch by following a career in the FBI. From where they stood, they could see the barn, the horses in the corral and Papa Baxter leaning against the fence with his head tilted to catch the warmth of the sun. It was a good life.

If Ty wanted to continue with the feds, he needed to become a supervisory agent real soon. He'd do a better job than Hurtado. Ty was smart and motivated and hadn't yet been consumed by the bureaucracy.

At the far end of the fence, Wade saw one of the Swain County Sheriff's Department vehicles turn onto the driveway. Near the house, the vehicle swerved and parked next to Samantha's SUV. Wade still couldn't tell who it was.

Ty groaned. "It's Caleb."

Any hope of claiming he was dead vanished. The rumor that he was still alive had spread faster than the wildfire. When he saw Deputy Caleb Schmidt jump out of his car and charge toward the front door, Wade pivoted and spoke to Hurtado. "If there's anything important I should know, tell me now."

Hurtado gave an annoyed huff. "Obviously, you're incapable of being patient. At least try to be courteous."

"Sir," Ty said as he stepped forward. "We're about

to be interrupted by Caleb Schmidt, a man who doesn't know the meaning of silence."

"One more thing from Morrissey," Hurtado said. "Before he was killed, the snitch told me there was something big going down."

Again, old news. Ty had already mentioned the smuggling of stolen weapons from the US Army base. "Did he have any details?"

"No location, but a time. Tomorrow night between nine and midnight."

The office door crashed open. Caleb came strutting inside with his thumbs hitched in his belt loops. In spite of his attempt to act cool, his breathing was rapid. His thick glasses were slightly askew. When he saw Wade, he froze.

Wade ground his rear molars together, preparing himself to be read the Caleb Schmidt version of the riot act. Instead, the old man flung his scrawny arms around Wade for a quick but ferocious hug.

"Glad to see you," Caleb muttered.

"Glad to be seen."

"If you ever pull a stunt like that again, I will kill you. I mean it. I don't make none of them there idle threats."

In his position, Wade would have felt the same.

Chapter Eighteen

After a heart-to-heart talk with Maggie Baxter, Sam found a quiet corner in an upstairs bedroom—the blue one with clouds painted across the ceiling—to call her parents. She had decided not to lie but to tell them as little as possible. Somehow, that plan got her started on an endless loop.

"Here's the deal, Dad. I need you and Mom to keep Jenny safe for a few days, a week at most."

"I thought you had a problem with the fire."

"The fire is ninety percent contained."

"Then it's okay if we bring Jenny back home."

That conclusion brought her back to "keep Jenny safe for a few days." And the circle started anew.

Her dad asked, "What kind of trouble are you in?"

She tried to demur. "I'd rather not say."

"I don't like that, Sammy girl, don't like it at all. I'm going to hire us a rental car, and we're heading back there as quick as we can."

"Stop!" There didn't seem to be an easy, gentle way to handle explosive news. "I don't want to lie to you."

"You'd better not."

"You've got to promise me, from the depths of your

heart, that you won't tell Jenny. She needs to hear this from me. In person."

"I promise."

She tried one more time to get him to change his mind, but he steadfastly refused. She decided to pull the pin on this grenade and let fly. "Wade isn't dead."

"Huh?"

"He faked his death and has been in witness protection."

"Huh?"

"There are some very dangerous cartel people after him, and he pretended to be dead so Jenny and I would be safe."

After a long pause, her dad said, "Run this by me again."

She told him again, filling in more of the blanks, and then again and again until finally he started repeating parts back to her, including the all-important promise not to tell Jenny.

"I won't bring Jenny back home," he said, "but I'm going to hire a rental car and stay within easy driving distance of your house until my Cessna is fixed. If you need this old cop, call me. I'll be there in just a few hours."

She figured that was the best assurance she could get. "You aren't old and you're a great lawman. Dad, you're the only cop I'd trust with my little girl."

After she disconnected the call, she pulled aside the blue curtain and looked out the window to the driveway in front of the ranch house. Two Swain County Sheriff's Department vehicles, including the gas-saving hybrid they were testing, drove toward the house. Then she noticed Deputy Schmidt's SUV parked next to hers. She had only six deputies. At least four of them were here.

The ace lawmen of Swain County had somehow figured out that Wade was alive and well and hanging out at the Baxter ranch. Would she be expected to coordinate with them? More likely, the boys would circle around Wade and beg him to come back and save them from the mean lady sheriff who made them take target practice once a week and insisted that paperwork be filed before they went home for the night.

She really didn't want to argue. If they wanted her gone, she'd go. Taking on the responsibilities of the sheriff's job had seemed like a good thing at the time. But it was thankless work, and she was tired. She pulled down the shades on the windows, closed the curtains and turned out the lights.

This bedroom had been designed for a child with the soothing blue color and the fluffy clouds painted overhead, but it was exactly what Sam needed—a comforting place where all the conflict and noises were locked out. She stretched out on one of the two twin-size beds. With the room darkened, the clouds on the ceiling became luminous decals of stars, a simple but magical detail.

The door handle turned, and her very own Prince Charming entered the room. While she was lying down and looking up, Wade seemed so tall that the top of his head brushed the stars. So handsome, he was strong enough to slay any dragon.

He sat on the edge of the twin bed and stroked a tendril of hair off her forehead. "You washed your hair."

"I smelled like a stinky old fireplace."

"And you changed clothes." He caught hold of the zipper pull on the orange Broncos sweatshirt she'd snatched from Ty's dresser. Wade tugged the zip lower. "Maybe you should try a different outfit."

"Are you being suggestive?"

"Should I be more obvious?" He gave a decisive yank on the zipper.

She slapped his hand, sat up on the bed and pulled the zipper back up. "This is a safe, magical room, made for a child. An innocent room. Do you see the stars on the ceiling? They're watching us."

"And so is everybody else. All the Swain County deputies, led by Caleb, are here."

"I saw part of the convoy arriving. I bet they're excited to see you."

"And ticked off." He exhaled a sigh. "That seems to be the typical response. I'm the guy everybody hates to love."

"An apt description," she said. He wasn't even trying to be agreeable, but she was nodding her head. "How was your talk with Hurtado?"

"I don't like the supervisory special agent any more than you do."

"You know what *SSA* spells backward?" She chuckled at her little joke. "You probably know him a lot better than I do. Every time I've talked to him, he's been phony."

"He's smug and arrogant. He acts like he's the big expert, but he's done a really poor job in getting this smuggling operation shut down. Morrissey was his snitch."

"And what did Morrissey tell him?"

"Here's the only useful piece of information. The

weapons that were stolen from the army base are going to be exchanged tomorrow night between nine and midnight."

"And we don't know where," she said. Otherwise, the FBI could call in the troops and set a trap.

"Not a clue."

He pushed himself off the bed and started pacing. In the dimly lit room, he looked like a muscular but confused shadow trying to decide where to alight.

She turned on the bedside lamp and got another lovely surprise. The lampshade rotated and flashed light silhouettes on the walls while a music box played "Hush, Little Baby."

"Adorable," she said. "I want Maggie to come to our house and decorate a room like this."

"For Jenny?"

"Maybe not. Our little Jenny wants to be a big girl who gets to do big-girl things. Like I told you, she wants to learn how to snowboard and ride horses. Doesn't have much use for playing with babyish things."

"Does she still like Gordo?"

"Of course." Her daddy had given her that special stuffed animal—a plump hippo with a goofy grin. "She can't go to sleep without Gordo."

"I can't wait to sit down with her and listen to one of her long, rambling stories. And I want to read to her, even if she wants the same book again and again. And yes to the horses. I'll teach my girl to snowboard and to ski."

When they talked about simple family things, it was as though he'd never left. They could pick up where they'd left off and move forward...except for the deadly threat on all their lives.

She couldn't lie back and enjoy the fake stars overhead. They needed answers. She gave herself a kick in the butt. "Did Hurtado have any plans?"

"I don't know. I left the briefing when he was only halfway through his agenda. But I have an idea. When Caleb showed up, I got inspired."

"I'm shocked, totally shocked." She rolled her eyes. "That has to be the first time in recorded history that the words *Caleb* and *inspired* were used in the same sentence."

"Unlikely? Yes. But this might be a bit of genius."

"Tell."

He sat on the other twin bed, placed his elbows on his knees and leaned toward her. "Do you think any of our deputies are part of the smuggling operation?"

The possibility had never presented itself in her mind. She had to think about it. There were different characteristics to different law-enforcement groups. The state patrol was standoffish and tended to be Lone Rangers. Undercover guys, like the men who worked for the DEA and ATF, were very cool and faced temptations every day. Aspen cops had a status thing going, while the Grand Junction law enforcement considered themselves to be more urban.

The small bunch that worked for the Swain County Sheriff's Department weren't cool or shiny or tough. They were earnest, tried to do the right thing and were a little bit nerdy.

She shrugged. "Nobody approached me to join their smuggling operations. Were you ever invited to that party?"

He shook his head. "I'd like to think it was my sterling rep as a straight shooter that kept the criminals from recruiting me, but I think it was more a matter of being in the wrong place at the right time."

"And your friendship with Ty," she reminded him. "If somebody approached you and you turned them down, Ty and the FBI would know about it."

"Whatever the reason," he said, "I think we can trust our deputies and the dispatchers."

"You could be right about that. What does that prove?"

"If anybody can sniff out crime in Swain County, it's our guys. We know *when* the next exchange of goods is taking place. All we need to do is find out *where*."

Talk about a long shot! Six deputies plus the two of them would try to find the roots of a smuggling operation in the hundred-and-sixty-square-mile area of Swain County, plus the neighboring counties that included hundreds of miles more of open territory. If by some crazy chance they actually found the smugglers, what would this hapless band do to take them down?

She got off the bed, took his hands and pulled him to his feet. "I guess we've got to start somewhere."

"And I have a plan B."

"Of course you do."

"The success of it depends on you," he said. "How's your relationship with Lieutenant Natchez?"

"Earlier today, I fired two bullets at him."

"Perfect."

WADE GATHERED HIS ragtag army of six deputies around the long table in the bunkhouse behind the ranch. The big two-story house where Maggie Baxter ran things was tidy, efficient and nicely decorated. The bunkhouse, which was full only a couple of times a year when they hired on extra help, was a barracks-like man cave with very little attempt at decoration and two wide-screen televisions, one at either end of the long structure.

The refrigerator was well stocked with beer. And Maggie had been kind enough to provide this law-enforcement crew with sandwiches, chips and two fresh-baked apple pies. Mama Baxter was on their side; Wade wished he could say the same for Ty and the FBI. Hurtado had warned him that they were dealing with a vicious cartel. Blood might be spilled. They had virtually no chance of success.

At least Wade and his band of misfits were taking action.

Their first order of business was food. Three or four ranch hands were also at the table, and everybody helped themselves.

Wade was surprised when Logan came through the door with two other guys. Ty's brother slapped Wade on the back and made introductions.

"What's this about?" Wade asked.

"Some of these men might want to help."

He lowered his voice. "I can't ask them to put their lives in danger."

"Did you forget that this is the West? The place where the locals form a posse and ride out after the bank robbers? Maybe we're not as wild as in the olden days, but we take care of our neighbors."

"What are you saying?"

"You might have a lot more deputies than you realize."

An unexpected turn of events, but he welcomed the extra help. Sitting at the table, he looked over at the two youngest deputies, both in their twenties. These two small-town boys were skillful when it came to search-and-rescue operations. Local motorists loved these guys.

Caleb Schmidt took a seat at Wade's left. As the man with the most seniority, he had standing. And he never lacked for enthusiasm or an opinion.

Samantha was talking quietly to the three other deputies, the men who thought of police work as their career, not because they harbored a passion for justice but rather they saw this as a steady job with decent benefits and an opportunity to help. He'd noticed that these three looked to Samantha for decision-making. Her rational style of leadership appealed to them.

After they dug into the food and beer, Wade stood at the end of the table. He wanted them to know what they were getting into. And he wanted to give them a chance to back out.

"One more time," he said, "I apologize to each and every one of you for inconveniences my death might have caused. My intention was never to hurt. I thought I was protecting my family and my friends."

"We heard you," Caleb said. "No more apologies."

"Before we get started," he said, "I want you all to know that this could be dangerous. One of our enemies in this smuggling operation is the Esteban cartel. This criminal organization has multinational reach. The scope of their cruelty and violence cannot be fully described. They've slaughtered whole villages of men, women and children. They're responsible for beheadings and mutilations. These are the monsters that haunt our nightmares, incapable of redemption or reason."

He looked up and down the table. Every person was quiet, thoughtful.

"The other end of this smuggling operation is even

more terrifying. You wouldn't know they were monsters. They look like us. Most of them are lawmen—cops, federal agents, state employees. You've been to parties with them, maybe even had them over to your house."

He thought of that barbecue at his home where Morrissey and Natchez were guests. "Most of you know that a state patrolman named Drew Morrissey was murdered. A big, friendly guy, he was a goof-off. And he was part of this smuggling operation. Not because he was particularly evil or cruel. He did it for one reason."

"For the money," Caleb said. "We've all been tempted. Makes me want to puke when I stop a speeder and he passes me a twenty with his driver's license and registration. That's how it starts. You take one little bribe and before you know it, you're working for the cartel."

Wade couldn't have said it better himself. He shook Caleb's hand. "I want to rip this smuggling operation apart. They've been working in Swain County and nearby areas for quite a while. I want them gone."

The two young deputies stood. "We're with you, Wade."

"The Baxters have been real understanding about letting us meet here. They've got the FBI in the parlor and us in the bunkhouse." Which, he thought, was appropriate. "If you want to be part of what I'm putting together, come to my house by three o'clock."

Samantha stood. "There's no shame in deciding you don't want to take on the monsters of the world. It's the sane decision. Nobody will think less of you if you don't show."

Wade stepped forward, took her hand and left the bunkhouse.

Chapter Nineteen

Sam hauled an armful of supplies into the kitchen of their house. Wade came behind her with more groceries. In their past life together, they entertained often, so she knew how to grab enough munchies to feed an army.

But this wasn't going to be a party. They wouldn't be playing games or trying to match up their single friends. She would probably be the only woman here, and none of the men thought of her that way, except Wade. She permitted herself a little smile. That was as it should be.

Their house would be the base of operations for tracking down the smugglers. That was, of course, if anyone showed up. Wade had given an inspiring speech, but he'd also been honest about the risks.

"Do you think anybody is going to show?" she asked.

"Caleb, for sure."

"I thought we should put him in charge of communications. Somebody needs to stay here and coordinate information."

He unloaded a few boxes of snack food into the large pantry between the kitchen and the mudroom. "I was hoping that you'd take on that responsibility."

Irritated, she placed a two-pound package of deli-sliced peppered turkey in the fridge and frowned at him.

"Do you want me to stay here because you don't think I can handle fieldwork? Or is it so I won't get hurt?"

"You want the truth?" he asked.

"Always." That was the only way she could trust him.

"I want to protect you. That doesn't mean I don't think you're capable. It's an instinct."

"Well, get over it." She placed bananas and Granny Smith apples in a bowl. "You're going to have to learn how to let me take care of myself. The same goes for Jenny. She's growing up and needs to be independent."

He threw up his hands. "Are you telling me I'm not allowed to take care of our little girl?"

"Taking care of her is one thing, but don't be a helicopter dad, always hovering around her."

"As it so happens," he said, "I know the meaning of that term. People in witness protection tend to watch a lot of television. And don't worry—I won't hover."

She shot him a grin. "I guess you're up on all the parenting techniques."

"Speaking of parents," he said, "you've had a couple of conversations with yours. What's up?"

She explained about the mechanical problems with the Cessna and then moved on to a deeper issue. "I told Dad that you're still alive."

He winced. "How angry is he?"

"That wasn't his response. He wants to help catch the bad guys. Just like all these other people from the Baxter ranch."

"We know good people," he said.

Caleb was the first to arrive, and he immediately made himself useful by brewing a pot of coffee.

Sam dashed upstairs to change clothes and put her hair in a braid so it wouldn't get in the way. After she'd thrown on a fresh pair of jeans and a white tank top under a plaid shirt, she checked her reflection in the mirror. She looked tough and competent, which was how she wanted Wade to see her.

Their extra-long bed stretched out in front of her like a promise. She couldn't wait until they were lying together in each other's arms, couldn't wait to hear him whisper her name, *Samantha, Samantha.* By the time she came downstairs again, three other deputies had arrived, and her house had been turned into a strategic battlefield. A huge topographical map was laid out on the dining room table. Quadrants marked off areas that should be searched.

The obvious problem was that they needed more people. The square miles to be covered were vast. And they were only a measly few.

Trying to narrow and focus their search, every man put in his bits of information. They actually knew a great deal. Being a deputy meant spending time in uncharted territory where people got lost or had cars break down. Where were the abandoned houses like the ones at Hanging Rock? Were there rental sites available? How was the fire going to impact their search?

"We don't know what the smugglers are going to take in exchange for the illegal arms," Wade said. "Their package could be small, like prescription drugs. Or it could be a truckload of human beings."

"What size are the weapons?" one of the deputies asked.

As they began calculating, she pushed open the sliding glass door and went onto the deck. The smoke from the wildfire was almost gone. A fresh breeze stroked her cheeks.

Then she saw the cars and trucks driving up the road to her house, kicking up a cloud of reddish dust. Logan was in the first truck. He leaned out and waved to her. There were probably five guys in the back of his truck. Four more cars brought up the rear. Wade's speech had been effective.

In the dining room, an air of solidarity prevailed. Plotting the areas to be searched was greatly enhanced by adding the cowboys from Baxter ranch who could patrol far and wide on horseback. More than once, she heard Wade telling them not to shoot first and ask questions later.

She heard what sounded like the *thwap-thwap-thwap* of a helicopter's rotors and went to the front window. When she saw the FBI chopper dipping down to land on a flat spot near the road, she couldn't believe it.

Wade came up beside her. "What do you think this is about?"

"Let's go find out."

When they walked out the front door, Logan joined them. He nudged Wade's shoulder. "What did I tell you? My brother can't stand being left out."

"I never thought he'd convince his boss."

Ty shoved open the chopper door and came toward them. He stopped a few paces in front of them. "You know that Hurtado does not approve of what I'm doing. Consider the chopper a gift horse, and you should never look a gift horse in the mouth."

"What should we do with it?" Wade asked.

"There's a couple of hours of daylight left," Ty said, "and this is probably the best way to get an overview of the burned acreage. Marshal Hobbs isn't going to let you go exploring on foot."

"I'll go with you," Logan said, stepping forward. "I've been thinking about getting one of these for the ranch. This could be a test drive. I'll be back here after dusk."

She watched them walk downhill toward the whirring blades. "Family is everything."

He nodded. "I need to call my sister."

"She is so totally going to kick your butt. Maybe you could record the call for me."

"Much as I hate to interrupt the fun time you're having by treating me like a jerk, I have another project for you."

"Natchez." She'd been thinking about him since Wade brought his name up. "Why me? And what do you want from him?"

"In case you hadn't noticed," he said, "he's real uncomfortable around you. Because the man is a fool, I think he underestimates you."

"Do you think he's one of the smugglers?"

"I'm willing to bet that good old Natchez has had a taste for the payoffs."

"What should I do?"

"Call him, and tell him that you hate my guts and you want to get out of this one-horse town. Tell him you want to make some serious cash, to meet with the smugglers."

"Will he believe that?"

"If you sell it right, he'll believe anything."

She appreciated that he was sending her off on a solo mission. "With all your protective instincts, I'm kind of surprised that you're willing to let me handle this on my own."

"Who said you'd be alone?"

Wade's bright idea was for him to hide in the car with her. After she got Natchez to talk, Wade would help her arrest him. Though she wouldn't admit it to him, she was relieved that he'd be close. Natchez acted the fool. But his swearing and intense tidiness might be a cover. He was organized enough to be the ringleader.

She placed the call. To her surprise, Natchez answered.

"I expected to get voice mail," she said.

"I always answer my calls," he said. "It's efficient. I expect you're calling about Morrissey's murder, and I've got nothing to report."

This wasn't going well. She needed to develop a more personal relationship. What was his first name? "You know, Trevor, I don't really mind when you swear."

"I'll be damned. Are you a dirty girl?"

"Maybe." She'd need a long soak in a scented bath after this conversation. "My husband doesn't understand that. I wish he'd had the good sense to stay dead."

After repeated swearing, he said, "You're kind of a surprise."

"There's something you might be able to help me with, Trevor," she purred into the phone. "I'm tired of living in this boring little burg. I want to make some cash, some real cash."

"I think I know what you're talking about," he said. "And there's no way I'd introduce you to those people."

Gotcha! "So you know who they are?"

"I didn't say that."

"But you did, Trevor. You said 'those people.'" And he sounded as if they were beneath him. Was he talking about the cartel or the locals? "I knew you'd be able to help me. You're well connected."

"I should go," he said.

She could almost hear him backpedaling over the phone. She had to offer him something special to keep him interested. "You know, with all these FBI guys running around, a girl tends to overhear things."

"What FBI guys?"

"You can see them flying around in their black helicopter. Take a gander out your window."

"I see them."

"If you introduce me to the people who can make me big bucks, I promise the FBI won't get in the way of the big deal that's going down tomorrow night."

"You know about tomorrow night?"

"Like I said, I hear things." She'd done the selling. Now she needed to be a closer. "Meet me tonight, Trevor. I'll come to your place."

"I don't know." Nerves trembled in his voice. "I just don't know."

"This is a onetime offer. I want an introduction that gets me into the smuggling operation."

"Okay, okay. You're on."

They arranged to meet tonight at ten o'clock at the Pine Cone Motel on the far end of Woodridge. When she ended the call, she couldn't help wondering. Were men really that gullible? Or did she have a creepy undercover talent that she'd never used before?

For the rest of the day and into the night, she helped Caleb send their guys out into the field and recorded when they reported back. The ranch hands were having the most fun playing posse. They each took a horse and went about fifteen miles from the Baxter ranch. There wasn't much farther they could go and make it back before nightfall.

The only viable leads came from what they observed when looking down from higher elevations. They pinpointed two ranches with high activity. When the deputies drove to the ranches to check them out, they found that one was having a family reunion and the other had set up a kitchen to feed the firefighters.

By nine o'clock, she was exhausted. Flirting with Trevor Natchez sounded like less fun than scrubbing toilets. First, she put in a good-night call to Jenny. Then she checked in with the fire marshal, who said the fire was still 90 percent contained, which meant he and his crew would be sticking around for a while longer.

At half past, she was in her SUV, with Wade lying across the seats in the back. He had tried to scrunch down on the passenger side, but his extra-large body wasn't meant to be concealed so easily.

"When we get there," he said, "you don't have to play any games with him. I don't like that he wanted you to come to a motel. What did you say to the guy, anyway?"

"I might have hinted that I thought his endless dirty talk was kind of sexy."

Wade groaned. "Leave your phone turned on so I can hear what's happening. You want to get the location for the smugglers' drop. And the name of the ringleader."

Not exactly an easy assignment. "And if he doesn't want to talk to me?"

"Back to the drawing board."

The Pine Cone Motel was full, as she expected it would be. The firefighters needed to have someplace to sleep. Natchez hadn't given her a room number, but his spotless Crown Vic was parked outside number seven, and a light shone from inside.

After syncing her phone with Wade's, she got out of

her car, went to Natchez's room and tapped on the door. "Trevor? Open up. It's me."

He didn't answer her knock, but the door moved inward when she pushed. It hadn't been properly closed. She snatched her hand away as though she'd touched a hot stove. Why would he leave the door open? Was he getting ice from the machine down the hall?

"I don't like this," she said aloud so Wade could hear. "Don't like it at all."

He was out of the SUV in a flash. His weapon was drawn and he tapped her holster to remind her that this might be a good time to be armed. Her fingers trembled as she wrapped them around the grip of her gun.

Wade shoved the door open. He went in hard and hot.

Natchez's body was neatly centered on the beige floral bedspread. There were two holes in his chest, just like Morrissey, but this was the primary crime scene. The state patrolman's uniform and the bed were saturated with blood.

She hadn't expected to scream.

Chapter Twenty

Wade pulled Samantha close and held her while she cut loose with a loud, piercing scream. He didn't blame her; the scene was horrific. Natchez lay in stillness. His eyes were closed. His face was peaceful. It looked as if he'd been sleeping when he was shot. The gore erupted across his chest, so much blood.

Samantha hiccuped a few sobs and stepped back, trying to regain control. "W-w-we should check his phone."

On the table beside the bed, they found his keys and his cell phone. The history of use showed that his only calls were between himself and his dispatcher and, of course, the call from Samantha. Natchez must have used a burner phone to communicate with the ringleader. Wade was certain that was who'd killed him. The ringleader was calling the shots.

A familiar face peered around the edge of the doorjamb. "Hello. Is anything wrong?"

Justin Hobbs stepped over the threshold, glanced at the body on the bed and averted his gaze. "My God."

"Are you staying here?" Wade asked.

"With many of the other firefighters." Hobbs peered at him, then blinked twice. His beard seemed to stand on end as he stared. "You're Wade, Sam's husband. I thought you were dead."

"I should explain," Samantha said.

As she walked toward him, her legs nearly buckled. She'd been through enough for one day. Dealing with this murder, which was clearly in Swain County jurisdiction, was going to take some time and coordinated effort. Natchez was a jerk, but his death needed to be investigated the right way.

Wade followed her and Hobbs outside. "I can handle this," he said. "Why don't you go home. Maybe Marshal Hobbs would be nice enough to give you a ride."

"I need to stay. I'm the sheriff, after all." Fighting back tears, she said, "Another murder investigation. That's got to be a record."

"It's not your fault," Wade said.

"This one is. He was in the wrong place at the wrong time, and I put him there." She leaned against the side of her SUV and glanced between the two men. "I'm in over my head. I'm drowning."

He'd never seen her so overwhelmed. Gently, he guided her to the SUV and opened the door to the bench seat in the rear. "I want you to lie down, Samantha. Get some sleep. You need it."

When he returned to the motel room where Natchez had been murdered, the fire marshal followed. Hobbs asked, "Anything I can do to help?"

"Thanks, but this is my problem."

"If you don't mind my asking, why did you pretend to be dead?"

"Witness protection." Wade knew he was being terse, but he'd told this story too many times already.

"Now the trial must be over, right?"

"Not exactly, but they have other evidence. My testimony isn't as important." Before the barrel-chested firefighter who actually resembled Smokey the Bear shuffled back to his room, Wade called out, "Do you have the fire contained?"

"It's just a couple of hot spots."

Wade reached into his pocket and pulled out his phone. Following Samantha's example at the Morrissey scene, he took photos of the crime scene. There didn't appear to be a murder weapon. He contacted the ambulance from Glenwood Springs and called Ty to ask about using the FBI crime lab for the autopsy.

He went through the procedures as though a murder investigation was something he did every day, talking to the manager in the motel office who hadn't seen anything strange and didn't have surveillance cameras. He interviewed several people who were staying at the Pine Cone Motel. Several came out of their rooms to see what had happened. Nobody saw anything useful.

When all of this was over, quiet little Swain County was going to have an exceptionally experienced forensic crew. On the other hand, he hoped these were skills he'd never have to use again.

Every so often, he'd check on Samantha sleeping in the back of her SUV with a blanket pulled up over her head. She needed the rest, desperately needed it. When he finally had all the details taken care of and the ambulance was carrying the body to Denver for autopsy, Wade climbed behind the wheel of her SUV.

He didn't want to drive with her lying on the seat; she'd fall off if he came to a sudden stop. "Come on, sleepy girl, wake up."

She didn't move, not an inch. What was wrong? Was

she sick? If anything had happened to her, he couldn't face it, couldn't go on. His sorry life would be over.

Leaping from the front seat, he went to the back and threw open the door. He grabbed a handful of blanket. Nothing there. She was gone.

A scrap of notebook paper fluttered to the ground. The writing was so sloppy that he could hardly read it.

If you want to see her alive, back off. No more search. No more trouble.

If this note came from the cartel, Samantha was already as good as dead. An empty feeling in the pit of his belly grew until numbness consumed his entire body. He was a shell, without strength or breath. He had lost the will to live.

He sank down on the curb outside the room where Natchez had been murdered. In a terrible irony, he knew for the first time what she'd gone through when he faked his death. And he couldn't tell her. This was the worst moment of his life, the greatest pain.

How could he lose her?

SAM COULDN'T SEE a thing. Her head was covered with a black hood, and duct tape covered her mouth. She inhaled through her nostrils, slowly, and then she exhaled. Accomplishing this simple act gave her great satisfaction, and she did it again.

Not yet awake, she felt as if she was caught at the edge of a nightmare and couldn't wake up. This couldn't be reality. It made no sense for her to be riding in the back of a truck with blankets piled on top of her. Where was she going?

She'd been drugged. That would explain why her brain was foggy. The last thing she remembered was falling asleep in the back of her car. No, wait—she remembered blood. There was a murder, another murder. The front of his uniform was drenched in blood. How could that be? If he was shot in the chest and didn't move, the blood would drain through the exit wounds in his back. He must have struggled, thrashed around. And then the killer arranged his body.

That scenario seemed worse. The kind of killer who could stand back and watch a man die was more sadistic than someone who came in, fired and left. Both were murderers. Both were horrible.

And she had to face the dawning realization that the murderer had bound her wrists and ankles. She was in the back of his truck. She could only hope that he would end her life quickly with two neat bullets to the chest.

Chapter Twenty-One

When he returned to the house, Wade spoke to no one. His private grief weighed too heavily on his shoulders. He could hardly make it upstairs to his bedroom, where he fell onto their extra-long bed. This was his fault. There was no one else he could blame.

He had taken his eyes off Samantha. Now she was gone.

His phone rang, and he snatched it, hoping to see that she was calling, imagining that she would tell him she was all right. It was an Unknown Caller.

He answered. "Who is this?"

"It's Ty. Where are you?"

"Why do you want to know?"

From the start, Wade had known that he should suspect Ty. Even if he was an old friend and they'd grown up together, it didn't mean that Ty hadn't taken on another role. He could be the ringleader.

There were three strikes against him. First, Ty was the one who came up with the faked-death scene. Second, he was high on the food chain in law enforcement. Third, he knew many of the locals from growing up in Swain County.

Having Ty turn out to be the ringleader might be a

positive thing because he loved Samantha and would never hurt her. Wade modulated his voice, removing all trace of hostility. "I'm home. I came directly here from the motel. Are you checking up on me? Making sure I'm not searching?"

"Something's wrong with you," Ty said. "I'll be there in a couple of minutes."

"Where are you?"

"At the ranch. Where else would I be?"

Being at the ranch didn't prove his innocence. The ringleader could send one of the guys who worked for him to kidnap Samantha. It wouldn't have taken much to grab her. They'd give her a quick poke with a sedative, pick her up and carry her to a waiting vehicle. The operation would take only a couple of minutes.

There had to be something Wade could do, but his brain wasn't working. He lay flat on the bed, staring up at the ceiling, running through suspects. His favorite was Hurtado, mostly because he didn't like the guy.

Everett Hurtado would make an effective ringleader. Not only was he able to misdirect the attentions of the FBI and other federal agencies, but he was accustomed to leadership. His only needs for keeping his dirty business operational were a couple of cell phones. And Hurtado would love the big bucks to be made in smuggling.

Wade ran through a couple of other lawmen. And then he thought of Justin Hobbs. The fire marshal had been on scene at the Pine Cone Motel. He was in frequent communication with Samantha.

Wade recalled the night Hobbs had popped over for a visit. At the time, it seemed as if he was getting ready to hit on Samantha. Maybe he'd been fishing for answers about her husband, trying to find out if Wade was still alive. Tonight when they met, Hobbs seemed surprised that Wade wasn't dead. Was he acting? With that damn beard in the way, who could tell?

Knowledge of his death was of key importance. The ringleader was responsible for the death of Morrissey the snitch and had planned to frame Wade by leaving his Colt .45 revolver at the scene. If that frame was going to work, Wade had to be alive. If Hobbs didn't know, he wasn't the ringleader.

Ty rapped on the bedroom door. "Wade? Are you okay, man? What's going on?"

The final proof appeared in Wade's mind. He had the answer. He hoped he'd be in time to save Samantha.

SAM DIDN'T KNOW how many hours she'd been held captive, but it seemed like a long time. The black hood still covered her head but the room seemed lighter. Dawn was beginning to break through the darkness.

She was lying on a bed. The ropes around her wrists were tethered to the bed frame. Her ankles were tied together but were not fastened to anything else. All of her wriggling around hadn't amounted to much. The cord around her wrists was looser but not enough to get free.

Her only real accomplishment was biting through the duct tape on her mouth so she could breathe. More oxygen to the brain served to sharpen her awareness of how much trouble she'd fallen into.

No doubt, she was a hostage. They were using her for leverage to force Wade's hand.

She scooted around on the bed so she was sitting near the frame, which seemed like a less vulnerable position than lying flat. If she could get the black hood off her face, she'd be able to gnaw at the cords.

The hood lifted as high as her chin. Twisting awkwardly and flipping her head, she got it higher. Finally, it was off. The dim light of early morning flooded her eyes.

She was in a small bedroom, lying on dirty sheets in a double bed. There were no photographs or pictures on the dull beige walls. Looking through the one window, she could tell that she was on the first floor. Though she couldn't see any other houses from the window, she called for help.

After her first hoarse shout, she waited. She hadn't heard anybody walking around in a long time. Had her captor left her here alone? She gave another yell.

Her throat was scratchy. The inside of her mouth tasted like cotton. If he had left her alone, it was certain that there were no nearby neighbors.

She concentrated on the cords that fastened her wrists to the bed frame.

BEFORE HE LEFT the house, Wade told Caleb to lie for him and tell anybody who called that he couldn't be reached. He pressed one of his last burner phones into Caleb's hand. "Then you call and tell me who is trying to find me."

"You can count on me."

Wade looked the aged deputy up and down. He was holding up better than most of the crew. He said, "I trust you." And he meant it.

He jumped into Ty's sleek black SUV. "We're going to Woodridge. To the courthouse."

Ty took off. "Do you mind telling me what we're doing? I know something's wrong. Where's Sam?"

Wade wasn't answering any questions until he had his proof. As far as he was concerned, Ty was still a suspect. "Why did you call me?"

"I wanted to let you know that we had an FBI forensic doctor at the Glenwood hospital. He did a preliminary autopsy on Natchez. The bullets that killed him came from a different gun than those that killed Morrissey."

Old news. "How much do you know about Justin Hobbs?"

"According to Mama, he's a real catch. If you hadn't returned from the dead, old Justin would have been making a play for Sam."

Wade hoped Hobbs's affection for Sam was real. He'd be less likely to hurt her. If he was the ringleader...

Ty parked in front of the courthouse and they dashed up the wide stone steps to the front door. Using Samantha's keys, Wade opened the front door. In the sheriff's office, he found what he was looking for. Among the many photographs of community groups, he located a picture that had been playing in the back of his mind since that day in Austin when he saw a familiar face.

Here he was...the face Wade had seen...the man he didn't know who had changed his life. He stood front and center in a group photo of a volunteer fire brigade. Standing beside him was Justin Hobbs.

"He's the ringleader," Wade said, "and he's holding Samantha hostage."

SAM HEARD THE noise from another part of the house. A door slammed. She heard him approaching her bedroom. It was too late to put the hood back on, but she didn't want to see the person who walked through the door. Her chance of survival would be significantly better if she didn't know him.

The bedroom door creaked open. "Good morning, Sam. I have a surprise for you."

"Justin?" She opened her eyes and looked into his heavily bearded face. "Could you untie me? My feet are numb."

"Wait until I tell you my news. After that, I'm guessing that you won't want to escape."

The hell I won't! Sam didn't care about the smuggling or the cartel or any of these other things. She just wanted to survive, wanted her life with Wade back.

Hobbs held up her telephone and pressed the play button. Jenny's voice came through loud and clear.

"Hi, Mommy," she said. "We're coming to see you right away. The fire marshal who came to my school last year and talked about fire safety gave us directions."

Sam's heart ached. "How could you?"

"It's about time that one of those school programs paid off."

"You tricked my daughter into trusting you."

"And your father, too." Hobbs checked his wristwatch. "They ought to be here in half an hour. Your father is quite the guy. He's been hovering around this area since yesterday, waiting to rush in and save the day. Reminds me of Wade. That's the kind of guy you like, right?"

"Tell me what you want." She would do anything to protect her daughter. "Just leave Jenny out of it."

"I want the money from this last smuggling score. All you have to do is stay here with your mom and dad and little Jenny, and don't tell anybody where the exchange will take place."

"Yes." She nodded vigorously. "I'll do whatever you say."

"That's the right attitude," he said. "I've got a little retirement home in Mexico where I'll be very comfortable."

She suppressed the hatred rising inside her as she looked down at the cords that bound her wrists. "Untie me, please."

"I don't have to tell you that if you try anything, it won't go well for Jenny."

"I understand."

"Even if you disable me, there are plenty of people who work for me. Four or five of them are coming here very soon. You'll like them. They're dressed as firefighters."

"Is that how you moved your men from place to place?"

"Everybody loves a firefighter." He started working on the knots that tied her ankles. "I'd give them a uniform and tell them not to talk much."

"May I ask a question?" She twisted her neck to see him. "Who broke into my house and stole Wade's gun?"

"That was Morrissey. I heard from an informant that your husband was the big-deal secret witness. I knew we had to do something when he escaped custody. I figured his first move would be to come home."

Her ankles were free. She struggled to wiggle her toes. It was going to take a little while to get the circulation back. "Who was your informant?"

"Doesn't matter," he said as he pulled the hood completely off her head and stripped off the remnants of the duct tape. "Morrissey stole the gun from your house, Wade's fancy copper-inlaid revolver. It was the perfect thing to use in framing your husband. All I needed was a dead body. Standing right there in front of me was a snitch for the FBI."

"Morrissey."

"I shot him in the back of my truck and drove him to the scene, setting up the supposed accident. I left some guys there to stage an ambush. The plan was for you or Ty to survive, and you'd have to arrest Wade based on the evidence."

"The gun," she said, remembering her mental struggle about hiding it. "How did you know I'd be in that area?"

"You told me all about it when we were calling back and forth. You told me where you were, and I set you up, Sam, told you about the hikers and directed you into the trap. I'm kind of surprised you didn't figure it out."

"I should have."

Before he started untying her hands, he took his handgun from the waistband of his jeans and placed it on the bedside. It was a powerful temptation. She thought about playing the innocent, trying to win his sympathy until she could grab the gun. Then what? He'd still have Jenny.

Her hands were free. He stepped back, leaving his gun unprotected. Too obvious. "Is this a test?"

"And you pass," he said as he snatched his gun. "Let's play house, Sam. I've got some eggs and bacon in the kitchen. Make me breakfast."

Visions of hot grease flying across the room danced behind her eyelids as she stumbled on her clumsy, frozen legs into a small outer room.

Behind her back, she heard him snap a clip into his automatic gun. "It wasn't loaded," she said.

"I'm not a fool."

The gun was now loaded and lethal. If she had another chance to get her hands on it, she could even the playing field. In the kitchen, there were many implements, like knives and heavy frying pans, that she could use to disable him.

Hurting him wasn't enough. If he had the slightest chance to take control again, he would harm her daughter. The only way she could be sure Jenny was safe would be to kill Hobbs.

His men would be here soon. She needed to act before they got here. Instead of attacking him, she took the carton of eggs from the refrigerator. "How many will be eating?"

"Make it scrambled eggs for five." He chuckled. "Aren't you going to ask me about the fire at Hanging Rock?"

He'd mentioned the cabins, but it was Wade's idea to go there and look around. "I suppose you had the cabin all set to start the fire."

"I'm a pro," he said.

From outside the house, she heard gunfire. Jenny! "What's that? What are they shooting at?"

As he went to the front window, he kept his gun aimed at her. "My men are shooting at something."

She silently prayed. *Not my parents. Not Jenny.*

"I know that fancy-ass black SUV," he said. "It's your friend Ty. And look who's he's got with him."

She didn't hesitate, not for one more second. With the outstanding aim of a woman who'd played softball every year of her life since she was six, she fired an egg at his face, then another and another. When he reflexively threw up his hands, she whacked him with the frying pan.

Hobbs was a big man. He didn't go down. Blindly, he charged toward her.

Sam was a big woman. She clubbed him again.

He sank onto a knee.

One more time.

He fell flat on his belly.

She grabbed his handgun and went to the front window. When she started firing at Hobbs's men, it was enough of a distraction for Ty and Wade to get them under control. As Ty aimed his semiautomatic rifle at them, the two that were still standing dropped their guns and raised hands over their heads.

Wade rushed toward the porch, and she met him there. He squeezed her tightly in his arms.

"I thought you were dead," he whispered.

"That makes us even."

She kissed him as if there was no tomorrow.

Ty interrupted, "A little help here. I could use some handcuffs."

"I'll get right on it," Wade said. "As soon as I tell this woman that I love her with all my heart."

A small voice called out, "Daddy?"

Sam saw her parents at the edge of the forest. Jenny broke away from them and raced toward her father. He scooped her into his arms and twirled her into the air above his head.

Sam wiped away a tear. Now everything was the way it should be. Their family was complete.

Epilogue

At the end of two full days of paperwork, Sheriff Sam printed the last of her reports and added it to the stack in the center of her desk at the courthouse. Cleaning up after the crime spree in Swain County was a huge job. She had witness statements, doctors' reports and autopsies, ballistics, photographs, arrest records, police reports and much more.

Using both hands, she pushed the stack toward Ty, who sat on the opposite side of her desk. "Here it is. Two murders, Morrissey and Natchez. Both were killed by Justin Hobbs. And I've included ballistics on the antique Colt .45 that Hobbs admitted he used in an attempt to frame Wade for killing Morrissey."

"There was another murder," Ty said, "the guy I shot on the road near the safe house."

"It's in there," she said, "including hospital reports on the other two wounded. Those two and the men Hobbs had at his cabin were all taken into custody and charged with assaulting federal officers. Plus, there were four more smugglers rounded up by the cowboy posse that Wade put together. Not to mention that the posse found the high-tech weaponry that was being smuggled to the Esteban cartel."

"Hobbs had us all fooled."

"All of you. Not me. I knew he was hiding something nasty under his big, thick beard."

"Funny thing," Ty said. "With his beard shaved, he looks like one of the cartel leaders. Blood is thicker than water. Their first contact with him was through family."

"Well, well, imagine that. Bad guys stick together."

Ty chuckled. "Proud of yourself, aren't you?"

"It's not often that a small county sheriff gets to show the FBI how to do their job."

Better yet, she was handing over responsibility for the investigation to the feds. Neither she nor Wade would be targeted by the cartel or the dirty cops. There might be some personal animosity. Sam wouldn't want to be left alone and unguarded in a room with Justin Hobbs, but he was going away for a very long time.

"Your talents—and Wade's—have been duly noted."

"Thank you, Special Agent Baxter." She pointed to the stack. "If the FBI needs copies, there's a machine down the hall outside the mayor's office."

"I'll pick my information off the computer."

"I don't think so." She'd heard horror stories about how hackers were constantly breaking into federal computers. "I don't want you to have access to my equipment."

At that moment, Wade and Jenny entered through the open door to her office. Her husband announced, "Back off, Ty. I'm the only one who gets access to her equipment."

Sam held out her arms and Jenny jumped onto her lap. "What have you and Daddy been up to? I haven't seen you since lunch."

"We went to the Roaring Fork," Jenny said.

That was the river where Wade had supposedly died. She shot him a glance. "I hope you were careful."

"We talked about water safety," Jenny said. "And we saw people in big yellow-and-orange rafts."

They still hadn't told their daughter how it was possible for her father to be dead and then be alive again. Those explanations would have to happen before she went back to school. For right now, Wade was using his time off to reestablish his relationship with his five-year-old daughter. As far as Sam could tell, that connection was going well...better than her own relationship with her husband.

She loved Wade, had never stopped loving him even when he was dead. Her words of forgiveness had been spoken, but it was going to take time for her to let go of her residual pain and anger.

"And we went shopping in Glenwood." Jenny gave her father a mischievous grin and placed her index finger across her lips. "It's a secret."

"Don't tell," he said as he scooped her off her mother's lap and set her down on the floor. "Would you take Ty into the outer office and draw him a picture of the rafters?"

Planting her fists on her skinny hips, she looked up at him. "You just want to talk to Mommy alone."

"Nothing gets past you."

Jenny took Ty's hand and pulled him into the other office. "Shut the door behind you, Uncle Ty. I bet they want to be kissing."

"Do they do that a lot?" Ty teased.

Jenny rolled her eyes. "All the time."

Wade came behind the desk and stood beside her. He gestured toward the paperwork stack. "Is this all of it?"

"Yes!" She blew a long, slow breath through her pursed lips. "In the past week, we've had more crime than in the entire history of Swain County, and that includes a holdup by Butch Cassidy and the Sundance Kid."

"You've been working hard." He flexed his fingers, went behind her chair, pushed her long braid aside and started a neck massage. "How's that feel?"

"Like the touch of an angel." As the tension in her shoulders popped and released, she moaned with pleasure. "A naughty angel."

"Being sheriff is a lot of work."

She'd been meaning to talk to him about the job. When he'd disappeared, he was sheriff. In his absence, she'd been duly elected to the position. "I kind of like it."

"You might want to think twice before you say you'll keep this work." He glided his hands down her arms, leaned down and nibbled at her earlobe, starting a crazy tickle that spread rapidly through her body. "You were almost killed this week."

"Most of the time, I like being sheriff. I'm not ready to retire."

"Glad to hear it," he said.

Though distracted by his touch, she was surprised to hear him agree with her. She rose to her feet, gazed into his light brown eyes and wrapped her arms around his neck. "I thought you wanted to take back your job."

"You're a good sheriff. Everybody says so. And it seems like a shame for you to give that up just because I'm here."

She totally agreed with him. "Why do I get the feeling that you're manipulating me? And if you are, please stop."

He raised his right hand as if taking an oath. "I will

never make plans without consulting you, my wife. Are you ready for a possible plan?"

"Tell me."

"Ty's boss, Everett Hurtado, made me an offer to work with the FBI. I'd get the safe house up and running. They want to use it more for consultations and meetings than as a place for protected witnesses. And they want me to set up an outdoor training program for agents."

"You'd be an FBI agent?"

"A consultant," he said. "Big difference. I wouldn't be involved in active investigations and, therefore, wouldn't be in danger."

This was beginning to sound too good to be true. "What about travel?"

"There might be some, but I'm my own boss and can always refuse to go."

She tasted his lips. "I like this plan of yours."

"I thought you might."

He deepened the kiss, and she experienced the swirling, mind-numbing satisfaction that only Wade could give her. Her body melted against his. Since she wasn't wearing her bulletproof vest today, she could feel the hard muscles of his chest and abdomen.

She exhaled a sigh. "I love you."

"But wait!" He swiveled her chair and sat her down in it. "There's more!"

When he dropped to one knee and took a black velvet box from his pocket, she felt her eyes grow wider and wider until they had to be as big as hubcaps. "What are you doing?"

He showed her the ring. "Samantha Calloway, will you marry me? Again."

"Renew our vows?"

"Yes."

A stunning piece of jewelry, the silver platinum ring glistened and the blue-tinted diamond sparkled. "Did Jenny help you pick this out?"

"She said it had to be blue like your eyes."

Sam slipped the ring on her finger. It was a perfect fit. And so were they.

* * * * *

He looked down and her eyes met his.

"There's no time to hesitate."

She pulled her hand free.

"Who are you?"

"No time. I'm here to get you out."

"How do I know that?"

"Look," he gritted out. "There's no time to offer proof. You have two choices. Trust me or..." He nodded his head backward, where it was obvious only death waited.

She stood there almost rocking on her heels. He could see the indecision, the unwillingness to trust any further, and he didn't blame her.

"I'm saying this only once more before I throw you over my shoulder. We can do it your way or we can do it mine."

SUSPECT WITNESS

BY
RYSHIA KENNIE

MILLS & BOON

First Published in Great Britain 2016
By Mills & Boon, an imprint of HarperCollins*Publishers*
1 London Bridge Street, London, SE1 9GF

© 2016 Patricia Detta

ISBN: 978-0-263-91896-0

46-0216

Our policy is to use papers that are natural, renewable and recyclable products and made from wood grown in sustainable forests. The logging and manufacturing processes conform to the legal environmental regulations of the country of origin.

Printed and bound in Spain
by CPI, Barcelona

Ryshia Kennie has received a writing award from the City of Regina, Saskatchewan, and also been a semi-finalist in the Kindle Book Awards. She finds that there's never a lack of places to set an edge-of-the-seat suspense, as prairie winters find her dreaming of warmer places for heart-stopping stories. They are places where deadly villains threaten intrepid heroes and heroines who battle for their right to live or even to love. For more, visit www.ryshiakennie.com.

For Ken—who led the journey through
Malaysia's Gunung Mulu caves with
the feeble light of a travel flashlight.

Our hiking boots were ankle-deep in bat guano and
each step was treacherous. I clutched the back of his
shirt as I couldn't always see in the fleeting light.

But the vast beauty of the cave
was worth a ton of bat guano.

Chapter One

Singapore—Saturday, October 10

She had been pretty once.

Now her skin gleamed in the glow of the fluorescent lights. A strand of auburn hair fell across a well-shaped brow and her lips held a glimmering trace of sherbet lip gloss.

"It's a shame, really," the coroner said as his sun-bronzed hand held the edge of the stark white sheet. "Life was just getting started. Twenty-five or there about." He shook his head. "I try to remember that every time I step out of the house. Enjoy the moment. You just never know. And in this job you're reminded of mortality every day." A strand of salt-and-pepper hair drifted across his forehead. "I try not to think about it or it would drive me crazy."

"True," Josh Sedovich said. "Any idea how she died?"

The coroner nodded. "She was hit by a blunt object to the back of the head. Surprising, I always thought Singapore so civilized until I moved here and took this job. Unfortunately, it's turned out no better than anywhere else."

"Why does it always end like this? On a temporary visa to see the world and, just like that, it's over." Josh ran his hand along the side of his neck. "It's damn hot in here."

"No air-conditioning," the coroner said. "Is she who you're looking for?"

"No. Fortunately not." He fisted his right hand. Not so fortunately for the unknown young woman on the coroner's slab.

Probable murder, potential arson and an unknown assassin. He'd been on the trail of this case for the past three weeks, and now one person was dead and still, miraculously, the witness lived. Not only lived but thrived over days that had turned into weeks and weeks into months. It wouldn't have happened had the FBI called him in sooner.

"Interesting that Victor has given you a hall pass. Maybe the fact that she's American, too. But more than likely not." The coroner looked at Josh with mild interest. "Private investigator..." He frowned. "I thought you would have to be a little more than that. CIA maybe. Or maybe I just watch too much television."

Josh slipped his hand into his pocket and looked away before meeting the coroner's gaze. "American? How do you know that?"

"Assumption on my part, but look at this." He pulled down the sheet, exposing the cadaver's torso, and pointed at her belly button. A steel stud pierced her navel; the steel was offset only by the red, white and blue of the American flag.

"Maybe," Josh said doubtfully. "But she might be a wannabe, too."

"Yeah, I know. Or her boyfriend was or, or... Still comes down to an unidentified body."

He straightened, turning to face Josh. "'Course, tattoos, earrings..." He trailed off, looking pointedly at the metal ace of spades in Josh's left ear. "Are rather a dime a dozen." He shook his head. "Don't understand it much. Must be the generation gap." An overhead fan kicked on. "What's this girl done? Any ideas on why someone murdered her?"

"Nothing that I know of." Josh flexed his fingers as he looked at the sad, lifeless figure. He reached over and took the corner of the sheet and pulled it up over her breasts. "Wrong place. Wrong time."

"Seems a little more than wrong place and time. Someone torched her apartment, but not before killing her." The coroner coughed into his gloved hand. "Heard that the original lease is in a different name, sublet. Can't get hold of the girl who signed the lease to tell us who she sublet to. Traveling Europe or some such idiocy."

"Just a minute." Josh held up his forefinger before turning his back and taking a few steps away. He pulled out the cell phone he'd bought at a local convenience store and hit Redial. "Yeah, Victor. I'll be there in a half hour, maybe less." He slipped the phone back into his pocket.

"Well, I suppose we'll know who she is soon enough." The coroner slid the drawer containing the body back into place and out of sight.

Twenty minutes later, Josh stepped over the charred threshold of the ruined apartment building. Outside, the cinder brick exterior was still intact but inside was a gutted mess. Water dripped from the ceiling and the acrid smell of burned plastic mixed with wood smoke and other synthetics.

He covered his mouth with the back of his hand and coughed.

"Josh Sedovich." Victor Chong held out his hand. It was a quick shake, more a formality than one with any feeling.

"Chong." He shook the man's hand for the second time that day. "Still can't convince you that a private investigator might get you more information than this team of officials you're set on?"

"No more than you could this morning."

"Definitely a case of arson," Victor confirmed with a shake of his head. His safety helmet was tucked under his arm and there were smudges of soot across his cheek. His dark hair was matted to his head and it was obvious that he had spent a great deal of time inside the smoking and charred remains. "Have you seen the body?"

"I did."

"And?" Victor arched a brow. "Was she the girl you're looking for? Your lost person?"

"No idea who she might be, but she isn't who I'm looking for." He glanced beyond Victor into the small studio apartment where she'd lived.

"Can't imagine hunting missing persons day in and day out. No variety."

"It's a job like any other," he said shortly.

"Now if that wasn't a false statement," Victor replied. "People go missing for all sorts of reasons, and I'll bet you've seen them all. So, best-case scenario that she's not in the morgue yet. I mean the one you're looking for. Obviously, the other... Well, we both know where she is."

"Best-case scenario, it wasn't her," Josh agreed, turning to look at the damage the fire had done. "Too bad about the identification bit. You would have made my job easier."

Victor shrugged. "Although identification isn't my problem, I still wouldn't mind having one up on Detective Tay. He's a prideful bugger, always rubbing my nose in it."

Josh stepped around Victor, his gaze taking in the cheaply papered walls, the hint of a vine pattern only partially concealed by soot and smoke. The tiny apartment was pretty much ruined. The water had destroyed what the fire hadn't.

"Interesting that the body wasn't burned at all. Now

it's just a matter of getting the right people to view her. And then we'll get that damn ID."

Josh breathed lightly as he stepped into the room. Victor carried on his one-way conversation as he followed. The smell of smoke was more intense here as it saturated the air and bit harshly into his sinuses. His stomach rolled. He looked with envy at the mask Victor donned as he stepped over a pool of water and sodden books that were scattered around a fallen bookcase.

The dull red spine of a hard cover copy of *Wuthering Heights* lay across the top of a box of paperbacks whose bright and torrid covers curled and swelled. The classic was like an old dog in the midst of a pack of pups. He skirted a small, nondescript, collapsed wooden table— more cardboard than wood, the kind purchased in discount box stores—and walked over to a small desk that stood untouched except for the damp soot that clung to it. The desk was different from the other furniture in the room. It looked older and had character. The patina was richer and darker, the legs had deep scrolls carved into them that swirled through the wood. He slipped on a glove and opened a side drawer. There was nothing but a collection of elastic bands, tape, pens and blank notepads. The heat had not gotten to this part of the room. He did a quick take of the other side drawer. This time it opened to a small line of files. His fingers flitted quickly through them, stopped and went back. From the corner of his eye he saw Victor watching. He wasn't sure how long Victor would allow his surreptitious view of the apartment before demanding that the fire investigative team and police take over. It was a lull in the investigation. The fire had only been out a few hours, and Josh was taking full advantage as he had done in other crime scenes in other countries throughout the world. It was all about speed and timing. He left the files and moved to the middle drawer.

He took out a blue leather folder and pushed the metal release. The folder opened; nothing was inside. He glanced over his shoulder. Victor was not looking. His attention went to the bottom side drawer, and his fingers skimmed quickly through the files.

He flipped through papers in a cardboard file. Empty—except one small sheet and a receipt. Both bore the name Erin and one Erin Kelley.

Tell Mike I took his last advice.

The note was written in a careful script, the letters fine, unlike a more masculine scroll that only confirmed what the signature said. The writer was Erin Kelley, or at least the woman currently calling herself that. The woman who had so recently been Erin Kelley Argon before she'd changed her passport and her last name. A twist of fate twenty-nine years ago had her parents on a business trip in Canada where her mother went into early labor. As a result, Erin qualified for citizenship in that country and when she'd run, she'd taken advantage of it. He took both pieces of evidence, folded them one-handed and slipped them into his pocket. He closed the drawer and opened the middle drawer and retraced the fine line he'd felt earlier. He pushed and something gave. He pulled open the drawer farther to reveal a hidden compartment.

"What do you have?" Victor was beside him. "The authorities only did a cursory look before they took the body away. And I just got here. So anything you can do to make our job easier." He pulled the thin edge of his moustache with a troubled look. "Although, really, I shouldn't be letting you do this."

Josh ignored the man as he took out an American driver's license and a passport. He flipped open the passport and it only confirmed what the first piece of ID had already told him. "Here's your identification. Emma Whyte. She had it well hidden against thieves."

"By jove. Good work, old chap."

Josh grimaced and rubbed the back of his neck. "Since when did you become a Brit, Vic?"

Victor scowled and glanced at his watch.

"What time is it?"

"Seven o'clock."

"It's been a long day. I'll leave you to it," Josh said. "She's obviously not the woman I was looking for."

"Good luck!" Victor told him genially.

Josh stepped over the threshold, seemingly empty-handed. Once outside, he dialed the number that would be in service for only a few more hours.

"It's not her," he said. "But she was here. Whoever the bastard is that they have on her tail, he now knows her last location."

"What's the matter? You sound off."

"Could be the last two years have been pretty much on the road."

"What, you're telling me you don't love it?"

"Not that much. After this, Vern, I need a vacation. I need to go home."

"To the RV? Josh you're not a family man and you live in a trailer."

His hand went into his pocket, his thumb smoothing the worn bead of a dime-store earring. "It's home, Vern. And family or not, it's time for me to take a break."

"Okay, fine."

He dropped the earring back into his pocket as a door slammed across the street. He walked away from the apartment building and around the corner to where an alley gave him a discreet view of the comings and goings around the apartment. "What gives with this case, Vern? There's another body. A woman. Every bloody assignment… I'm so damned sick of seeing women dead. At least this time she wasn't raped. Not that that is any better. Dead is dead."

"You're taking it personally," Vern Ferguson, the director of Josh's branch in the CIA said.

He turned away from the street and looked down the tight, concrete-bordered alley. Sometimes it was hard not to take it personally. He drew in a breath, held it a few seconds longer than necessary. "You said you have something new? What is it, Vern?" His gaze roamed the area—the overflowing garbage bin, the tiger-striped dog snuffling through the refuse. "I don't think there's much time. We could be talking hours, minutes… Who knows?"

"Intelligence has her in Georgetown, Malaysia."

"Georgetown. Damn it, Vern. Too bad you didn't have that for me sooner. You know the Anarchists don't waste time. They're not just any biker gang. As it is she's been running for five months."

"Yeah, I know," Vern said with a hitch in his voice that was part wheeze, part cough. "She's tired and with the trial going forward, they won't stop."

"Right, and they want her dead, and odds are they're on their way. Fortunately, no one knows where in Georgetown yet."

"Then quit wasting time on the damn phone."

Josh grimaced as he clicked off and tossed the phone into a nearby garbage can.

Chapter Two

"Give Respect, Get Respect." Erin Kelley repeated the words as she wrote the phrase on the chalkboard and ended with a sweeping flourish. Her fingers shook and she had to stop. She ran her tongue along her lower lip, her back to the class. But even writing the word *respect* sent a slight tremor through her. The chalk dust clung uncomfortably to her sweaty palm.

The temperature was unseasonably warm and this early in the morning the heat was already unbearable in the small, cramped room. A finger of light skittered across the blackboard, briefly illuminating the words. She mentally shrank from the light as if under a searchlight, as if they'd found her after all these months. Impossible, she reminded herself as the chalk sweated in her hand, and the children shifted anxiously behind her. And as she had done so many times before, she reminded herself that she was safe, that her trail was cold. Enough time had elapsed. They'd never find her. They were no longer interested. And as she did at odd times throughout any given day, she considered the truth of those beliefs and whether she was really safe, whether these children were safe. One day, she knew, despite her hopes, the answer would have her on the run again but that wasn't today.

She put down the chalk and turned to face the class.

"Today, we're going to learn about respect," she said in English. The school's curriculum was taught in English to children who were already bilingual, fluent in both Malay and English, and who, in many cases, if they hadn't already, would master a third or even fourth language in their lifetime.

At the back of the room a heavyset boy shifted in his seat. Beside him, a sullen-faced classmate shuffled papers across his desk. And at the front one boy whispered furtively to another. The rest of the boys eyed her uneasily. They knew what was coming. There wasn't a boy who had missed the taunting in the schoolyard and not one who didn't know what was going to happen as a result. She had made it all perfectly clear from her first day.

She fixed her gaze on the targets of this lecture. The two culprits dressed in crisply pressed navy pants with matching jackets, white shirts and sleek haircuts stared back without a flicker of emotion. They were both the sons of successful Malaysian businessmen, and neither lacked for pride or esteem. They were children of wealth and privilege with attitudes she had struggled to control since her arrival. Yesterday, their attitudes had threatened to harm another student. It was a scenario that played out in schoolyards across the globe and through the decades. They had taunted a slight, studious boy on the playground. She bit back the scathing words she wanted to say. Bullying aside, they were still only children. But for a second she saw another classroom a world away, and another child and a small girl pummeling another.

Leave my sister alone!

The skinny, carrot-haired girl stuck in her mind, running through reel after reel. The knobby knees, the brilliant hair, the circle of taunting children. And always she stood screaming those words, running intervention as she grabbed and punched and pulled hair, freeing her sister from the circle of tormentors—over and over again.

Her gaze went to the thin boy in the front of the class. He wasn't looking at her. Instead, he was fumbling through his backpack, which was emblazoned with a variety of action figures.

"Before we begin today's lesson, who would like to volunteer to go tell Mr. Daniel that the air conditioner isn't working?"

"They've shut it off, Miss," Ian said. "They always do in October."

"Besides, Mr. Daniel's left." Isaac waved his hand frantically in the air even as he spoke.

"On an errand," Ian added.

"In your new car," Isaac finished. He was fascinated by vehicles of any sort and had followed her into school last week pestering her with details of her new vehicle purchase and clearly unimpressed with what had impressed her; gas mileage.

"Right. I didn't realize he was leaving this soon." She pulled at the back of her cotton blouse, which was beginning to stick. She wiped the back of her hand across her damp brow as her eyes drifted to the parking lot and she thought of Daniel. Friend or not, she wasn't apt to lend out her vehicle on a whim, but Daniel hadn't asked. Instead, he'd planned to use public transport and lose over a half a day's pay to attend a dental appointment. Knowing the pain the tooth was causing him and that he was too proud to ask for help, she'd offered him her car. Insisted, really.

"So, let's begin." She swept a hand to the blackboard. "Respect."

The class of ten- and eleven-year-old boys in their fourth year of the six-year Malaysian primary school system should have been sweating and fidgeting. Instead, they now sat with backs straight, their eyes fixed on her.

"Anyone know what that means?" She placed her hands on the back of her chair. The sunlight seemed to shift and for a moment blinded her. She pushed the small crystal bowl to the front of her desk. The orchid and the bowl were a birthday gift from a group of teachers she'd had lunch with since she'd arrived. They'd presented the gift yesterday and even had sung a round of "Happy Birthday." Except that her birthday wasn't yesterday, nor was it this month. Her birthday was months past and a lifetime away.

"He's a loser." A boy stood up. His height and classic good looks belied his age.

The boy in question sat slouched over his desk, his untidy mop of black hair hanging forward and hiding his face from the class. She looked away and instead forced her gaze to the boy who had just spoken.

"Sit!" she snapped at Jefri. The boy was one of a small, tight-knit group who thought his family's wealth placed him a tier above everyone else. "No one's a loser."

Out of the corner of her eye she saw a flicker of motion. Something moved in the parking lot. She allowed her attention to divert momentarily. Her heart thumped.

"Miss Kelley?" Jefri's voice was insistent and still had the high notes of childhood, despite the fact that at almost twelve, he stood tall enough to face her eye to eye.

"Just a minute." She motioned the boy to sit down. Outside the heat rose in shimmering waves from the pavement as the shadow cast by the voluptuous canopy of an ancient rain tree fell short of cooling the overheated tar. In the parking lot, her new lemon-yellow Naza Sutera gleamed. Daniel hadn't left yet.

Her hand curled on her desk, her nails biting into her palm. A familiar figure moved with an easy walk toward her car, and whatever or whoever had caught her attention previously was gone. She breathed out a sigh as she recognized the school custodian, Daniel.

She turned her attention back to the class as she pointed to the chalkboard. "Shall we read this together?"

"Give Respect. Get Respect," the boys repeated, their childish voices rising solemnly to the occasion, some looking rather sullen, while others repeated dutifully as they did everything she asked.

"So, now we'll discuss what that means. I want—"

A blast of light exploded outside with a roar that rattled the windows and knocked the remainder of her sentence into eternity, where it would remain forgotten. Somewhere outside the room someone screamed.

A door slammed.

"Stay where you are. Sit down, all of you. Now!"

She rushed to the window even as the children jumped from their seats.

Flames shot into the air, smoke billowed, obscuring the parking lot, the grass. "Oh, my God!" She took a stumbling step backward. Her body seemed to freeze in position.

"Miss Kelley?" a small voice questioned her.

"Did you see that?" someone else shouted.

The class, she'd almost forgotten... A boy pushed in beside her, fighting for window space.

Voices chattered in the hallway.

She needed to secure the room. Protect the children.

"Sit!" she repeated as she swung around. "Stay away from the door!" She grabbed the edge of the desk and yanked it in that direction. But already the door had flung open and children scattered into the hallway.

"They're here," she whispered.

Chapter Three

Flames shot in the air as Josh closed the space between him and the fireball that had once been a vehicle. Black smoke billowed through the flames, and the smell of gas and burning metal filled the parking lot. And there was a hint of something else, the putrid sweet scent of burning flesh.

No.

He shielded his eyes from the intense glare and grimaced at the sight of the blackened hulk behind the wheel. He watched silently, aware of two things in that instant— that the corpse was too big to be her and that the outlaw biker gang, the Anarchists, had found her. He backed up and returned to the shelter of a canopy of pepper vines that fronted the edge of the school and provided a leafy shelter. He had no qualms about moving out of sight now that he knew the victim was beyond his help. His attention settled briefly on the burning vehicle. Chaos erupted from the building as children yelled and shrieked. The sharp commands of authority cut through the mass of voices as two female teachers attempted to control a mob of children. He hovered at the corner of the building, away from the main crush, out of sight of curious eyes.

He edged forward. The children milled excitedly, some cupping their hands over their eyes to get a better view.

An older, gray-haired woman in a suit jacket and skirt was hurling orders and pointing inside. When one boy headed for the steps, she yanked him back by the collar of his navy blue school uniform. Josh's gaze went to the other exit.

"Where are you?" He pushed the knit cap back from his forehead and glanced at the car and the fire that continued to burn bright and hot. He turned his attention back to the school and debated rounding the building and entering through the back. But that would serve no purpose. He was well aware that a face-to-face encounter, especially now, would have her running. He'd come too far to lose her.

"Come on," he encouraged his absent quarry. He wondered how she'd managed to survive as long as she had. From what he could see she had only a rudimentary knowledge of the art of disappearing and a bucket of pure luck. That was about to change.

"Daniel!"

It was a woman's voice, clear with a sweet edge despite the shock that so obviously laced through the words.

"There you are," he said under his breath. She had changed her name, her nationality and her look, but he would know her anywhere. Her hair was now a pallid blond contained in an elegant updo that he recognized as an attempt to add years to her youthful face. But even at a distance he would recognize those eyes and those cheekbones. He'd studied that face for hours, memorized it as he did for every job. Except this time he had wanted to know so many other things, such as what her voice sounded like. Now he knew.

Her gaze seemed to fix on the scene. He inched closer.

A movement out of the corner of his eye had him turning, and as he did he saw that one of the children had broken from the cluster and was moving much too close to the vehicle.

"Damn it," he swore. The flames were licking at the vehicle and there was no way of knowing if the gas tank had gone with the first explosion. He moved fast, forgetting about keeping to the fringes or keeping his head low. He grabbed the child and rolled with him, sideways and away from the hot, still-popping metal.

The boy squirmed, and Josh pinned the youngster with one hand. "It might explode again. Stay back unless you want to die." He repeated the command in Malay for good measure.

The boy nodded. Josh let the boy up and watched as he rushed back to his friends, who were all huddled a safe distance away. There was a look of hero worship in the group as the boys gathered around him. The boy was obviously considered a hero for undertaking such a risky business as getting close to the car or possibly being tackled by a strange man, or maybe a combination of the two. The adults were moving out of synch. One woman corralled another group of boys while another was frantically talking on her cell. Near the entrance of the school he could see two others, but all of their attention was focused on the vehicle, and all of them seemed to be moving in a disjointed fashion or not at all.

Josh diverted his attention back to the vehicle. The smoke curled thick and black, and in the distance he could hear the wailing sirens. The canopy of a lone rain tree threw shadows over the shrinking fire in the parking lot, its arthritic trunk standing thick and knotted, a silent silhouette. Across the street a woman clutched the handles of her pedal-powered pushcart, the vibrant pink, yellow and red flowers muted in the gathering smoke. On the main street cars continued to move in a steady stream as if smoke and fire were a normal part of their daily commute.

He scowled. He'd been so close. It had been gut instinct to check the primary schools in Georgetown, suspecting she would hunker down, consider herself safe again for a time. On Sunday, with the help of a local investigator that he'd met on a previous assignment, he'd acquired access to and checked the records of every school in the city that taught in English and that had acquired a foreign female teacher in the past few months.

He'd gone to her apartment just as school would be beginning for the day. While he was fairly certain that they'd located her, he'd hoped to find something that might prove that the woman they'd found in school records was her. He'd jimmied the building's back door. Fortunately the building was old and unalarmed, but who he suspected was the building's owner had found him just as he left her apartment. In fact, he had just closed and locked the door, leaving it as he had found it including the small piece of tissue tucked in the latch, meant to alert her to an intruder. It had taken a bit of acting to back out of that situation, but he'd had what he wanted—confirmation that she was the teacher he was seeking and—what he'd thought at the time was an interesting tidbit of information—that she was the owner of a new Naza Sutera.

In the distance, the Penang hills cast a sinister shadow as they cradled one against the other, their dark protrusions muted by distance. His gaze cruised across the bystanders, did a mental calculation of faces, numbers, positions. Nothing.

Josh gritted his teeth over the expletive that wouldn't change the reality.

She was gone.

Chapter Four

Erin was fighting for breath as she rounded the corner and stood out of sight of the school. A lorry swished past belching exhaust as a convoy of motorcyclists followed close behind. It seemed as though they were all fighting for space as a truck jammed in behind the cyclists and the loud red of Coca-Cola overlaid it all as a delivery truck squeezed into the street. A horn honked and a bicyclist swerved as pedestrians weaved their way through the intersection's traffic snarl.

Her jaw was clenched so tight it ached, and her hand worried the strap of the bag as her eyes strained for a cab to flag. One broke with the traffic and pulled to the curb. She rushed to meet it, throwing open the door and flinging herself inside.

"Focus," she muttered. She fired off her address in panicked words that she had to repeat when the driver turned around with a puzzled look.

Behind her, flames still punctured the otherwise quiet late-morning sky as sirens wailed and trouble inched closer.

"Daniel," she whispered. She dashed a tear away and unclenched her hands. She looked out the window as sun glared through the windscreen. A motorcycle pulled up beside the cab, a chopper. The driver's legs were propped up as he sat back on the low-slung seat. He turned, a dusty-brown beard covering much of his swarthy face, and smiled. The smile was not one of friendship. It was a leer, maybe, or worse. She hit the door lock.

She swallowed and clenched her free hand so tight that her nails dug into her palm. Her throat closed and her eyes burned with unshed tears.

She'd hated to run but she didn't have a choice. The conversation with Mike Olesk had made that fact clear. A retired police officer who had been a friend of her father's and a man she hadn't seen in years, Mike had been the only person she could think of whom she could trust and who might help her sort out her options. The conversation that ensued was one she would never forget, for it had changed her life.

He tapped ashes into a glass ashtray, the Hollywood emblem once sharply emblazoned on it now blurred with ashes. "I know how these things go down. The authorities make promises. But face it, on this one we're talking local police up against the Anarchists. They don't stand a chance. If it were the feds it would be a different matter."

"Why isn't it?" Her stomach turned over, anticipating what he would say.

"It will be soon. The local authorities will be calling you in for questioning, unless you come forward first. I suspect you maybe have a day, maybe less."

"No," she said shortly. "I can't. I won't answer their questions."

"You know you don't have a choice. Why are you balking at this, Erin?"

She shook her head.

"It would be for the best. They could charge you with obstruction of justice."

"I'd go to jail?" There'd be safety in jail.

"Maybe, maybe not." He coughed, the sound deep and achy in the silence between them. "Word's out that the Anarchists will do anything to ensure their leader, Derrick Reese, doesn't serve time. Maybe if I put in a word with the sheriff's office we could have this thing escalated to a federal level. We could live with that."

"I can't."

He rubbed the bridge of his nose with his thumb. "If we don't do that, if you run, that only makes you guilty of a crime."

"I can't. I'll run. Can you help me?"

"Erin. Are you out of your mind? Did you hear what I just told you? If I can get to the feds, if you admit everything, they can keep you safe."

"They'll want me to testify," she repeated, her heart thumping.

"Of course."

"Under oath?"

"Under oath," he agreed. "Erin, what is this all about? Who are you protecting?"

Silence hung between them.

"Who was it, Mike? Who turned me in?"

He took a long drag on a hand-rolled cigarette, his thick brows drawing down over narrow eyes.

"Word has it that only this morning that no-good boyfriend of yours squealed louder than a pig facing a luau."

"Steven," she whispered. And despite everything, the betrayal still hurt. She couldn't trust anyone, not with the truth, not with who was really the witness.

Smoke curled around them and her nose tickled. She wanted to sneeze but instead she coughed.

"Mike, I can't give you details. Just trust me. I have to run. I need to disappear."

"Erin?"

"Mike. Please, can you help me? It's life or death. Please, just trust me."

He stood there looking at her for a long time before he nodded. *"For how long?"*

"I don't know," she said quietly. *"As long as it takes."*

"Come." He motioned with one hand. She followed him and together they worked out a plan.

She shuddered. She ached to go home, to where it all began—San Diego. And she knew she might never go home again.

She opened her eyes and for a moment she froze, thoughts of home driven from her mind.

"The children," she murmured. She would have stayed for them, if it had been necessary. But the children were safe. She'd made sure of that. The principal had corralled many of them before they'd exited the building. The ones who had managed to slip outside were under the watchful eyes of two senior teachers.

She'd miss them, even the troublesome ones. Her life had become one of loss, of regret—it was what she hadn't expected of a life on the run, or more aptly what she hadn't thought of until the reality hit.

Focus, she reminded herself as the cab swung onto the congested street that she called home. Overhead, signs advertising products of the East and West vied for attention as the cab pushed farther into the crowded streets, and she wondered if this had been an error in judgment. Should she have gone directly to the airport? Were they on her trail even now? Or did they think her dead?

They.

She had been running from the faceless they for too long.

She could see the Victorian elegance of a former British mansion, the timeless beauty of its stone exterior a sign that she was almost home. She took courage from the familiar sight as the building pushed its stately presence into a world that seemed to be fighting for space. It was as if it refused to relinquish the hold it once had had, standing rock solid as the world around it changed.

The cab swung around the corner and the landscape changed again. If there was anything she loved about Georgetown it was how the old laced its presence through the new, how British traditions merged with Malay. She had purposely taken an apartment relatively close to the school within the hustle and bustle of daily life in Georgetown. Her apartment was a low-slung building in a cluttered section of the city where shops and open-air stalls dotted the landscape and fronted the more traditional brick-and-mortar buildings behind them. She'd loved this area from the first moment she'd laid eyes on it.

Not today.

Today, even under the brilliant afternoon sun, it seemed flush with shadows. On the sidewalk a man walked in a djellaba as his leather sandals skimmed easily across the concrete. His wife walked by his side in her traditional burka, her face and her thoughts hidden from the world by a layer of cloth and a veil. It wasn't an uncommon sight in Georgetown. Yet today, despite the fact that he held her hand—it all seemed to take on a sinister edge. Erin turned away to look out the opposite window.

The cab pulled over, and as she opened the door, the scent of curry intermingled with the smell of sewer. It was familiar and had begun to remind her of home, of here. After two months Georgetown felt comfortable, safe. *Had*, she thought with regret.

"Could you wait, please?" she requested as she stepped out of the cab.

Inside the apartment building, the narrow hallway with its faded morning glory wallpaper was empty. Only the chatter of a television set coming through one door and the clunking of the ancient washing machine down the hall broke the quiet. She stopped at the dark wood door at the end of the hallway. For a minute it was as if she wasn't here, as if this nightmare had never happened.

Daniel, she thought, and a sob hitched deep inside her and threatened her control. She took a deep breath. She needed to focus on running, but she could only think of Daniel. He was one of the few friends she'd made in Georgetown, and he'd still be alive if she hadn't loaned him her car. He hadn't asked to borrow it any more than he'd asked to die. It had all been her fault.

Her fault. Those two words kept reeling through her mind.

Stop it, she told herself. *Just stop it*. Now wasn't the time for recriminations or even grieving. She had to get out before she jeopardized someone else's life.

Erin reached for the knob and hesitated. She ran her tongue along her bottom lip. She looked down at the key in her hand. This time when she reached she touched the heavy brass knob, but then dropped her hand and took a step back. A small knot of white tissue lay on the floor. She worried her fingers against her palms, staring at that tiny piece of tissue.

"Erin."

She jumped, bit back a shriek and swung around.

"Yong, you scared me."

"There was someone asking for you earlier today. Did they find you?" the apartment owner asked. His face was downcast, and his slight shoulders slouched as they always did. "I'm sorry. After he left I opened your door just to do a check. We've had to replace some of the locks in the building." He shrugged. "I didn't go in, but I wanted to make sure your lock was working, that it couldn't be easily compromised. Besides, I'm sorry if he was a friend of yours, but I didn't like the look of him. And a double check is never a bad idea."

She unclenched her hand and took a step back. "I thought someone had been here."

"I thought you might." He smiled. "The old tissue in the door frame trick. Not a bad idea for a single woman. Not that we have much trouble with break-ins but you never know." He cleared his throat, the sound raspy and raw in the narrow hallway. "Just glad you haven't needed it."

"Thanks, Yong. I don't know what I'd do without you."

"No trouble," Yong said, but his eyes narrowed and he took a step closer. "You're all right?"

"Fine. Thank you." She turned the key over in her hand.

"That doesn't sound fine to me. Remember, like I've said, you need anything. I have daughters your age. But you know that. You met one of them." He hesitated. "You're sure nothing's wrong?"

"I'm sure."

"Okay," he said and turned away, jingling keys in his hand.

"Yong."

"Yeah." He stopped.

"What did he look like? The man, I mean." She fumbled with words and struggled to keep the tremor out of her voice.

"A big guy, six feet, maybe more. Hard to tell from my view down here." He chuckled. "I don't know. Not bad-looking." He paused. "Why? You think you might know him?"

"Was he Malay?" she asked.

"Don't think so. Had an accent, not Aussie or anything. Something else."

"Thanks." She hadn't asked his hair color or his race or... Did it matter? She knew he wasn't Malay. If he got close enough for her to see him, did she stand a chance? She had to get out of here and fast. But she needed to know. She had to ask at least one of those questions. "What color was his hair?"

"Don't know. He was wearing one of those knitted caps."

He jangled his keys, his sneaker-clad feet almost twitching as he answered her. "Look, I don't think he'll be back. And I'll be keeping a closer eye on things."

Her hand shook as it went to the door frame.

"No worries," he said over his shoulder as he headed down the hallway and to his own apartment.

"No worries," she repeated.

She turned the key in the lock with fingers that still shook. She stood in the doorway for a minute, then two. She pushed the door open wider. Her eyes darted back and forth, taking in micro snapshots of the room. Behind her a door slammed, and she jumped.

Hesitantly, she leaned one hand against the door frame as if that would ground her, make everything normal or turn back the clock. But nothing changed. The cot folded down from the wall, the kitchenette was jammed against the opposite wall, the tiny television in the far corner. Through the narrow window that faced the street, she could see the cab waiting.

"This is it," she murmured. "This is goodbye." She wiped the back of her hands across both eyes. She took a breath and then another, pulled out a tissue and blew her nose.

She grabbed her bag from the top shelf of the closet, tore clothes from hangers and emptied her drawers. Within a few minutes she was packed.

She never looked back as she closed the door behind her, as if this was just another day, and hurried out the door and into the waiting cab.

"The airport, please," she said. Her hand knotted around the straps of her knapsack and a small bag that carried her few personal items as she perched on the edge of her seat. She pressed her free hand to her temple as if that would still the headache that was beginning to beat dully and then dropped it to clutch the seat in front of her.

JOSH SLIPPED OUT the back entrance of the school and tucked the brochure he'd stolen from her classroom into his pocket. He would disappear as silently as he had arrived, leaving the retreating flames and tamped-down chaos to the authorities. He glanced at his watch, which functioned as a GPS as well as registered the time among other things. He hadn't expected the car bomb. As a precaution, he'd planned to mount a small tracking device on her car that would have followed her anywhere she went.

The victim—collateral damage. It was the only way to think of such things without losing it. He'd seen a number of breakdowns in the field from either mental or emotional stress; he didn't plan to become one of them.

Collateral damage.

School caretaker. That information hadn't been too hard to obtain. He'd overheard the hysterical words of a female teacher, confirmed that the car was his target's and that she'd lent it out, confirmed that Erin Argon was still alive.

Would she flee by land or air? Where? He considered the trajectory of her five-month flight. She'd begun her flight fueled by fear and misguided advice rather than immediate danger. Lucky and wily, her changed name and Canadian passport had kept her hidden until these past few weeks when he had been assigned the case. Still, she was damn lucky, and he knew he had little time to find her before the Anarchists beat him to it.

Luck aside it was amazing what she had accomplished and how easily she had slipped out of sight. So far she had crossed no fewer than ten international borders. Other than the weeks in Singapore, this had been the only place where she had settled. So where would a woman go who had crossed continents and countries, who had thought she was safe and who now had to come up with an alternate plan?

He was under her skin. An inkling of doubt rose at that thought. Doubt that maybe it was the other way around. He shrugged it off. She was an assignment, nothing more. He'd studied her, he knew her. She was tired. She'd go somewhere to regroup, to come up with a plan and another place to hide, because this time she had run, more than likely, without a plan. Where would she go? He touched the brochure in his pocket and wondered if it could be as easy as that.

"It's a risk," he muttered and smiled. There wasn't anything better than a risk; throw in one of his infamous hunches and he was betting that he was bang on right. After all, who else would know that she was fascinated by Malaysia's bat caves in Gunung Mulu National Park? He was guessing she had kept that information to herself. He certainly wouldn't have suspected it if she hadn't left her canvas satchel and run, taking nothing from her classroom but her purse. And if he hadn't snuck into her classroom before he left he would never have known, either, for he would never have found her brochure on the Mulu Caves and literally stumbled on to where he was now sure she planned to go next.

He jumped in a cab and gave the driver the order for

the airport even as his mind churned through the options. She was panicked. Would she take the slow route out of here or just hop a plane? He suspected the latter. If she were smart, and so far she'd proven she was, a few transfers around the country and her trail would become a little grayer, a little more difficult to follow. Keep on doing that and she could disappear. He needed to get to the airport to confirm he was right and get a ticket on that same plane. He leaned back.

"Damn," he muttered as his thoughts went back to the one man she'd reached out to, the man who had been the catalyst to send Erin Kelley Argon on her five-month flight.

"Mike Olesk, we finally meet."

He held out his hand.

"I don't have time for this," the grizzle-faced burn-out said.

"You used to be a city cop," Josh said.

"What's it to you?"

"I'm with the CIA." He held out his identification.

"And you want to know about Erin."

Josh's lips tightened. "I didn't expect it would be this easy," he said drily. He seriously hadn't thought the man would admit to knowing her, never mind that he would just blurt out her name.

"That's about all I'm going to tell you," he said with a surly edge to his voice.

"She's in danger," Josh said. "And you have the power to help me find her."

"How do I know you are who you say you are?"

"I could get a warrant," he said, but it was only a mild threat.

"You don't have time now, do you? The trial begins in a little more than a month. They need Erin, and the

Anarchists need her dead. She's the witness that can put them all away." Mike shook his head.

"Why?"

"As if you don't know. She witnessed a murder, and it wasn't just any murder, was it? No, the gang leader up and shoots what looks like the gang's link to crime-based money out of Europe." He ran a hand through hair that shone with grease. *"You're not the only one in the know, and you're not the only one hunting Erin."*

"How well do you know her?" Josh asked quietly. There was something else going on here or at least he suspected so. Information was flowing too quickly, and that, he had learned during his six years in the field, was always suspect.

Mike looked surprised and there was a secretive cast to his bloodshot brown eyes. *"Not that well. I knew her as a kid when her father and I worked together. As an adult, we lost touch until... Well, until she came to me for help."*

"And you helped her disappear."

"Something like that. But I don't know where she is now. I haven't heard from her in months."

"Fourteen days," he muttered as outside the traffic continued to flash by. That was the number of days since he had spoken to Mike Olesk, and then had cobbled together her flight path that had taken him to Singapore and finally to this point.

Mulu Caves in Gunung Mulu National Park. He opened the brochure. The glossy pictures would have been enticing in another situation. The information gave the usual condensed and carefully edited descriptions, all of it what he already knew. The park was isolated and accessible only by a ten-hour boat ride or a small plane. It was the perfect place to hide, but it was also the perfect place for a trap. He suspected she hadn't thought of that; she hadn't had time.

He looked out the window and smiled.

She was in his sights. He wasn't in hers.

Chapter Five

In the past hour Josh had laid a false trail from Miri, Malaysia, through Beijing and then to Hong Kong, a hotel registration here in Erin Kelley's name, a car rental there. But that trail would delay the men who were after her only for so long—a day, maybe two.

"They're offering ten million for the kill, Josh." Vern folded his arms, his feet propped on the desk, his florid skin at odds with his blond hair. *"Fortunately, the first man out of the gate isn't one of the best."*

The passage of time since that conversation seemed nominal considering all that had transpired. Josh shifted his pack and artfully dodged milling passengers in Miri's airport, all the while taking in the change in her appearance. Despite the fact that her new hair color gleamed a startling blue black and wire-rimmed glasses glinted beneath the artificial light and hid her vivid blue eyes, he still recognized her. Her frame was thinner, more fragile than her pictures had indicated, and the blue-black wig made her delicate skin look pale and gave the illusion of fragility. It was an amateurish attempt at a quick disguise, but it was effective for now. In fact, the black hair color was genius in a population where the average person was dark haired and dark skinned. It made her blend in just a bit more. Unfortunately, she hadn't had time or hadn't thought of the pallor of her skin accentuated against the unnaturally dark hair.

He shrugged. It would do and sometimes on the run, that was all you had. He imagined she'd be pulling out hair dye when they reached the Gunung Mulu National Park. It wasn't a bad idea and it was all he had or, he amended, she had, at least until he developed some kind of rapport with her.

Erin Kelley Argon.

He had followed her flight halfway across the world and watched her survive despite the odds. Her path hadn't been as simple to pick up as he'd first thought it would be. He'd been surprised at every turn. At times she'd shown gut intelligence for flight, as if she had done this at some other time in her life. Despite having help and advice from Mike Olesk, alone she had still gone through the steps with a polish that hadn't left one misstep. That was evident in the fact that the Anarchists hadn't expanded their search off the continental United States until shortly before he'd been deployed.

Yet nothing in the history he had gone over said she had ever had a reason to run, to hide. Until the murder, she'd led a normal life.

He was still in awe of those initial moments of her disappearance. Her flight had been brilliant, classic even. She'd put everything in place before running. She'd left San Diego and legally changed her name, dropped her last name while still in the country and in a matter of weeks had obtained a passport in her new name and country. And when she'd run, she hadn't flown but instead had zigzagged north into Canada and taken a train across that country. But what he'd least expected was the creativity that followed. She'd jumped a container ship and taken a convoluted path before finally arriving in Eastern Europe.

He had followed her journey as he had prepared for this assignment with an almost morbid fascination. She had kept him awake nights as he'd admired the ingenuity this woman had put into her escape.

A movement caught his eye.

She was at the ticket counter. He took a step forward, his gaze locked on her and then veered left. He had to transform from Josh Sedovich, CIA agent, to just Josh, tourist. He headed to the washroom and his own change of appearance.

ERIN TOOK A deep breath as she tried to portray a casual traveler. It wasn't easy considering everything that had happened. This was the third flight since this morning's tragedy. She was lucky there had been room on the flight to Miri, and now she hoped her luck would hold out again on the flight to the Gunung Mulu National Park and its legendary caves.

"Just made it."

The voice behind her was male and too close.

She turned to face a shock of dark curly hair and brown eyes that sparkled with humor, yet something more serious seemed to lurk there. He was clean-shaven and attractive in a boyish kind of way. Still, she took an involuntary step back even as she took in his knee-length beige shorts and white T-shirt with Kuala Lumpur's skyline emblazoned across it. Only an overly enthusiastic tourist would actually wear a T-shirt like that, never mind the socks. Yet in this world, her new world, nothing was a given. Nothing was as it appeared and no one was safe. It had been a harsh reminder, today's lesson—short and brutal. She blinked back tears. She had to act as if everything was normal, as if she was no different than anyone else.

She offered him a half smile.

"You did," she agreed as she assessed and discarded the man behind her. She'd never seen him before and his dress screamed tourist. He was no threat.

She turned away as the couple ahead of her moved from the counter and the clerk motioned her forward. She stepped up, dutifully provided her weight and that of her luggage, and within minutes was checked in.

"When do we board?" she asked.

The clerk swung around to where a clock face ticked the minutes. It was two o'clock. "Fifteen minutes," he replied. "Through that gate."

Outside the tarmac made this morning's classroom feel cool. Heat shimmered and distorted the landscape. Even the low-lying shrubs that skirted the edges of the pavement appeared to be wilting in the heat. The distant hills rose in a scalloped frame of shadowed images that were fronted by patches of emerald-green forests and stretches of clay in hues of rust. Ahead of her stood a small prop plane with Malaysia emblazoned in red and blue lettering on its narrow metal frame.

As they lined up to board the plane, Erin could feel every breath and her heart seemed to thump loud enough to be heard.

"It's hot today, again. Odd," she muttered.

"Excuse me?" the man with the so-uncool T-shirt asked.

"Oh, I… I'm sorry. I was talking to myself. Bad habit."

"Traveling alone does it to one. Do it myself," he said cheerfully.

"I suppose." She tried to keep her attention on him. She eased her hold on her bags.

"A way to self-medicate," he said. "Talking to oneself. At least, so I was told. Not sure what exactly one is medicating, but there it is—self-help. All I know."

"Thanks," she said with what she hoped was a smile. She pushed a strand of hair out of her eyes and felt the sweat that she knew must be glistening on her forehead.

"It is unusually hot," he added.

She offered a half smile and held back as he and the others inched forward, waiting for bags to be loaded.

"Next!"

A bag was thrown onto the scale.

A heavyset man followed the suitcase, stepping onto the scale.

It was a pattern—weigh luggage, weigh passenger.

"Small plane—they have to juggle the weight." It was T-shirt man, as she'd begun to think of him.

"Next."

"After you," he said and accompanied his words with a slight sweep of his hand motioning her forward as they reached the front of the line.

"Thank you." Her hand tightened on her bags and she blinked and blinked again. She bit her lip and her hand stopped shaking. She turned her attention to him, noticing that he was taller than she'd first thought, but his broad build gave the illusion of a shorter frame. As she'd determined before, he was good-looking, but more than likely a bit of a goof if his souvenir T-shirt, too-long shorts and tennis shoes with socks were any indication. Yet he wasn't as boyish-looking as she had thought. In fact, he wasn't boyish-looking at all. In the sunlight, his features were almost craggy in a roguish kind of way.

"No worries," he said.

"No worries," she repeated.

She glanced around as she took her seat. No additional passengers, just the same ones she'd already accounted for. There was no one who might pose a threat. The passengers included an older couple with a slight camera addiction, judging from the camera bags that dangled around both their necks. Both carried a few extra pounds that were not the well-toned form she assumed would be required of a hit man. She shuddered at the thought.

She'd come close, too close.

She turned her attention back to the occupants of the small plane. The other couple, both male, was obviously excited about the trip and even more obviously in love. Both were slight and short in stature, and effeminate, one more than the other. Definitely not hit men material. No threat there, either. She folded her arms under her chest and looked out the window, but instead her thoughts went to the past and her family.

"You can't leave us Erin." Tears swam in Sarah's eyes.

"There's no choice, Sarah. You can't breathe a word of what happened."

"But Erin, you can't leave. I won't let you."

"There's no choice," she repeated as she put an arm around her sister, hugging her close. *"You're pregnant and that changes everything."*

"You said I was a fool," Sarah said. *"And you were right."*

"The baby's real, Sarah. And whether I agree with your decisions in getting to this state, or who you chose to have a baby with…"

"Father absentee," Sarah muttered. *"I think I'm off men, possibly for life."*

"I'll protect you both, and the only way to do that is for me to get out of here."

"But your job?"

"Not permanent. I'm substituting at a variety of schools."

"But you love the kids. You live for your work."

"There's no other choice, Sarah. If I don't leave the Anarchists will hunt us down."

"Instead, they'll only hunt you," Sarah said sadly. "I can't talk you out of this insanity?"

"You can't." She hugged Sarah. "We'll be in touch."

"I love you, sis," Sarah said.

The engine vibrated the small plane, and as it cut into a turn that seemed to shift passengers and luggage alike, Erin held her breath.

She pinched her fingers together, her nails biting into skin. She looked out the window. Beneath them the forest canopy sprawled in lush greenery hugging ragged limestone cliffs that punctured the jungle floor with primitive ease. The forest appeared endless, and for a brief moment Erin allowed herself to be caught up in the natural beauty of this place. While her gut tightened as she remembered that she'd be isolated, alone and only temporarily safe, temporarily out of sight. She needed a plan and she needed it quickly.

"Completely awesome, isn't it?" said the man who had waited in line behind her.

"It is," she agreed as ahead of them the two couples admired the view out their respective windows, the two men silently watching the passing scenery, and the husband and wife taking an endless stream of pictures.

"Name's Josh," he said easily.

"Erin," she supplied reluctantly. So far she'd managed to dodge conversation with any of the other passengers. She looked at him. She had to be sure he was no threat. She reminded herself that if he were out to kill her, he would have done so, unless, of course, he was waiting for the plane to land and for anonymity. But if that were the case, he wouldn't have been wearing that ridiculous T-shirt.

You're seeing danger where none exists, she told herself. Still, she had to make sure he was safe. Nothing in his demeanor suggested a threat of any kind. But she'd learned early on that danger came quickly and unexpectedly.

How long would it be safe to stay here? She knew the answer even as she asked the question. Not long, a matter of days until she got a plan together. She had to get out of Malaysia, get across the border to another country and safety. She needed to sketch a path, a number of flights within the border, before leaving Malaysia for good. She needed a plan and a map, and she had fled without either.

She took a deep, shaky breath. It had been a huge misjudgment, an error. She had thought she was safe. She had let down her guard. Now one innocent person was dead and she was running without direction.

"Something wrong?" Josh leaned forward, concern reflected in the furrows in his forehead.

Damn, she thought. He'd been watching her and she hadn't noticed.

"You're afraid of flying?"

The roar of the engine seemed to fill the small cabin.

She wished that was all it was. Instead of replying, she remained with her gaze riveted on the window and on land—a new challenge.

"We're about to land. See." He pointed. "It won't be long. You'll be fine."

"I..." She began to assure him and to deny any fear of flying, and then stopped. The new Erin could not afford to offer too much information, too much familiarity. Lies were her new truth. It had taken her months to become comfortable with that, and still it rang false. She still had to remind herself. Lies weren't who she was. The old Erin had been open, trusting, honest... No more. She took a breath, put a smile on her face and met him head-on. "Thank you. This whole small plane thing makes me a bit queasy."

"Used to do the same to me," he agreed. But this time when he looked at her there was something darker and more intense in the look that seemed to belie the flippancy that had seemed second nature to him.

She shivered.

"Are you cold?" This time his brows almost met over the question.

"I'm fine."

The plane began its descent and the afternoon sun gleamed on the dense greenery, adding a sparkle-like affect. Another time it might have been amazing. Now, she could feel Josh's eyes on her. She sighed. That was all she needed—a man's interest.

Or did she?

She shifted in her seat and eyed him from the corner of her eye. A plan began to form. Her hand drifted to the window frame. She was a woman alone, on the run. That was what they were looking for. That was how she had left. An American posing as a Canadian, one who taught school and didn't fit here. They'd looked in the schoolyards, and they'd found her.

Once.

They'd find her again.

Traveling alone made her stand out. She had to change her name again and her identity, but right in this moment, there was nothing to do but forge ahead with who she had become. But there was something she could change.

She looked over at Josh, and he smiled almost hopefully.

Maybe that was the best cover of all. She hated being alone, yet, oddly, she had become used to it. While she didn't like it, she didn't feel as uncomfortable as she had in the beginning. Of course, the beginning had been laced with so much fear. The fear was still there, but it was like white noise, something that had become her daily companion, a familiar entity that reminded her not to trust.

She'd trusted and Daniel had died.

Chapter Six

Josh stepped onto the metal stairs of the plane's exit ramp. He was right behind Erin, her black wig gleaming like a beacon in the late-afternoon sun. He looked to the right and left as he matched his steps to hers. The tarmac stretched out, cut through the relentless jungle that closed in around them. The resort was built well above the ground and away from the unpredictability of nature in a satellite of stilt-legged buildings adjoined by wooden walkways. It was rustic in an elegant fashion.

"Heard the king of Monaco stayed here. Or maybe it was a prince. Not sure, royalty of some kind," the older woman with a camera dangling from a leather strap around her neck said to the man who stood beside her sporting a camera of his own.

A resort that had housed royalty, Josh thought. That was new since he last visited, and reassuring. The logistics of security had already been tested.

While he considered these things, his attention never turned from Erin. He was aware of every movement, of the fact that she now stood in line just ahead of him. He watched as her fingernails scraped against the strap of a small canvas bag, making an odd rough-edged sound, the only sign that she was nervous.

His gaze shifted slightly ahead of her to the couple

closest to them, and his biggest concern because of that, because of proximity. They had matching hard-shelled suitcases on wheels—oversized and, he suspected, over-packed. The luggage was a fairly good indicator that this trip was the most risky of their travels, for the luggage almost screamed safe and their demeanor capped his assessment. They were no threat.

There was a low hum of chatter around them as the passengers stared at the amazing backdrop the distant cliffs made as they pierced their off-white talons through the lush green jungle. He watched the tourists, listening to what they said, how they interacted with each other, mentally recording all. It was humans who would cause any problems in the future, not scenery. Because of that, he didn't care for limestone peaks or bat caves except as a strategic means of escape, places to hide if the worst-case scenario occurred. In the meantime, what he cared about were the nooks and crannies where an assassin could lurk. Again, he scoured the disembarking passengers and moved on to the resort crew that waited on the edge of the empty runway with a minivan to take those less limber up to the resort.

His gaze slid over the employee at the head of the line. The man was lean, sun-bronzed and approximately five foot four. He was dressed in pristine white cotton pants and a T-shirt with the Royal Mulu Resort logo emblazoned on it. Instinct told him he was no threat, but he'd wait to pass judgment once he had the evidence to back up that initial determination.

The last bag was unloaded and he saw Erin take a step toward it.

He hurried forward as she reached for an oversized knapsack.

"Let me take that." He lifted the bag as he made the

comment, leaving her no option but to graciously accept. "Mulu is more beautiful than the brochure promised."

She gave him a look that could only be called leery.

"I never anticipated this." He swept his arm in a half circle. "Did you?" He didn't even consider how inane the comment was. It didn't fit who he was, but it fit his current persona. He'd just have to watch it so as not to go overboard with it.

"It is, but then that's why I came here. As I imagine you did, too."

"Actually," he said, "I'd never heard of Mulu until a friend enlightened me. I didn't even make a reservation." He shrugged. "I don't like to travel like that, but..."

"No reservation? Really?"

She only looked mildly interested and far from trusting.

"Did you reserve ahead?" he asked and felt her eyes on her bag.

"Yes, of course." She frowned. Her eyes narrowed as they met his and her lips were compressed in a fine line. "You are lucky it's October. One of the few months where there's less tourists." She held out her hand for her bag.

"You're sure? I can take it."

Her hand brushed his. Something shifted in her gaze and her lips softened.

"It's heavy. Let me," he said.

"Thanks," she replied as she led the way with a determined and slight sway to her hips, which despite her slim figure were seductively curvy.

Overhead a bird screeched. The shadow of the bird's startled flight cut across them as it dove, giving a view of glossy black tail feathers before it disappeared into the lush jungle. She jumped and slipped on the wooden walkway, which was slick from a recent rain. He took her arm, steadying her.

"Careful," he warned as she looked at him with an expression of fear mixed with gratitude. There was a haunted look in her eyes, or maybe he imagined it, for the look was as quickly gone, and replaced by the determination he'd seen earlier, an emotion that consistently emanated from her.

"I can take it now." She reached for her bag.

"You're sure. There's no need…"

Their eyes clashed, and he handed her bag to her. "I could have taken it the rest of the way."

"You could have," she agreed. "But I prefer not."

She gave him a smile that took some of the edge off her words, and then turned with the bag slung over her shoulder, the straps gripped with one white-knuckled hand as she followed the two men who were already a few yards ahead. Two minutes later he was holding open the glass-plated door to the reception area for her as a rush of air-conditioning swirled around them.

"Well, we're here," he said as he graciously waited for the woman behind him to enter before relinquishing the door to a heavyset gray-haired man who was towing a wheeled suitcase behind him.

"We are," she said over her shoulder and strode determinedly toward the reception desk without a backward glance.

"WE HAVE YOU booked for a double occupancy." The desk clerk looked up and then over at Josh as if he were the missing double. "As you requested."

"That's right," Erin said. "My boyfriend will be joining me later." Her eyes slid to Josh and her hand slipped through the strap of the bag. Her eyes flitted to where a round, white-faced clock hummed on the wall behind the reception desk.

Four o'clock.

She sneaked another peek at Josh and saw only admiration in his gaze. Despite the wire-rimmed glasses and tacky T-shirt, he wasn't as geeky as she'd first thought. In fact, there was something about him that she couldn't quite put her finger on. She gathered her passport and held it in an iron grip.

She looked away but felt his eyes on her.

"Boyfriend?" he asked, disappointment etching his words.

She nodded as her gaze flitted to his. There was an intensity there, a knowing that belied the unbecoming tourist T-shirt. There was smoke in his eyes that seemed to pierce through the lens of his black-rimmed glasses and a ruggedness to the face behind the frames.

"This place is amazing," he said as he turned and looked one way and then the other, clearly overwhelmed. She suspected he was an infrequent traveler.

Her lips twitched, and she almost smiled.

"I'll see you around," she said as she left him to check in and followed the concierge out the door.

Five minutes later she scanned her room for exits. The airy, sunlit room held a wicker desk and chair and a comfortable-looking queen-size bed, but those were minor points. What was important were the window, the door and what was outside. From what she could see, barring the front entrance, the only exit was the window that looked out onto a narrow catwalk, a thin bamboo walkway that might have been used by resort employees. She glanced at the window. It would do in an emergency. First she had to determine if she could open it or if she would need to break the glass. If the latter were the case, she would need something handy to break the glass with.

She opened the stained bamboo closet door. Inside was nothing but a row of old-fashioned wire hangers. She ran a thumb over one, thinking that these hangers could be used as a weapon if necessary. They weren't much, but they'd be better than facing any threat empty-handed.

Her hand quivered. Whoever was after her was more sophisticated than coat hangers. They'd blown up a car. They meant business, and they meant to kill her. It was as Mike had said and she hadn't wanted to believe—only worse. A slight headache began to pulse low in the base of her skull. She missed her friends, her family, her apartment—and she missed her cat.

She'd delivered Edgar to her sister the day before she'd run. Sarah had been sworn to silence and Mike to vigilance. They'd both be fine. The cat would be well cared for, spoiled and more than likely a few pounds over his ideal weight by the time she got home, and her sister would have had the baby she shouldn't be having. A single woman with no career aspirations and no man willing to stick around wasn't the ideal candidate for motherhood. But that was Erin's opinion, not Sarah's.

Home.

Her thumbnail pinched into the palm of her hand.

"Focus," she reminded herself as the wave of homesickness, loss and despair washed through her. She took her mind from other places back to the moment and to reworking the plan. She couldn't worry about family or friends or even cats; there was nothing she could do for them but stay away and stay alive.

She looked at the closet, closed the doors and went through her list of defenses. The list was meager. She had pepper spray from a night market stall. Other than a self-defense course she'd taken with another primary grade teacher, she had little in her favor.

As she thought through the events of the past few days, she realized that she had to get out of the country in a very short time. This escape was only temporary. She didn't know how good the people hired to find her were, but she suspected they might be very good. They'd found the school she'd worked in, they'd found her new identity and they'd attempted to kill her.

"Stay calm," she reminded herself. But there seemed no end in sight and no one she could approach for help.

She looked at her watch as if that would give her the answers that weren't forthcoming.

Her headache was escalating.

She sat down on the bed. She'd run three quarters of the way around the globe and they'd found her. She'd changed her appearance yet again. And she'd been on a cash-only basis since leaving home. She needed to do more.

She wasn't sure where she was going next, but she knew what she needed in the short term while she was here.

Her nails bit into the palms of her hands. She relaxed her hands and took a breath—panicking would get her nowhere.

"Damn boyfriend dumped you," she murmured with a laugh that held no humor at all. "And then along came Josh." She hated every aspect of this story, from its very necessity to its needy woman overtones to using an innocent man—possibly toying with his affections. All of it was distasteful and all of it was necessary. She pulled a box of hair dye from her pack.

Josh Sedovich, an easy man to reel in. She thought that without arrogance but instead with the thoughts of an attractive woman who knew she was attractive.

She wouldn't hurt him, just engage in some harmless flirtation—the illusion of a couple.

She sucked in a deep breath. Her life was an illusion, an illusion that hurt.

Chapter Seven

Josh shielded his eyes. Despite the threat of rain later in the day, the sun beat hot and relentless even in late afternoon. This was the least popular time of year, as the rain made things muggy and uncomfortable. It wasn't usual for numbers to drop too much, but with renovations on some of the more distant accommodations, tourism was noticeably down. That was good news—less activity to monitor, fewer potential incoming threats.

The drone of a plane's engine pierced the sultry heat. It was on schedule. He watched as the plane landed.

He'd just gotten word that, as he had suspected, the last hit had been by one of the Anarchists's gang members. Bobbie Xavier was not the brightest tool in the shed, but he was one of the deadliest. Josh had gotten confirmation that his diversion had worked. Bobbie was on his way to Hong Kong.

But with the recent news the stakes had just gone up. The Anarchists had hired someone else, a man who wouldn't work in tandem with Bobbie, and one who wouldn't depend on luck or the mistakes of a woman who had never had to disappear before. The man was a professional. He had a record of success that ended in a trail of death, and he had a record of outsourcing. That meant the numbers on her trail could and more likely would, go up.

That meant that there might not just be one. In the near future, there might be two or three. They needed to get out of here, maybe sooner than he'd previously thought.

Sid Mylo was not someone to take lightly. Why the hell were they hiring someone with Sid's capabilities to go after someone like Erin? Sure, she had been on the run for five months, but—and that was the next mystery— why had it taken them that long to send someone after her? Until now they had depended on the muscle of the various club members across the states as the alert had gone out and the nets had gone up. But they hadn't looked outside the continental United States.

"Erin Argon," he muttered. It was the real woman he would be bringing back, not the actress Erin Kelley. He wondered how she could have gotten herself into this mess. She didn't look like the type to date bikers. But that was exactly what she'd done.

He knew some women got off on that. Some dated criminals slated for death row, sought out men who were bent on destruction, their own as well as that of others. But it was rather disconcerting to think that a primary-school teacher would spend her free time with men who had questionable ethics. Drug dealers, pimps and murderers—and that was only the beginning of the crimes that could be attributed to various members of the Anarchists. It didn't seem to fit anything he knew about her. And whether she'd learned her lesson after one colossal mistake, he didn't know. Only she knew that. And it wasn't something he needed to know. That knowledge would no more save her than hiding out in Mulu would.

He pulled open the door of the hotel lobby.

The concierge stood by the desk. His brown pants and jacket seemed to fade into the background. But his posture and wide smile, despite his solid but short stature, made him immediately stand out.

Their eyes met and held in a moment of understanding before the concierge looked away.

Josh waited a few minutes, glancing through a display of pamphlets before turning to the concierge. "Must be nice to work here."

He looped his thumbs into the belt loops of his shorts. In listening range was an older couple that seemed to be involved in their own discussion, but they glanced over at him with what he thought of as a tourist's curiosity.

"Yes, sir." The concierge met his gaze this time with a rather puzzled expression, as if he didn't know where the question was leading.

"Josh." He held out his hand. "Three," he mouthed. It was the number of days, maximum, that he planned to stay before getting Erin out of here.

"Tenuk," the concierge said with a rather solemn grace and tapped his finger silently, one, two, three. It was confirmation, nothing else.

Josh moved to the back of the lobby. His gaze grazed the bank of pamphlets against one wall while he kept a discreet eye on the comings and goings of staff and guests in the lobby.

The woman behind the desk was reading, but she shoved the book under the counter as the door opened, announcing more guests. An older couple checked in with more noise and fluff than their entrance warranted. The man was balding and sweating, the woman was thick set, easily as tall as the man, and both carried themselves in a way that spoke of never having been denied.

There was nothing more to be learned here. Josh dropped the pamphlet, glanced briefly at Tenuk and opened the door.

Outside, he lowered his sunglasses. The polarized lenses provided some privacy, hiding his eyes from scrutiny. It was ninety-two degrees, hotter than normal. He moved away from the hotel entrance and to the side where he could discreetly watch the new arrivals.

He pushed the ball cap he'd just purchased in the gift shop off his forehead and wiped at a nonexistent line of sweat. About one hundred feet away a couple sat at an outdoor bar drinking what looked like a highball of some sort—rum and Coke, he suspected.

The reception door opened with a slightly gritty sound that spoke of a need of attention, adjustment of the hinges possibly. Tenuk came up beside him. The two of them stood there for a moment in silence, taking in the comings and goings of the resort and their position in it.

"Is the flight that just arrived from Miri also the last flight out?" Josh asked. It was a pointless question meant only to cloud their real purpose should anyone be listening. He already knew the answer; both of them did. There wasn't anything about the resort's transportation that he hadn't been briefed on. What he didn't know were the people who worked here or the guests who were currently in residence. Or, more importantly, those who might be in transit to the resort.

"There are two more."

Josh nodded.

"Your accommodation is acceptable, sir?" His sun-bronzed face was scarred and pockmarked, his frame small but solid. Tenuk Laksana was one of the best of Malaysia's special forces, or so Josh has been told.

"Of course. Exactly as I expected. Better," he said with enthusiasm.

"It's clear," Tenuk said as he leaned sideways against the railing.

"One plane in since ours," he said. Behind them was jungle, in front was a supply cabin and farther away he could see the glimmer of the pool. At the far end of the resort a couple threw a ball for their toddler, and in the pool a heavyset woman was doing laps.

"Another expected in half an hour. I double-checked the roster. A group of senior tourists arriving from Bangkok." He shoved his hands in his pockets. "Six in all and on the next roster, four young women who are scheduled to begin work here tomorrow."

"The wild cards are the dormitories," Josh said, referring to the hostels that housed backpackers in a dormitory-style room.

"True enough. That's where the budget travelers stay, and there's usually more of them. Fortunately, you have luck on your side. The home stay and dormitory are closed for maintenance."

"Manageable," Josh replied. "If we'd had to deal with the home stays…" He thought of the area where locals managed various types of tourist accommodation just outside the main resort, and where many were under renovation as a result of the park's recent accommodation safety mandates. "Despite the season, the tourism would have increased."

"Meaning more security issues. Still, even without them it's a rough assignment," Tenuk said with a smile.

"Seen worse," he said shortly.

"Maybe, but she's lucky to still be alive."

Josh couldn't disagree with that. Fortunately, he'd found her before her luck had run out. If it hadn't been for her slips, it would have taken longer, but making friends in Singapore had been her first error. Emma Whyte was in a morgue because of her association with Erin Kelley Argon. It wasn't a pretty fact, but it was one that separated the professional from the amateur. A professional never would have made that mistake.

"Ten million," Tenuk hissed under his breath. "That's a lot of money, and I imagine the ante could go up. Where the hell are the Anarchists getting that kind of money?"

Josh ran a thumb along the railing. They were alone in this far corner of the resort. No one could hear this conversation, and still he was reluctant to say. If Tenuk didn't know where the money was coming from, it wasn't up to him to fill in the gaps.

"Word has it that their reach has stretched into Europe," Tenuk said. He laced his fingers together, cracked his knuckles. He dropped his hands and shrugged his shoulders. "The trial should prove interesting."

Josh nodded. "An understatement."

"They're flush with money. We're having problems here, too."

"This trial could be a watershed."

"You hope," Tenuk said. "They're getting a stream of funding from somewhere, and with the leader about to go on trial, anything could happen. Any way you look at it, the authorities need to cut off the funds."

"Can't disagree." Josh nodded.

"This witness can put a stop to it all. If the Anarchists' leader is nailed for Enrique's murder…" Tenuk rubbed his chin. "The murder of a European billionaire provides that link, proof even, especially when the murderer was the leader of the Anarchists."

"She couldn't have got caught up with worse," Josh agreed.

"The change of name was smart, but the ability to acquire a Canadian passport was a fortuitous stroke of luck on her part," Tenuk said thoughtfully.

"Unfortunately, the smokescreen wasn't deep enough. She's run out of time."

"Yeah, true enough. She's an amateur who didn't know she needed to change her skin more than once." Tenuk shifted and turned around to look into the jungle. "So far it's all clear. Not sure how long this window will stay open." He swung back around. "The killer running gave her some breathing space. I suppose it really gave the Anarchists room, as well. They weren't feeling any heat." He chuckled at his own joke. "Never suspected she'd left the States, did they?"

"Nope," Josh agreed.

"And now they have. I don't envy your job," Tenuk said. "A biker gang and your own FBI both desperate to find her. And you, man, where does that put you?"

Right in the middle, Josh thought. "On the firing line," he said as he turned away, his mouth a straight line as he gazed into the seemingly impermeable jungle.

"But I suspect that's where you like to be."

"And you don't?" Josh replied flatly, his attention shifting back to Tenuk.

"I suppose." Tenuk shrugged.

"Is the plane ready?"

"Plane?"

"Today, tomorrow and then out. Enough time to gain her trust, although earlier would be better. Considering how she is, what she knows, that might not be possible."

Tenuk looked pained. "This is the first I'm hearing of it."

"Nothing was arranged." There was a flat edge to his words and his mind ran through the ramifications of the oversight. "Vern was going to handle it."

"You're sure?"

He hadn't followed up. There hadn't been time. He

began to rework the possibilities. They couldn't stay any longer. He'd get in touch with Vern immediately. Too much time here was risky. "What's the word from Georgetown?"

"The disappearance of a local teacher and the explosion has made news." Tenuk pushed back from the railing. "That doesn't give you, or us, much time. There's a lot of money up for grabs." He rubbed his thumb against his chin. "Another mistake like the last and she's dead. Getting too close to people and then the car…" He shook his head. "She's lucky."

Josh couldn't disagree with that. But he understood what she'd done and why she'd done it, too. The need for stability, a place to call home—the need to blend. But she had blended too well. She'd blended right into sight.

Chapter Eight

Josh looked at his watch.

Six o'clock. They'd landed over two hours ago and he was now established in a room three doors from hers.

Dinnertime.

He pushed the empty bag of peanuts aside and stood up. Outside there was silence. He sat back down.

His mind shifted to the faulty intelligence that had brought her to this point.

There'd been a spotty internet trail. Other than a few communications out of a Thai resort four months ago that unfortunately for Emma Whyte had led to Singapore, there had been nothing. Only silence. But it had been enough to give him a direction and a continent: Asia.

"You're on your last legs," he murmured.

He put on the glasses and pulled on the baseball cap emblazoned with the words Mulu Caves. He angled the hat, tipping it slightly back from his face.

He grabbed what they called a man-purse or satchel. To him it was a purse, a distasteful and currently useful accessory. He slung it over his shoulder. He glanced in the mirror. If one didn't look at his buff arms or notice his tan, and if he kept his lips softened to detract from the hard line of his chin, he could pass as a typical tourist. No threat.

There was the distinct click of a door being opened. He

glanced at the monitor strapped to his wrist. It looked like a regular watch but it was far from that. It could function as speakers for a listening device, act as a GPS and still tell time. It also could be programmed for myriad other things, which he hadn't had time to configure before he'd been on the road for this assignment.

He stood up, gave her a minute or two to get a jump on him, and then opened the door. The heat of the afternoon had shifted to a muggy feel, and the earthy smell of rain permeated the air. But the rain was only a fine mist, warm and balmy. He began a leisurely walk along the wooden decking that bordered the cottages and fed them all into the main areas of the resort.

He turned the corner at the end of the line of cottages just as she entered the dining room. He took his time, looking here and there, running a finger along the wooden railway and all the time covertly watching.

Josh frowned as he reassessed the dining area for the second time that day. Natural light spilled in through a bank of windows that lined every side of the rectangular building. If there were trouble, there was little to no protection there. His hand went to the collar on his golf shirt and he adjusted one lapel so that it stood up slightly. The material clung in the heat and itched uncomfortably. The glasses slid and he pushed them back up with his thumb.

He reached for the door, gave the glass plate a push just as a shadow passed behind him.

Josh spun around, dropping his hand and touching the handle of his gun.

There was no one there. Yet someone had been. He'd felt it with an instinct that was rarely wrong.

There was movement to his left.

He shifted, turning sideways, presenting a smaller target as he scanned the resort. Four older couples in the distance, standing around—probably having a conversation about what they were going to do tomorrow.

Not the problem. He'd seen them come in.

His gaze went to where two men were talking, their voices raised and slightly slurred.

Something shifted again and seemed to move in the rapidly dwindling light. It was in the forest that bracketed this raised resort. That was where the trouble was, where he had always known it would be. He just hadn't expected it so soon.

Branches bent and twisted as a nearby tree shifted in a slight breeze. He eased forward, ready to confront, ready to—

A woman screamed.

He swung around and saw the same three backpackers he'd seen earlier, twentysomethings who were staying at the resort tonight. Tenuk had told him it was a one-night splurge. They weren't the problem. He could see that in the freeze frame in which they stood, as they turned startled faces in the direction of the scream.

He dropped his hand and headed toward the group and the origin of the scream.

"I've got this." It was Tenuk. His hand rested briefly on his arm, staying him. "I think I have an idea what the problem is. Nothing serious. Go have supper."

Josh watched Tenuk disappear among the backpackers, who seemed to overwhelm him in size and appeared as though they could easily overpower him. That was if Tenuk were a man of ordinary means, but as a member of Malaysian Special Forces he could take down a man or two with ease, just using his hands.

He stood there for a minute, a frown on his face as the backpackers scattered and he had a clear view as Tenuk spoke to the screaming woman and gestured to the ground. Even in the gathering dusk, Josh could see the problem. It was now clear that the scream had been nothing but the woman coming in unexpected contact with the resort's mascot—a foot-long gecko.

Tenuk. He'd appeared out of nowhere. As if he'd been watching Josh.

He stood there for a minute, maybe two, just watching—thinking, gathering information.

Finally, he turned and strode the short distance to the dining room. He opened the door and entered the large space. The windows he had noticed earlier ran the length of two walls and seemed to frame the second exit on the far side of the room. Tropical trees filled the northeast and southwest corners. The room was over half-full, and he noted approvingly that Erin had taken a seat by one of the potted plants, nearest the exit, as well as the kitchen.

He folded his hands behind his back and scanned the room, checking out each of the occupants, hoping the image he presented was that of a regular diner scouting out a table.

At the opposite corner and farthest away was a sixty-ish couple, leaning forward and deep in conversation, a bottle of wine listing in a wine bucket beside them. To the right and fifteen feet away was the couple he'd watched check in not two hours ago. They chatted with another couple, who appeared to be in their midforties and whom he'd already filed as nonthreatening. In the center was a family with two small children. The woman had vibrant red hair that he'd noticed the moment he'd entered. It was like a beacon—that and her laugh. He frowned. Children were dangerous in a situation such as this. They were wild cards that could become a danger to themselves and to everyone around them. Closer and to his right was another couple, Japanese; he'd heard that they were taking a vacation from their corporate jobs.

Erin looked up and smiled at him.

He smiled back and headed toward her.

"Hello," he said with what he hoped was an easygoing, guy-next-door smile. He glanced around, fidgeted and then smiled at her again. "Wow. It's a big place."

"It is," she said and put down her menu.

"I should find a seat," he said and started to turn and walk away.

C'mon, he thought, *work with me*.

Then he thought of something and turned back. "Have you been here long? I mean, have you ordered yet?" he asked, one hand on the back of the empty chair at a nearby table but his eyes were on her. He pulled out the chair and sat down at the table next to her.

"No, I haven't." Her eyes grazed over him, and she looked ready to say something before she looked away.

Instead, she leaned forward, her arms crossed and her elbows touching the table. She wasn't as thin as he'd thought. Her cleavage was deep and creamy smooth and… He drew his gaze away.

He picked up the menu and then put it down as the waiter stopped and asked what he'd like to drink. He ordered a Coke and then picked up the menu. He looked over at her. She was tapping a finger on the table.

"It's strange," he added, a note of hesitation in his voice. "I don't usually eat alone." He cleared his throat, kept his eyes on the menu even as he felt her eyes on him.

"Join me," she said.

He looked over at her, and she looked at him with a frown and less welcome in her face than her invitation justified.

"You don't mind?"

"No, of course not. I don't like eating alone. I imagine you don't, either."

"I don't." Actually, he did. He enjoyed being alone. His job demanded that he did.

"Your boyfriend's not joining you?" he asked.

"I…" She hesitated, glanced behind her and then straight at Josh.

Again he was caught, mesmerized, by the intense blue of her eyes. They were an identifying mark that pegged her immediately, a unique color that one could not fail to notice. He wondered why she hadn't obtained contacts to change the color. That fact sifted into a series of others as he noticed her hair was shorter than it had been even at the airport, shoulder length, blue black in the muted light. The wig was gone. He looked over her shoulder where a breeze seemed to move the umbrella tree whose branches hung wild and bushy near the exit. He looked away—it was nothing, no threat. He stood up and moved over to her table where he sat down across from her.

"He doesn't exist," he suggested softly as he set the menu down in front of him and looked seriously at her. He held up his hand. "I'm sorry, I didn't mean to imply…" He let the words trail off. "I just read in *Lonely Planet* of how in areas like this, young women were advised to pretend to be with a boyfriend. And I thought that maybe, that's what…"

She shook her head, looking slightly chagrined. "It's all right."

He leaned forward. "Smart move on your part." He leaned back and dropped his hands on the table, his posture open, nonthreatening. "A woman traveling alone is, especially in remote areas like this, not always wise."

"You're right and for the reason you just stated." But

even as she said it her lips thinned and she sat back, crossing her arms across her chest.

"Look, I didn't mean any offense."

"None taken. I'm on sabbatical and I've always wanted to see the caves." She shrugged, and he admired her ability to spin an off-the-cuff yarn. "None of my friends were into it, so I decided it's now or never."

"Can't say I blame you," he agreed. "I'm kind of a similar story. Just wanted a bit of adventure before winter sets in."

"Adventure," she repeated and it was as if she were turning the word over in her mind. "Yes, it is an adventure to travel to a place so remote. Most of my friends would never consider it."

"It's the perfect place." He almost grimaced at the word *perfect*. "At least from my limited experience. I'm from Coal City, Illinois. Well, that's where I grew up. You?"

"Toronto," she said softly, and he wasn't sure but he detected an edge to her voice.

"Toronto," he acknowledged. "Canada," he said with a hint of doubt in his voice. He was, after all, Josh, naive tourist, with little interest in much more than whether the Cubs would win this season and what he would choose for supper tonight on his first adventurous trip. She didn't need to know that not only did he know where Toronto was and how many miles it was from the American border, he could pinpoint every major and many minor cities in Canada and in more than a hundred other countries, as well. He also could tell her that Toronto was the fourth largest metropolis in North America and list the three that preceded it and a laundry list of those that followed.

His thoughts shifted.

Toronto.

It was brilliant. He'd thought that earlier. That the city

she'd flown out of to get to the first exit off the continent had become the one she declared as her home base. Not true, of course. He knew that she'd spent little more than the time it took to change transport before she had been on her way again.

He'd followed her trajectory from San Diego to Vancouver, Canada, where she'd arrived by bus, and then taken the train across that country before she'd taken another bus in a series of transfers out of Toronto to St. John's, Newfoundland. From there she'd taken a container ship halfway around the globe. He suspected at the time, as he still did now, that she had been making the trail as long and as distant from its source as she could. It was a logical assumption. Something an intelligent person would do, and Erin Kelley was definitely intelligent. She'd graduated high school at fifteen and a half, and finished a degree in education at nineteen. By the time she was twenty-three she had a Master's degree in education and a string of schools she'd substituted at. Fast forward six years and it brought them to this point.

"I've always wanted to go to Niagara Falls," he said. "Can't imagine what it would be like to have something like that right in the city. I imagine you'd go every day if you could."

"Not exactly in the city," she replied, and a dimple appeared in one cheek as she looked at him with an almost lighthearted look on her face.

"No?" he asked, feigning a boyish innocence combined with blatant geographical ignorance. The kind of person he deplored. "I thought it was only a taxi ride from the city center."

"Eighty miles southwest. And considering traffic around the city, well, it's not a relaxing ride. Definitely unaffordable by cab."

A crash came from the kitchen, the thud of something heavy hitting the floor. Josh schooled himself only to swing around in his chair when instinct would have had him lurching to his feet. Muffled curses and someone shouting, though he couldn't make out the words as the sound level had dropped, but they had a berating tone. Other diners were watching with animated interest to see who or what might emerge from the kitchen.

Erin was on her feet. Her face was taut, all color gone. She was closer to the edge than he had previously thought.

"Someone's supper hit the trash," the British man to their right said with a small laugh.

His gaze swept the room. Everyone else went back to their meals when nothing else happened. Josh kept one eye on Erin and one on the kitchen. He saw the back of the chef and the raised arms. Erin looked stricken, as if she would bolt at any second. He had to treat this seriously, secure the area, a big step in the trajectory of their relationship and gaining the trust he needed.

He placed his hand over hers. "Calamity in the kitchen," he said. "I'll go check. I paid my dues in a commercial kitchen as a teenager."

As he stood, he noticed her knuckles were white and he suspected that she didn't realize how tightly her hands gripped the edge of the table.

Relief seemed to flood her face even as her gaze flicked to the exit. She was staying on top of things. *Good girl,* he thought. *Keep your eyes on the exit at all times. But don't bolt—not yet.*

"It's nothing, I'm sure," he said. This was the first chance he'd had to place the thought in her head that he could protect her.

It was a big break and a big first step to being Erin Argon's boyfriend and getting her the hell out of here before everything broke loose.

Chapter Nine

Erin took a deep breath.

The only thing pinning her to the chair was the unwanted attention continuing to stand would draw to herself and, oddly, Josh's calm reaction. She'd pushed her chair slightly at an angle so she could see both the kitchen and the exit and took a series of deep breaths.

A string of words, what sounded from their inflection like curses of some kind, emanated from the kitchen. As the closest table to the kitchen, she got the benefit of the amplified kitchen noise. The rest of the diners had already lost interest. She leaned on her arms, her hands grasping her elbows, in an attempt to control her chattering nerves. She watched as the chef excitedly waved a wooden spoon and a smaller man said something that was so toned down as to be equally as incomprehensible. Her gaze shifted to Josh, who was in the middle saying something. But now it was difficult to hear. The only thing she knew for sure was that they weren't speaking English. And she only knew that from catching the odd word. Words she didn't understand.

She wondered how he knew what was being said and then realized he probably didn't. But it didn't matter. His manner was what was getting their attention. She'd noticed that about him, his calm presence that under normal circumstances she would have instinctively trusted. Except she'd learned over these past months to trust no one but Mike, who was now out of contact. She was on her own.

He shrugged as he came back. "Someone's dinner is going to be a little late. Steak burned. And the rest..." He shrugged. "On the floor."

"That's it?" she asked and was relieved that the tremor that had shot through her body since the first inkling of trouble was now silent.

"That's it," he agreed as he sat down. "Bit of competition between the chef and his help." Josh laughed. "Worse, he's from the Czech Republic and when he gets excited he reverts to his native tongue. I had to jump in, as all anyone understood was anger. Once I got through to him that he'd flipped languages and no one understood him..." He shrugged. "He switched to English and everything was good."

"You spoke to him in Czech? Is that what you're saying?" Surprise ran through her. It wasn't a common second language, at least not where she was from. "And you know that how?"

"Born there," he said easily. "First generation Czech, too young to remember the place, though. Folks left before I was even talking."

She hadn't expected that. Josh seemed solid, made at home geek, born in America. Now he was telling her he had a bit of an exotic past. Dark hair curled around his ears, and somehow she hadn't noticed the chiseled planes in his face or the sharp intelligence in his eyes. There had been so much about him that had been hidden by the ball cap and the dark, slightly unflattering glasses. Her heart raced momentarily considering what else she might have missed—who he was and his threat potential. She met his eyes head-on.

"You never went back?"

He shrugged. "Once. It's a long story and the history of the region is boring dinner talk."

"So you grew up in the United States, but…" She couldn't help staring at the new Josh. She looked away.

"But I speak Czech," he said easily. "You know how it is when your parents are from somewhere else." He laughed. "No, I suppose you don't." He shrugged. "They spoke Czech at home, to each other, so I got a pretty good handle on the language."

"Oh," she said. Darkness had settled around them. It seemed to draw long fingers into the room, meshing on the edges of the light, threatening to take over. She gave herself a small shake. Her imagination was in overdrive again.

But she couldn't seem to help it. She hated this time of day. It made her feel vulnerable somehow. Yet despite the jarring incident in the kitchen, the darkness and this morning's tragedy, she felt calmer than she'd felt all day.

He picked up the menu, held it for a minute as if he wanted to say something. His thumb tapped against the glossy cardboard, his fingernail white and well-manicured.

She supposed that went along with who he was, a citified man. A man whose closest brush with nature would be the boardwalk leading to the caves.

He opened the menu and glanced briefly over the top of it. "I'm not sure what to choose."

Her menu lay in front of her. She picked it up and opened it, glancing through the choices.

"The problem is I like everything that's on here." He lowered the menu and smiled at her.

She couldn't help but offer him a tentative smile back.

There was so little that was threatening about him, and she'd already deemed him a nonthreat, she reminded herself. She wouldn't be sitting here with him otherwise. And more than likely, considering who was after her, he would have liquefied her by now if that had been his plan. She shuddered. *Liquefy.* It was an outrageous word, a movie word—nothing more.

"Are you cold?"

"No, I'm fine. Thanks." She lowered the menu and looked at him, surprised for a moment at the knowing that lurked deep in his brown eyes. And just as quickly, that sense of knowledge was gone and his eyes hid nothing more intense than the smile he offered her.

Keep your distance.

"What made you come to Malaysia?" He set down the menu. "I mean alone. That must have been difficult."

You have no idea.

She'd hated being alone, and in Singapore she'd stumbled on a woman who had briefly become a friend: Emma. She'd enjoyed Emma's company in the short time she had been there and had been grateful for a place to stay. But when she'd left, she'd disappeared, leaving only a brief note. Nothing online, nothing traceable. She'd followed that rule, Mike's rule, to the letter. Georgetown was where she'd made her mistake. Tears pricked the backs of her eyes, and she willed them away with a mental effort that she'd honed these past months. Tears were counterproductive, and she hadn't cried since she'd crossed the US border, possibly for the last time. The back of her neck felt hot and her stomach tightened. She took a breath and fought for the feeling of normalcy, for the ability to project the illusion. This time, getting close would only be an illusion and she'd pull away before anything could happen. She wouldn't make that mistake again.

"I'm sorry," he said. "I've made you uncomfortable."

"No, it's all right. I've just had some bad news."

"Anything I can do?"

"No." She shook her head. "Nothing that won't re-solve itself."

"Good then," he said. "Man, I'm starved. Did you notice the special of the day? It might be a better alternative than this darn menu." He shook his head. "Never give a hun-gry man too many choices, not when they all look good."

"No, I..." She shook her head, relieved to change the subject. She hadn't really looked at the menu. She'd lifted it up, held it in front of her for enough minutes to have read it, but the truth was that she hadn't even given a thought to it. Less than eight hours ago a man had died in an explosion meant for her. She couldn't focus, couldn't get it out of her mind. She blinked. She had to stop thinking about it. For-ward was the only option. "I'm not particularly hungry."

"Pizza," he said with a smile.

She drew in a quiet breath and smiled.

"Would you like to share the standard, pepperoni, Ital-ian sausage—"

"Mushrooms," she finished and laughed. She hoped the laugh had sounded natural. But then she was hyper-critical of her acting ability, knowing what failure to put on a good act could mean.

"Mushrooms," he agreed. "Goes without saying. You're in?"

"Definitely. I'll share, but nothing large unless you're hungry."

"And a small salad," he added.

She nodded gratefully. She hadn't had pizza in months. Not that it hadn't been available, but she hadn't done more than go to school and return to her small apartment to eat and sleep before starting the routine again the next day.

She'd stayed low, stayed off the streets. That was until just a week ago when she'd begun to go out a little, lead a normal life, think the heat was off.

She'd been mistaken.

She looked up and met his straightforward, almost honest gaze. He was exactly as she'd originally judged him to be—safe. There didn't seem to be anything nefarious or dangerous about him.

She toyed with her napkin and then dropped it. She needed to take charge, take the lead.

"Have you booked any tours?" she asked as she set her menu aside. But before he could answer, the waiter was at their table requesting their orders.

"Medium pizza." Josh listed the ingredients. "And a Greek salad." Josh smiled at her. "Greek is good?"

"Of course," she said with more cheer in her voice than she was feeling. "How did you know?" The words slipped out. She drew in a breath. That was unacceptable and could lead to mistakes.

"Know what?"

"Which salad I like." She shook her head, giving herself a mental shake, as well. "Of course you didn't. That was a ridiculous thing to say."

"I'm sorry, I should have asked." Josh's lips pressed together and he cracked his knuckles as if overcome by a case of nerves.

"It's all right. No worries, really."

"Doesn't everyone like Greek?" Josh asked and there was a look of puzzlement on his face.

Geeky and safe, she thought with not so much emphasis on the first as there had been when she'd first seen him.

Instead, the word *safe* seemed to ring in her mind, and for once in her long flight she had the odd sense of coming home.

DESPITE WHAT JOSH thought of the actions that had brought Erin to this place, there was something that drew her to him. Maybe it was the self-deprecating smile on her face that he found sexy or her lips that were full and beautifully kissable.

He shouldn't be thinking about her like that, like anything but an assignment. But it had been a long time since he'd been in a relationship that was anything but a one-night stand. This assignment had ridden tight on the back of another that had taken him through central Europe. There had been no thought or time for women or clandestine affairs. There was no time for such now.

A look behind him confirmed that the older couple to their left and one table behind were finishing their desert. The accent in their voices, mannerisms and the bits of conversation he caught indicated that they came from northern England. The man had a pallid look to him but a strong jaw line that spoke of someone who could be relied on in a pinch. He watched as they spoke and how they gestured. Married, he guessed with accuracy that rarely failed. Longstanding, he also suspected from the way they sat in long, easy moments of silence. To his right, two men were focused only on each other, and as he watched, one's hand covered the others. They had been the ones with the ultra-conservative luggage and now their conversation was intense, every look, every movement, focused on each other. He'd ruled them out earlier as no threat.

"Were you planning to go to the caves tomorrow?" he asked, turning his attention back to her.

"I suppose," she said. "No." She shook her head with a smile. "Definitely. Why else would I be here? I'm sorry. I was distracted." She threaded the fingers of one hand through those of the other.

You're not too sure about any trip, because that's not why you're here.

Her thinly arched brows met slightly closer together as she turned her attention back to him. The eyebrows were only part of her disguise but an effective part. Past girlfriends and keen observation had him recognizing a cosmetically altered brow. It was an obvious attempt to make the natural arch of her brows into something else.

She leaned forward, her body language encouraging him, and he knew immediately that her thoughts were aligning with his. She was setting him up to be the temporary boyfriend, the smokescreen, taking her out of the role of single woman traveling alone. It was all becoming too easy. Of course, this could all be the proverbial calm before the storm.

"Shall we?" he asked as he slid the payment folder to the center of the table.

"I really wish you'd let me…"

"Gentleman's prerogative," he said with a slightly suggestive smile.

Ten minutes later they were at her door. He bent down, meaning to give her a friendly kiss on the cheek. Instead, she put her hands lightly on his shoulders and turned her head, kissing him full on the lips—a closed-mouth kiss but a kiss just the same.

"Good night, Josh," she whispered as she turned and unlocked the door.

Bravo, he thought. She'd taken charge of the situation, stepped in and made the first move, placing him in position to be the boyfriend she needed. It was a brilliant strategy and damn fine work for an amateur. And he tried not to think of how much willpower it had taken not to do more than just kiss her. He had been tempted like he hadn't in a very long time. He imagined what she would taste like, what her curves would feel like against him instead of the teasing brush that had been reality.

Instead, he continued to pretend he was a naive tourist and whispered, "Good night," before turning and heading back the way they had come.

Chapter Ten

The rock gleamed, stark and impenetrable by the light of Josh's flashlight. It was just before midnight and his watch alarm would rouse him to announce the beginning of a new day in less than five hours.

For a second he took in the caves through the eyes of a tourist. Clearwater Cave, at over one hundred miles in explored length, was once thought to be the longest cave in the world. The sheer grandeur of nature's beauty carved in rock was awe inspiring even at midnight by the light of a flashlight. But natural beauty and inspiration were not what he was looking for.

"I hope to hell this is all redundant information," he muttered. So far he'd marked off the pathway, checked out both Deer and Wind Caves with the intent of ending this night's tour here, at the one cave that could circumvent trouble better than either the walkway—too visible—or the jungle—too impenetrable.

The mouth of Clearwater Cave loomed large, a hollowed black monolith that was intimidating by the light of day, never mind against the backdrop of the night sky. The system went on for miles with individual caves linking up to others giving the illusion of a singular cave. While he'd been here before on another assignment more than four years ago, he had only explored these caves virtually.

The assignment had been over within hours, the targets easily disposed of.

The light grazed the rough rock, gray-brown and dense with the wear of time. Like the two caves that had come before, this one had walkways that made it easy for the amateur to explore with the added safety of a guide. What would make escape more difficult were all the places off the walkway, the nooks and crannies that could hide a killer.

In other circumstances he would be impressed by the magnitude of it all. The cave was as massive and awe inspiring as the brochure had promised. He shone his flashlight into the dark depths, but the light couldn't touch the outer reaches of the cave. It was that large. He returned the light to the walkway. He skimmed a hand along the rail that kept the tourists safely away from the vast middle of the cave where rough rock outcroppings and stalagmites made exploration treacherous.

A snake slithered along the railing. The flood of light had disturbed its nighttime hunt, and its slim length gleamed an eerie blue black in the artificial light. Josh pushed forward, ignoring the cave-racer snake, a nonpoisonous variety that fed mostly on bats. The information rattled through his mind even as he passed the reptile. The only snakes he was interested in were those of the warm-blooded variety.

His flashlight skirted over the walls where insects crawled through crevices. Other creatures hid there, as well, but nowhere that his light hit was there a crevice large enough to hide a man. The light swept the walkway and across into the main part of the cave where stalagmites and craters peppered the cave floor, which was slick with bat guano. It was there where the danger would hide, and it was also there where they could escape if need be.

He needed a handle on all exit points no matter how difficult an exit it might prove. The only thing he didn't plan to check was walking out. For that would involve getting through thick jungle and climbing limestone cliffs. It was an arduous trip that only the fittest would attempt. It wasn't an option easily scouted, and it wasn't one he planned to take, not with a woman who had no experience rock climbing.

He bent down, grabbed the top of the railing and swung over. He landed with a small thump on the soft mat of the cave floor. The light continued to skim over time-smoothed rock, musty with the damp that had settled like a second skin. The dank blackness thickened and surrounded him as he stepped tentatively along the slick floor, the bat guano feet deep in places.

At the back of this cave was a river, one he hadn't needed to check out on the one previous visit, for that had been a different kind of assignment. The river was part of a convoluted underground water system that was thought to have created the caves. More important, it was a probable escape hatch. One he hoped they wouldn't need.

Ahead there was a deeper, impenetrable blackness, one that wasn't touched by the moonlit-streaked night that was faltering the farther he was from the entrance. The darkness seemed to draw tight around him, the silence continually broken by the squeaks of thousands of bats.

He slipped and caught his balance. The light shifted wildly, skirting across the rock.

"Damn it," he muttered through clenched teeth. He could easily lose his balance, slide and fall into what was basically a giant bat toilet. The smell, considering it all, wasn't bad. Instead, it was a dank, rich, slightly fetid scent. He'd smelled worse on other assignments in other places. Much worse. And for a second he remembered the spoils of war, and the horror of rotting corpses in the midst of insurgencies in poverty-ridden countries.

"Fifty," he muttered, counting off his steps. Each was approximately a two-foot advance into the cave. According to the map, the first access to the underground river would be a matter of following the wooden walkway along the perimeter of the cave.

He stopped and switched off the light. There was a different sound now, a feeling to the vast emptiness that hadn't been there before. He switched on the light and peered into the blackness. There was nothing beyond where the sliver of light from the flashlight splashed. He turned around. The entrance was more than one hundred feet back, where the last of the evening light had vanished. There the moon shone down and provided some light, some reprieve. The darkness, the hollow rock that held so much unseen life, all of it was a challenge that ran a sliver of fear along his backbone and made his whole being come alive.

"Sixty-three." He counted off his steps under his breath, his attention focused again on the immediate surroundings. The cave was off-limits this late at night. Tourists were to keep away from the caves at these hours. They were dangerous, and they'd all been given a copy of the rules, printed in tourist pamphlets and reiterated by resort staff. It had been clear from the beginning. People had died in these caves by not following the rules. It was the standard mantra, and it worked. The mass of people believed and followed rules, fearful of the consequences of noncompliance. It wasn't that people hadn't died, but the dangers were not as excessive or as common as tourists were led to believe. But it worked for the majority. Traveling in safe groups and staying at a safe resort was enough adventure for the average city dweller.

The darkness was changing slightly. There was a different feel to it. The light shone on what appeared to be a dip and a narrowing of the walls and an increased feel of dampness in the air.

He continued to count off his steps as the light skittered over a rock ledge that smoothed out into an odd-looking beach, minus the sand. Around him was the chilly dampness of a place that never saw the sun. Ahead of him was a calm, but he suspected deceptive, band of water. The river ran underground through much of this cave, except here where it opened up, skirting rock and eventually leading to the outside. Here, no bats shifted in the dark, only other creatures of the night, rats and other rodents, snakes and the insects that made their home along the rock banks of this strange cave river—all of them, for now, harmless.

The flashlight was waterproof, as was the knapsack on his back. He clipped the flashlight to a reinforced rope that hung around his neck, peeled off his jacket followed by his shirt and put them both into his knapsack. He hadn't been much of a swimmer until he'd joined the CIA and become a field agent; then it had become a necessary skill. He took a deep breath and cracked his knuckles.

One foot slipped into the water as his hand touched the ledge, and he took a deep breath before dropping into the river without another thought. Research had given him all the information he needed. The water closed around him and for a second a tremor of warning ran through him, for it felt like a trap.

He treaded water before taking a breath and heading into the murky unknown with long, powerful strokes. The water was invigorating, not chilly but not warm, either. He dived under, circumventing the rock that skimmed across the first stretch of the river and came up for breath ten feet away where the rock peeled back and only bracketed the sides of the river, closing in on either side, darker than the night that surrounded it, more ominous. For it was there that he could see the occasional gleam of the nocturnal cave dwellers' eyes as they watched and somehow seemed to monitor his progress.

The air changed as the river exited from the dank confines of the cave. It was a river where guides brought the more adventurous tourists to swim. A thrill he suspected for some. Water dripped from his hair and he shook his head, scattering droplets around him. He boosted himself over the ledge and stood up. It hadn't been an arduous swim, not for him. But the question was, could she do it? What he'd learned of her was that she'd had swimming lessons as a child, nothing much past beginner classes but enough to know the basics. So what kind of swimmer was she? He could take her clinging to his back if necessary, but would it be necessary?

He glanced at his watch—12:40 a.m.

His arm scraped against an outcropping of limestone. Water dripped into his eyes, and he pushed his hair back with splayed fingers. There was no indication of danger yet, but time was running out. Two special agents had arranged to meet them in Georgetown, and from there they would get her back to the States and placed in the witness protection program, leaving him to deal with the Anarchists' man or men, as it might be.

It was a good plan as such plans went, still untried and subject to variables they had yet to anticipate.

The evening air basked warmly around him, and he knew he'd be dry in minutes. And as he began the walk back to the resort, his thoughts were on Erin and the most difficult part of his assignment still ahead. There was little time and because of that a premium on establishing trust.

Chapter Eleven

Tuesday, October 13

"Thirty," Erin muttered through clenched teeth as she powered through another push-up. Full push-up, no woman's version. She'd graduated into the real thing over two months ago. Push-ups, sit-ups, running in place—now it was all part of her daily regimen.

The sun streaked through the window, the early morning rays already heating the little room as the fan twirled overhead. She thought about turning on the air conditioner as she stood up and looked at her watch: 5:30 a.m.

"You'd be an hour from getting up in the old days," she said and shook her head. "Talking to myself. When will that ever end?"

She turned her mind off distracting thoughts and instead concentrated on fifteen minutes of jogging in place.

Twenty minutes later she was untying her ponytail and reaching for the shower knob.

"Japan," she murmured. "That's far enough away." She put her hand under the water, checking the temperature. "Train for part of the way, maybe through Bangkok." She stepped into the shower. "English as a second language. Emma said everyone was doing it there, in Japan. I'd blend into a sea of Westerners." She grabbed the soap and hummed a tuneless verse, made up for all she knew. It didn't belong to a song she could think of.

Water sluiced down her body as she soaped and lathered and absently noticed how her curves were less full, firmer. Her soft, desk-formed body had transformed into an athlete's body, and despite the fact that it had been of necessity she was beginning to appreciate it.

She reached down and turned off the water.

"You have to stay focused," she reminded herself.

A bird whistled outside and then followed with a strange warble and the gecko that seemed to reside in her room continued its cricket-like chirp. Otherwise everything was quiet.

She looked out the window where she could see dense jungle on the other side of the walkway. With a second-from-the-end room, and the room beside her newly vacated, she had a privacy that the others did not. It was something she suspected could be advantageous to someone in her situation. She could easily run, hide in the jungle.

Dressed, she grabbed her bag and opened the door even as she took a deep, troubled breath. Leaves rustled and the S-path of a lizard imprinted on the thick foliage beneath the wooden walkway. Erin shivered. She disliked reptiles of any kind.

Soon she was in the hotel gift shop and five minutes later, she fingered a map she'd purchased there. It was a fairly decent map. If nothing else it showed the proximity of the Mulu caves in relation to the rest of Malaysia.

"Don't go anywhere without a back door, a way out." She whispered the words that Mike had emphasized again and again during the flurry of activity that had led to her flight. Thoughts of home and family overwhelmed her. She would be an aunt by now if Sarah had had the baby.

She pushed thoughts of home from her mind. Home distracted her and took her out of the moment. She became less observant and more vulnerable as a result. She'd learned that on a train through the Black Sea region in Russia when her pouch had almost gone missing. She'd closed her eyes at the wrong moment, drifted into a catnap with thoughts of home lulling her and only by chance had she awoken in time to stop the man attempting to cut her pouch free from her waist with a knife. She'd screamed and for the first time on her flight, drawn attention to herself. It was enough to have the man slink back to his seat as if nothing had happened. She'd huddled in hers and exited immediately at the next stop. Since then, she'd beefed up security on the pouch that carried everything of importance. A wire cord that couldn't be easily cut had replaced the leather one, and the pouch itself was now out of view, under her clothes.

"Erin!"

She turned as Josh flagged her down with a one-armed wave.

"You're a long way away. Daydreaming?" His voice had a teasing note.

"No, I'm fine. I was just…" Her fingers trembled. *Damn it*, she thought. *Get it together.*

"Erin?" He moved closer, and the faint scent of pine that might be shaving gel and fresh air wafted around her. She noticed the definition of his upper arm, like that of a man who worked out—one who was fit. She frowned but didn't move away.

"What's wrong?"

She tried to smile. "Nothing…"

Everything. I'm running. I'm alone and I'm terrified for my family, for myself.

The thoughts ran through her mind even as she wrestled them into submission.

"You're sure?" Concern played across his face.

"Yes. Just feeling a little down."

"Classic single traveler syndrome. Being alone, I mean. It can bum you out." His voice was low and smooth, self-assured like it hadn't been before.

Her palms were slick with sweat from the heat and something else that she refused to give credence to. She moved away, disconcerted. Everything about him was tough and toned. And all of that brought her up short.

His eyes were a cinnamon color and she was drawn to them like this was the first time she'd seen them. The sunlight glinted on a steel stud in his left ear.

Who was Josh Sedovich?

"Josh?" His name was tentative on her lips. He wasn't the geek he'd presented himself to be, that much was becoming clear. Or was it? Had her imagination just gone into overdrive? She'd had moments of this throughout the past five months. It was suspicion where in the end no suspicion was warranted. But it was better than the alternative—what had happened in Georgetown could never happen again. No one else must die because of her.

She clenched her fists, her nails digging deep. This was so hard. That was why in Georgetown it had been such a relief to strike up casual friendships.

Daniel.

"It wasn't your fault."

"What?" *What the heck? Was he reading her mind?*

"Whatever it is that's bothering you. It's not your fault."

She bit back a sigh of relief. Except that soon it would be common knowledge. Especially now that she had disappeared. Only she hadn't. She was registered under the name she'd used in Georgetown. She needed a new alias and she needed it soon.

Local teacher's car explodes.

The headline was as clear in her mind as if he had said it or as if the news line had flashed before her eyes. Her heart raced and she had to quell the urge to bolt.

Three days. It seemed like forever, and she could only hope that it was soon enough.

"So WHAT DO you do when you're not vacationing?" Erin asked that afternoon.

Josh looked at the worn tips of his hiking boots, boots that had seen many mountains. He'd hiked mountain trails and rock climbed and on one assignment he'd even parachuted from a plane. It was all part of the job.

"Civic administrator," he replied. It was a fairly dull career that no one tended to ask further questions about. "You?"

"I teach," she said as if that general term covered it all.

"If I were to guess I'd say grade school," he said with a smile. "You look like you'd be good with kids."

She looked at him, startled, and he wondered if he had pushed her too hard.

"Just a guess." He shrugged.

"You're right," she said softly. There was a note of pride in her voice. "I love kids," she said. "It's why I chose grade school education." She hesitated.

He smiled. It was an easy conversation that surprised him, as it had been unplanned. "The only kids I know are those of a good friend of mine. Suzette calls me the drop-in, spoil-them-to-death uncle." He shrugged. "They call me uncle even though I'm not."

"Sounds like you enjoy them."

"I do but I don't get them. Don't see enough kids, I

guess, to be able to relate. But they do seem to love me, at least from the way they scream and jump all over me when I arrive." He shrugged. "Could be the gifts I bring."

"I've always loved kids," Erin said softly.

"Is that regret I hear?"

"No, I... No, not really."

He sat down on the edge of a lounge chair. "What brought you here?"

"Teaching English as a second language," she said without hesitation. "I began the whole journey because of that and then unexpectedly got an opportunity to teach at a private primary school. It was a temporary fill-in." There was a tight set to her mouth and a sorrowful look in her eyes.

"So, planning to go home?"

Her lips tightened and pain seemed to dance briefly in her eyes before she met his with a dazzling smile. "I may travel for a bit first."

His eyes locked with hers. The startling sapphire blue held a hint of smoky mystery that hadn't been there before. He dropped his gaze and wished he hadn't stopped at the milky white skin where one collarbone pushed up against the delicate film of her blouse, and the rise of her breasts forced him to look away.

"Josh? I'm curious—the earring. Why the ace of spades?"

"A reminder," he said shortly, more shortly than he'd intended.

"Really," she said. "The ace of spades—the highest card in the deck and the death card. Interesting choice."

The highest card always wins, he thought. *Even over death.*

She smiled at him and placed a hand on his wrist. The touch was featherlight, and for a minute it was as if there was nothing else, only the two of them.

"I'm planning to go to Deer Cave and see the bats. Leaving at four. I imagine that will be enough time. I want to enjoy the hike, stop, take some pictures."

It took him a second to realize what she had said. His senses were still so full of her touch, her nearness.

She stood up.

"Alone?" *Not in this lifetime*, he thought grimly. He glanced at his watch. Sid Mylo had outsourced as he'd thought he would. Tenuk had just confirmed that at least one man in addition to Bobbie had arrived in Asia via Hong Kong. There was no word on Sid, and that was what worried him. They were still safe despite being stuck here longer than he'd planned. Tenuk had watches posted. Still, he wasn't taking a chance. She wouldn't be alone. Not that there wouldn't be other tourists. Strangers. It wouldn't happen. He was on her like glue.

"Want to come along?"

"I'd love to." He inwardly cringed at the use of the word *love*. It was not a word, except in the context of a relationship with a woman, that he would use to describe anything. It was a girly word that didn't fit into his world, but it fitted his current persona. He stood up. He admired the casual way in which she had thrown out the invitation. She was not as street blind as he had thought, but not nearly street savvy enough. At least her asking had saved him manipulating the invitation.

She rubbed her bottom lip with her tongue, an endearing habit that he noticed she did when she was out of her element. A habit that was not something forced or put on, and not something a professional should ever do. But she wasn't a professional.

For a moment, as the silence shrouded them, the jungle seemed to close in around them.

"I'll meet you here." She lifted her wrist and looked at

her watch. "In, say, an hour? I'd like to leave early, well before four even, take my time along the walk."

"Sounds good. Do you have a map?" The question was redundant—he had mapped and tracked the area, and the layout was clear in his mind, not to mention the walkway that was impossible to get lost on.

"Yes," she said. "No worries. I'm good with a map."

"Well, at least someone is," he said in his best Josh the Geek voice.

He watched her leave with a slight swing of her hips and realized for the first time that when this assignment was over he wasn't so sure he could just walk away without a second thought.

"Get it together, Sedovich," he muttered as the revolver tucked in the waistband of his pants pressed against his back, and his mind began to go over the intricate layout of the cave that contained the intriguing underground river.

His gaze followed her even as he made sure she wasn't aware of his vigilance. But the truth was that he wouldn't let her out of his sight.

Chapter Twelve

"This is amazing," Erin said as she snapped a picture an hour and a half later. "Josh?" She looked at him with a slight frown. "Can you believe this? Look." Her finger brushed along the wooden rail on the walkway within inches of a stick insect—its long, wood-like body was motionless as it seemed poised to wait and see what they might do next. She slipped a small disposable camera from her pocket and took a picture.

Fine lines bracketed her mouth. They hadn't been there in the pictures he had seen of her before her flight.

He pulled his gaze to her eyes where interest and something else sparked. They both knew what the something else was—fear, anxiety, the threat of death that haunted her.

"It is," he agreed and shadowed her as he pulled out the cheap camera he'd purchased in a market in Singapore.

"Special forces took out a man in Kuala Lumpur," Tenuk said as the morning sun cast a glare from behind.

"Dead?"

"Unfortunately," Tenuk said. *"No answers from a corpse and no word who or what might be following him."*

"Too close. I need to get her out of here. I've got to get hold of Wade."

"That might be exactly what they expect. Sit tight. Let's keep to the original plan for now.".

He shook his head. The conversation with Tenuk had only been this morning. He had rethought logistics but found Tenuk was right. The Malaysian Special Forces kill had taken the assassins back a step. He turned his attention to Erin and hurried to join her, but she was already heading up the walkway as if the Mulu bat cave was the most important tourist attraction that she would ever see.

"Hey, stop for a minute." He puffed as if the ten minutes of easy walking combined with an additional twenty minutes of power walking had exhausted him. "Slow down."

She stopped and turned around, one hand on her hip. But as their eyes met she looked suddenly confused, as though she wasn't sure who he was.

"Slow down?" She took a step toward him. "You're not out of breath. In fact, you don't sound strained at all despite the heat." She backtracked another few steps. "You must work out."

"I do." He hesitated. "When I have the chance."

"I suppose that explains it." But there was doubt in her voice as she wiped the sheen of sweat from her forehead.

He shrugged. "I've started running." Actually, he trained in heat—ran marathons in weather almost as hot as this. And hours at the gym made the mile they'd gone in ninety-degree heat nothing. He should have dabbed a bit of water from his water bottle on his forehead, given the illusion of sweat. It was a glaring error.

Damn, he thought. He'd been distracted. She'd distracted him. That had never happened before, and it couldn't happen now. But the line between feigning interest and having an interest seemed to be thinning despite his efforts.

They took their time for the next stretch of the walk-way. It was an easy walk, the earlier power walking unnecessary considering how much time she'd allowed. She had been pushing his limits, testing him, he suspected. And again, that had surprised him. There was more to her, more layers than he had expected.

And as he thought that she turned around, fixing him with those blue eyes of hers that made him think of other things, things that had no place between them.

"I don't think it's that much farther."

In fact, it wasn't. It was fifty yards straight ahead. It had been dark last night, but that and past experience told him everything he needed to know. There was a path in and out, but they could go farther if necessary, to another cave where their options of getting out increased in the form of the underground cavern he'd explored only last night. Not the best option but an exit strategy should it be needed.

"You're sure?" he asked as if none of those thoughts ran through his mind.

She waved a map, the typical over-glossed, underdetailed resort pamphlet.

"Erin."

"What?" She swung around to look at him.

She smiled in a way that in another life would have drawn him. He would have been all over getting to know her. But here the game they played was much more complicated.

His fingers brushed her shoulder and for a moment it felt as though the world stopped as electricity seemed to dance between them. She shivered beneath his touch, turning to face him, almost in slow motion. He ached to hold her, but a movement just over her left shoulder took that ache away. For a moment his breath stopped and his whole being stilled.

Silence beat between them as the plush rise of her breast pressed against his arm. He was aware of it like he was so many other details, but his full attention was focused on labeling the movement as danger or...

He drew in a quiet breath and pointed to his left, in the direction where the flattened grass in the shape of an S indicated the predator was nonhuman. It was a lizard.

They continued along the wooden walk. His senses were now in overdrive. The dense foliage was problematic, but he'd known that going in. The air was humid, thick like the plant-choked jungle that seemed to reach and tantalize and even tease. Anything could hide in there as the lizard had already proven.

Beneath the walkway was a land mine of natural threats. The giant lizards that weaved easily through the long grass, the insects that were oversized and loud and screeched from their green sanctuary while humans were confined to the resort's boardwalks for their own safety, he suspected, more than for the protection of the environment. He felt rather like an animal in a cage, except he was free to escape the boundaries of the wooden railing at any time and at his own peril.

He peered over the railing. The ground was more than ten feet down and lush with tall grass. When he tilted his head and looked up, vines wound around the trees, a green labyrinth of plant life. The jungle provided a screen, a screen that he didn't like.

He hurried to close the distance between them as she made her way determinedly along the path. And he thought again of how easily she became a tourist rather than a woman on the run. There had been only amateur acting in the background he'd been briefed on, yet she appeared to be acting very well.

As if to dispute that thought, she turned around and there was a look of panic in her eyes. "I've got to go back."

"Back?" He was puzzled. "But we're almost there."

"Claustrophobia," she said as she pushed past him. "I… The thought of a tight, enclosed space…" Her hands clenched, and he could see her knuckles were white. "I thought I could do this. It was so long ago when I planned this trip."

Claustrophobia? He questioned that immediately. Her voice sounded strained but not panicked, not the terror of a phobia. There had been no mention of that in any of the comprehensive research he'd received.

"Claustrophobia?" he repeated. "You're sure?"

"I… I just can't do it, Josh."

It didn't fit her profile, not the textbook version or the real. For the space of a few seconds he was stumped, and then realized what it was: loss of control—an environment that she couldn't choreograph.

"Excuse, excuse." A small man came up to them, his companion a few feet away. They'd been walking at a leisurely pace but now they were walking fast; he'd been monitoring their progress since he'd first become aware of them more than ten minutes ago. It had taken them that long to catch up.

He gritted his teeth. "Yes?" he asked with forced politeness.

"Can you read this, please?" The man held out a brochure similar to the one Erin carried.

No threat. He'd determined that hours ago, since their arrival. They'd arrived on the flight after theirs. They were a couple, five years married, celebrating an anniversary before returning to corporate jobs in Tokyo. The only issue was that they were tourists whose first language was Japanese. It had been Tenuk who had gotten that bit of information. Between the two of them they were cobbling together a profile on each of the guests.

He looked at the pamphlet they were holding.

"I speak English," the man explained. "Reading, not as well."

"What do you need?"

"When does Deer Cave close?"

Josh glanced through the pamphlet and immediately saw the problem. Despite a long and drawn out history and current facts, there were no times of viewing. It was obviously a printing screwup that the resort had failed to catch.

"The tours have stopped for today. We're on our own." He smiled at them. "The best show is still to come. The bats will emerge just before dusk." He glanced at the sky, saw that the sun had shifted and settled lower. "You can follow us if you'd like."

"Thank you," the man said solemnly. The woman again said nothing. Instead, she nervously bit her nails and stood in the shadows just behind the man's right shoulder. She seemed rather timid as if...

He watched the man put a hand on the nervous woman's arm, giving her a silent message, a warning maybe. Josh felt his whole body tense, prepared to defend, to interject. He watched for the woman's reaction.

Any sign of fear in her demeanor and he was prepared to jump in. His eyes met the woman's. Here was the moment of truth. Her gaze was soulful, her eyes a deep rich brown that held no fear and no hurt. Instead, she smiled, one that was tentative but not trembling.

She put her hand in the crook of the man's arm.

Josh blew out a breath. If there was one thing that could send him off the straight trajectory of a mission, it was a woman who wasn't being treated well. He had been raised by a mother who had fled that kind of abuse. At the time he'd been too young to do anything. But when he was older, he'd paid his father a visit and let him know exactly what he thought of him. While there'd been nothing physical, the last words he'd left his father had, in a way, been like blows.

His hand slipped into his pocket. He fingered the worn beads, a single earring, not even a pair. That was all he had left to remind him of the fragility of life.

"Josh?"

He swung around to find Erin beside him. He'd taken his eyes off her—lost track of her position. He blinked to clear his mind.

There was still panic in her eyes but it was muted by a look of determination that was accented in the thin line of her usually full lips. "I'm sorry. That was silly of me. I do want to see the bats. And the cave, too, but I suppose that will be tomorrow as tours are done for the day." The tremor in her voice wasn't put on.

He put a hand on her waist, half expecting her to brush it off. She didn't, and something felt right about his hand being there. They barely knew each other, were little more than strangers, yet they needed to be so much more. His touch moved from a light brushing of his fingers to something more solid. He could feel her firm, warm flesh beneath the thin blouse, the well-toned and slim lines that held not an inch of extra flesh, evidence of the physical toning she had done in these months of flight.

"Let's do this," she said. She moved a few inches away, and he was forced to drop his hand.

Behind them the couple spoke in excited undertones as they hurried behind them, and they all walked at a fast pace. They had ten minutes to make the final quarter mile hike to the observatory.

He adjusted his ball cap and took the rear.

Chapter Thirteen

This wasn't a good idea, Erin thought. Dusk was approaching and they were heading deeper into the jungle. It didn't matter that it was a quite civilized, wide wooden plank walkway that kept them away from the jungle's depths. It was still a place that was foreign, unknown. If anyone was following her, if someone had landed at the resort, then she was here, trapped.

Trapped.

What had compelled her to take this hike knowing the possibilities of what might happen? Whoever was after her would know by now that she hadn't died in the car explosion in Georgetown. Whoever was following her more than likely knew who had died and who she was.

How soon would they come after her?

It came to her as she fought off the tendrils of panic, that the jungle and the approaching dark provided cover both for the hunter and the hunted.

Where had she read that?

It didn't matter.

She glanced at Josh. She liked him. In another time or place he would be a friend. But that wasn't what surprised her. What surprised her was that she found herself attracted to him. That was an emotion that in her current circumstance she had no time for and one she had to ignore.

Despite feelings of friendship or the desire to get close, if the worst happened, she reminded herself she needed to run and not consider the rest, the others on this trail. She had to remember Sarah and what would happen if they knew what her sister had seen.

But there were others and she would endanger them.

She'd run. That thought played over and over in her mind.

But in Georgetown there'd been no choice, no survivors, no one to save.

Tears threatened, and she struggled to hold them off. Daniel.

He wouldn't leave her mind and that was right. It had been her fault. If she hadn't befriended him, hadn't gotten the car or loaned it to him...

If.

She took a deep breath. She had to remain focused. She folded her arms as, despite the heat, a chill seemed to drift through her.

"Are you okay?"

Josh was right beside her. She wasn't sure how he had gotten there, and that thought was disconcerting.

"Yes." But the word was drawn out, not said with any confidence. And there was something odd in the way he looked at her. As if he understood...

"It'll be fine," he said without hesitation. "No matter what else is going on in your life, this is the chance of a lifetime."

Something had changed. There was an innuendo in his voice, as if he knew what she was afraid of. Of course, that was ridiculous. No one knew, no one except those who wanted her dead and a few others.

He steadied her with one hand on her arm. His grip was gentle, yet she suspected she wouldn't be able to break it. This wasn't the geek Josh she was comfortable with. This man was different. He made her heart race and her palms sweat.

"The heat," she murmured. What was wrong with her? It wasn't the heat and it wasn't claustrophobia. But she couldn't seem to quell her reluctance to move forward, to go anywhere near this cave. But it wasn't just the cave that was giving her jitters. It was her inability to control her racing heart every time he came near.

She could feel him behind her now, hear the sound of his feet on the wood, smell the faint scent of soap and something tangy, unlike earlier, it was something she couldn't identify it was so subtle. It toyed with her senses and sent odd tingles down her spine. She looked out over the railing where trees and vines seemed to twist, mesh and weave together into one writhing mass, where the animals—mammals, reptiles and birds alike—weaved through the tangled world of plants. The jungle was never ending, bracketed only by the distant limestone spears that punctured all that green and offered more treasures to the adventurous hiker. They also offered another way in.

Something tight twisted in her gut.

A bang sounded to her left, and she jumped and bit back a scream.

Behind her the woman screamed and then silence abruptly followed. Erin realized they hadn't exchanged names. It seemed wrong and haunting, and they were strange thoughts to flit through her mind in the few seconds it took before Josh had a grip on her arm and pushed her behind him.

"What...?" She wanted to break free, wanted to run.

"Quiet," he commanded in a voice that again didn't mesh with the man she had come to know. As he stayed her with one hand, she suspected he would restrain her if she moved at all.

He scanned the area, his hand on his side, the other continuing to hold her back. She looked down and saw the hint of dull black metal, a gun. His shirt shifted and then there was nothing.

Ridiculous. She had imagined the whole thing, not the bang, but the gun. There was no reason for him to be armed. He was an administrator and a reluctant tourist. It was ludicrous to think anything else. Still, her mind went back to that moment even as she stayed behind him and felt oddly safe.

It was a full minute before he released her, turning around at the same time. "Another damn lizard and a snapped-off branch." He pointed to the swaying grass and a tree branch that was lying half against the tree and half on the forest floor. Beyond that was the S-shaped trail of trampled foliage left behind by a reptile that was deceptively fast for its size.

"Monitor most likely."

She swallowed heavily as she thought of the lizard that could grow to six feet or more and was common in the area.

"Erin?"

"I'm all right, really," she snapped and immediately regretted the edge to her voice. "Maybe I... I just need some water."

"Here." He handed her an unopened bottle.

"No, that's yours." She reached into her pack. Nothing. She'd forgotten to pack water. That was inexcusable; she couldn't afford to forget any more than she could afford to be unobservant.

"I have two. Just in case," he said with a smile, breaking into her thoughts.

She looked at him with a combination of surprise and gratitude. "You must have been a Boy Scout as a kid." She'd obviously imagined the gun. She needed to take a step back. His earring caught her eye—ace of spades. She was seeing danger everywhere.

"Something like that," he said easily.

She looked into his eyes and for an odd moment she felt a little less alone. She wanted to get out of here, but instead she took a step closer to him, as if he could protect her.

Ridiculous, she told herself. There was no knight in shining armor. It was just her. She was alone.

Two days.

That was the amount of time he had to hold this position. Keep her here and keep her safe before a plane arrived to get them out.

The resort plane was unfeasible. Public transport, especially by plane, was just that, public and not the option he wanted. They needed to go back the way they had come, and transferring flights to do it was not wise. His thoughts backtracked to the previous night.

"What the hell happened to our ride out?" Josh asked, the cheap cell small and slippery in his hand.

"Too chancy. They've infiltrated Kuala Lumpur. One man for sure who could take your transport out at the knees," Vern replied.

"Good to know," Josh said drily.

"Bad news, pal. I know. Here's what you need to know. Sid Mylo is in Bangkok and with his lead out of the picture, it's slowed him down. And taking the man in Kuala Lumpur is only a matter of time."

"Meantime, there's intelligence in Bangkok. He'll get answers," Josh replied, his grip tight on the cell.

"Maybe. But we've been feeding him some bad leads, too. Hopefully he's picking those up."

"Hopefully. And if he isn't?"

"Then you do what you're paid to do. Get her the hell out of there," Vern replied.

"Reassuring," Josh muttered and disconnected. There wasn't much else to say. Bangkok was too close and their ride out feeling too far away. Right now there weren't any other options.

That had all been last night and a million miles away, or so he wished.

"Josh. You're not listening." There was a note of condemnation in her voice.

"Beautiful, aren't they?" he said, his attention again on her as the first stream of bats began their early evening exit for feeding. The sky soon darkened with more and more bats as they emerged from the enormous cave that he knew could easily hold a 747.

His eyes went skyward as one hand rested lightly on her shoulder.

She didn't push his hand away; instead, her attention remained on the sky and the bats coming out of the cave in one awe-inspiring, massive cloud. He looked in that direction but what he thought of was how her skin was warm, how the jut of her shoulder teased his palm, how her skin might feel like silk. He let his attention stray only slightly before he reeled it in, keeping an eye on the movements around him while appearing to marvel at the sight that everyone else was enthralled with.

She was watching—appearing to watch, anyway, but he knew that her mind wasn't really there. He could feel it in the tense way she held herself. He would have liked to know what she was thinking. He assumed she was still fearful, still considering her options, still thinking about when she needed to bolt. What he knew for sure was that she was tense. He wanted to knead the soft skin and ease the tension from her.

He put his free hand over his eyes as if to get a better view. It was an amazing sight, but one he'd seen on a previous mission during which he'd killed two rogue former KGB agents. His familiarity with Malaysia was one of the reasons he'd been called on.

The wrinkle-lipped bats were a black mass. Their squeaking seemed to fill the evening sky. In a way it was oddly surreal. The cloud of bats made him feel as if he were a tourist like the others. He reached for her hand, tentatively brushing his palm against her fingers. She didn't flinch or pull her hand away. His index finger brushed against her thumb. She tensed, and he held his breath, hoping she'd allow that one bit of contact.

They stood watching wave after wave of bats exit the cave. Their wings seemed to chafe the evening sky, their squeals echoing hollowly around them.

"Unbelievable," she said when the last of the animals trailed from the cave. The Japanese couple smiled at them and chatted happily as they followed behind on the long hike back.

Thirty minutes later they were at the resort. In a way it had all been oddly anticlimactic.

Josh looked at his watch.

Time was slipping away.

Chapter Fourteen

Wednesday, October 14, Mulu

"I need a fly-in at exactly 19:00 hours, eight hours from now."

"You've made contact. Got her panting after you."

"Made contact," Josh said shortly. He didn't have time for Wade's chauvinistic and rather outdated humor, but Wade was from another generation and despite a youthful appearance, a few decades older than Josh's twenty-eight. That aside, Wade was his and Erin's ticket out of this place.

"You're okay?" Wade asked. "Haven't heard from you in months."

"Back-to-back assignments."

"Look, we'll talk after this. Get together. I've missed you, buddy."

"Sounds like a plan," Josh replied. He thought back to his conversation with Vern and what he'd learned and how it was not something to be shared with Wade. "I could use a few drinks, some laughs."

"Say no more."

Josh disconnected, thinking how much he missed just the friendship side of their relationship. Wade Gair had flown him in and out of hot spots since he'd first become a CIA operative. The two of them had trained together, military training first and then the more specialized training for the infiltration that their jobs demanded. Wade had been a latecomer to the CIA, arriving after a career in policing. In that time, and despite their age difference, they had become not just colleagues but friends.

His hand grazed the rail. It was muggy from the rain the previous night. The jungle was oddly quiet, which he found disturbing, almost ominous. A gecko skirted along the opposite railing and a multi-colored parrot-size bird stared at him from a nearby tree. He had no idea what kind of bird it was. He only knew that it was no threat and gorgeous. He scanned the area ahead. The pool was to his right, bracketed by lounge chairs and bordered by concrete. The rectangle of crystalline blue seemed to stretch endlessly. Empty, it was mesmerizingly still. A door shut on the main common area and a slight woman wearing the colorless dress of an employee came out carrying a tray. Again, no threat.

The click of a latch, and he turned but knew without a visual it was Erin.

She frowned when she saw him. There was something else in her look that had him pushing away from the railing, going to her.

"What's wrong?"

"I've looked everywhere. The common area, out here, everywhere…"

"Everywhere?" Had he lost his touch? How had she ended up out here without his knowledge? Without… There was no time for second-guessing. "What did you lose?"

"A picture." She hesitated as if she were going to say something else and then thought better of it.

"Picture?" His brows drew together. Considering everything that had happened to her, he couldn't comprehend the importance of one picture.

"My father. He died when I was young. I know it may sound silly, but I carry his picture with me." She hesitated. "I always have. And now it's gone." There was a haunted look in her eyes and a pallor to her face that made him realize that this was real, a fear unlike the case of claustrophobia-that-wasn't yesterday. Whatever it was that was attached to that picture was as real as her flight to Mulu. And, he realized, despite the gravity of her situation, in this moment possibly more important.

He thought of the beaded earring in his pocket. He'd carried it for five years now, almost since he'd first joined the CIA. A talisman that he'd admitted to no one and a reminder of his mother who'd died five years ago, the victim of a home invasion and brutal rape.

"Did you have it after the Deer Cave yesterday?"

"I'm not sure."

He glanced at his watch, although in a pinch he could approximate time by the position of the sun. There was no tour going to Deer Cave this morning and no tourists going on their own. He'd spoken to Tenuk and gotten a full account of the day's activities. A group of tourists was going with a guide to one of the farther caves. They'd left more than an hour ago. Since the resort wasn't at peak capacity, there were only a few left behind.

"I'm going to Deer Cave," she said with determination and as if she had read his mind. "I can't lose that picture."

"Erin, I don't think you—"

"That I should go there? Alone," she finished as if they were an old married couple. "It's okay, Josh. Broad daylight."

He pushed away from the railing. He didn't like the

idea of her heading anywhere alone, especially to one of the caves. It wouldn't happen.

"I have to go, Josh." And there was steel in her voice. "That picture is everything to me. There are no others."

"What do you mean? It's not digital? Scanned?"

She shook her head.

No others. Josh was flabbergasted. In this day of computers, that there wasn't a scanned picture on a disk drive somewhere was unfathomable.

"I have a copy on my computer, but this one..." She bit her lip again. "He gave it to me. He..."

He got it. Her father had touched it with his hands. And while that might seem overly sentimental to others, he could see the importance. He knew from his research that her father had died of a brain aneurysm when Erin was twelve.

He could see it was important enough for her to forget the danger that was so close, important enough for her to focus on the search rather than her plan to leave. The exit strategy was clear. He'd seen the map in her bag. Smart, using a physical map rather than relying on traceable technology. But her plan wouldn't happen. She'd be out of here before she took action into her own hands. By the end of today she'd know who he was and welcome his protection. It was a comforting thought, but one way or another she was leaving tonight. In the meantime, they were still in the clear. Tenuk had reported less than thirty minutes ago that his sources along the river had seen nothing. So he'd humor her on a mission that he could see was of high sentimental importance.

Within the past thirty minutes, the first plane of the day had landed as scheduled and before it landed a quick background check on all of them had brought up nothing but innocuous tourists—two Americans, both women and neither travelling together, a French single woman and a Malaysian couple with two kids. And the pilot had been doing this run for a long time, his skin swarthy from years of sun, his eyes hidden within the folds of skin that had wrinkled in late middle age. None of them was a threat, yet going back on this path was ill-advised despite the signs pointing otherwise. It wasn't facts he'd garnered but rather a gut reaction. He'd learned to trust gut reactions every bit as much, but how did he explain that to Erin. Truth at this point could damage the trust he'd already built between them.

"I often think if Dad hadn't died, my sister, Sarah…" She hesitated. "I'm sorry. You don't know her and now I'm burdening you with stupid family history."

"It's not stupid if it means something to you," he assured her. He knew she had booked a boat ticket tomorrow. There was no way she was leaving here by boat or any other means by herself. He had hours to reveal the truth and get her to buy in. He pushed the thoughts aside and smiled encouragingly. "Tell me."

"Sarah had a tough time growing up. She didn't fit. She was shy, introspective, different—and kids bullied her." She shook her head. "Look, I'm sorry. You don't know what I'm talking about and it's not relevant."

He merely nodded. He knew exactly who Sarah was. Four years younger than Erin and the reason she was on the run. There was nothing he didn't know about her, including that her sister was now in protective custody.

"If you want to talk about it," he ventured.

"No." She waved her hand. "I'm sorry. It's just… I have to find that picture."

Thirty minutes later they were back on the path heading to Deer Cave.

They didn't go far or fast. She moved slowly, her attention shifting from right to left and into the dense foliage that bracketed the path. He had never seen her so jumpy, not even on that first day after all the horror of the explosion. Even then, despite the haunted look in her eyes, she had projected a composure that he had admired. Now he could see the tension in the way her shoulders were set and in her silence. And it was not over men with guns and a death wish, but rather one simple photograph. In a way it was as oddly endearing as it was disconcerting.

"I can't lose it," she muttered, twisting her hands together.

His gaze swept the jungle, the walkway and her.

"Tell me about your father," he said as a way to disperse some of the tension. She was working herself into a state that threatened to be exhausting.

"I wasn't close to him," she said through tight lips.

That surprised him considering her reaction to the missing picture.

"I know." She laughed, a dry, humorless sound that sent a sliver of warning straight to his gut. "You're wondering, why am I in such a knot about this picture?" She stopped, stuffed her hands into the pockets of her shorts and looked somewhere past him, as if the answer were in the ever-changing yet never-changing jungle.

"He was your father. Understandable."

"I think it was because I missed so much. I never really knew him. He was on the road a good portion of my childhood." She pulled her hands from her pockets. "This is all irrelevant. We're wasting time. The tours begin in an hour. It won't be so easy to look at our leisure then."

"But if you don't find the picture you still have the memory."

She stopped and swung around. "Thanks, Josh." She hesitated. "For everything."

"I haven't done much—"

"You've done more than you know," she interrupted with a hand on his arm. Her touch was hot and connected in a way that he wanted to reciprocate, to touch her back, to press her against the railing, to…

He put his hands on her upper arms, pulling her closer.

She didn't stop him. Instead, there was an oddly puzzled look, a softer cast to her gaze.

His right hand cupped her cheek and his lips met hers. His tongue caressed the velvet skin, parting it as his hand moved downward, slipping along her ribs, flirting with the edge of her breast, imagining what it would be like to taste her there.

She moaned, and he pulled her closer, his crotch hard and tight against her belly, his arm around her waist, his tongue plundering her mouth.

Security.

Damn it, he thought.

"I'm sorry." He pushed her gently away, steadying her but putting distance between them with his arms.

She pulled away from him, stumbled back, her eyes confused and clouded.

"Sorry?" she asked, and her hand swept the curve of her waist and then dropped. "I… You're right. That shouldn't have happened."

"I hope this doesn't stand in the way of our friendship."

"No." She stumbled. "No. Of course not. I shouldn't have, either. I…I need to find that picture."

He took her hand. "C'mon, let's keep going."

It was minutes of silence, of him trailing her, watching her and watching the jungle around them before he spoke.

"Where are you going after here?" It was an inane question, but it was safe.

"I'm not sure," she said. Her eyes scanned the walk as

if the picture would miraculously appear in the middle of a path that had seen too many footprints since yesterday.

And from the tone of her voice he knew that she was sure.

It was almost time to reveal the truth. That her destination was not what she thought, and he was not who she believed.

Almost.

A ray of sun shone down and seemed not only blindingly bright but reminded him of their narrow time frame, how the morning was already aging out, and the situation that could heat up at any minute. He looked left, then right, his hand ready to grab his weapon at any time.

They were at the mouth of Deer Cave. The jungle was oddly quiet and the bats safe in their rooftop hollows, sleeping until the rush for feeding tonight. It seemed despite millions of breathing, sleeping bats, they were alone.

"I hate to say it, but that picture is more than likely lost."

"It can't be, Josh." She shook her head.

"You didn't go into this cave, so there's no point going in now." And despite his words and the hint that she had a choice, there was none. She wouldn't be entering that cave with or without him.

"You're right." She hugged her arms to her chest and looked so forlorn he almost took her into his arms without thought.

A crack broke the tension of his thoughts. The sound was foreign and unlike the sounds that he had heard in the time they had been at the resort. He tensed, prepared to act, to protect her.

One hand was on his gun, the other on her elbow.

There was a split second of silence and then a branch snapped hollowly as something shrieked in the heart of the forest. The crack was followed by a flash of light and an echo that volleyed in the brush, reverberating through the dense foliage that closed around them. A warning, a missed shot. He suspected the latter and dove into action.

"Get down!"

He had her around the waist, hitting the ground first and rolling with her. He lifted his head from where they lay flat to the wooden walkway. There was silence. Worse, he couldn't see through the thick canopy of long-leafed plants and tall grass that bordered the walkway and seemed to close in around them. They blocked any view he might have. He didn't know what view the shooter had.

Josh had his Glock in one hand. He silently indicated that she should remain where she was. Her eyes confirmed that she understood. She lay motionless, but he could feel her tension and knew she was poised to run.

He scanned the area, searching. The whisper of the jungle began to heat up and something shrilled again, as if warning of change, of danger deep in its depths.

He drew in a tense breath as he considered what that single shot had meant. Was it a warning or a way of drawing them out and off the path? It was all the data he had, and he had to make a decision. To remain on the wooden boardwalk was to remain in the open—a target. They had to get back to the resort, to safety.

His analysis was broken by another shot to the left, but seemingly distant enough that Josh suspected the shooter was firing at random. The odds were high that he didn't have a clear view of them, any more than they did of him. But the second shot was too close and within seconds of that shot, Josh had his arm around her and was again rolling along the wooden pathway to the right and toward a dip that took them closer to the jungle floor. With the shots coming from behind them, there was no way they could go back the way they came. They had to move ahead, and the nearby cave was no option.

He thought of the river in Clearwater Cave, a back entrance that could lead them to the resort and potentially to safety. Safety, that was, if he could keep the target unharmed and stop their pursuer.

He ran through the layout of the cave, the path and the suspected location of the shooter. They were far enough ahead, and the pathway angled for a few hundred feet in a way that would be to their advantage. And with the pursuer behind them, they were being pushed forward and that made forward the logical way to go. He couldn't judge the distance, but whoever it was, was well concealed by jungle.

He rose with a tight grip on her hand.

"Let's move."

He met resistance but he'd expected that and was ready to power through. He turned and with gritted teeth said, "Look, Erin, I know who you are."

"Who are you?" she whispered, her voice tight, almost strangled.

"CIA."

"No." The word was small and soft in the vastness of the jungle.

She seemed paralyzed with disbelief, fright—he wasn't sure which. He needed to pull her out of it. Shock her.

"They want you dead." He took her arm. "I'm here to make sure that doesn't happen."

She seemed unable to comprehend what he was saying. He went for a figurative slap.

"Emma is dead." He didn't have to qualify with a surname. Her look told him everything he needed to know. She knew who Emma was.

Her face went pale, paler than it had been only seconds before.

The words were shocking, but he knew she needed something to galvanize her into action. It was a brutal way for her to find out about the woman who had been an acquaintance—a friend, he suspected. But he didn't have time to use pretty words or soothe her shattered calm. He had to get her up and get them moving. They'd been discovered and they needed to get the hell out fast.

She pulled her hand free.

"Look," he gritted. "There's no time to offer proof. You have two choices. Trust me or..." He nodded his head backward where it was obvious only death waited.

She stood there almost rocking on her heels. He could see the indecision, the unwillingness to trust any further, and he didn't blame her.

It had been seconds really that she wavered, although it seemed longer. Suddenly, her indecision was gone. Now he no longer had to tug at her—she was moving alongside him, pushing ahead, running. They were moving along the boardwalk path that had once seemed so civilized, so harmless, so...

He could hear her breaths, heavy with an edge that bordered on labored. He had her running full-out.

One minute and then two; he knew it wasn't physical exhaustion that would take her down quickly but the emotional panic that overlaid it all. She wasn't trained to deal with a flight-or-fight moment, no matter how much she'd upped her exercise routine.

Four minutes in they rounded a familiar bend where the walkway's elevation lowered. His gaze cast down into the jungle, waiting for the break when the jungle met the path.

He stopped suddenly. They couldn't run forever. They

needed shelter, and that shelter was looming ahead of them in the sweating foliage of the rain forest.

"Are you okay?" he asked.

She nodded, panting, and in her glazed, fear-stricken eyes he saw, or maybe hoped he saw something that hadn't been there before—trust edged with a little desperation.

He went to ground, dropping to the wooden walkway, pulling her down beside him, their feet dangling over the rich vine-and-brush-layered jungle. Here it was a little less dense. And only a few feet away they could get lost. He would have to carefully follow the walkway above them.

They were on the other side from where the shot had come. They could hide as easily as their pursuer. He doubted if whoever was after them had any more jungle knowledge than he did. If it was Sid, he suspected from his notes on the man, less. But that aside the man was good and would make up for it in other areas.

"Jump!"

She nodded, and with that he pushed off, her hand firmly in his, her body aligned perfectly with his. They landed with a thump. He released her hand as he rolled and was immediately on his feet. He held out his hand; there was no hesitation as she gave him hers. He helped her to her feet and began to jog ahead to where the trees grew thicker, the foliage deeper, where they might be more hidden. Still, the noise of their movements couldn't be covered. Instead of the thud of hikers on wood, there was the rustle of brush being moved aside and a different sound to their footsteps. He looked up and could see the path directly to his right. The sun was screened by the walkway and shadows were thick in the foliage. But still it felt too open.

"This way," he hissed. "To Clearwater Cave," he said in answer to her unspoken question.

She didn't say anything, and he admired the fact that she instinctively knew to be silent, to keep up.

The cave was where he had the best chance of defending them and where they had the best chance of escape. But that cave was twenty minutes away on a walk. That time would be shortened by a run but through jungle and with her smaller steps and endurance, it was still a good distance away. Overhead there were only jungle sounds— a bird calling for a mate, the thud of a branch dropping to the forest floor—but behind them there was nothing.

It was over ten minutes before they stood below the cave and another minute before they had climbed the steps and were at the entrance of the cave. Behind them there had been silence more disturbing than the earlier gunshot.

He held her back with one arm around her waist.

A minute, two passed.

He nodded to her and they stepped into the damp coolness, the rustle of bats overhead and the feeling that they had entered another world.

He silently counted their steps as soon as they passed the entrance and the light began to fade. A generator sat at the entrance to provide light for the tours. It wasn't running. Instead, there was an uneasy stillness filled with the rustling of the creatures of the dark and the bats. Their presence was everywhere as the darkness closed in, as he and Erin moved away from the entrance and the light faded. He continued to count their steps.

Twenty.

Thirty-five.

Her palm was warm and trusting against his. Briefly, he wondered how much of that was illusion, his want of her trust, and how much was real. It didn't matter. He shifted his hand, taking a stronger grip on hers. The fetid scent of the other occupants of this cave was oddly comforting, as if the bats stood between them and danger.

Forty-five.

They were smaller steps than he had taken before. He'd factored that in the previous night—her steps weren't as large as his and he was already pushing her to her limits and about to ask for more.

Fifty.

Not far enough to be safe from gunfire but far enough to be out of sight in the shadowy darkness. He hugged them as close to the inside railing as they could get, she on the inside, near the rock, and he on the outside, where danger could lurk. He'd considered going directly to their area of least defense because it was also the one that cloaked them the best as no light reached there. But it meant going across the uncharted floor where the stalagmites made walking treacherous. That wasn't for her.

A shadow moved in the entrance that was now well behind them. Still, it was a light-filled beacon although the light no longer reached them.

Josh's hand went to the Glock. "Get down," he hissed. "And keep moving."

A shot rang out.

The small flashlight he carried had subtly marked their path not just for them but the killer who was following them. Another shot this time to his left.

He clicked off the beam.

A sliver of light cut through the darkness. It wasn't sunlight and it came from the entrance.

"Run!"

Chapter Fifteen

He could feel her eyes on him and sensed the fear vibrating from her. There was no time for comfort, for consoling. "Go." He tried to couch as much confidence as he could in his voice. If he could he would have taken her fear and eliminated it like he eventually would their pursuer.

"Stay on the walkway to the river," he said in a harsh whisper as he gave her a slight push and then moved forward, placing himself between her and whoever was after them. He could see a shadow at the entrance, the outline of a man. He lifted his Glock and shot—a warning more than anything.

The answering shots rang out—one, two, three. Josh counted them off so he could time as closely as possible the moment when a reload would be needed. And while he counted he turned and ran, following Erin, heading for the river and their escape.

Ten shots.

If he'd guessed right, there were five to seven bullets left depending on what kind of magazine the bastard had. His mind reeled with possibilities. He stopped, assessing the situation.

Nothing. Only silence.

He moved forward quietly now, waiting, listening. Then he deliberately kicked a rock that pitched forward landing hollowly somewhere ahead of him. Another shot. There were four to six left. He couldn't be sure. He scuffled his feet, not too much to create suspicion that this might be a diversion, but enough to focus the killer's attention on him rather than on Erin.

The silence was too long.

The bastard was reloading.

Erin was far enough ahead, out of range. He could hear her moving forward as he'd instructed, but he could no longer see her.

He leaned down, felt around for another rock, picked up one and then two. He threw one. The stone rattled in a hollow clatter just ahead of him and to his left as it bounced along the cave floor. He hit the ground as another shot fired in the direction of the rock he'd just thrown.

There was a deathly stillness that seemed strangely alive, as if the cave breathed around him.

He threw the second rock and began to move forward toward the river. There was an odd whirring like a faint clapping, seeming more distant than it was, as the bats were disturbed and a few began to fly around.

He bent down, jumping lightly off the walkway and to the floor of the cave. He moved carefully, quietly, picking his way along the treacherous floor, heading to the river and Erin.

He counted his steps, choreographing them to the night before. He was within fifty feet of the river. Already he could sense it by the increase in moisture in the air and that odd smell that wasn't quite as dank as the rest of the cave. He stopped, looked behind as something moved to his left.

A light flickered briefly but long enough for him to pinpoint their tracker. He fired. There was a thud, then the sound of something falling. He'd made contact. At least, he hoped he had.

Seconds ticked by and there was nothing, only a hollow emptiness, silence so deep that it had him silencing his own movements, listening and looking ahead for Erin.

Was whoever pursued them gravely injured?

Dead?

He moved forward as the cave floor smoothed out and the ceiling lowered. He couldn't see her. "Be there," he muttered and hoped that she hadn't veered off the path, that he hadn't missed her.

Where was she?

"Josh," she whispered very close to him.

He reached up toward the walkway, where he could see the dim glimmer of flesh. His fingers brushed against her hand. He could see the whites of her eyes in the dark, in the muted flare of his flashlight as he shone it through his sleeve. And what he saw looked stark and very afraid.

He gave her hand a gentle tug, felt her nod in understanding as she scooted to the edge of the walkway, dangled her legs over as he reached up and lifted her down. Behind them the silence was somehow more ominous than anything that had come before. He took her hand and they began to pick their way forward. The sound of water dripping overhead and the dank cool feel of the rock intensified as they came closer to the river. He squeezed her hand, trying to transfer courage to her or at the least trust in him. For what he was about to ask her to do, swim in the dark, and finally going underwater. Doing that might take all the courage she had.

Behind them, there were no shots and Josh wished there had been. Then at least he could have tracked the bastard, known if he was getting closer or had gotten lucky and killed him.

"Can you swim?" he asked.

"No. I took lessons, but…"

"No?" He stopped, and she bumped into him. Lessons. She should be able to swim. Irrelevant. She couldn't. He redirected his mind from the problem to the solution.

She clutched his hand so tightly that he thought he would lose feeling. "I can float, but…" Her voice shook.

Gently, he unpeeled her fingers from his. "I'll do the swimming for both of us."

Her breath was soft, hitching in the bleak darkness. Behind them a killer might still lurk and there was no time to bolster her courage. They had to get out of here, fear or not.

He took a breath, his mind checking off the options, the alternatives. There was none. There was only one thing to do.

He squeezed her hand as they turned around a large boulder, the final marker that told him they were there. His hand felt along now in the darkness. He flicked on his flashlight as they were now shielded from the entrance and from the killer by distance and the twists and turns they had taken to get here.

If his calculation was right, they would soon be within a few feet from where the cave floor opened up and the underground river began.

Around them the damp, dank walls seemed to almost breathe a collective sigh. Beside him, he could hear Erin's soft, almost hitching breathing. His hand went to her arm and in the process brushed the soft rise of her breast. He felt the rapid beat of her heart, and the warm, sweet scent that was distinctly her seemed to surround him. He couldn't help it—in this microsecond lull of safety, he pulled her tight against him, pressed his lips against hers. The kiss was hard and deep as his tongue explored her mouth, and she clung to him, her heart pounding against his. Behind him he could hear the steady drip of water, see nothing but darkness and smell the musty scent of water too long in an enclosed space.

He broke the kiss, his hands on her shoulder. "Hang on to me and don't let go no matter what happens."

He bent down and felt her hands on his shoulders and her legs close around his waist. "It's underwater. Take a deep breath when I tell you."

One minute was what he had timed for this first leg. An eternity for anyone who hadn't practiced holding their breath for any length of time, especially in a situation where fear made the body crave more oxygen. He ran a hand along her forearm. "Ready?"

"Ready."

He felt her draw in her breath and her slight weight press against his back. He took a breath. Turned and nodded to her before he jumped in with her clinging to his back.

The initial push into the water was more difficult than he'd thought. Suddenly her weight seemed heavier, more than he anticipated, and his shin scraped against rock. Pain sliced through him, stabbing up his leg, and he hoped it was nothing serious.

Water closed over his head as they went under.

The water was surprisingly warm as they sank. Warmer than he remembered it being the previous night. He began making powerful strokes, pushing them upward and forward. His lungs began to burn as they pushed toward the point where he knew that they would begin to ache for lack of oxygen. He hoped she could hang on until they broke the surface.

He counted seconds as he had done when he had run the first trial of this water escape. He allowed for an extra few seconds, knowing he was swimming slower with Erin on his back.

Twenty-one.

Twenty-two.

Twenty-three.

Water pressed heavily on him and now her weight seemed so light as not to be there. The only reassurance that she was still there was her arm that was around his neck and pressing so hard that it hurt. He reached up and brushed her forearm with his hand, a silent warning to change her grip. She shifted her arm, taking the pressure off his throat.

Twenty-four.

Twenty-five.

They were just beneath the surface now. He was within half a minute of reaching his endurance and that meant she was at the end of hers.

Thirty.

Thirty-one.

He'd mentally counted out forty when he forced them above the surface to where they were out of the main interior of the cave, into the quiet subsidiary that led through tight rock, another turn that was completely under the rock and then out into another cave area and finally close to the entrance of the resort and hopefully safety.

She gasped, her grip on him tight as he surfaced. He wanted to ask if she was okay, but he could only tentatively squeeze one hand and suck in a silent breath as he took long, sure strokes, floating and pushing forward in turns, as the water seemed to close in around them, insulating them from the danger that lurked behind. Ahead he could see light and hoped nothing was there to meet them or they would be screwed. His mind ran through the options.

His muscles screamed now with the extra weight. Swimming had never been his forte. She shifted, and he gritted his teeth, expecting her to lose her grip and slide off. He prepared for rescue. Instead, her grip tightened.

She was every bit as tenacious as he, he thought with an inward smile. They'd make it out. All he had to do was keep swimming. Behind them there was a disturbing silence filled only by the lap of water.

There was no going backward, no turning to face anyone. There was only escape in that slash of light ahead of him. From there he needed a plan and he kept swimming, his mind on a plan of action that would get her the hell out of here.

"Take a breath. We're going under one more time."

Her answer was a tightening of her grip on his shoulders.

"On three."

Water closed around them as tight and as urgent as his thoughts. He had to move fast, get to the resort and get her out. But two things stood in the way of that: the gunman behind him and the woman on his back. Of the two things, it was the woman he was most concerned about. A life-and-death matter was one thing, but when they emerged from this cave how would he convince her that he was the only way to safety?

Chapter Sixteen

Erin clung to his back, one hand now fisting his shirt, her other arm around his neck. Was she holding too tight? Would she choke him? Should she let go, and if she did would she drown? They were crazy thoughts, uncontrolled, and she couldn't stop them. The thoughts, the fear, all of it ran rampant through her.

Her eyes were pinched shut.

She was underwater, unable to breathe, unable to move, her only chance of survival, Josh.

Hair twisted across her face, covering her nose like a sheet of plastic wrap. Her cheeks puffed out like those of a blowfish. She was too terrified to release her grip on his shirt, or maybe it was his shoulder that her nails were now digging into, she didn't know. All she knew was that she wasn't letting go, ever.

She wanted to drag in air. Her lungs burned and fear made her want to breathe in the worst way.

Her hand gripped his shirt so hard that her fingers ached.

In the swirl of water that threatened to drown her the past flooded her mind as if it were more comfortable than the present and the reality that they could both die.

She could hear the taunts of the children.

That had been so long ago. She'd been eleven.

She could see her sister's frightened face.

She could feel her own fear that day.

"No," she'd screamed as she'd watched almost in slow motion. Water had nearly killed her sister. Those children had pushed her off the bridge. Pushed her sister into the river. She was back again, in that river, struggling to save her sister. Then, the only thing she'd had was luck on her side and a river with wide, shallow shoals along its banks.

She opened her eyes and reality flooded in. She squeezed them shut. Her lungs begged for air and she wrestled the fear that demanded she take a breath, underwater or not.

She shifted and found herself sliding. There was a moment of panic as the water seemed to pull at her, trying to tear her away before his hand reached back and steadied her.

She locked her ankles around his middle. Well-toned, hard, the impressions flitted through her mind as easily as the water ran over her skin, caressing it in an odd way, disturbingly cool and detached. Water ran slickly between his skin and hers, making her hold on him tenuous. She concentrated on hanging on, surviving this moment, getting out of the water and not getting shot. As for the rest... She needed a plan and, damn it, it appeared she might have run out of options. Her plan was him and clinging to him. This wasn't a plan. This was desperation.

They broke the surface and she struggled to draw air, gasping and fighting for control. Her lungs ached and she coughed, but her hold on him was almost unbreakable. He was swimming with slow, strong strokes, taking them away from the threat behind them.

"Hang on," he said in a hoarse whisper, as if that command were necessary, as if she would let go before he got them the hell out of this river.

To her right, not three feet away, was a ledge that seemed to slice through the water. It was narrow, she suspected too narrow for two. The entrance was close. She could see light maybe twenty feet ahead. Water still stood between them and the exit, and for a moment they seemed to bob in a swirl of current that came out of nowhere. Water lapped over her face, and she choked, fought to bite back a cough that might alert whoever was pursuing them of their presence.

Her pursuer.

A tremor ran through her at the unnecessary reminder.

"Grab the ledge. Can you get it?" he asked, breaking into her thoughts.

Her hand reached out. Her fingers shook. She took a breath. There was no time for hesitation. She felt slick rock. She wouldn't be able to hold on. She…

"Use me as a float."

Not following his instruction wasn't a choice; surviving was. She couldn't think. She reached out. Her heart hammered.

She couldn't do this.

She was starting to slide and there was only one place to go—under.

Then her hands were on the ledge, she was half-off his back. It felt as if a quarter of her body lay on the ledge, and her fingernails clawed rock, while the weight of her body threatened to drag her back down into the darkness, into the river alone—without Josh.

Where was he?

"Josh." She wanted to yell. Instead, it was only a terrified whisper as she was shoved from beneath, pushed, hands on her butt pushing her up and…

She managed to get a grip on the edge of rock and pulled herself the remainder of the way out of the water finally, scrambling, trying to push her legs over the ledge, and within seconds she was there. The slick rock was cool beneath her wet clothes. Her heart hammered, and she searched the water. There was no one, he was...

Gone!

"Damn, Josh..." She wanted to scream his name, as the terror of what and who pursued her beat down on her, hard, relentless and deadly in the darkness.

She was terrified for herself, for him. She couldn't go back into that water, not alone.

Had he drowned?

Left her?

She almost choked on her fear.

Then he broke the surface. She could see him faintly, the outline, the idea of him. Her heart hammered in a way it never had before. She had been afraid like she'd never been before.

She took a deep breath as he reached up and pulled himself out of the water, landing with an odd thump on the ledge beside her.

She thought he'd disappeared, left—worse, drowned—and she was alone. It frightened her like nothing in the months of flight from the Anarchists had. She'd feared for his safety, for his life. And for the first time she'd feared that she couldn't do this alone.

A shiver raced through her.

"Erin." His finger trailed softly, reassuringly along her cheek. He flicked on the flashlight, illuminating her face and lifting the shadows from his eyes.

She clutched her arms beneath her breasts and looked away from him. She scanned the area for where they would go next. Another shiver shook her. Ahead was the pool where many tourists often ended their tour of the caves. At least that's what he had said. Everything she knew about how to get out of here was what Josh had said.

She'd never felt so helpless, so dependent. She took in a quick gulping breath and squeezed her hands into fists. She unlocked her hands, biting back another shiver.

He stood up, water dripping from his hair and from his clothing, and his presence seemed to fill the narrow ledge. He held out his hand.

She didn't take it, not immediately. The truth was she couldn't stand. Her legs were shaking too much. She willed the shaking to stop. But just thinking it, just taking a deep breath didn't steady her nerves, not that quickly and they didn't have time. She knew that.

"We've got to keep going," he said in that short, decisive way that was nothing like the Josh of their initial meetings. "Details later."

She nodded.

This was a man not used to being ignored. This was a man used to being in charge.

Josh was no tourist. He'd made that quite clear. But the question that threatened her very safety was what did he want? The only thing that was clear was that in the moment he wanted her alive.

Alive was what she'd fought for all these months. She took the hand Josh offered and for the moment, for as long as it was necessary, she gave him her trust.

Chapter Seventeen

The cave was directly behind them and a pool of water in front. The sun was blinding after the darkness of the cave and the blackness of the underground river. Now they stood poised on a rock ledge fifteen feet up and faced more water.

"Jump," he ordered.

Despite the command, he knew she couldn't, not immediately. She was faced with two terrifying options—potential death behind them and the fear of water, and its association with death, in front of her. He could feel the fear and doubt and see that she was frozen. It was a normal reaction, instinctive—the will to survive. But she had no choice. The grip on her hand told her so. He tried to communicate everything he couldn't say into that palm-to-palm connection. He squeezed her hand once, looked at her and said, "You can do this. One, two…"

"Three."

The counting was what kept him focused, grounded and he hoped it did the same for her. It was a fleeting thought as they were in the air on three, leaping from the ledge that skirted a small opening from the cave into a pool of water, crystal clear and cool. Again, water closed over their heads. He could feel her fingernails biting into the back of his hand. He squeezed her hand, his other arm pushing them back up.

They broke the surface. His hand still had an iron grip on hers as he turned to face her, one arm holding her up, the other treading water. Her face was red as she fought not to gasp for air, trying to remain silent, aware that there was still a threat somewhere behind them.

He wiped a drop of water from his brow and then traced a finger gently down her cheek.

"That man…" she began and she shivered despite the warm evening air.

He knew she was biting back panic, and still he slammed her with the truth.

"Dead," he said bluntly. Although for the flight through the river he'd maintained a belief that they were still being followed, known the possibility existed and pushed himself because of it, now there was no reason to believe so. There would have been more shots if the man weren't dead. Instead, there had been silence for too many minutes. And prior there'd been an odd thud, the sound of a body falling, hard to confuse with anything else.

She nodded, her teeth worrying her bottom lip. The water lapped at their waists as they waded out. As she stepped out of the water, he let go of her hand.

"We'll circumvent the resort, go in off the trail. Go to my room. It's the safest right now," he said.

"Is it true?" She hesitated, her face almost pained. "What you said? That you're CIA?"

He knew that his silence was all the answer she needed.

Her face seemed to lose color. If she had been pale before, her face was a death mask now. It was as if every bit of emotion, of life, had been sucked out of her.

"I'm here to take you home," he added in case that hadn't been clear.

She shook her head violently and took a stumbling step back.

He reached out to her, and she knocked his hand away, her wet hair swinging across her cheek and making an odd slapping sound.

"The Anarchists won't touch you. You're safe. You'll be in protective custody."

"No!"

"I'm afraid you don't understand, Erin. You don't have a choice."

"I'm under arrest?"

"No, of course not. But you're not free to go, either. I'll accompany you the whole way." He held her gaze. "Let me get you out of Mulu." He stepped back from the reality of the rest of where he was taking her. "I know you have plans, but the river is not safe."

Surprise was in her eyes and in the lift of her brow.

"The man who was tracking you wasn't their best." He shook his head. "And there's someone else, another assassin en route."

"More than one… Oh, my God." She squatted down, defeated.

He suspected her legs were unable to hold her and he felt for her. She was one small woman, untrained in this kind of thing, with men after her who were able to track and take out the most skilled individuals.

"I can't do this. There's no place where they won't find me."

"There's one place," he replied.

"Where?"

He held out his hand. "With me."

She looked up at him and gave him a single nod of her head and, he suspected, all the trust she had in that moment.

She gave him her hand.

If her trust wouldn't last beyond getting her out of Mulu, he'd face that later. In the meantime, he wasn't sure how much he trusted her new resolve. He definitely wasn't releasing her hand. He'd learned a long time ago not to trust any of his assignments. And that was all she was, an assignment. And if he told himself that often enough, he hoped it might be true.

"Josh!"

Her cry had him immediately on guard as he instinctively looked up.

Maybe forty feet away and twenty feet up, metal glinted in the light that dodged through the trees and it was clear that an armed man stood on the ledge. He stood slightly to the side, protected by the nondescript rock that hung into the jungle's vast reach. Josh registered size, hair color and matched him to a previous glimpse he'd gotten of their pursuer as his hand reached for his gun and his other pushed Erin behind him.

One shot and then two, the man dropped, his gun clattered partway down the rocks.

"Dead?" a small voice asked behind him.

"Dead," he confirmed as he spun her around. "Let's get out of here."

But only a few minutes into the hike that would take them back to the resort, she stopped, and he suspected she might be at her limit. They were alone except for the virulent life that hid in the jungle surrounding them.

"He's dead," she whispered. "Were there two?"

"No." He'd made a mistake. He'd thought he'd killed him once; he'd been wrong. His right hand clenched into a fist.

Unacceptable.

"Same man. He wasn't dead. He is now."

Tentatively, he touched her arm, the bare skin like velvet beneath his fingers. He'd dragged her through hell and she had said little. He tilted her chin with a forefinger, concerned that maybe she was in shock.

"Erin?"

Her lips quivered and a tear slipped down her cheek. He hadn't expected that; he suspected neither of them had.

"I'm out of my league," she murmured as her weight pressed against him as if her body had no will of its own. She looked up, and he looked down and somewhere in the middle their lips met. And once it had begun, he couldn't stop it. It was as if the shock and trauma that had just occurred needed the reaffirmation of life—they were alive. They had survived. The thoughts were only blips on his radar for her lips were full and moist against his. One hand skimmed the warm satin of her breast. Her nipple pebbled against his hand, and he realized she was braless.

He didn't say anything. He didn't need to. What he needed to do was get his hand off her breast, to lead them forward. There was no place for sexual antics with a dead man behind them. There was no place anywhere.

But he wanted the feel of her skin against his. Wanted it worse than he could remember ever wanting anything in his life. The danger, here in a place where this shouldn't happen and most of all with her—a woman whose curves he'd only imagined and had tentatively only explored the edges. His groin tightened at the thought of holding her, exploring her.

The timing was wrong.

He'd had his share of one-night stands and short-term relationships. He'd given his heart to no woman. And he definitely hadn't given his heart to Erin, but he suspected rather belatedly that while he might not have offered it, she might very well be in the process of a covert operation and be stealing it out from under him.

No.

She was a woman, not a covert operation. He pushed away and with the danger behind them gone, he began to move forward, not looking backward at her face, not willing to see what her eyes might reveal.

She was an assignment, no more, and while he wasn't willing to give his heart, he was more than willing to share his body.

Chapter Eighteen

One down. How many more to go?

He had pushed her to her limit and beyond, but they had finally made it back to the resort and relative safety. Josh's mind raced even as his senses were attuned to everything around him.

They entered the resort from the back. It was quiet as many of the tours were still an hour or two from completion. He looked at Erin. She was pale despite her time in Asia. Her hair hung free of its earlier ponytail. One piece of dark hair had dried into a curl and the rest hung straight. It was an odd thing to notice yet it was a relief to touch the edge of normal if only for a second.

"You're all right?" he asked softly.

She nodded as if speaking might be too much effort. She'd been quiet the whole walk back, as had he. He'd been planning and considering his next move; he suspected she might have been doing the same. He wanted to tell her there was no need. Instead, he had maintained the silence.

Tenuk met them, his hands fisted by his sides. "Son of a bitch! I didn't think you'd make it out. I was about to go in after you."

"We did. What the hell happened? We were compromised. We had the all clear." He looked Tenuk directly in the eye. "You gave it to us."

"I know." Tenuk shook his head. "Like you said, I gave that to you this morning. Damn it!" His fist clenched. "Faulty intelligence. No excuse. I'm just thankful you made it out alive."

Josh watched Tenuk closely while he listened for any changes around him.

"Came in on foot and by river. Took out two of my men before I was alerted that he'd slipped through the net." Tenuk ran a thick hand through his hair. "I didn't find out soon enough to warn you. I take it you managed. No injuries, I mean."

"I managed," Josh said.

"Can't keep all angles covered. I know that now. The river and the jungle, it's too easy to come in under the wire."

"Makes sense. Just wish you'd been aware of that sooner. Would have saved me a lot of grief." What he had to remember were the men the Anarchists had now hired were more than likely every bit as experienced in tracking and slipping under the wire as he was. Josh bent his head back as perspiration peppered the nape of his neck. The heat had dried his hair. "You might want to do something about the body in the pool outside Clearwater."

"I'll handle it," Tenuk replied.

He could feel Erin stiffen beside him.

"No other alerts?" he asked Tenuk as he took her hand, ran a thumb down her palm, trying to instill some sort of calm, of confidence.

Confidence? Calm?

What was he thinking? She'd just been shot at, had run for her life, been through a cave river and watched a man die. She was probably so shell-shocked she'd never be the same.

She squeezed his hand as if trying to convey the opposite.

"No. I've got the river covered. In fact, I've hired a couple of the men from the local tribes. They'll be better at it than any of us. I doubt this time anyone will be able to slip by. As far as the flights in are concerned, we've been monitoring that for a while." He nodded. "As I know you have. No other way except…" He glanced back to the quartz cliffs that punched jagged outlines in the crystalline sky.

"The back way, which means rock climbing and jungle trekking," Josh finished for him. "Not an improbability."

"You're right. We're on it."

"I hope to hell you are," Josh replied. "This was too close."

"You've got to get her out of here," Tenuk said. "That's the only way she's going to be safe."

"In the meantime, this can't happen again."

"It won't," Tenuk said grimly.

"That goes without saying," Josh replied and looked at Erin, trying to silently reassure her and thankful that she hadn't added her thoughts to the discussion. He wished she wasn't here, that she were someplace where danger was only a part of fictional entertainment. And conversely he was glad she was here, where he could see her and know she was safe. He wanted her physically by his side from here on in.

"You're all right?" he asked Erin again.

She looked from him to Tenuk, fear and hope in her eyes.

"Fine, for now. A little shook up."

"An understatement, I'd imagine," Tenuk put in.

"We'll get you out of here, Erin. Trust us."

She nodded. "I suppose I don't have much choice."

"A woman of common sense and logic." Tenuk's laugh fell flat. "The resort is clear," he said to Josh. "I suggest you keep her in your room until it's time to take off. I'll give you the signal."

"Same as before."

"Same." Tenuk smiled and winked at Erin.

She said nothing, neither acknowledging nor ignoring Tenuk's rather fresh gesture. Josh suspected that it was Tenuk's way of making Erin feel more comfortable in a situation that had to be anything but comfortable.

He put a hand on her shoulder in comfort and reassurance. They would talk more when Tenuk left, and he hoped the hand on her shoulder silently told her that.

He felt the tension in her and wished he could explain more than he planned to, enough to make her comfortable, less in the dark. So much of what he did was under the table. The bird whistles that Tenuk had used through their three-day stay here to alert him to her comings and goings once she was outside her room, the furtive communications with Wade, the arrangements to get her out of here. All were things he could not reveal.

"It will be okay. You'll see. I'm getting you out of here," Josh said as they headed for his room.

He felt her tense and realized his error.

She looked up at him with haunted eyes and she said nothing.

But the tension that seemed to strum from her said everything.

Out of here, no matter what he said before, meant home, to the States, to San Diego where it had all begun.

Chapter Nineteen

He opened the door and guided her in, his hand on the curve of her waist. She turned to look at him with resignation and, despite everything she'd just been through and heard, or maybe because of it, what he suspected was distrust.

"We'll wait here in my room for Tenuk to give us the all clear. I don't want you alone or at least out of sight." Tension rippled between them.

"I can't believe it. The river isn't safe. A boat trip... I thought..." She shivered and pushed a thread of hair from her brow. "That's how I meant to get out." She shook her head. "I never thought danger would come that way. I should have."

Her shoulders shook, and she wrapped her arms under her chest as if to self-comfort. It had been too much. She was a civilian, a grade-school teacher, unprepared for such trauma.

"The hit man, killer, whatever you want to call him, obviously thought the same. As Tenuk verified, that was the way he slipped in." His hand still rested on her waist as he tried to instill confidence in her, ease her jitters, and at a minimum, let her know that he was there for her in any way she needed him. He needed her to keep it together during these next hours. And if she could do that, he'd get her out of here, keep her safe.

But as before he was blindsided by the feel of her, by the heat that ran through his palm as he touched her and by the desire that her nearness aroused. He dropped his hand and closed the door.

"Have a seat," he offered, for he could see her fingers trembling as she tried to hold them rigid at her side.

She was destroying his equilibrium. He didn't do damsels in distress, not literally and not figuratively. He'd lifted many people out of sticky foreign jams but never an attractive woman whose curves had pressed up against him one too many times and whose body he couldn't help but notice.

He told himself that he couldn't think such thoughts. Attraction was dangerous in the field. She was the object of his rescue, nothing more. To think anything else endangered them both.

"You've been through hell, and I don't mean just today, Erin Kelley Argon," he said.

She ran a finger along the blind and then pulled the cord, closing off the outside world. "I don't suppose we should leave them open."

She turned to look at him with traces of fear still in her eyes, and he only wanted to fold her in his arms and never let her go.

"I think I need you to say it again," she whispered. "Who you are."

"Josh Sedovich, just like I said. CIA."

Her eyes were as blue as a clear winter day, and troubled. He closed the distance between them.

"Erin." His hands dropped to her shoulders. He imagined the silky skin beneath the thin cotton and instead pressed his lips to hers, pushing them open, tasting her.

A faint sweetness flirted with his tongue as he pulled her tight against his chest. Her lips were soft and yielding. Her tongue tentatively touched his as her body leaned into his.

Her palm skimmed almost flirtatiously against his forearm. The scent of something like jasmine seemed to waft from her. And all the adrenaline that had rushed through him earlier now settled in his groin. He bit back a groan and along with that the urge to bend her backward over his arm.

Instead, he pulled her closer, his hands slipping from her waist to cup her bottom, lush even through the rough cotton pants, and he drew her even closer as he dipped her back and his lips again claimed hers.

A soft moan escaped her, and his tongue plunged deeper, wanting to duplicate that somewhere else, knowing it was too soon. Her breasts pressed against him, warm, giving, suggesting so many other possibilities, and he only wanted to rip off the clothes that stood between them.

"How did you get hooked up with trash?" he breathed. It was a sentence that forced his mind to reality, an attempt to control his wayward body.

She went still.

Her silence seemed to echo between them. She pushed against his chest, taking a step back, her jaw set.

"Trash," she repeated. Her face was taut and almost expressionless. Her hand reached out, and she slapped him, the sound loud and cold in the room. The slap seemed to vibrate between them as they stood unmoving in a face-off of indecision on her part and of silent respect on his. She was like a deer on the highway, unsure if it should run or freeze, and it was his fault. He had made a beautiful moment ugly. A moment that had taken her away from the fear and panic she had so recently experienced had now been destroyed.

"I'm sorry. That was uncalled for," she said after a full minute went by during which neither of them moved.

His cheek stung but it was a minor assault considering everything she'd been through.

"Completely understandable. You've been through a lot. And..." Diplomacy, he reminded himself even as he voiced his thoughts.

She looked at him with eyes wide and troubled. He wanted to hold her, to stroke her, to... He took a step back. He wanted to do more than get her out of here and into the hands of the legal system. He wanted... He bit back the last of his thoughts. It didn't matter what he wanted. He couldn't have her, not any more than he'd had, and that had been a mistake.

"In your shoes I may have done the same."

"I doubt if you would have ever been in my shoes," she said softly.

It was a truth he couldn't disagree with. Instead, he said, "It's real, Erin. I mean who I am, why I'm here." Outside the afternoon was drifting to a close and the resort was quiet. He'd considered suggesting that they go to the dining room, but all things considered, he thought it would be best to remain here, quiet and out of sight until Wade arrived. They'd missed lunch. He'd notify Tenuk, get a meal brought over.

"You do this for a living. You're an expert." It was a redundant statement that he suspected she needed to say to grasp everything that had happened. She clenched the fist of her right hand before looking up at him. "My luck ran out, didn't it?"

He couldn't disagree with her there, not on either point.

If the Anarchists hadn't delayed, if their leader hadn't escaped capture for so many months, it would have been different. As it was, she'd had a reprieve. That aside, he had to admit she'd been good, the slip out of the States brilliant in her method of transportation. The rest, the access to another passport, was the luck of birth.

"We have a window, Erin. Like you heard, we'll be out of here tonight." He took her hand. "Are you hungry?"

"No, I..." She shook her head. "I'm not hungry, not in the least." She looked at him with eyes that were wide and pleading. "I can't go back, not to the States."

"You've got to get out of Mulu. What happened this afternoon will keep happening until they succeed." If it was possible, her face went even paler. He didn't need to mention the fact that the local authorities would be on this soon, too. He'd already staved them off, temporarily.

"Until they..."

She held up her hand. "No, Josh. Don't say it. I know. I wake up every morning knowing this could be my last." She shook her head. "I never thought it would come to this. That not only Daniel but Emma would be dead because of me."

"Not because of you," he said, although in a way what she said was true.

"No?" She looked up at him with pain in her eyes. "She befriended me, offered me a place to stay for a week, and I left her that damn note."

"She didn't send it on."

"You knew?"

"I found it when I went to the apartment. Mike never saw that note."

"It doesn't matter. She died because she knew me. And Daniel, too." Her voice seemed to crumble, break up as if she could stand no more. She folded her arms, wrapping them around her chest.

"Erin. It wasn't you. It's the Anarchists and those they hire."

"I shouldn't have run."

"You had no choice." He reached for her, pulling her to him. She was stiff in his arms. He knew why she had run, knew about Sarah, but he needed to hear it in her own words. For then he would know that he had her complete trust.

"I can't go back." She pulled away, her lips set. "No one else must die because of me."

"And to stay overseas would be worse. You're flirting with death. They'll go after you and eventually everyone you know."

Her face went pale. "No."

"Yes," he said firmly. "I'm sorry, Erin, but this just isn't about you. Not anymore."

"I can't go home," she said.

"We're going to Georgetown for now." There was a no-argument tone in his voice.

"Georgetown? You're kidding me. I… They…" She shook her head. "No."

"You have to, Erin. No one's looking in Georgetown. Not now. It's the safest landing place out of here. And it's temporary, but…" He glanced at the window as if there might be someone listening but really he only wanted to give her a moment to absorb the reality. "Georgetown is safe despite what happened. The man who tried to kill you there…" Again, he paused for effect. "He followed you here."

"He's dead," she whispered.

"He is, and like I said there are others after him. Better, more experienced, no fail rates."

She frowned, and her eyes flitted from him to the door. "That man you were speaking to here…"

"Tenuk."

"He's the concierge and yet…"

"Malaysian Special Forces. He and a few of his men have been on watch these last few days. We're in the clear for now, but I can't guarantee how long that might last. We've got no choice but to get you out of Mulu tonight."

"You're sure?"

"As sure as I can be," he said. He fingered the handle of his gun and watched as her eyes followed. "I'll protect you, Erin. That's why I'm here." He'd repeat that fact as many times as she needed it to be repeated. He knew what shock did to a person, and she'd been through more in the past hours than many people had in a lifetime.

She crossed her arms and then dropped them. Her eyes didn't have that sparkle, that edge that he was so used to. Instead, there was a look of resignation on her face.

"Erin, let's get you safe." He took her upper arms, felt the silken, well-toned flesh, looked into her eyes and said, "Georgetown is the least likely point of discovery." Return to the place you'd fled. He'd used the same tactic in other assignments.

"I don't have many options, do I?"

"Not at the moment. From Georgetown we'll get you out of Malaysia," he replied as he sat her gently on the edge of the bed.

She folded her arms as if that would offer some comfort to the overwhelming thought of what the future held. And he knew what she was thinking: a return to the States where she suspected that the danger still hadn't been mitigated. She was loyal and she would not expose her sister to danger. But now wasn't the time to reveal all that he knew, including where Sarah was at this moment.

She held up her hand. "Look, I'm still shaking, and you do this for a living?"

"It's not always so dramatic."

"I can't imagine worrying, the possibility that some-one you love might die, that…" Her eyes glistened with unshed tears.

"You're not talking about me are you?" Josh asked as he traced his thumb along the corner of her eye and wiped away the tear.

"No." She shook her head. "My brother died doing what he loved—heli-skiing. We begged him to not go that day. And he did." Silence hung briefly between them. "It destroyed my mother. In and out of therapy… What he did, it was horrible that he died, but what that did to my mother… So unfair."

"Tragic," he agreed. "But no more unfair than run-ning with shady men who end up having you leave your family behind and live a false life overseas. Is that fair to those who care about you?" She'd provided him with the appropriate time to finally dig under her skin, draw a bit of blood and hopefully expose the truth.

"It wasn't like that. You know that, don't you?"

He said nothing.

"I know what you're trying to do. And I hate it." Her laugh was dry, mirthless. "But we have time to waste, and I want to know about you. I like you and putting your-self in danger with every—" She stopped as if pondering. "What do they call it? Assignment?"

"Close enough. It's a thrill, I suppose, and a job. Maybe a bit of both and difficult to explain." And he wasn't sure why he was allowing the shift in topic except that know-ing about him might make it safe for her to reveal more about herself. "Maybe that was too simplistic. I suppose, for me it's more about giving back to others what my par-ents never had—security. On a trip home to Czechoslovakia when I was five they were detained for months. My mother was never the same after, neither was my father. A loving relationship basically crumpled before my eyes and became instead, abusive. I didn't want that to happen to anyone else. I suppose that was my underlying motivator to do this—not the thrill." He turned away. "At least that's what I said going in. One year later my motivation changed completely. My mother was raped and murdered in a home invasion." His eyes narrowed and for a moment he looked away. "It could have been any house on the block. They chose hers." He swallowed heavily. "Fate."

"I'm sorry. I didn't realize."

"Enough of my past," he said. They had little time and he needed information. "When was the last time you heard from Mike Olesk?"

Erin started and her mouth tightened.

"What's wrong?"

She ran her hands down her upper arms as if that would ward off the chill.

"Tell me," Josh said as his arm went around her shoulders, drawing her against his side.

"If you're thinking that Mike had anything to do with this, with finding me, then you're wrong. Mike would never do that. Ever," she said as if for emphasis. "He was my father's friend. When we were younger, he was like an uncle. We lost touch after my father died. He worked in law enforcement. He knew how to keep quiet."

"And he wasn't around for a lot of years until you contacted him," Josh said. "But as an old family friend, you trusted him," he guessed.

He wondered if that trust had been misplaced. People had been turned for surprisingly small amounts of money, and the money in question here was much more than that. But for now it was only a suspicion like any other. "When did he contact you last, Erin?"

"I got an email from him after leaving Singapore. It said simply, King of Malaysia. You know, referring to King George II, who Georgetown was named for."

"Mike told you to come to Malaysia, to Georgetown?" It was a question that lacked the element of surprise. He had seen this coming. Did it mean Mike Olesk was involved? He couldn't rule it out.

"Mike had nothing to do with this, if that's what you're thinking." She faced him, her fists clenched. "He wanted me to be able to lie low for a while. He got me safely to Georgetown. And he was right. I was safe for a long time. He had nothing to do with any of it, not with Daniel or Emma." She shook her head, and tears filmed her eyes. "That was over two months ago that he contacted me. The last time I ever heard from him. The last…" Her voice broke up as emotion got the better of her.

This time he didn't try to comfort her, didn't put his arm around her. He instinctively knew that she needed space.

Two months for the Anarchists to find Mike, maybe a bit of time for them to come up with the right amount of money. It was possible, even probable. He remembered the shifty look of the older man's eyes, as if Mike were keeping a secret.

"It's okay. Trust me. I'll get you out of here." It was all he could say for now. The last thing he needed was for her to fall apart. But as he met Erin's troubled eyes, he realized that falling apart was not an option. Her eyes were filmed with tears but her shoulders were set in a stoic angle. She'd hold it together. He could count on that.

He ran his finger along her cheek, wiping a tear that escaped.

"Don't," he said thickly. "Don't cry. It's all going to work out."

She looked up at him and connected in a way that snaked hotly through him as he saw more trust in her eyes than anyone had given him in a long time. He leaned down and kissed her, his hand caressing her cheek, feeling her softness and yet sensing an iron core—an iron core that they'd need to see their way through.

Chapter Twenty

"You can't outrun them," Josh said as his hand rested on her forearm, strong and warm. A shiver ran through her. "You have to face this thing. It's the only way it will ever end."

She stood up and turned away from him, hating every word he said for it was the truth. "You know, don't you?"

"About what happened that night?" He walked over to the window, raised the blind with his forefinger and looked out. Then he went to the door, opened it and looked around. He came back and sat down beside her. "I was briefed before I left."

"Briefed," she murmured. "It all sounds so cold...so clinical."

He shrugged.

She knew he wouldn't disagree with her assessment. She suspected that it was his strong willpower that allowed him to put his emotions and personal judgments to the background, and allowed him to do this kind of work.

"They think you're a witness who will help pin a murder charge on the leader of one of the most influential biker gangs in the world. They assume, apparently, that your testimony is doubly important because it is also proof of what was already suspected—the gang's high-priced connections and funding out of Europe." He folded his arms, his six-foot-plus frame intimidating, she imagined, if you didn't know how much he cared. "While that's not exactly how it came down, and not quite your reason for running, I just can't see how you got involved with them. Was it the thrill? What drives a woman like you to fall in with a biker gang, especially one as notorious as the Anarchists?"

"It wasn't like that." She shook her head, ignoring the other implications.

He reached over and covered the back of her hand with his. "Tell me how it really happened. Not how it was reported." His voice was a low growl that sent a shiver down her spine.

She took a breath.

She needed him for now—to get out of Mulu. That was it. There was nothing else. After that they would part ways and she would flee—alone, as she had for the past five months. There was no other choice. Fear ran through her about what he wasn't telling her. Did he know about Sarah? He wasn't saying, and she couldn't ask without arousing his curiosity. She couldn't take the chance and she couldn't ask the question.

Her mind went to that night as it had done over and over again during the months since it had happened.

She remembered odd things about that spring evening, the buzz of a fly that had somehow gotten into the car. The rich smell of living things in full bloom overlaid by the sweet, rather wistful scent of lilac. It was festival time and Cinco de Mayo was only a week away.

She remembered the house, a stately two-story Spanish Colonial set on ten acres just outside San Diego. She'd gone there knowing her boyfriend Steven would be there. Unfortunately, Sarah had insisted she should come along. Sarah, who had been almost four months pregnant.

"The smell of blood," she whispered. "It was horrible. I'll never forget…"

"Why didn't you report it?" Josh asked, breaking into her thoughts.

She looked at him, caught in her memories, and it took a second to bring herself to the present and a question she suspected would be difficult for an outsider to understand. She took a breath. "Steven, he wasn't there like he promised and then he showed up outside as I was leaving, almost out of nowhere. Told me it was unfortunate and tragic and that he didn't want me involved. He said that he'd report it to the police immediately, tell them that he'd stumbled on it. Not mention my name."

"And you believed him?"

"I wouldn't have in other circumstances but then— well, it was traumatic. I only wanted to go home where it was safe." She shook her head. "At least where I thought it was safe."

"Let me guess. He didn't report it?"

"I didn't see Steven again after that day."

"And you didn't file your report, either?"

"No, by the time I realized that Steven hadn't, I knew who had died and what I'd seen. I identified the men from pictures on the news report and after that I spoke to Mike."

She thought of all that had transpired what seemed a lifetime ago. It had all happened so quickly. One day she had been fielding teaching gigs as a substitute teacher in San Diego and the next minute she had been running for her life. Mike was the only person she trusted with what she saw, or rather, what Sarah had seen. Even with him she hadn't told him the truth of who was the witness. Even then she had tried to protect Sarah. Mike had laid out her options. He had briefed her on how to disappear.

He'd given her tips, and she'd cobbled the details together herself. But it had been Mike who had guided her. And with no experience in such things, she had taken his advice and began to consider the worst possibility she could imagine. Leaving her home and running.

"YOU'RE NOT HOW I imagined you'd be," Josh said.

"How did you imagine me?" Erin asked. Her heart thumped a little extra beat as she anticipated what he might say, how he had thought of her. Worse, how he might think of her now. Steven and all that he had drawn her into had not been her best moment.

He paced the room and then stopped. "It isn't a flattering picture, Erin. I have to say that."

"I imagine it's not," she said quietly. "To say my exboyfriend was a mistake is an understatement."

He nodded. "After reading the report I thought you might be a bit ditzy but intelligent. Perpetually drawn to the allure of adventure, to the bad boy. Textbook. And after I spoke to Mike, well, I…"

Her stomach clenched at the thought of that.

"He said you were naive. That you had first real boyfriend syndrome. Finished school too young and were sheltered, spoiled even."

"He said all that?" The enormity of what Josh was saying was too much to take in. And oddly it was Josh's word she trusted. Mike, the old friend of her father's, one of the last few reminders of her father—to think he had said those things was a breach of trust, and a smackdown she'd never seen coming.

She stood up, went to the window and then turned away, too disheartened to lift the blind or look out. "I was never any of that."

"Never?"

She whirled around. "You know nothing about me," she said through clenched teeth, the memories fresh. She looked at him and saw compassion flirting in the depths of his eyes. She swallowed, cleared her throat and said, "And yet you assume everything."

"Then enlighten me."

"I don't know if I can."

"Trust me," he said softly.

She took a breath. "Steven never wore the colors or dressed like a biker, at least when he was with me. Not until that night." She shook her head. "Of course, I knew before that, that something wasn't right, that Steven wasn't just a regular guy. I'd seen his friends, heard some of their talk and put some of it together. I knew he was a biker. I just didn't know he was an Anarchist."

"Tell me about it." His voice was gruff with a raw edge. "About that night. The night that Antonio Enrique died."

Antonio Enrique. The Spanish billionaire was proof of the Anarchists' ties to old money and the European funding connection. And his death was what would take the leader of the Anarchists down—for murder.

She gripped the windowsill as she turned away from him. "I planned to break up with Steven. I wanted nothing to do with him or the gang. But…" She leaned one hip against the sill, her face turned sideways to him. "I would have broken up anyway if Steven had a normal career. He wasn't my type of guy."

"Steven Decker," Josh mused. "Arrested three weeks ago attempting to cross the Mexican border near Tijuana. Drug running." There was nothing but disdain in his voice. "I suspect there may be other charges pending."

The news shocked her but emotionally she felt nothing. She'd never loved him and the thought of who he was and what she'd been to him made her sick. But arrested? She couldn't imagine the free-spirited man she'd known behind bars. She didn't want to imagine any of it. She wanted to hit Rewind.

"It was inevitable. What puzzles me was what you saw in him." He frowned as he looked at her. "You're into bad-boy types?"

She shook her head, and her hair slapped across one cheek. "No. God, no. Like I said, I didn't know that was what he was. I met him at a movie. Actually, I spilled my popcorn into his lap. I thought there was nothing bad about him."

"A movie?"

"You don't believe me?"

"Unfortunately, I do."

"Steven." She shook her head. "He didn't even like to be called Steve. He had a motorcycle, a Harley, but that's no different than a thousand other bikers in California. The only thing that was strange is that I never saw where he lived. He always picked me up, and we would go different places." There was a look on her face that almost made him want to believe her, almost. "I didn't know." She hesitated. "I should have."

"But at some point you found out," he encouraged. "I read the report but a report is nothing more than a dry collection of facts. And…"

She pushed a strand of hair from her face, slipping it behind her ear. "You've been briefed, as you call it. So I suspect you know most of it already."

"I do." He nodded. "But I'd like if you'd tell me yourself."

And she did, starting with their first date to that fateful night.

"It was horrible. I didn't see much. I heard arguing and

I saw their faces briefly." She swallowed, hating the lies she'd told, hating all of it.

"So how did you put it all together?"

"Like I said, a news report that night and then…"

"That's not how it came down, is it?" he said with a hard edge in his voice.

She looked up at him and saw something in his eyes, something that frightened her. "No." She shook her head. "That's exactly how it happened."

This time she couldn't look at him for he would see the fright in her eyes.

"You weren't alone, were you?" He paused and silence filled the room. "There's a witness to that murder, but it wasn't you. Was it, Erin?"

"What do you mean?"

"You're protecting someone. I hoped you would tell me who—voluntarily."

Silence dragged between them as her eyes averted his and dodged to the gleaming wooden floor.

"It's Sarah, isn't it? Your sister."

She stood paralyzed, her hand gripping the sill.

"I know you didn't witness that murder. That you're protecting Sarah, but what I don't know is why."

"Is she…" Her voice was choked.

"She's safe. She's in protective custody. They won't get her. Either her or, what was the damn cat's name?"

"Edgar." Relief flooded her voice. Was he telling her the truth? What reason did he have to lie? "Sarah's safe?"

"Protected 24/7 by our best."

"How long have you known…has the CIA known?"

"FBI, you mean. It was their gig until you stepped off American soil. That's where I came in."

Her knees threatened to give out and she had to consciously breathe to regain control.

"Are you okay?" Josh asked as his hand rested gently on her shoulder. The heat of it seemed to burn through the light cotton material and she wanted to turn and lean closer into his arms, into the comfort of his embrace. But now wasn't the time.

"How did you find her?"

"I don't know the details of that," Josh said. "The only detail I'm concerned about right now is you." There was an undercurrent in his voice that sent a tremor through her. "Tell me what really happened."

She shook her head. It was all so difficult.

He drew her into his arms.

"I care about you, Erin. More than I should. I wouldn't lie to you about Sarah. I know she's important to you."

She looked at him and met the truth in his eyes.

She took in a breath and as he held her she told him what had happened that day. Her voice was steady but she thought that it might only be his arms around her that held her up.

"Sarah heard scuffling and like a fool she went in. And that's when the murder happened. She saw the leader of the Anarchists turn, saw his face in a mirror and, thank God, he didn't see her."

"Giving you the perfect opportunity to run in her place," Josh said. "Very brave, but…"

"Stupid."

"No, not that," Josh said quietly and drew a strand of hair from her face.

She looked up at him and felt hope that maybe with him she could face anything, including the Anarchists.

Together.

She pulled away from him and took a step back.

She tried to reel in her emotions, corral them, but it was impossible. In three days she had done the unfathomable. In the wrong time and place and with the wrong man, worse, one she knew little about, she had done the unthinkable.

It couldn't be, but no amount of wishing made it go away.

She'd fallen in love.

Chapter Twenty-One

Erin drew in a long breath. It seemed as though her knees wouldn't hold her, and she found herself again in his arms. She should pull away. She knew that as well as she knew that she didn't have the will to combat what might follow.

"It's going to be all right. I've got you."

She turned her face into his shoulder as pent-up emotion, relief, tension, all of it seemed to flood through her. She wasn't sure she could have stood without the support of his arm around her waist.

"Sarah's safe?" She shivered as she looked at him. She so wanted to believe that it was true, but it seemed impossible. It had been too long coming, yet, this man had risked his life and saved them both, and he was willing to put his life on the line again.

"She's well taken care of. She couldn't be safer. So tell me," he said. "Why didn't you file a report, despite what Steve Decker said?"

"I wanted to, but Sarah was adamant that we shouldn't. She told me she'd heard begging, that the victim…" She swallowed hard. "Was begging for his life. She saw chaps and leathers, too. Bikers. She was sure of it. But what she was also sure of after watching a news report later that night was that she'd watched the leader of the Anarchists murder someone." She shook her head. "I mean the Anarchists, well, they terrified me, especially after I spoke to Mike." She looked up at him. "They won't stop looking." It wasn't a question but a fact that she had feared through her entire flight.

"And Steven?"

She shook her head. "He was there, like I said. He showed up as I was leaving the house."

"Explains why the Anarchists went after you."

She shook her head. "I never wanted to believe that of him, but who else could it have been? And Mike, he confirmed it." She took a breath. "Thank God he never saw Sarah."

"So he was saving his own skin."

"I suppose so. Saved me the breakup speech." She smiled shakily.

"Circumstances worked against you," he said.

"Enough of Steven. How do we stop them?"

"At this point, we don't. Specifically, you don't," he said. "That's why you need me."

"Oh, God." She seemed to fold into herself, her heart beating too loud, too fast. Everything seeming so futile.

His arms were tight around her, and she shuddered.

"You're going to make it. I promise. But it's time to go home."

"Home," she murmured as his lips met hers, and for the first time it felt as though it could be a possibility as her arms went around his neck. Her breasts pressed tight against the muscled ribbing of his chest. All of it felt so right even when the timing was so completely wrong, even when he was wrong. The wrong man. She couldn't imagine the chances he took, the day-to-day complications of what he did for a living. It was incomprehensible. But more incomprehensible were her feelings for him. She shouldn't have them. She didn't know him.

"You're safe, baby," he said against her lips as she wrapped her arms around his neck.

She wanted to melt into him, and for a moment what awaited them outside this resort was forgotten. All the doubts, the possibilities of the future melted into the present. There was only this man, this moment and a relief so intense that as it shifted into passion, everything seemed to implode.

His hand ran down the light cotton material of her blouse, slipped beneath the hem. Skin on skin, his hand warm and rough. She wanted that hand there. She wanted more. She...

"Josh..."

She slipped free. It wasn't that easy. It couldn't be. She'd been running too long. She moved a few steps away as if in distance there would be answers, salvation, something.

His hands were on her shoulders, solid and comforting and sensual, even though it was nothing more than the touch of a hand through cloth.

He pulled her close, her derriere cupped against his thighs.

He ran his hand along her side, curving at her waist and settled it on her hip.

"I haven't wanted a woman like I want you in a long time," he whispered, his breath hot and scintillating against her ear. She shivered against him, against the hardness that pressed against her and called for her to turn and offer him everything she had. She stayed with her back to him and let his hands go where they would.

His hand circled her belly and slid upward. Her blouse slipped off one shoulder. The buttons of her blouse were undone. A warm hand covered her naked breast and she didn't know how they had gotten to this point, except that she wanted to turn in to him and was held firmly against his hips, at his mercy, as his fingers toyed with her nipples and as her breathing came just a little hotter and just a little faster.

She barely noticed as her blouse fell to the ground, landing in a puddle at her ankles. His hands dropped lower, to the curve of her waist, her hips, the V between her legs, holding her there, making her arch and want to turn and reach for him.

"Josh."

Behind them a breeze lifted the canvas blind, rustling in the tight heat that seemed to settle around them.

She hesitated as everything that had happened and that she had yet to face slipped to the background and passion threatened to consume her.

He nuzzled her earlobe, the soft caress making her shudder even as she shook her head.

"I want you," she murmured as her fingers ran tentatively down the hard muscle of his broad back. Her hand dropped.

"There can never be anything between us, Josh. This is just an illusion, a place where I should never be and a place where you always are. A dangerous place."

His hand stilled between her legs as she wept, wanting him.

"You're too risky."

He ran a thumb over her nipple.

Pinpoints of pleasure ran through her. "Men like you…"

She pulled away from him before it was too late, before passion swept reason out of reach.

"And who or what, exactly, are men like me?"

She picked up her blouse and pulled it on. She took her

time gathering her disjointed thoughts, breathing slowly and getting her traitorous body under control.

She did up the last button before meeting his eyes.

"Men who thrive on adrenaline, on fast-paced lives and equally fast-paced relationships. Men who will never own a home and mow a front lawn." She looked away, one hand working through the fingers of another and then she looked at him, seeing the truth in his eyes.

"Erin…"

"It's true, isn't it? I bet you don't even have a pet or a neighbor you know or…"

"An RV just outside of Tampa," he said and walked to the window. He stood there for a long moment, his dark hair curling over his collar, his shoulders broad and tapering to slim hips.

He was everything she wanted in a man, yet everything she didn't. He was danger, and he was compassion. She'd never seen that in any man.

"A camping trailer?" She smiled and shook her head. "Wouldn't an apartment work better?"

"It's a little bigger than that. And as far as portability, well, I liked the allure of the open road at the time I bought it. As it is, it's been in an RV park just outside Tampa for the last five years." He leaned one hip against the windowsill. "I've gotten used to the small space and knowing that if I feel like it I can move it at any time." He cleared his throat and pushed away from the sill. "Except I've never felt like it. Like moving."

"But you're not a stay-at-home kind of guy?"

"Not lately," he admitted. "I'm not home a lot, but I am handy, if that helps. At least my friends think so."

"Handy?"

"I spent the last vacation plumbing a friend's bathroom." He ran a hand through his hair. "Seems like years ago."

He smiled at her and it seemed odd, the smile and even the conversation, considering what they had just gone through and where they'd just been.

"I know, hard to believe."

"It is," she replied. The image of him raising that gun, of the man…falling and… She closed her eyes. She couldn't think of it. It was hard, even after seeing him in action, to think that the gentle, unassuming man she had met was capable of those things or worse. And if he weren't capable of those things, it was even harder to face the other truth, that she would now be dead.

"It's all been too much. I'm sorry," he said and his voice had a gruff edge. "I would change all of this if I could."

"How do you do this day in and day out one assignment after another?"

He shrugged. "I suppose I was drawn to it after spending my youth traveling the globe. I left home after two years of college and spent a couple of years traveling. And, of course, what happened to my family when they were detained."

She digested all of that. "I can't even begin to imagine. Does it fulfill you?"

"Some days," he said honestly. "And other days I'm not sure if I shouldn't be doing something else."

"But you didn't finish college?"

"One day I may finish. In the meantime, life has been my university."

"A rather tough way to get an education." She laced her fingers together.

"Erin." His voice was gruff, and then she was in his arms and he was holding her and it felt so good, so safe.

The scent of him was warm with the clean scent of the outdoors. His chest was solid against her, comforting.

The chirp of a jungle insect seemed to knife through the room, and Erin shuddered, remembering who and what might be out there, maybe not nearby, not yet… but soon.

"I'm sorry you had to see any of that," he said.

"Don't be," she replied. "You saved my life."

"Just part of the job," he said as he strode across the room, putting distance between them. A whistle rather like the call of a bird had Josh opening the door. She watched as he nodded to someone she couldn't see. He opened the door wider, and Tenuk stood a few feet back from the doorway, looking serious.

"I'm going with Tenuk—five minutes. I won't be out of sight of the room."

"You want me to stay here…alone?"

He stepped back and placed his hands on her shoulders. "It'll be all right. We're close to getting you the hell out of here."

Hell, she thought. That was what she had been through and as she met the sincerity in his eyes she realized, that hell might be what she would be facing when all this was over.

When she went home, to Sarah, to the safe house.

When she was home—without him.

Chapter Twenty-Two

Early evening, Wednesday, October 14

"Just heard from Wade," Tenuk said. "Georgetown is out of the question."

"Why?" Josh snapped.

"Wade would be here in under an hour, but he's reported a major foul up at the airport. A crash has Georgetown's runways closed and emergency measures in place. I suspect it won't be much longer before Wade gets around that, but he's not going to be here as scheduled."

"How soon?"

"Another couple of hours." Tenuk shrugged and handed Josh a small slip of paper. "Here's the numbers of the plane. Don't ask me how Wade got them before he got on the plane. Or for that matter how he contacted me. Only thing you need to know is that's our plane. Be sure to destroy this in the usual manner." Josh nodded. He'd chewed and swallowed more than his share of paper.

IT WAS NEAR nine o'clock before they heard the buzz of a small plane, an Otter, similar to the ones the resort used. Josh went outside, and Erin could see from the window as he looked upward.

"It's time to get out," he said, leaving the door open behind him.

Erin hesitated.

It was the moment of truth, when she gave him her trust not just in this moment but all of it going forward. It was a lot to ask considering everything that had gone before, how long she'd depended solely on herself. She hesitated, taking in his sun-burnished good looks, the cap and tourist T-shirt gone. The plain black T-shirt defined his flat belly, defined his muscle—reminded her that he was all man.

Too much man.

Too much risk.

"Erin." His voice broke into her thoughts, his hand warm yet oddly commanding on her forearm. "This is it. The plane is here. Stay close. It should be clear but…"

His hand slid from her forearm as he held out his hand. "We're going to have to hurry."

Despite her thoughts she hesitated only briefly, and as she did the impact of it all whirled through her mind. This was life changing, epic, and it would affect both her and Sarah. What if she were wrong?

"Move," he said, and his tone suggested that there was no possibility of hesitation.

His grip went back to her arm as he propelled her forward. "The next man destined to try to take you out is on his way. He was seen up river not that long ago. Remember what I told you earlier? More deadly than anyone who has tracked you before."

She swallowed heavily, digesting that information, trying to stay calm.

Outside, they hurried along the wooden pathway. She could sense Josh's tension in the tight grip he had on her hand. He nodded at a maid who moved lightly along the boardwalk, a bag of cleaning supplies over her arm. She was the only person they met on their walk to the tarmac. As they left the wooden walk it almost seemed like the verdant green jungle had taken on an ugliness that was foreign, where once, or maybe in another time and place, it had been beautiful.

Her imagination was in overdrive.

She took a breath. The jungle seemed to be the same, rich and thick, full of the calls of the birds. But the rustling in the brush no longer signified something amazing, possibly camera worthy like wildlife. Instead, it felt as if it was a trap that housed a game of life and death.

The grip on her hand was so tight she could feel the bones shift.

"Josh," she protested.

The jungle seemed to breathe around them, the darkness providing another layer, one of danger. There was nothing to see but thick shadows. Something shrieked deep in the jungle's depths and she jumped as a shiver ran across her spine. Whoever the next tracker was he could be in the jungle, and they would never know until it was too late.

They stepped off the walkway heading for the tarmac.

They were out in the open, exposed. Her palms were damp, and a knot in the pit of her stomach that combined with the sour taste in her mouth made her fight against the urge to throw up.

She looked ahead. The plane was on the runway, the shadow of the pilot in the cockpit and the propellers going. The plane was ready to take off.

Time was running out. She could feel it in the short gasps of breath, in the pounding of her heart, in the sweat that slicked her palm against his.

It had been so few hours since they'd made a run for their lives through the cave and now it threatened to begin again.

Erin gasped for breath and saw the door to the plane open, a weathered-looking, blond-haired man flagging them in a one-armed wave.

"Hurry." Josh's command was overlaid with urgency as he moved faster and for a second she was unable to keep up and then she stumbled.

Josh pulled her to her feet, quickly, easily and with no words of concern. There was no time.

The pilot was out of the plane, opening the door and waiting for them to get in.

"Josh. King of the grand exit," he said. "Good to see you, man."

"Wade. Good to get the hell out of here," Josh said as he helped Erin in.

The interior of the plane had a heavy, musty odor as if it had been in the jungle too long. She pushed a canvas tarp aside and crawled into the farthest seat from the door. She looked out the window, but there was little to see as it was smeared and streaked with what looked like dirt. She clenched her hand, her nails biting into her palm and held back the urge to ask questions.

Josh and Wade were settling themselves in and before long the plane was taxiing down the runway, and they were off.

"Where to after Georgetown?" she asked.

"Georgetown? Not in this plane, sweetheart." Wade turned around and smiled at her.

He looked at Josh. "You heard?"

"Tenuk told me. Anything else?"

"What?" Erin's heart thumped and her mouth went

dry. They had agreed to Georgetown. Not quite agreed, she admitted to herself, but she'd been comfortable with that option. Josh had made her comfortable with it and now he was changing it. She looked at Josh, demanding an answer as her eyes clashed with his. What else had Tenuk told him that she hadn't heard?

"Plane crash on the main runway. Officials are all over the area and the city is crawling with overhyped media. We've got to take you to a safe zone for now." Josh looked back, his concern evident as his eyes searched hers. "I'm sorry, Erin. Things are moving too fast, and I didn't get a chance to tell you."

But even as he apologized her mind was going back to that one word. *Safe*, the word that kept coming up, but looking at Josh and hearing the diversion, she was beginning to feel less than safe.

"What's the change? Tenuk didn't know what you had in mind," Josh asked with confidence in his tone that eased Erin's mind at the thought of a diversion.

"Pulau, Langkawi," Wade said. "Honeymooners island. Trite but effective."

Josh nodded. "How long?"

"We'll get another plane in by tomorrow afternoon to get you out."

"Have you been in contact with Vern?"

Erin pushed her hands against her belly as the plane lifted into the air. Her stomach seemed to drop with the increase in altitude. She didn't feel comfortable. She didn't like this, not knowing Wade, not knowing about the conversation with Tenuk and realizing that there was a lot that Josh might be doing that she wasn't aware of. Suddenly trust seemed like a shaky position to be in. She was running blind—trusting that he would save her. She didn't like it.

He looked back at her with a reassuring smile. "Vern is who I report to. The one who got me into this. Wade here…"

"Private contractor," Wade said as the plane banked into a turn.

"Give or take. A wild card who works for the CIA."

"You blew my cover," Wade complained.

It was a brief moment of lightheartedness in the midst of a black unreality.

"It'll be okay, babe," Josh murmured under his breath.

In her heart that was all she wanted, to rewind the mess that her life had become and to have it all boil down to a word so simple.

Babe.

BRIEFLY SHE CLOSED her eyes as if that would return her equilibrium and establish a more normal reality. She was on the run and this time she was no longer in control. Truthfully, she hadn't been in control for a while, maybe since she'd first laid eyes on Josh. She shivered as Josh turned and his hand settled on her lower arm.

"Despite how this looks, it will be okay." But his voice was grim.

"How can you be so sure that I couldn't have carried on without you?" She looked straight ahead, her eyes averted, her body almost vibrating with tension.

It was an outrageous thing to say considering everything that had happened. She would have been dead in Clearwater Cave or even before. She shuddered, not knowing what had pushed her to say such a thing.

He had rescued her. They both knew that.

"For one, you can't stay on the run anymore. It's only a matter of time before they'd take you to ground. And two, the FBI will protect you. You'll be safe with them."

She shifted back, against the wall of the plane as if that would offer any protection. Despite everything that had happened, somehow she still harbored doubt.

Fear ran through her. No matter what had come before, she'd made the wrong decision. Despite what she had said, despite trust, despite everything, she couldn't go home. Ever.

"You'll be safe. We'll keep you safe," Josh said.

She shivered.

"There isn't a choice." His gaze was solid and confident. "I hate to say this but…"

"Say it, Josh," she said and she fisted her hand as if that would protect her in some way against what was to come.

"You're in our custody whether you like it or not."

She'd known that. He'd as much as said it an hour ago, but she'd known it before that. It was the inevitable cost of life, her life. She'd accomplished the most important thing. Sarah was safe. There was a point where she had to trust, where she couldn't run anymore, not by herself—this was the point where she faced it all.

"Where do we go from Langkawi?" Her heart seemed to stop in her chest at the thought of the answer. She knew what he would say, where he was taking her. He'd told her, yet she had to ask again and again, as if that would make it palatable. As if by hearing the word she could imagine it as the place before she had run. A part of her past where there was nothing dark and deadly awaiting, where the risk had been mitigated. She wanted to believe that in the worst way.

"Home," Josh replied. "You know without me saying it again. There isn't any other choice."

Her stomach tightened at the thought, even though there was also a rush of jubilation at the idea of seeing her family again. But then that wouldn't happen, she'd be in a safe house along with her sister and as Josh had stated, not the same house, either. She'd be there until the trial was over and a conviction took place. And if a conviction didn't take place… It didn't bear thinking about.

Fear sliced through her with icy discomfort and she took a breath as she looked at him. She could see the jut of his jaw, the firm line of his lips and the determination in his eye. And something changed for her looking at him like that, strong, yet so vulnerable. He would always do what was right, no matter the cost. Her heart did a small thump as she realized how close she was to saying yes to everything he might offer, yet he had offered her nothing except returning her safely home.

Home.

In another time, another place—another way, it would have been everything.

"I'll keep you safe," he repeated.

His words were reassuring, and they shifted the paradigm of reality. They made everything real and right. How had it happened in such a short time, that she had fallen for him, fallen for the wrong man, in the wrong place? Wrong in every way. The risk her brother had taken was small in comparison to what this man did for a living. She couldn't risk it. She couldn't… But there was no stopping it. She loved him. She'd already admitted that, to herself, anyway.

"No worries, Erin. You're in good hands," Wade put in. "I've worked with this guy for half a decade now. There isn't any better. Except *moi*."

"Bastard, fishing for favors again," Josh said, but with a light edge in his voice.

She looked from one to the other, but already her thoughts were moving ahead. What to do when she got to Langkawi? He'd said she was in custody. Did she trust him? Could she? Were there any other options? She was so conflicted—trusting on one hand, distrustful on the other. Fear was the only emotion that seemed constant.

"If you run you'll jeopardize everything, not just yourself, but Sarah, too," he whispered as he leaned back to look at her. "You're going to make it. I promise. It's time to go home."

Her heart seemed to stop.

She looked at Josh. Now he was talking to Wade. They were speaking in undertones, and she could hear none of what was being said over the roar of the engine. She leaned forward, and Josh turned.

"You're all right?"

"Fine."

Her ears clogged as twenty minutes later they began their descent. And for the rest of their time in the air little had been spoken.

Another five minutes, maybe ten, and they stood alone on the tarmac, Wade and the plane gone.

"You'll be fine, babe." Josh leaned over and kissed her.

She took a step back. She wasn't too sure she wanted him or any of his romantic overtures. Not now. Not ever. They—couldn't be.

She spun around, away from him. She didn't need her thoughts full of anything but keeping out of reach of the Anarchists. She didn't need her thoughts full of him.

A small Malay man in a *longyi* that had a brown-and-white tie-dyed look to it came up to them, maneuvering easily in the long cotton wrap, his plastic flip-flops snapping against the pavement. He spoke to Josh with words that Erin didn't understand and that only upped her nervousness. Somehow those moments on the plane had seemed safe and now on the ground it was as if the danger breathed around her. Her nails bit into her palms as she looked at the black stretch of pavement lit by the runway lights. In the distance she could hear the waves crashing rhythmically onto the shore.

An island. She wasn't sure what Mike would say about that. She wished she could speak to him. She suspected he wouldn't like it. But Mike may have betrayed her...

It didn't bear thinking about.

She had to trust.

Josh.

He was still speaking words she didn't understand. They were words that would affect her future. She didn't take her eyes off him, as if that would change whatever was being decided. Josh nodded and the two men parted.

Josh came over. "We're here overnight. Pickup is arranged, as Wade said, tomorrow afternoon."

"It's safe?" It was a ridiculous question. Obviously it was safe. They wouldn't be here if it weren't.

He nodded. "For now we're a honeymooning couple. Enjoying sights, spending too much time indoors with..." He looked at her and winked. "With each other."

She crossed her arms.

"Kidding." He touched her elbow. "Look, I'm sorry. I was trying to lighten the mood just a bit. You can relax, at least for now."

"It's the *for now* that I'm worried about."

"Don't. That's why I'm here." His arm curved around her waist.

"We have no luggage."

He turned her around and there, sitting on the tarmac, were two dusty blue, hard-shelled suitcases that hadn't been there before.

"Unbelievable." She looked at Josh as a second thought came to mind. "Now where?"

"A cab to the nearest hotel, which is just around the

bend." He released his hold on her waist. "And a cab, my love, is right over there."

She turned but for a moment her eye caught on the lush greenery that was highlighted faintly in the artificial light and reflected the jungle that was so tight and thick that it seemed to choke her as it sprawled around them. Something screeched, and what sounded like a scream followed.

She jumped and muffled a shriek with a hand over her mouth. "I'm sorry. I just... I've never heard anything like it."

"Monkey. The island is full of them," Josh said as he picked up both suitcases.

"Let me carry—" she began, determined to be of some help.

"What kind of husband would I be if our honeymoon started out with you carrying the bags?" he asked with a small smile.

Her smile reflected his. "Not great, I suppose." She looked across the tarmac to the cab. "Okay then." She took a breath and stood tall. It would take all her focus to appear normal. A few minutes later she was wrestling with the sliding door of the van.

Josh reached over her shoulder. "Let me," he said as the door slid open in an uneven jerk. Erin got in and Josh threw in the bags. The driver grunted once, said something that she couldn't understand as Josh closed the door with a slam.

The ten-minute cab ride was silent. The driver's speed and maneuvering of the dated van that served as a cab was painfully slow. They passed only one other vehicle. It was all that broke the drive except for the vehicle's headlights and the lights from the resorts that offered peeks of the endless stretches of jungle on the inland side and the views of the ocean that stretched out beyond them on the left. If this had been any other time, if this were a normal vacation, if they had been a normal couple—it would have been ideal.

She looked at Josh, his face tense and alert, his classic good looks underscored by the courage and integrity he'd already shown her. He was a man who worked in the trenches and put his life on the line every day. He was the man who said he could save her after five months on the road when she thought that no one could.

The cab pulled into a graveled lane where a yard light revealed a low-slung building that was cloaked in weathered pink siding. A sign announced the resort's name in a slight right-handed list. To the left and about a hundred feet away, edging toward the nearby ocean, another yard light revealed a two-story, milk-white structure with five rooms up and another five down and stairs leading up to individual units. There was no one in sight. Early fall was the slowest season and this slightly run-down affair would not be a tourist's first choice.

"This is it?" she asked, though it really didn't matter. She hopped out behind him, watched as he spoke briefly to a short, balding man and then reached for their suitcases.

In minutes the door to their room was open, the keys were in Josh's hands and they were alone.

The room was desperately tiny. At first she wasn't sure how they and their bags would fit. Josh dropped their suitcases between two small, legless beds that were really only a pair of mattresses on the floor. Outside, there was a little veranda, enough room for the white plastic chair and the pot of dying flowers that now occupied it. A flight of stairs led to a path that the owner said went through low-lying brush and over to the beach. Even in the dark it was clear this location was idyllic. Had they been honeymooners, she could imagine appreciating it despite the accommodation's rustic edge.

"Romantic enough for you, love?"

"Cut it out," she demanded. Considering everything, she wasn't in the mood for teasing. "In another life this room would have been Flintstones funny. Unfortunately, now not so much." She pressed a forefinger to her temple, hoping to ward off another headache.

"This has been hard on you."

"You think?" she said and immediately recanted. "I'm sorry."

"Don't apologize for what you can't help."

"All right, I won't." She plunked down on the bed, sitting cross-legged only inches above the floor. "So what now?"

"We spend tonight here and then we head to the Malaysian mainland by small plane tomorrow afternoon."

"Back to our place of origin?"

"Not quite. We head to Kuala Lumpur and from there it's only a matter of a couple of stops and you're home." He shrugged. "I didn't plan this segment. Wade did. He claims with a little help from Vern. Considering the foul-up in Georgetown, this segment makes sense."

"Vern?" she asked, wanting to know more than the little he'd told her on the plane.

"The man who gave me this assignment. He's safely stateside. But he's who I report to when this is all done."

"A boss?"

"More or less."

She pinched her bottom lip with her thumb and forefinger as she thought about the logistics of everything.

"Stop it. Quit thinking so much," he said as he sat down beside her.

"We're safe here?" It was a moot point, but somehow

the question made it real, made the thought of safety something she could entertain.

"I think so." He put a hand on her thigh.

"Think?" She leaned closer into him, as it felt safer with him near.

"Nothing is guaranteed. But it's the option we thought safest."

Safest, she thought looking at him, feeling herself falling for the lure of his warm cinnamon eyes, breathing in the scent that was uniquely him—fresh air and something that smelled vaguely like pine—and feeling on edge and uncomfortable and only wanting...

She couldn't admit what she wanted.

He wasn't safe.

They weren't safe.

Nothing could ever be safe again.

Chapter Twenty-Three

"I don't know how you do this," Erin said. "This kind of assignment over and over. This kind of danger." She took a breath. "That's what I am, right? An assignment." She stood up. She rubbed her palms, as if the friction would ease her thoughts.

"I won't lie to you. That's what you were in the beginning," he admitted. "No more." He took her hand, pulling her down on the edge of the bed. The room was so tiny that a chair wouldn't fit now that their suitcases had been set down.

"I don't know what will happen when this is over, Erin, but I care for you. More than I should—more than I ever have before."

"I'm not sure how to take that," she said with a glimmer of a smile and wiped her eyes with the back of her hand. "But I'm glad you're here. Without you I wouldn't have made it."

He nodded. There was no need to say anything. There was more truth in what she said than she might ever know.

She turned to face him, her lips still quivering, and he cupped her face between his hands and kissed her. He could taste the salt of her tears between them, slicking his lips. His tongue caressed her lips as it ran along them devouring her tears and then devouring her. He ran his hand along the sleek skin of her neck, resting where he could feel the distant and rapid beat of her heart.

She was so much more than an assignment. She'd been more almost from the beginning. But what he felt for her could be dangerous, especially as they danced one step ahead of danger. They couldn't afford any distraction or any hesitation.

He sat back, his hand on her shoulder, his thumb caressing her collarbone. "I'll get you out of here, Erin, but you can't hesitate, question me—ever. That's important. Promise me that. No hesitation ever again, not now that you know who I am and why I'm here."

"I…"

"Hesitation can be lethal," he said grimly. "The Anarchists have a bounty on your head. Ten million dollars."

"Ten million." For a moment she was quiet. When she turned to look at him, shock was in her eyes. "That's unbelievable, a staggering sum."

"You didn't know?" He was surprised at that.

"No. I haven't been in touch with anyone at home for a long time. You said there was another assassin and that he'd been outsourced. How good is he?"

His thumb stopped skimming along her collarbone. He knew what she was asking. Was Sid better than he was? Could Josh stop him if they met face-to-face?

He shook his head. "Like I said earlier, he's never failed. Word is he's not alone. I need to get you home where there are the resources to keep you safe."

Seconds seemed to tick by and felt more like minutes. Outside, the silence seemed to whisper of danger.

How far did her trust reach? His gaze met hers. He wanted to explain to her what she meant to him. Yet he didn't know himself. He only knew that no matter what danger they danced around, he would protect her with his life.

"It's a game for you." She frowned. "I don't mean like that, but I think you live for the challenge. That every assignment is like that for you, including this one."

"Never that, Erin." His hand covered hers. "You mean more to me than that." He lifted the palm of her hand to his lips and brushed a kiss across it. "I don't know how it happened, but I think I've fallen for you."

"Fallen?"

Her hand remained in his.

"Fallen," he repeated, surprising himself.

He kissed her then, parting her lips, her body pressing against his, the feel of her soft against his chest, the need for more was overwhelming.

More wasn't where they should be going. They had no future. He couldn't compromise her like that. He couldn't, wouldn't...

He let her go and dropped his hands.

"I'm sorry."

She shifted away from him. "Do you know that my sister, Sarah, was pregnant?"

It was a statement that seemed to come out of nowhere, and he didn't know what to say. Instead, he said nothing.

"I wasn't happy about it. The guy was a mistake, as she says. Not in the picture. She's too unsettled and she's going to be raising a child as a single parent. I should be there for her, instead..." She choked back a sob but a tear slipped from beneath her lashes.

He wiped it away with his thumb. It had been too much for her. He knew that. Most civilians would have collapsed by now. Not Erin.

She looked at him. Her eyes shimmered with unshed tears. "I'm probably an aunt now, and I may never know if it's even a boy or a girl. You know, despite all my original misgivings, I want to know that." She shook her head. "I'm sorry. I'm not usually a crier and that's all I seem to be doing."

He smiled at her, taking her hands in both of his. "She had the baby and both of them are healthy and well."

"Oh, my God." Her hand went to her mouth. "Why didn't you tell me sooner? I'm an aunt." She laughed a rather startled giggle.

"She had the baby ten days ago from what I've heard. A boy." He squeezed her hands. "She was placed under protective custody two weeks ago and we had to pull one of our female field workers in—midwife in a previous profession."

"A boy," she murmured. She looked up at him, and he could see the questions in her eyes, her doubt that it was true and that they were both safe.

"They're both fine, Erin. I promise."

"I believe you," she said. "It's just that… He'd have a name already I suppose…"

"Liam," Josh said. "The baby's name is Liam." His hand covered hers. He knew what a shock this was for her. Not having family near, with a mother who was troubled and needy, with little concern for her adult children's lives, it had made the sisters close. It had surprised him when he'd first discovered that particular piece of her life. It was not how it had been with his mother but every family was different.

Silence hung between them.

He let her lead, knowing she was overwhelmed, and sad that she had missed it all. "She's okay? They're both okay?"

"More than fine. Big baby, from what I heard." He shrugged. "No idea of weight, hair color or lack thereof, so don't ask. Sarah has been prepping for the trial. She's going to testify."

"No." She stood up. "She can't do it. I won't..." She stopped.

He took her hand and pulled her back down beside him. "It's going to be fine. We just have to get you home."

"It's been so long since home has been anything more than a word, a moving target I could never reach. At least that's how it all felt. I know it hasn't been that long but..."

Josh put an arm around her shoulder. She felt right there, leaning against him. She fit. Like they were meant to be together. But he'd known that hours ago; it was only now that he admitted it.

"I'm sorry, I shouldn't have..." she said as she pulled away and stood up.

He followed her, brought her back against his chest, the feel of her heart beating like the quiver of a small, frightened animal. Yet she was no frightened animal. She was a grown woman, courageous and one who had hours ago hit the wall of her endurance.

His lips brushed hers, the feel of them achingly soft. Her breath was warm and seductive and his tongue caressed her lips, teasing them open. He brought her body close to his, relishing the soft feel of it against him. His hand dipped down the slim waist and over the seductive curve of her hips. She fitted against him as if she'd been meant only for him. The thought brought a rush of passion and desire and his hands only wanted to strip her of the clothes that stood between them, to plunder and make her his.

He couldn't do that—she was too vulnerable. He'd be taking advantage.

She cupped his face with her hands and kissed him.

It was a kiss that removed any doubts, and he kissed

her back. He took charge, pushing her hands aside and wrapping his arms around her.

But she met him kiss for kiss, her tongue sending shivers through him as she tasted his lips, his neck. Her fingers were like pulse points of heat on his skin as she ran them under his T-shirt, flirting with his firm belly, going upward. He bent down, his lips meeting hers, his hands beginning to undo the buttons of her blouse.

"I'm stronger than you think. I survived five months on the road," she whispered, her breath hot against his neck.

"You were amazing. I couldn't help but admire what you did. The container ship, brilliant." He pushed her blouse partway off her shoulders.

She pushed his T-shirt up as her fingers roamed over his muscled chest.

"Josh?" Her hand dropped.

"Don't stop now." It was all he could think to say.

"I didn't plan to," she said in an oddly breathy voice. "I just want to rid us of this T-shirt. It's getting in the way." She took a step back and pulled an arm free of her blouse.

"You're a mind reader," he said as her blouse fell to the ground and was soon joined by his T-shirt. He cupped her breast. Her nipple pressed hard against his palm—and he was hard. She was caressing him, and it was too much. His hand closed over hers.

He unzipped her shorts, pulling them down.

"Let me," she said but instead she reached for him and within seconds there were no clothes between them.

The small room seemed too much, everything was too close—the world seemed to stop and then in a way, impossibly, heat up. She was like no other woman—he felt out of control and he didn't want that, yet he wanted it all—all of her.

He bent her backward over his arm, his lips ravaging

hers, claiming one breast and then the other. She pulled him down to the mattress where her hands also slipped down to where he held on to his control by a thread.

He pulled away from her, pinning her hands as he trailed kisses down her throat, the same way she had done to him so many minutes earlier.

He cupped her hip, running a thumb along the inside of her leg.

Where this was going—there could be nothing after. His job, his lifestyle…she abhorred risk. She'd said so.

He wanted her more than the job. It was a random thought, something that flitted through the mire of desire.

His hand held her breast, toying with her nipple as his other hand explored farther, running fingers between her legs, caressing her until she told him in a way words never could how ready she was.

"There's no turning back, Erin."

Had he said that? He wasn't one to second-guess anything and most especially sex, but with her it was different. With her he wanted it to be perfect. And it was, as she rode him to ecstasy.

And when it was all over, they lay silently side by side, but after a few minutes he leaned over and kissed her, and she ran her hands over his body and he needed no convincing that they should begin it all again.

And as the night deepened, the threats and the thought of death were liquefied in the heat of passion.

Chapter Twenty-Four

Thursday, October 15, 4:00 a.m.

She slept curled up as if in a cocoon. Her knees were pulled up to her stomach, her feet were curled around his, her plush derriere pushed against his groin and teasing him to begin it all over again.

He shifted away.

There were other things to consider despite his readiness, despite his body's driving reminder that he wanted her and he wanted her now. He'd been awake the past hour going through the events of the evening, through the details of their escape from Mulu and backward further to that afternoon. It was a procedure he followed in every assignment, covering all the bases, making sure he'd missed nothing. He'd gone back to that evening, to the plane and to Wade. There he found the inconsistency, the niggling moment of doubt that made him consider possibilities that he once would have thought implausible.

No more.

Now he suspected they'd been compromised. That was always a possibility and not a shocking one to realize. But it was the man he suspected that made him not want to believe.

He stood up. There were times when he had to follow his gut and this was one of those times. Something told him to check the status of the Georgetown airport directly with the airport authorities. He headed down to the hotel's shabby office and within ten minutes he was back, the expression on his face grave. The airport had never been closed—there was no accident, no crash. Yet, Wade had admitted on the flight that he'd personally informed Tenuk of the Georgetown Malaysia's temporary closure. There was no reason for Wade to admit that to him unless he was so secure in his lie that he could accept sole responsibility.

"Damn it," he muttered and his fist clenched as he realized what Wade had done. It had been hidden by Wade's habit of dressing more like the locals in tropical climates and wearing a long-sleeved cotton shirt despite the heat. He swore that it kept him cooler than exposed skin. He remembered what he should have noticed then, the small tattoo, covered by his sleeve. It was nothing noticeable, not to anyone else and for a while, not even to him. It had been that tidbit of information that one takes in but doesn't acknowledge until later. He should have been aware of it immediately. But there'd been too much going on.

No. He shook his head. That was leeway you gave the ordinary man. It wasn't something he gave himself.

"One day if I can ever retire, I'm getting a tattoo," Wade had said, a year ago on another beach, in another time—a different assignment. "On my wrist. Freedom. And then I'm getting the hell out. Thing of it is, I don't think that time will ever come. My retirement dreams are too pricey."

Wade had dreamed big and retirement had been a nonentity for him. He'd said many times that his ex-wives cost him too much in alimony and three kids still in college drained him of everything he made.

But somehow Wade had found the money; the tattoo proved it. He couldn't believe he'd missed that tattoo, but thinking back now, it had been inconspicuous, small and almost flesh-colored. He suspected it would be enhanced later—when Wade was truly free. But now he'd realized what he'd missed. The small bird positioned like a rocket taking off on his friend's wrist was a glaring oversight. The thought made him more than uneasy and he still wanted to deny it but what clinched it all was the check on the status of Georgetown's airport over the past few hours. It had all been a ruse.

He'd come back to bed, to check on Erin, to hold her and to think.

Tenuk.

He had repeated the information from Wade. It was his job to check. Why hadn't he?

And then there was Mike Olesk, the man who had given Erin the idea to run. Mike Olesk was the man who had told her to go to Georgetown and to the place where she had been compromised.

They were no longer safe. Wade and possibly Mike Olesk had turned. Whether there were others, no matter how many there might be, didn't matter. Not now. The only thing that mattered was that they were on their own and they had to get the hell out of here.

His hand brushed her shoulder. He lifted a strand of hair and stroked along her arm, trying to ease her from sleep to wakefulness without scaring her. She shifted but didn't wake up. Another time he would have smiled at the thought for it was another sign that she trusted him and that she felt safe.

He looked at his watch.

He had no idea how much time they had, but he suspected Wade's promised afternoon pickup was null and void. The tattoo raised all kinds of flags including an intuition that screamed danger. It was an intuition that he had learned not to ignore.

She turned over and blinked, looking at him with a sleepy, passion-dredged gaze.

"You have to get up, get dressed."

"What?" She sat up. She was awake in an instant, a skill he suspected she'd learned early on in her flight.

"We're getting out," he said in a throaty whisper. "We've been compromised."

"Wade?" she whispered.

He looked at her startled. "What...?"

"Women's intuition and the look on your face. You look devastated. Only a friend can do that. He was a friend, wasn't he?"

"I thought so."

"What happened?"

"No time for explanations. Except to say I think he's run into a pot of money that will make him a free man."

"The ten million?" She frowned.

"Exactly. That and a little tattoo on his wrist that says he's a free man—able to retire early." He held out his hand, lifting her off the bed. "Wade doesn't—didn't," he corrected, "have that kind of money."

She frowned. "You're sure?"

"I'm not so sure of anything right now. Except that we need to get out."

She reached down, grabbed her shorts and top.

Moonlight stripped patterns of faint light across the small room and seemed to highlight the urgency by casting her face in shadows.

"You're safe, Erin," he said, sensing her inner qualms. "I won't let anything or anyone harm you. I promise."

"Josh." She laid a hand on his arm. "I know that and

I trust you, but you've got to know that you can rely on me, too."

"Fair enough."

Fifteen minutes later they were on the path leading to the beach. The night sky was just beginning to lighten.

Damn, he thought, he would have preferred the cover of complete darkness. They'd have to move fast.

"What now?" she asked as they trekked along the hard path that led to the beach.

"Tenuk arranged a fishing boat. It's waiting to get us off this damn island before we're trapped here," Josh said, squeezing her hand. That was one problem solved. Tenuk had followed up with the Georgetown airport and discovered Wade's lie. He'd been notified by Tenuk only five minutes ago that there was a breach in security and that another Special Forces agent would be meeting them by boat to get them off the island. The conversation had made it clear that Tenuk wasn't his problem. In fact, the information Tenuk provided only confirmed what he already knew—that the leak was somewhere else. And all of it circled back to Wade. There was a hollow feeling in his gut at the thought, but it was nothing he could dwell on. He had to focus on their current situation.

He could see a figure down the beach more than sixty feet away and faint in the darkness. Beside him, Erin rubbed her elbows, her arms folded as if protecting herself.

"Get down," he hissed. "Just in case."

She sank down into the sand, and he knew that if nothing else she would feel less exposed.

The man who had met them at the airport emerged from a thicket of scrub brush maybe twenty-five feet ahead.

"Stay here," he said to Erin. "Stay down," he repeated

before he went over to the small man who appeared to be wearing the same *longyi* he had worn earlier.

"The boat is waiting," the man said in Malay. He waved his hands as he spoke.

Josh nodded, listened as he was briefed on logistics and then turned to go back and get Erin. It was time, time to get her out.

"C'mon, Erin, we've got ourselves a trip booked." He kept his voice light, trying to dispel all the fear and urgency that already had her on edge. "We're taking a boat out of here." He repeated that information as if confirming what he already knew and what he had so recently told her. Maybe in repeating the fact that they were getting out, he could keep her focused—calm. Except, he was surprised as he looked at her, to see that she was looking completely together. The earlier tears were gone, as were any questions or doubts about his motives. She was quietly moving beside him, shadowing him. He couldn't ask for more. "Do you have any motion sickness tablets?"

"Yes, but…"

"Take them. We're in a small boat on a sea known for making people ill."

She stopped and opened her pack. The leather pouch he knew had a steel cord that she told him had remained around her waist through her entire trip. She took a pill and handed him one.

He shook his head, returning it to her. "No. They make me sleepy."

"And you need your wits about you." She dropped both pills back into the container. "You need me to be alert, too, and I don't normally get sick."

They headed down the beach. The sand seemed to stretch endlessly on either side, highlighted by a half-moon that lit a strip of the beach and aided by the rapidly lightening sky. Sixty feet down the beach and another forty feet from shore, a weathered fishing boat waited. It was smaller than he'd expected, not much more than thirty feet in length. He frowned and considered the size of the ferries that plied the Andaman Sea along the Malaysian coastline. This boat was much smaller. It could be a rough ride even in a bigger boat. This one might make it a bit more arduous, but there was no choice.

In the distance he could see the gleam of red of the outboard motor and then the light slipped and the boat fell into the shadows. Jungle bracketed them to the right, screening and providing a border between the beach and whatever lay beyond.

"Move quickly," Josh said as he prodded her with his hand in the small of her back.

He'd purposely put himself between her and the jungle, because it was from there that trouble would come. His hand fingered his Glock and his gaze ran along the perimeter to where jungle briefly met sand and their waiting transport.

Waves swept onto the shore, not overly large but with enough weight to make a constant crashing sound that broke the stillness. Unfortunately it masked the sound of other things, other dangers. The boat was maybe seventy feet away now, anchored just off shore. The driver would be there to meet them in five minutes, hopefully less. At least that was what his intelligence source here had said, and it was what Tenuk had communicated to him.

He didn't like it.

They were too open. He considered heading toward the jungle, crouching there until their driver showed up. But five minutes wasn't that long and he knew the man who would be taking them in this boat. And he knew that he wouldn't be a minute less than the five minutes, they'd been told.

As those thoughts crossed his mind there was the sound of gunshot and a flash. It lit a spot in the jungle, pinpointing where the shot had been fired.

"Damn!" He hissed as a slice of pain drove through his left arm.

"Josh?" Erin's voice was barely audible.

"Get down!" He pushed her to the sand with one arm. His other arm was numb but already beginning to throb. He knew debilitating pain would happen soon, and he knew he had to power through.

The shot had come from not thirty feet to their right, from the shelter of the jungle.

Find cover.

Get out of the open.

The thoughts jammed together in the seconds that followed as he flattened her to the sand, as they crawled forward, the rough grains digging into his elbows. She was right beside him, matching him inch for inch, watching him as he tried to keep his injured arm away from the sand, from pressure—the pain so fresh it threatened to take him down.

"We're going to stand up and when we do, run straight toward the boat. Then we're going to hit the water, go under and swim the rest of the way underwater to the boat."

"You can't, Josh. You're injured. And I—"

"Run," Josh commanded a moment later.

Flashes of light, this time closer, maybe twenty feet to their right.

More gunshots.

She had a grip on his good arm, pulling him along, as he kept his back to the jungle, between her and the shooter.

Something hot and warm trailed down his arm, and his breath was coming too heavy. He was bleeding. He didn't know how bad it was, and he couldn't think about it. His head spun, he was light-headed—loss of blood, maybe shock. He couldn't let it take him down.

"Josh."

"Keep going," he hissed, squeezing her hand, freeing his arm.

"You're bleeding."

She stumbled, and he grabbed her with his good arm. He tasted blood as he bit the inside of his lip, matching the pain in his arm with something more acute—a temporary block he'd learned a long time ago, one pain, no matter how small, temporarily masking another.

A man rose from the underbrush not forty feet to their right. Heavyset, he was dressed in what looked like fatigues, with dark hair and an even darker outline of a gun.

Erin screamed and then covered her mouth.

As the man raised his gun, Josh dropped Erin's hand and raised his Glock. His hand wavered for a moment and one blast of gunfire followed another. The dark shadow on the edge of the jungle fell. And it was as if everything went still.

"I doubt he was alone," he said and he couldn't keep the pain from his voice.

"Lean on me," she said.

He gripped her shoulder with his left hand and even that was painful. He shifted his gun and for a minute the pain put him off balance. He eased up as he realized that his fingers were biting into her flesh. "I'm sorry."

"Don't be," she whispered. "Let's just get you to that boat."

He clenched his teeth. This wasn't how it was supposed to be. And again he leaned on her as pain tore through his arm and blood pooled in his palm before dropping to the sand.

"Thank goodness for the morning workouts." She laughed, a strained sound in the shifting and rapidly lifting darkness.

He let go of her shoulder and stood straight. They couldn't get to the boat and defend themselves like this. Blood streamed down his side.

"Give me your gun," she said.

"What?" Now he was sweating, and again the world seemed to spin. His hand went to the Glock. "No way. I'll be fine."

"You're in no shape to use it and if there's someone else… If he's not dead…"

A shot sounded to their right. She was flattened to the sand, he was on top of her, firing back. It was the only way to keep her safe, as uncomfortable as it might be for her, his body a shield for hers.

Silence. Seconds ticked by, a minute—the silence continued.

He rolled off her.

"You're all right?" He would have helped her up, but his damn arm was now almost useless and the other was occupied with the gun.

He could see the raw fear in her eyes and that fear was mixed with disbelief and something else: determination.

She didn't ask for the gun again. He suspected that was a moot point now. The only point that was relevant was to get to that boat. "We need to get out of here now!"

"You're bleeding." She seemed fixated on that. He supposed that was normal. Shock maybe.

"It's not that bad, Erin. It just needs a bandage and an aspirin—maybe a stitch or two. We'll have plenty of time once we're on the water."

A shot, this time to the left, and he could almost feel the heat of the bullet.

"Hell!" Josh muttered and they hit the sand again. He rolled with her, his arm around her, the gun pointing out, away from her.

Once.

Twice.

This time he was careful to keep his weight from her, but it wasn't easy and he wasn't one hundred percent successful. He knew from her stifled groan that he had crushed her into the sand. He rolled again, this time his injured arm took their combined weight and he grunted as pain shot through him. Then they were positioned flat-out on their bellies. A perfect position to take aim, and this time he needed to get their pursuer. He'd already determined that his thought of more than one was wrong. There was one and there wasn't going to be another chance. Here the jungle met the beach in a triangle, bringing the cover the sniper was enjoying closer to them. Flattened to the sand, they had a chance.

One shot.

Two.

Three.

Again, the shots were coming from ahead and slightly to their left. Now they were against the lower brush that straggled on the outer edges of the jungle as foliage met sand and came close to the ocean.

Complete cover finally.

Josh lifted up, pressing on one elbow, covering Erin as he fired back. He estimated that the sniper was less than twenty feet away. An answering volley again from the left and just behind them as their Malay fisherman joined in. He counted off as silence settled on the beach.

He rose to his knees, pulling her up with him. Blood

was streaming down his arm. The boat engine droned in the sudden quiet.

"Let's go." He pulled her to her feet.

"Oh, my God," she muttered, her hair wild and tangled, falling across her face. Her hand shook in his. "You're okay?"

"That's my line. I'm fine. Let's get moving." He pushed her in front of him, putting himself again between her and the beach. The boat was so close now, not twelve feet off shore. He plunged into the water after her. It was warm on his ankles and he wanted to ram his aching arm into it.

Instead, he pushed her ahead of him while the boat bobbed in the water.

There was silence between them, and he tossed the plan to swim for it. The boat was closer than he thought.

"An armed fisherman?" she asked with a touch of humor in her voice as she reached for the ladder.

He smiled at the effort to find humor in a situation that was outside the reality of a schoolteacher's norm. He supposed the past five months had all been out of her norm. "Malaysian Special Forces," he explained.

"Fisherman on the side." The Malay man smiled and reached a hand over the boat, helping Erin in. He then reached a hand to Josh.

"At least they didn't get your shooting arm," he said as Josh swung into the boat with a grunt.

Within seconds they were away from the beach and from the danger that had threatened their lives.

"Who were they?" she asked.

"I don't know," he replied. "I can only assume it was another bounty hunter, executioner, whatever you want to call it, sent by the Anarchists."

"Thank God we didn't have to swim underwater," she said.

"That was the least of your worries." His smile was tight as he held his bad arm.

The boat swung around and headed into the warming light of early morning. The ocean was shadowed and silent.

He grimaced as another pain shot through him and his arm throbbed. Blood seeped through his fingers.

"I need something to wrap this with. Your blouse is cotton."

"I've got one better," she replied. She opened her pouch and pulled out a roll of fabric bandage.

"Is there anything you don't keep in there?" he asked and bit his lip as he pushed the sleeve of his T-shirt higher and pain shot through him.

"Fortunately I took some first aid," she muttered. "It's bad, but looks like the bullet went straight through."

He clenched his teeth as she bound the wound, and the blood seeped slowly around the edges.

Erin finished and then held the back of her hand under her nose.

The smell of the fish, the roll of the waves—he imagined it was all getting to her.

"Feeling queasy?"

She nodded. "But I'm still voting no on anti-nausea medication."

"Don't feel shy about taking it later. This ride's rough, like I said, and we've only just begun."

"Where are we going?"

He admired the fact that it was the first time she'd asked that question. She had allowed him to take her from apparent safety into danger and with no idea where they might be going.

"We're going to Thailand. It's our only option, Erin."

Ten minutes in and Josh's arm was a dull throb. Everyone was quiet. Erin, he imagined, was immersed in her own thoughts. He had been going over the logistics of what had just happened and Bob, as he preferred to be called, was concentrating on guiding the boat in a sea that was far from placid. Even in daybreak the water was thick and dark, the waves battering against them. The throb of the engine and the slap of waves was the only sound and it was eerie.

"We're going to make it, babe."

"I know," she said with a smile that quivered. "I never doubted you."

THEY'D BEEN AT sea for over an hour. Erin wasn't sure how much more she could endure without giving in and taking something to stop her stomach from heaving. She reached over and placed a hand on Josh's good arm as if doing that would somehow settle her stomach and her nerves. His heat seemed to transfer back to her, to give her confidence. The only thing it didn't do was stop the roiling in her stomach that was a combination of fear and motion sickness. His hand covered hers, and she took a temporary breath of relief. She could make out a fishing boat farther out to sea and watched as it disappeared into the horizon.

Relief swept through Erin, and she released her grip on Josh's arm. She hadn't realized she'd been holding on so tightly, but she was still imprisoned by his hand.

"You're all right?"

"Fine," she assured him. "How's the arm?"

"Hurts like a bitch, but the bleeding slowed down." He held out his arm where no more blood had seeped through the bandage since she'd first applied the wrap. He leaned over and squeezed her hand with his good one. "You're going to be fine."

"I know." She smiled faintly back at him. And what

she knew was that if they made it safely home, it was all thanks to Josh. She couldn't think of it, of what lay behind and even what lay ahead. "You're going to be fine, too."

"Thanks to you," he said.

"The least I could do," she said and smiled. "Seeing as you wouldn't hand over the gun." She paused. "I can use it, you know."

"I never doubted," he replied. "But I appreciate your bandaging skills more."

Bob turned the boat closer to land, and she could see that he was angling toward shore. The voyage was almost over. They weren't safe but soon...

"Not much farther," Josh confirmed.

Another wave of nausea ran through her. She swallowed and turned to him. "I'll be happy once we get off this boat." He squeezed her hand and said something, she presumed in Malay, to Bob. And she was reminded of how accomplished Josh was, that he wasn't just bilingual but trilingual and possibly more, that there was much about Josh that she didn't know, that she would never know. For no matter how she looked at it, they could never be a couple. Josh was a man without home or family, who was definitely much too risky to love.

Well over an hour after they left Langkawi behind they were on land, in another country.

Thailand.

In the distance she could see a longboat, and to the right the distant speck of the boat that had brought them here. Ahead there was nothing to differentiate this strip of beach from the one they had just left. It was deserted, sheltered by jungle that acted as a backdrop.

Around them was the salty scent of ocean. The morning sun gleamed across it as the beach seemed to stretch endlessly.

"Let's get off this beach," Josh said, taking her hand and moving forward and toward a break in the jungle that had been hidden by rock and foliage. It was a small rock outcropping where the greenery fell back and sand and rock replaced it. They made their way around the cliff where the jungle fell away and open land stretched in front of them.

"Your arm?"

"Can wait. We've got a rendezvous out of here."

Overhead, there was a sound that was distant and vaguely familiar.

"Helicopter," Josh said shortly. "I notified Vern. Wade's been taken out of commission. They're extracting us."

"Extracting?"

"This way." He had her hand in a grip that suggested there was no time for questions. "It's taking us up to Trang. A city in Thailand," he answered her silent question. "Where we're taking a plane out."

"You're in no shape…"

"The Anarchists have pulled out the stops. There's no choice. Thailand is no longer any safer than Malaysia. The only place where you're safe is in custody in the States. We can control things better there. I'm in no shape to do it here."

Wind kicked up overhead as the helicopter lost altitude over the beach.

Then it was landing, wind lifting the sand, spinning it, throwing grit into their eyes. Through squinted eyes she could see the pilot, a silhouette against the glass.

It was all too surreal. Erin's throat was dry and she couldn't have spoken if she had wanted to. She was moving on autopilot, trusting that Josh would get them out. And she supposed that he trusted the shadowy figure in the helicopter and the fact that he could get them some-where safe.

Home.

Was home safe?

Was anywhere safe?

They were on board even as the questions swirled.

As they settled in their seats, the pilot reached into a canvas bag at his side and pulled out a manila envelope. "Here."

Josh took the packet, and the pilot turned around, ad-justing his headset.

Erin pulled the safety strap over her shoulder as the helicopter lifted, tilting as it gained altitude. She glanced at Josh, curious as to what he had, what this meant and yet feeling too overwhelmed to ask.

"New ID," Josh said as he handed her passport.

"British," she said with a frown. "Ann Worthington? I don't…"

"Sound British? But you've acted."

She knew that what he said wasn't a question, that the research he'd obviously done would have more than likely shown that she'd taken an acting class in university; and while it wasn't a passion or even a hobby, she had acted in more than a few plays.

She nodded. "Amateur."

"And in real life you were good enough at acting to disappear, resurfacing as someone else."

She nodded again.

"So now, say as little as possible. And worse case, you've been living abroad, the accent diluted as a result."

She knew that she looked doubtful.

"It's the last time. We'll be on a secure flight home by later this morning. And the trial begins in early November," he said over the noise of the engine. "The fake ID is only an extra precaution. I doubt if you'll need it."

Her smile was one of relief as they spoke briefly and easily of other things, their conversation bracketed and secure within the noise that separated them from the pilot.

"A month." Her heart beat hard in her chest.

"And it's over. There's enough evidence with what Sarah saw."

"I hate the thought of that."

"I know." His hand covered hers. "And once she's testified…"

"I disappear," she finished for him. "But I disappear with Sarah."

"Maybe," he replied. "But if you have to disappear again, you won't be disappearing alone."

"What are you suggesting?"

His lips claimed hers and he drew her against him. "You're mine and nothing's going to change that."

"You're awfully confident."

"Confidence has gotten me out of a jam or two."

"That's what I'm afraid of, Josh," she said honestly. "What you call a jam."

The ocean sprawled an azure blue to their left, and to their right, as the helicopter tilted into a turn, the morning sun reminding them of a new day as it glared through the window. A new day where there was another land and the hope of home.

His good hand settled over hers. "Maybe I've had enough danger for one lifetime."

Chapter Twenty-Five

Wednesday, November 17

Guilty—the leader of the Anarchists was going down.

"You're safe," Josh whispered in her ear. "Sarah's safe. It's over."

"Safe?" Was there such a thing?

"Yes, safe," he repeated firmly. "And without Sarah testifying. That's the beauty of it all."

She looked around. It was hard to believe. The plain, cream-colored walls hadn't changed. The box-like apartment had been her home for a month. Outside, snow was falling lightly. The weather was colder than normal for midfall in Whitefish, Montana. This was where she'd been detained, hidden while they were stateside. It was the first time she'd seen Josh since coming home and she'd missed him more than she wanted to admit, more than she'd thought possible.

"There are no others. The Anarchists have been taken out at the knees. There's nothing you can do to them. And it turns out that one of their members turned state's evidence. They never needed Sarah."

"All of it was for nothing," she murmured.

"Except that no one knew that it would come to that."

His arm settled over her shoulders, drawing her up against him. "What Sarah saw now means nothing."

"Thank goodness," she murmured, leaning into him and all that he offered.

"No more worries."

"An understatement," she said and turned to him with a smile.

His hand covered hers. "No more running."

Her smile broadened. Just that morning, in anticipation of this very news, she'd agreed to a full-time teaching job with kindergarten children. It was halfway across the country from her sister and her new nephew, but at least Tampa was in the country. Her days of running were behind her.

"It was too bad about Wade," she murmured. "You trusted him."

"To a point. But truly, in that line of work you doubt everyone."

She noted the past tense, wondered at it for a moment and moved on.

"Even Mike." She sighed. "I can't believe that he was that far in debt or that he was able to be bribed."

"He had a gambling problem but he didn't cave in until the last minute. He swore that he thought you'd be safe by then, that you'd left Georgetown. He'd never imagined you'd still be there." He cleared his throat. "If that's any justification."

She shook her head. She'd lost contact with Mike after she'd arrived in Georgetown. That had been his last bit of advice—go deep and break contact. Now she realized that in an odd way he'd given her a head start before offering up what he knew for what money he could get. In an odd way he'd protected her before betraying her.

"I trusted him. But he wasn't a friend. As an adult I wasn't close to him. Should that make me feel any better?"

"Betrayal is betrayal. He's going to be facing a court date of his own, if that's any consolation. As for Wade, I suspect early retirement isn't in the cards for him, either. Can't say I feel sorry about that one. He had you facing an executioner for a paltry sum, not even the full reward."

"Paltry?"

"It's just money. History tells us how little that can be worth at the whim of a government—think Vietnam or Cambodia. There were times in the twentieth century when their currency meant nothing. Millionaires became paupers overnight at the whim of a corrupt government. It can happen anywhere."

"Josh." She squeezed his hand. "It's all right to feel like crap because your friend betrayed you. No need to divert with a history lesson."

"Divert?" He smiled slightly. "You're right. Wade took me out at the knees, at least for a day or two. I didn't expect that of him. But you're wrong about one thing. Like I said before, he wasn't a close friend."

"Still, like you said, betrayal is betrayal. He endangered you and would have had me killed for money. It's unbelievable." And she thought of how, for Josh, it was all about making it right. She knew without him saying it that the money had always been secondary.

"Maybe after all this we need a vacation," Josh suggested. He looked at her with a rather impish expression on his face.

"Vacation?" The thought of flying, of going anywhere after all the months of travel, of flight, was off-putting. She'd put the Canadian and British passports into safe-keeping, but she'd yet to pull out her American passport. She had no desire to go anywhere.

"I thought maybe a spa."

"Spa?" The thought of Josh going to a spa, of him enjoying the experience, was improbable. The fact that he would do it for her was, well, it was a self-sacrificing gesture.

"Something wrong with that?"

"Maybe a real trip."

He laughed, the sound deep and throaty. "Maybe we need to meet somewhere in the middle."

"Maybe," she agreed.

He reached over, pulling her to him. The strength and ease with which he did it attested to how quickly he'd healed. Stitches and a round of antibiotics had replaced her field dressing, and now there was only a scar to remind them of the bullet that was meant to kill.

"Maybe? Time alone doesn't sound romantic to you?"

"That spa you mentioned?" She grinned up at him. "I don't know."

"We'd be together." He drew an arm around her shoulder. "And while we're speaking of that, I have a surprise for you." He looked at the clock on the wall.

"A surprise?" She looked up at him just as his lips met hers, teasing them in a light flirtatious kiss, as she wrapped her arms around his neck deepening the kiss and drawing more as she met him kiss for kiss. It was he that drew away first, holding her at arm's length.

"First, the surprise," he said, his voice thick with passion. He ran a forefinger over her lower lip. "For any more kisses, I will want to take you to bed at a completely inappropriate time."

"Inappropriate?"

A knock at the door had Josh turning, his hand going to his gun—instinctively putting Erin behind him.

"Time?" Josh asked.

"Ten minutes to midnight," a male voice responded.

Erin's heart skipped a beat, both at the ritual and at the knowledge that the phrasing meant that there was another agent, a bodyguard on the other side, and what that might mean.

Josh put a hand on her shoulder. "Precautionary," he said as he went to the door and opened it. A broad, dark-haired man silently filled the doorway before nodding at Josh and stepping back.

"Sarah!" Erin breathed as a slight, young woman with an anxious expression took a step forward and then another. Her strawberry-blond hair was tied back in an understated bun, and she held a baby wrapped tightly in a pale green blanket. She was hunched almost protectively over it.

For a minute emotion and shock kept her standing, staring at her sister and the small bundle she held.

A slow smile spread over Sarah's face as she bridged the distance between them.

Erin threw her arms wide, drawing her sister into an awkward hug, conscious of the baby between them. "I can't believe you're here. That you're safe." She took a step back, her hands still on Sarah's shoulders.

Tears filled Sarah's eyes. "Thanks to you. I can't thank you enough. Erin…" She choked on the words. "You could have died. I was so scared."

"But I didn't," Erin said firmly.

Sarah shook her head. "I prayed every night for you, between that and the fact that you're the smartest person I know and the best, I knew you had to make it."

"Sarah…" Erin felt her face flush at the compliments and with the joy of seeing her sister after so many months.

"And it's finally over." Sarah shifted the bundle in her arms and looked back at the man who hovered in the doorway. "Almost."

"My nephew?" Erin breathed and wiped her eyes with the back of her hand.

"Liam," Sarah said and smiled as she pulled the blanket back.

"The name suits him," Erin said as she looked down at the baby with the dusting of reddish-blond hair whose face furrowed while he continued to sleep.

"It was Grandfather's."

"I know," Erin replied, for the first time contemplating the significance of that name and feeling surprise that Sarah had cared enough about their ancestry to use it. She suspected that the past few months had changed many things for Sarah and that with the baby there were more changes to come. She smiled as Liam's tiny hand grabbed her pinky. His eyes opened briefly and met hers as if acknowledging her before they closed again. "I'm an aunt," she said and she knew in that moment that she was hooked. "And I'll spoil you rotten," she whispered to the now sleeping baby. "Promise."

It was two hours later, and Sarah had gone back to the hotel with the FBI agent who would shadow her until sentencing was complete. Josh had confirmed that would be a few days from now. They sat together on the stiff little couch that Erin had good-naturedly complained about on more than one occasion.

"I won't miss this place," she said softly.

"You'll love Tampa," he promised.

She looked at him and laughed. "But not the RV." But she wasn't moving to the RV. She had her own place for now, a job, a soon anticipated reunion with her cat, Edgar, and a life that she knew would include him.

"I love you, babe," he said, his voice deep with promise.

She leaned her head against his shoulder. "You're still too risky to love," she said in a flirtatious whisper.

"Maybe not." Outside, the streetlights winked on. "I suspect I'm too risky *not* to love."

Her lips met his in a kiss that was hot and yearning and spoke to a future that lay wide and open in front of them.

* * * * *

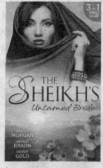

MILLS & BOON®

Let us take you back in time with our Medieval Brides...

The Novice Bride – Carol Townend

The Dumont Bride – Terri Brisbin

The Lord's Forced Bride – Anne Herries

The Warrior's Princess Bride – Meriel Fuller

The Overlord's Bride – Margaret Moore

Templar Knight, Forbidden Bride – Lynna Banning

Order yours at
www.millsandboon.co.uk/medievalbrides

16_MB519

MILLS & BOON®

Why shop at millsandboon.co.uk?

Each year, thousands of romance readers find their perfect read at millsandboon.co.uk. That's because we're passionate about bringing you the very best romantic fiction. Here are some of the advantages of shopping at www.millsandboon.co.uk:

✱ **Get new books first**—you'll be able to buy your favourite books one month before they hit the shops

✱ **Get exclusive discounts**—you'll also be able to buy our specially created monthly collections, with up to 50% off the RRP

✱ **Find your favourite authors**—latest news, interviews and new releases for all your favourite authors and series on our website, plus ideas for what to try next

✱ **Join in**—once you've bought your favourite books, don't forget to register with us to rate, review and join in the discussions

Visit **www.millsandboon.co.uk**
for all this and more today!